Enjoy the read. Can't
wait fu feedback
Love
Carlie.

A
DARKER
HORSE

Carline Bouilhet

A DARKER HORSE
Copyright © CARLINE BOUILHET 2017

First published by Zeus Publications 2017
http://www.zeus-publications.com
P.O. Box 2554
Burleigh M.D.C.
QLD. 4220
Australia.

The National Library of Australia Cataloguing-in-Publication

Author: Bouilhet, Carline.

Title: A darker horse

ISBN: 978-0-6480998-1-9 (paperback)

Subjects: Crime fiction
Horse racing – Australia—fiction
Horse farms—Australia--fiction

To my sister, Gwendoline,
for gifting me a magical insight into life in the desert.

Acknowledgements

My heartfelt thanks to John Matthews
for patiently leafing through the manuscript
to correct factual errors.

To Dr Patricia Marechal-Ross,
my deepest appreciation for casting a critical eye
on every sentence and offering invaluable suggestions.

I am also most grateful for a youth
where riding horses was part of the course
and for my wonderful Australian friends
who helped me celebrate Melbourne Cup year after year.

Other books by this author

Halibut Cove, SPRA, New York, 2011

The Fleuron Connection, Green Olive Press, 2013

FOREWORD AND WARNING

A Darker Horse is a work of fiction and a product of the author's imagination. Any similarities with people, dead or alive, and events, past or present, are purely coincidental, even though true events may have been inspiring.

While the intrigue is spun against the glamorous world of horseracing, its aim was never to enlighten with its insights the trainers, breeders, jockeys, stewards or any other professionals who derive their livelihood from what has long been called the Sport of Kings.

Its aim was always to entertain the occasional punters, the men and women of all creeds and ages who attend the races for the unique atmosphere, the distinctive ambiance and the matchless excitement; for those who, once a year, on the second Tuesday of November, stop all work at 11 am, spend a small fortune on hats and boutonnieres, and wait with bated breath for the clock to strike three; and for anyone who admires these most noble of animals, once meant to roam free across the plains of most continents.

The author hopes to be forgiven for taking some factual liberties which may have stretched the boundaries of reality to enter the realm of possibilities.

CHAPTER I

In the last six weeks, Arielle LaSalle's favourite mare had started to bag up, with her udder visibly swelling. A five-year-old solid dark bay horse with a spritely temperament, Dauphine had bonded with her rider since her birth. Together, they had tallied an impressive number of races and everyone hoped that her best traits would be passed on to her progeny. Watching her, Arielle worried about her maiden foaling. For the past few days, she had lovingly brushed the horse to calm her down, sometimes twice daily. Until yesterday, when she had finally noticed her nipples waxing – a sure indicator that the foal would be born in a day or two – she had regularly sponged her udder and teats so that the foal would nurse easily. After spending hours cleaning one of the dozen large birthing stalls available at Chantilly Farms, and laying soft, dry straw on the ground for the mare's comfort, she was now impatiently waiting for her waters to break, braiding and wrapping her long black tail in the meantime. Outside, a quarter-moon hung high in the sky.

Arielle caressed the horse's muzzle, but the latter remained unresponsive to the familiar gesture, whipping her head around as if human touch was too much for her to bear. In the dimly lit stall, Arielle suddenly heard the unmistakable gushing of water: Dauphine's placenta sac had just broken and the mare instinctively began to lie down on her side. Within minutes, powerful contractions racked the swollen horse, her legs twitching. She groaned and whined as she did so, her nostrils flared. Arielle quickly punched in the veterinarian Nathan Heather's number into her mobile phone: the local surgeon had promised he would be there within minutes to offer assistance when the time came. Under normal circumstances, he would have offered to wait up with her, but he had had a trying day at a nearby farm, resulting in a stallion being put to sleep, a decision which always tugged at his heartstrings.

Mesmerised, Arielle witnessed one delicate front hoof poke out, quickly followed by another, both covered by a rubbery coating. Through the wet glaze she observed the full length of the front legs slide out, immediately followed by nose and head: one last push and the foal lay at its mother's feet. The mare paused, remaining immobile, snorting noisily, her breathing still laboured, contractions still racking her body. Puzzled, Arielle wondered why the mare did not stand up immediately. Tentatively, she approached her to see what the matter could be. Minutes ticked by but Dauphine still laid on her side, her eyes wild and panicked. Could there be another foal? Could Dauphine's difficulties of the past few days be due to carrying twins?

As per the instructions given by Nathan earlier that day, she promptly lubricated her hand and arm and bravely slid it down the mare's birth canal. The horse didn't protest at the invasive but gentle gesture. The young woman soon grasped a foot and then another, tugging at them, slowly pulling them towards her until the head and shoulders finally appeared. Gently, steadily, she continued to slowly pull out a second foal. Behind her, Nathan whistled softly.

"Well done, Arielle!"

Covered in a wet, slick substance, Arielle looked up at her lover, her eyes shining bright, emotion choking her.

"Now let her rest and bond with her young," he coached.

The exhausted mare nonetheless stood up within minutes, the sudden movement breaking the umbilical cord. She looked down at the two foals lying at her feet, circling them once and sniffing the air, before studiously licking each foal clean and nuzzling them. Nathan quickly reached for the iodine solution to coat the foals' navels and began to carefully sponge off both mother and foals, Arielle silently following suit.

"We still need to wait for Dauphine to evacuate the placenta and make sure the foals stand up. Are you all right?" asked Nathan minutes later, looking at Arielle's tired face.

"Look at them: they are so beautiful. They are as black as their father! And look, they have their mother's unusual markings. I just can't believe there are two of them..." whispered Arielle in awe, her eyes moist and her lips trembling. "I never cease to find this experience amazing," she added, watching the firstborn tap his forelegs together as if trying to judge how he would sustain his weight.

She laughed softly when he tried to stand once again, falling and rolling back on his side. After a few more comical attempts he finally stood under the approving eye of his proud mother. On the other hand, the second-born foal had remained alarmingly inert, his head rolling from side to side, calmly observing the proceedings. Distraught by his inactivity, the mare came around, nuzzling him repetitively, nudging him over and over again, as if trying to convince him to attempt to stand, but all for naught. Worried, Nathan and Arielle finally approached the colt cautiously, aware that the mare may at any moment unpredictably react to their undesirable interference.

Large liquid eyes, the colour of dark chocolate, stared into Arielle's own and the foal tentatively sniffed the air around her, taking in her soapy scent now mixed with sweat, fear and fatigue.

"Come on, little one," begged Arielle, "please stand up."

At the sound of her voice, the foal retracted its forelegs underneath his torso. It was now obvious to both observers that the second foal was not only smaller in size but also much weaker than the first, his long legs almost too fragile to support his weight on their own. It took another three hours of failed attempts and nervous pleadings before the foal finally stood and joined his twin and mother in the small paddock outside the birthing stall. Pre-dawn already crackled when they began nursing. With the birthing ritual finally over, Arielle lit a cigarette and watched them play, hopeful that despite the obvious difference in initial birth size, both colts would now survive.

5

Their coat was a true black, with just a white irregular blaze resembling an upside comma in-between their eyes. The only true visible difference between them was that one had a coronet on each front leg, right above the hoof, while the other failed to display such distinctive markings. In Arielle's eyes, they were both gorgeous specimens yet, from experience, she already feared that when her father, Guillaume de la Selle, owner of Chantilly Farms, came and inspected the newborn foals later that morning, the second twin might not meet with his approval. She sensed that due to its smaller than normal size, he might not reach expectations and be disregarded outright as a potential runner.

Unlike his diminutive daughter, William LaSalle, born Guillaume de la Selle, dominated most gatherings through his stature alone. Standing above 6'2", with a physique most athletes would envy, the 62-year-old man exuded charm and charisma. He had immigrated to Australia at the age of 30, when, following the aftermath of a much publicised court case, he had been forced to leave behind his ancestors' chateau known for its sprawling grounds and majestic riding stables. Indeed, the Haras de la Selle, located outside a small hamlet in Brittany, had been in his paternal family for generations. The 37 hectares of the breeding farm were as accessible from Lorient Airport and the train station as they were from the ferry at Roscoff, the ideal location facilitating travel across the Channel for his prized champions. A long gravelled driveway led visitors to the 15th century two-storey mansion, which anchored the site with its high-pitched roof and quarry-stone walls covered in molten reds and green ivy. Tall elegant topiaries framed the front entrance. At the back of the house, a wide sandstone terrace offered vistas across rolling hills of verdant pasture all the way up to the river, which ran lengthwise through the property.

On a regular basis, his family horses had run the Grand Prix de Paris and the Prix de l'Arc de Triomphe at Longchamp and had won, more than once, both the prestigious Prix de Diane and the sought-after Prix du Jockey Club. They had also competed on several occasions in the United Arab Emirates where he had even come to befriend the President, and Sheikh Maktoum bin Rashid Al Maktoum's first cousin, Sheikh Hamdam, who was as passionate about horses as the Emir. However, when Guillaume, celebrating his latest win on the Chantilly racecourse, witnessed the murder of Marcel Francisco, head of the Unione Corse, while dining with his parents at L'Ecume des Jours, a popular but upscale crêperie tucked away in a back street of Roscoff, his days had been numbered.

In 1967, the gangland wars against the powerful Guarani clan, the former ruling dynasty of the Corsican Mafia, had already raged for two years, sparked by competition over casino revenues and horse track betting. After handling a particularly messy first course of moules marinières, Guillaume had just excused himself from the table to wash his hands when five gunmen, armed with machine guns, had barged into the otherwise virtually deserted dining room. Midweek, besides the notorious Marcel Francisco, dining at the back of the restaurant with his vast entourage, the only other diners had been two young English couples. In the melee that followed, all bystanders and restaurant staff alike had been killed by stray bullets. Alerted by the commotion, Guillaume had run to the front room but at the sight of gunfire had stopped short, watching the entire scene from behind a two-way mirror at the back of the bar. Once the gunmen had fled, he had called the police.

Later on, he identified one by one the members of the Guarani clan responsible for the massacre; none had bothered wearing a mask since they had been convinced they had not left any witness behind. In doing so, his personal safety had been immediately compromised. To seal the prosecution's case, he had bravely agreed to testify in court, bartering his testimony against a new identity and a one-way ticket to Australia. To save his life from retribution he'd indeed had little choice but erase all traces of his existence going forward. With its owners murdered and the only heir safely overseas, the Haras de la Selle was finally sold through a complicated sleigh of hands, through lawyers and offshore firms so that the proceeds of Guillaume's inheritance could never be traced back to him. Selling his prized champions had been the hardest of all, but then he had been well aware that a mere investigation into bloodlines could potentially bring killers to his doorstep once again. He had also been doomed to change his family name: his new Australian passport claimed he was now William LaSalle, born in Switzerland. On the day he had boarded for Australian shores, he had nonetheless adamantly refused to part with the thickly bound leather photo album which stored the souvenirs of his former life.

It wasn't long before the handsome and accomplished young Frenchman met his match in young, attractive Sarah Seymour, whose family owned a successful winery with vast abutting lands in the Hunter Valley, an easy three-hour ride from Sydney. A graceful, dark-haired beauty, Sarah was as petite as Guillaume was tall, as fine boned as he was athletic, but it was her passion for horses, which won his heart first and foremost. As a wedding dowry, Sarah's parents gifted their only child 3000 acres of undulating hills and rich alluvial flats. Guillaume's inheritance allowed the couple to build on it their very own dream: an impressive stud farm dominated by a two-storey quarry-stone house, the design inspiration for which had been none other than Guillaume's own childhood dwelling back in France. Thirty years later, the impressive Chantilly Farms was amongst the most respected in the country, with Guillaume earning along the way both the respect and the trust of his peers. However, tragedy had struck when, one year after their fairytale wedding, Sarah had become pregnant with twin girls.

Since Sarah, three years younger than her husband, had breezed through the first six months of pregnancy, no one had anticipated any complications. However, weeks before delivery, a routine check-up had shown mild distress in the unborn babies. Hours later, her obstetrician had advocated an emergency caesarean, denying her former romantic wish for a natural birth. The twins had unfortunately shared the same amniotic sac, and, apparently, the nuchal cord of one baby had accidentally wrapped tightly around the neck of the other. By the time the twins were extracted, Arielle was alive but her twin had failed to draw a single breath. Six weeks premature, Arielle came into a world which was already mourning what would never be. Her identical twin sister, Murielle, was buried in an intimate ceremony before she even came out of hospital. Arielle would be Guillaume's only child: indeed, despite his pleadings, Sarah had adamantly refused to face the prospect of a possible repeat ordeal. Two years later, ovarian cancer radiation had forever removed the topic from their conversations. The ghost of depression soon followed Sarah around.

Gradually, Chantilly Farms' mistress began to withdraw from social activities. She rarely stepped outside the beautiful home she had so lovingly created with her husband, except to tend to her magnificent gardens. Sarah's obsessive protectiveness of her surviving child had led to home schooling and to a certain amount of confinement for the young child. In her opinion, local schools had lacked in scholastic distinctions, anyway. The mere suggestion of possibly sending Arielle away to boarding school had been abhorrent. Deprived of normal social interactions for a young girl, and with horses as her only companions, a reserved and tenacious Arielle had early on become a fearless and accomplished rider. Since her weight and height were ideal for a jockey, it was soon apparent that it would be a profession in which she could excel. In any case, by age 16, the 5'5" foot, slim and delicately boned Arielle, as strong willed as her father and as stubborn as her mother, wouldn't have had it any other way.

Professional female jockeys were still a rare breed when she began racing, but her choice of career made sense for everyone who had ever seen her on the back of a horse. The day after her 18th birthday, she had already started racing as an apprentice jockey, having earned within six months her license in racing. With her indenture a given, she won plenty of country races in

Groups One and Two. However, Guillaume, who, over the years, had watched the loneliness creep in his daughter's eyes, stopped her élan, claiming that she shouldn't yet rush into the demanding career. He insisted she took some time out instead in order to reflect on what she really wanted to do with her life. Moreover, he argued that, regardless of her ultimate decision, she would most benefit from a stint living abroad, where she could learn something about the world at large and discover how to conduct herself without constant supervision. Despite his wife's vociferous protests, Guillaume remained inflexible: it was time for Arielle to be exposed to the world beyond Chantilly's gates and break free from her enforced solitude. He agreed though that her safety remained paramount. To reach his objectives, and after considerable soul searching, he finally decided to contact the one man in whom he still held absolute trust.

Guillaume had met Sheikh Hamdam decades earlier when the young man had come with his uncle to broker a deal at the Haras de la Selle. Indeed, Sheikh Maktoum bin Rashid Al Maktoum, first president of the United Emirates, had been responsible for introducing the Arab world to international horseracing. He had long admired the breeding practices held by Guillaume's own father, and the two men had discussed at length how the Dubai ruler could play a major role in raising the industry's standards in his part of the world. During their time together, the two adolescents had formed a bond of friendship which they cultivated on every track where their families' horses ran, as well as plenty of polo fields across Europe. Later they even attended the same English university, albeit pursuing different disciplines.

When Guillaume's parents were assassinated, Hamdam had followed the harrowing trial week after week. Unbeknown to Guillaume, and with his uncle's blessing, he had put his considerable resources to keep his friend safe from harm, mistrusting the police's ability to shield him from the Unione Corsica's far-reaching clutches. In the aftermath, he had even purchased most of his friend's horses when the latter had been forced to flee the country. Over the years, Hamdam had intuited that Chantilly Farms were Guillaume's new venture in the southern hemisphere. To his trained eye, recognising his friend's telltale methods had not been difficult. His only regret was that Guillaume's and his family's safety implied that they would most likely never cross paths again. Thus, when the old-fashioned hand-written letter reached him mid-December, requesting that he take the young Arielle under his wing, Hamdam had not hesitated.

A first-class round-trip ticket on Emirates Airlines in Arielle's name arrived merely a week later. In his note, waiving Guillaume's objections in regards to such a generous gift, Hamdam had explained that such a ticket would simply prevent anyone from tracing back its origins. Arielle had been both overjoyed and apprehensive by the speed of the planning. The two old friends had worked fast: she would celebrate New Year Eve's at home and be on a flight abroad the very next day.

As befitted his position, Hamdam, only slightly older than Guillaume, had married four wives. The first wife, whom he wedded at the age of 21, had been heralded as the perfect choice: the marriage had been described as politically astute, since it strengthened the ties of the small Arab state with its Qatar neighbour. Shy and uneducated, Sheikha Maitha had kept a low profile in society, strictly adhering to the traditions and culture of the Muslim state, which limited her interactions with men. She had nonetheless given her husband five children in the first few years of her marriage. Once his succession had been properly insured, the ambitious Emirati had been free to marry his English-born girlfriend: he had met her at a mixer between Cambridge, where he had been enrolled in the MBA program, and the Royal College of London, where she had pursued studies in international politics. Having waited for him patiently for half a decade, Catherina had happily converted and had readily moved to Dubai after the much-publicised nuptials.

His intellectual equal, she was the woman most often seen by his side on the international social scene. Her blonde hair, fair skin and slim figure continued to turn heads wherever they went. A passionate fashionista, she had however stumped most criticism by creating her own exclusive fashion label, designing the most beautiful abayas her contemporaries had ever laid eyes on. Her husband had been proud of her accomplishments, and her exclusive by-appointment-only shops dotted Dubai's most prestigious malls. When Hamdam had married once again, barely four years later, she had been most unhappy; her protests though had fallen on deaf ears.

Indeed, Catherina had proven unable to carry children to term and a healthy brood was the standard by which successful marriages were held. Hassa, Hamdam's third wife, had been purely chosen for her child-bearing capacities, and remained as withdrawn from public life as Maitha had been. Sharing exactly the same values and background, the two women, not unexpectedly, formed a strong bond of friendship, further alienating Catherina. As a peace offering and to soften Catherina's growing resentment, Hamdam bought, in her name only, a two-storey penthouse in Central London where she took to sojourn with and without him. But when her husband, at age 60, had wed for the fourth time a woman now 33 years his junior, she began spending more and more time abroad, under the pretext of taking her fashion label – Eclipse – to major capital cities around the world.

Sheikh Marwan bin Saeed Al Sharqi from Fujairah had been pleased to pledge his youngest daughter to the Dubai ruler's first cousin. Latifah had just blown the candles on her 17th birthday cake when she had met Hamdam, already past his prime, during an official function held at the Emirates Palace in Abu Dhabi. In the course of the evening, he had been introduced to the unusually tall, light-skinned woman with the huge brown eyes speckled with gold. She had held his gaze a fraction longer than etiquette would have suggested and he swore that she had been somehow laughing at him under her veil. Intrigued, he had begun to pursue her through the appropriate channels. Through what he deemed a most desirable union, his uncle had once again applauded his choice since it strengthened the Al Falasi clan political ties with his neighbours: Hamdam had known only too well how important it was for him to maintain allies in the politically volatile region.

On his wedding night, the first time they had been alone with one another since the termed courtship began, Hamdam requested his young bride disrobe in front of him, while he sat on the edge of the bed, fully clothed. He had expected the usual display of tears and reticence synonymous with young virgins, but she had surprised him, letting her robes fall slowly, until they pooled graciously at her feet, the scent of her aromatic oud filling the room as she did so. Even though she had kept her eyes carefully downcast during her disrobing, she had nonetheless managed to be effortlessly provocative. Hamdam had been delighted.

When she finally stood in her glorious nakedness in front of him, a hand modestly covering her smooth and perfectly waxed pubis, he had signalled for her to approach him. She had stopped barely a foot away, had levelled her gaze at him and smiled.

"Aren't you scared?" he had asked curiously, unnerved by her composure, so unexpected in someone so young and so innocent.

"Why should I be? Your reputation precedes you. You're rumoured to be a gentle and honourable man. But I hope not too gentle," she had added flirtatiously, casting him a sideways glance to gauge his reaction.

"You're absolutely enchanting!" Hamdam had exclaimed. "What would please you, my child, as a betrothal gift?"

"You may not like what I have to say," she had replied quickly, uncertainty flickering in her eyes for the first time.

"Why don't you try me anyway?" Hamdam had riposted, amused by her boldness.

After a minute's silence, during which it had been obvious she weighed the pros and cons of her answer, Latifah had sighed almost loudly.

"My wish is to become as educated as Catherina," she had begun hesitantly.

Hamdam, unsure he had heard her correctly, had simply stared at her, unintelligible words forming on his lips. Finally clearing his throat, he asked her to repeat herself.

"Are you referring to Catherina, as in Sheikha Catherina, my second wife?"

"The one and only. I'd like to pursue studies in Islamic Studies first of all, but also in foreign languages, like French, and English, and Italian," she had announced brightly, words tumbling down hurriedly. "That's what my heart really desires above all else as a wedding gift, if you'd be ever so generous," she had pleaded, her eyes cajoling.

Since all his previous wives had predictably drawn long lists of jewels and expensive objects, Hamdam, taken aback at the unusual request, had smiled broadly.

"For the second time tonight you've surprised me, my dear. I'll honour your request but since you're not old enough to go to university on your own, I'm sure you'll see no objection in being tutored here at the palace. Shall we start next week, after our honeymoon?"

Her features suddenly alight in puerile delight, and her eyes shining bright with excitement, Latifah, forgetting she was stark naked and had known the man sitting on the edge of the monumental bed for less than a few hours, had jumped to his neck and kissed him unabashedly on the mouth. Hamdam had laughed wholeheartedly at her unbridled enthusiasm and clutched her into his arms, the fire in his loins now matched by the warmth in his heart.

Ten years later, he looked back at his wedding gift as the best investment he had ever made. Latifah had proved to be a natural linguist. Her aptitude at absorbing foreign languages had been nothing short of amazing. Now at age 27, besides Arabic, she spoke a non-accentuated English, French like a well-to-do Parisian, Italian like a Milanese but also Spanish, Portuguese and most unexpectedly of all, Japanese, a language she had pursued only because she had loved the food. When, one day, during a politically delicate conversation debated during dinner back at the house, she had inadvertently noticed that the translators had put their own spin on her husband's words, she had discreetly warned him and helped him save face. Ever since, her skills had become most useful during her husband's meetings with foreign investors. She was now often seen as part of his entourage during business negotiations. Many of his interlocutors remained blissfully unaware of who she really was until it was often too late.

So when Guillaume had requested his help, Hamdam had known right away that Latifah would make the perfect chaperone for his friend's only daughter. Entrusted with the task, Latifah had been thrilled: not only did she welcome the company, since the opportunity to befriend foreign women was rare in her circles, but she was also well aware that the responsibility would afford her more personal freedom, at least temporarily. In her wildest dreams though, never did she imagine that the presence of the Australian-born young woman would propel her into the rarefied circles of international racing. Guillaume, in his letter, had indeed failed to share with his friend his daughter's prowess in the saddle; officially, she was to fly to Dubai to attend university and officiously to start living like a woman her age. It was her chance to put racing on the back burner for the first time, and he had not cared to prejudice her stay.

Arielle spent her last week in Sydney shopping with her reluctant mother: Guillaume had insisted she carried with her a wardrobe suited to the intolerably hot desert climate and appropriate for her entry into high society. He had spared no expense in her complete makeover. Whatever she might have forgotten, they agreed she could easily acquire overseas.

15

According to her mother, still dismissive of the entire idea, Emirati women did little more than shopping anyway, and she would have plenty of time to metamorphose into a Cinderella. Thus, in a matter of days, Arielle traded her jeans and jodhpurs for fashionable dresses, and her riding boots for high-heeled sandals. She nonetheless managed to sneak a pair of each in her brand new luggage. Hamdam had also arranged for a two-year student visa, a time during which she was not expected to come home. Secretly though, and regardless of her father's good intentions, Arielle had hoped she would still find plenty of opportunities to ride: riding was really all she'd ever found pleasure in, and taking it away from her seemed like a cruel and unjust punishment.

The 13-hour flight to Dubai had afforded Arielle complete comfort. She had marvelled at the clever design of her first-class cabin, with everything she could ever want within arms' length. Despite the butterflies fluttering in her stomach, she had even managed a seven-hour uninterrupted sleep. She arrived at her destination fully refreshed, ready to face the unknown. As soon as she stepped off the plane, a woman she had judged to be in her mid-thirties, with a white head scarf and impeccably cut suit, had manoeuvred her out of the line of passengers, straight onto a golf cart and through Customs. Before Arielle could even get her bearings, she had spotted her bags on the carousel. Before she could make a move to retrieve them, her minder had snapped her fingers and a Pakistani man, hovering nearby, had quickly hoisted her bags off the conveyor belt and onto a trolley. By the time she had walked through the airport doors, her bags had already disappeared into the trunk of an awaiting limousine.

Upon spotting her, the uniformed chauffeur, standing at attention by the back door, smiled at her. As he made no move to open it, Arielle, unsettled, stood rooted on the spot, unsure what to do next. Seconds later, the rear-tinted window scrolled down and a perfectly oval face framed by large black sunglasses peered out.

"Arielle, are you going to stare at the car long or climb in?" chimed a warm and friendly voice. At that very minute, the chauffeur opened the door and Arielle slid inside the leather banquette next to an elegant woman clad in a light linen suit, a silk scarf draped loosely over her head and around her shoulders. Immediately the stranger removed her glasses and embraced Arielle tightly.

"Hi, I'm Latifah. Welcome to Dubai. I trust you had a nice flight?"

"Hi, I'm Arielle but you already know that. Yes, I enjoyed my flight, thank you," the words stumbling out awkwardly.

"Is there something the matter?" asked Latifah, sensing her companion's uneasiness.

"Well, to tell you the truth, I imagined you a lot older. I was sure you'd be covered in black from head to toe and I can't believe how perfect your English is!" apologised Arielle.

Latifah laughed easily.

"So you live up to your reputation: I was warned that Australians are quite direct in their speech!"

Arielle blushed: she couldn't believe she had already made a faux pas in the first few minutes of her arrival. Latifah, aware of her embarrassment, was quick to rectify the situation.

"As you noticed, I didn't step out of the car and didn't come to welcome you at the arrival gates. You're right; I would have had to wear a full abaya for that and be accompanied by a male family member. But I wonder why you thought I'd be older."

"Please don't think of me as rude, but isn't your husband my father's friend? And since Papa left his forties behind a couple of decades ago, I made a stupid assumption..." railed Arielle, mortified once again.

"I'm the fourth wife. Fourth wives are usually a lot younger than their husbands. I was a tad younger than you are now when I was wedded. That was 10 years ago."

Eager to change the subject and reeling at her father for conveniently leaving out that his friend had four wives, a glaring omission in her mind, Arielle asked her whether she had any children.

"Not yet. Do you?"

It was Arielle's turn to laugh.

"It'd imply that I ever got to approach a suitable man at any distance," she confessed wryly. "The men at Chantilly Farms are mostly too old or too weird," she added in lieu of a full-blown explanation.

Latifah looked her over.

"Wouldn't you have met boys your own age at school?"

"Impossible to do when you're home schooled! No luck there I'm afraid, and I suspect my mother chose my tutors old and ugly on purpose," replied Arielle, amused at the memory.

"I guess that we both made assumptions about the other," corrected Latifah. "I think you and I have much to learn from each other. I've been looking forward to being your chaperone but I had no idea it would be to the letter of the word," she added with a wry smile.

"May I ask you some questions before we get to your house?"

"I'd be surprised and disappointed if you didn't have any, unless you have hidden the fact that you're also a Muslim?"

"Not likely! I'm sorry," Arielle stammered, realising how offensive it may have sounded. "So do you all live in the same house? I mean you and the other three wives?" she continued eagerly, hoping Latifah had not noticed her gaffe once again.

"We all live under the same roof but in different quarters. We are requested to get along socially, but we aren't each other's best friends, that's for sure. It isn't as if Hamdam asked anyone concerned for permission to get married to anyone else; we aren't Mormons. Catherina, his second wife, resents the two women who came after her. However, I get along with the first wife, who took me more or less under her wing; I'm the same age as her oldest son, so she never saw me as a threat. The third wife, Fatimah, ignores me completely: she is busy breeding as was the first. Catherina, from what I've gathered, couldn't have children. She has suffered a few miscarriages and has never been able to carry a child to term, but she loves Hamdam and he loves her back. Besides, Hamdam already has 10 children. It's enough to carry on the name. I'll have to give him one or two children in the next few years but right now he isn't pressuring me, which is the way I like it."

"It must be quite difficult," observed Arielle sympathetically.

"You'll be the judge. Here, we're almost home," said Latifah as the limousine turned right into the Palm Jumeirah.

"Here is the Palm and there, at the end, you can see the unmistakable Atlantis complex. Hamdam's uncle was responsible for its development. It's promoted as the eighth wonder of the world. We live on the water, right at the far end of the top branch for lack of a better definition."

Arielle was no longer listening, glued to the window, mesmerised by the sight stretching in front of her. The car slowed down in front of intricately designed iron gates which slowly swung open on their approach. An explosion of multi-coloured bougainvillea covered the four-metre-high walls. The car finally stopped in front of marble steps under a canopied roof flanked by impressive columns. The young woman, followed closely by Arielle, sauntered up the stairs. A valet opened wide the majestic verdigris-bronze double front doors. Outside of hotel lobbies and cathedrals Arielle had never seen such dazzling heights in an entrance foyer. The domed ceiling was the latest application in refractive glass, letting in the sunlight whilst deflecting the heat of the day. She spun around, murmuring "Wow" as she did so. She had yet to notice the tall and imposing dark-haired man who had just walked in.

"Arielle!" boomed a rich low voice behind her. Arielle spun around to find herself literally face to face with a rather attractive man, despite his slightly crooked nose and receding hairline. She deemed him to be in his early sixties. With a closed cropped beard, and dressed in an impeccable snow-white kandura falling gracefully off his broad shoulders, his stature was not unlike her father's. A benign smile in an open face beamed down at her. She bowed and extended her hand, uncertain as to how she was supposed to greet the man she was certain was no other than Hamdam himself, but he swooped her off the floor and kissed her on both cheeks in a very European manner.

"I can see so much of your father in you!" he exclaimed, putting her back down and looking at her up and down from head to toe.

"Welcome to my home! I trust Latifah has taken good care of you so far? How was your trip?"

"Everything was fine. Thank you so much. Your wife has been most welcoming," replied Arielle somewhat formally.

"So tell me, you take after your dad in looks but do you also take after him in the saddle?" questioned Hamdam, delving straight into his personal interests and referring back to Guillaume's former reputation as an exemplary polo player. His friend had not only followed in his father's footsteps in breeding and training horses but had also derived great pride and enjoyment competing during heated matches.

"Oh no! I'm much better than my father!" replied Arielle without a trace of conceit.

Hamdam shot her a quick look, his thick eyebrows raised in surprise. Latifah secretly repressed a smile: Arabic women would never dare compare themselves to a man, regardless of the circumstances, especially in the company of other men. She knew instantly that her husband would regard the girl's response as impudent. Yet, so far, she had not detected in the latter any sense of entitlement, falseness or misplaced pride and so, curious, she waited to see how the scene played out.

"Would William agree with your assessment?" inquired Hamdam, careful not to call his friend by his birth name and wary to leave any hint of sarcasm out of his tone.

"Everyone agrees, not just him," replied Arielle, still blissfully ignorant that her replies had left everyone aghast.

"Well, we'll just have to put you to the test, wont' we? Do you play polo like your old man or is dressage more your style?"

"Neither," laughed Arielle, amused by the idea. "I race thoroughbreds."

In the vast hall, time stood still, everyone frozen into place, mouths agape, holding their breath. Hamdam's astonishment knew no boundaries.

"A well-kept secret, I'm sure," stammered the otherwise uber-confident businessman.

"It really depends on who you talk to," replied Arielle lightly. "Actually, I was hoping I'd be able to ride whilst I'm here; horses have been my life and two years without jumping on a saddle seem like an eternity."

"I'm sure we'll be able to accede to your desires. Perhaps you'll be able to teach Latifah to ride. So far I haven't been able to make her go near the stables."

"I'd be delighted. In fact, I'll do anything to repay your kind hospitality."

"Well, there will be plenty of time for that. Meanwhile, Latifah will show you to your quarters. I'll expect you for dinner around nine. You'll meet my other wives then. Again, welcome to Dubai and to my home. If you need anything just ask me. And I'll see what I can do about those horses of yours."

While Latifah was showing Arielle to her rooms, located in the female guest quarters, and with his curiosity deeply aroused, Hamdam jumped on the internet to Google the temporary addition to his household. He hadn't been shocked as much by Arielle's assertion that she was better in the saddle than his old friend than by her claim she raced thoroughbreds. Surely she was mistaken. Women simply didn't make it as jockeys. On the other hand, it was true that she had the right bone structure, the ideal height and was certainly born and bred in the right environment. What he soon found out astounded him: Arielle LaSalle was recognised in racing circles all over Australia as the most promising jockey ever to show up on the circuit. The fact she was a female only added to her allure and reputation. The young woman had not spoken in vain: she had stated a simple fact. Hamdam immediately wondered how he could take advantage of the situation. On impulse he dialled his uncle's private number. The conversation that followed would forever change the young woman's destiny.

CHAPTER II

C hantilly Farms continued to prosper during Arielle's time abroad. Guillaume's horses had twice won the Caulfield Cup and had thus been automatically selected to run in the prestigious Melbourne Cup. Black Fizz, a black colt with distinctive white stockings on all four legs, had even come in second place, earning Chantilly Farms' owner a sizeable chunk of the prize money. Despite their good fortune, Guillaume and Sarah, known to their friends simply as Will and Sarah, terribly missed their daughter, throwing themselves into their work to forget her absence. As a result they had grown closer to each other, rekindling the romance which had vanished from their relationship ever since Arielle's birth. Even depression had lifted its hold on Sarah's heart, when she came to accept that her overbearing protectiveness could not change the outcome she had feared for so long: children were meant to fly the coop, experience the world at large and grow into adults. You couldn't protect them forever from illness, strife, accidents, failure, heartbreaks or even death. It was the nature of the beast and their lives to live. Yet it had taken her 18 years to heed the lesson.

After all those years, and due to her sole daughter's absence, she had finally come to accept that Murielle's death – Arielle's twin – had been a tragic accident, with no one to blame, and that nothing could have prevented it. She had finally conceded that distance would have little bearing on her personal safety since tragedies could happen at home just as well. To keep a sense of closeness to the daughter she had agreed not to contact whilst she was abroad, Sarah had nonetheless taken to read online, and daily, the *Gulf News* and *Gulf Today* newspapers to avidly collect any news. Both parents had been proud of her unexpected early accomplishments: Arielle had won both the Dubai Gold Cup and the United Emirates Derby and her wins had made headlines. Now, after nearly two years abroad, the prodigal child was returning home. Her parents could not wait.

The reunion at the arrival gate at Sydney International Airport was nothing short of cathartic. Guillaume marvelled at the changes in his daughter. Arielle had blossomed into a real beauty, her large green eyes enhanced by a light tan, her long auburn hair cascading in soft curls around a finely chiselled face which had lost the soft roundness of childhood. She appeared more mature, more self possessed and every hint of wistfulness had disappeared from her eyes. Likewise, Sarah could not get enough of her, kissing her incessantly, firing question after question all the way back to Chantilly Farms. The moon was already high in the sky by the time they reached the famous gates. After a celebratory drink Arielle soon begged off to bed, thoroughly exhausted.

For Arielle, returning home was like stepping back in time: the house and her bedroom were exactly as she remembered them. Her parents had not aged either, except that her mother looked happier somehow, the haunted look in her eyes suddenly gone, the fine lines around her mouth proof to many smiles, not bitterness. For a few minutes, as she put her clothes away, she delighted in the notion of sleeping in her own bed once again, underneath the safety of her parents' roof. She had missed it all so often, had dreamed about it for so long that she could hardly believe that she was finally back on home soil. However, sleeping alone once again unnerved her. Nonetheless, she soon fell into a dreamless sleep, wondering what her future would now hold.

Over the next few years, it became abundantly clear to everyone what a serious advantage it really was for Guillaume to have his own daughter ride most of his protégés across the finish line. Now nearing 30, Arielle had often ridden the winning horse across prestigious races all over the country, the tack room at Chantilly Farms filled with her trophies and ribbons. She lived for the races, with the adrenalin-charged atmosphere, but never let her passion overcome her sensibility. Arielle refused to buy into the game of ego and fame, unlike most of the people she came across. Her notoriety and beauty though had earned her many suitors, yet she had found most of them shallow and vain, more interested in her wealth and her celebrity status than the person she really was. They also always came short when she unfailingly compared them to her first love, whose torch kept burning deep in her heart.

She had nonetheless met veterinary surgeon, Nathan Heathers, a few months earlier. The young man, older than her by just a few years, had first come to the house to introduce himself, having recently moved his practice into town. Mutual physical attraction aside, Nathan had been one of the few men she had come in contact with who hadn't in some way been indebted to her parents. Regardless of how close she was to her formidable father, she had longed for some independence from his ever-growing influence. Straight shooter Nathan had nicely fit the bill. Moreover, both in looks and in temperament, he stood as polar opposite to the man to whom she had once given her heart. To date, their relationship had been uncomplicated, a sharp contrast to her first love which had been layered with complexity.

On the morning after she had delivered Dauphine's twin colts, they were both sitting on the paddock's fence, watching the two colts nurse. They were still waiting for Guillaume to show.

"Good morning, my cherie! Not too tired? How did it go?" inquired Guillaume as he walked up noiselessly behind the couple perched on the wooden railings.

Surprised she hadn't heard him approach, Arielle turned around quickly to face her father and affectionately pecked him on both cheeks. Nathan shook his hand.

"Your daughter handled it like a pro. You should be proud of her. She had to assist in the birth of the second foal though as it wasn't coming as naturally as one would have hoped for," Nathan explained.

"A twin birth? Is that him?" queried Guillaume, pointing at the smaller yet perfectly proportioned animal.

"Isn't he beautiful?" cooed Arielle, looking longingly at the black colt cantering around the paddock.

"Won't be any good for racing though," determined Guillaume, shaking his head, after observing him for just a few minutes.

"Oh, come on, Papa! He's small, I'll grant you that, but it doesn't mean he can't race! Only time will tell!"

"The prognostic isn't good: not only is he smaller in size and thus unlikely to meet the height requirements when the time comes, but his frailty is far from a desirable trait in a sprinter. If you want to keep him as your own, you're welcome to it. You even deserve it, but at this point, I'll only proceed with the registration of the other one. Discussion is closed. I need to go back inside now, I've much to do. Any other problems I should be aware of?" he asked, turning his full attention to Nathan.

"No, sir. They are both nursing fine and so far this season's foals are all progressing nicely."

"Great. I'll see you both at the house for breakfast in 15 minutes. Darling, I think you should get cleaned up first: you look an absolute mess," observed Guillaume, taking in his daughter's soiled T-shirt, muddy jeans and matted hair. After looking down at her clothes, Arielle sheepishly shook her head and broke down in musical laughter.

"I see what you mean. Nate, let me take a shower first but please join us for breakfast," she added, winking at her boyfriend.

The three of them walked back to the house in animated conversation, the two men still weighing the pros and cons of whether to register both colts with the racing authorities. By the time both men reached the front door of the house, a decision had been made.

"There is truly something of a witch in you," admired Nathan a few weeks later as he neared the spot where Arielle, balanced on the fence, watched the young colt she had playfully named Obsession canter around the paddock. Indeed, after attending to the branding of all new colts on the property, the veterinarian had come looking for her.

"You're a true horse whisperer," he added, seeing the black colt come up to the fence to nuzzle in Arielle's long auburn hair as soon as he spotted her. Imitating his brother, Obsidian, his twin, had also walked up to the fence yet had stopped at a respectful distance, with the watchful mare, Dauphine, placidly observing the proceedings.

"I bet that in another four months you'll be able to begin halter-training with this one! Unbelievable!"

"Another four months you reckon?" replied Arielle mischievously. She reached out to the spritely colt and caressed his ears and nose, all the while emitting a low clicking noise by tapping her tongue against the roof of her mouth. The colt whined and snorted and put up one of his front legs on the fence.

"He's saying hi," she said with a smile and, without waiting for Nathan's reaction, jumped inside the paddock and motioned for the weanling to follow her. Without hesitation the animal pranced around, remaining a couple of paces behind her, accelerating when she did, breaking short when she stopped.

"Wow! Very impressive!" yelled out Nathan. "Destined for the circus rather than the track? What about Obsidian? Did you get him to perform the same tricks?"

"Dad has started imprinting him and you know I can't really interfere with the process. I've to let him do what he wants to do with him. On the other hand, Obsession is mine and I spend a lot of time with him. Dauphine even let me sleep in the barn with the three of them last night!"

"And a true obsession it has become! Probably why you stood me up?"

"Oh! I'm so sorry, Nate! I completely forgot we had a date. Can I make it up to you?" she exclaimed apologetically.

"I'm sure you can, but it may require for you to stay away from your baby for a few hours."

"Let's do it tonight. I'll come to your place. We can order dinner or I could pick up some dishes at the delicatessen on the way and I'll bring a couple of bottle of wine from my grandparents' estate. How does that sound?"

"Perfect, as long as I don't slip your mind once again," replied Nathan ruefully. "I've got to go. Pandora Estates want me to check on a few of their mares, all close to foaling. I'll see you at eight."

He kissed her on her soft fleshy lips. "I can't wait," he murmured in her ear, breaking away. Arielle watched him rev up his truck and disappear along the driveway. If she wished to hang on to him, she'd better keep her word. She wondered once again what he saw in her since she saw herself as irrevocably flawed.

Indeed, despite her riding accomplishments, Arielle was plagued with deep-seated insecurities. Despite her lively nature and her innate ability to endear those around her, she masked a pervasive sadness with humour, hiding behind a cheerful facade. Moreover, her secluded childhood on the farm had early on hindered her capacity to relate to men other than her father and the farm hands who worked around the vast property. As time wore on, most of them had come to treat her like a younger sister, her diminutive size frequently mistaken for youth. Her open face, lit by large almond-shaped green eyes speckled with gold, pert nose, full sensual mouth, shoulder-length light auburn hair, blemish-free olive skin, fragile bone structure, boundless energy and easy laugh did the rest. Her stint in the United Arab Emirates in her early twenties had taught her to continue keeping men at arm's length even though, at the time, she had graced the party circuit with great enthusiasm, eventually shedding the remnants of her childhood in the bed of one particularly beautiful Arab man. When she had returned home nursing a broken heart, for years she had simply sworn off men, at least until Nathan had shown up on her doorstep.

It hadn't been until her return from overseas that her parents had finally revealed the circumstances of her birth. A couple of weeks after her return, following a particularly emotional 21st birthday dinner, she had once again pressed her mother for details. Indeed, Arielle had forever wondered why, right on her birthday, her mother religiously scheduled a trip to the cemetery early in the morning, refusing any company, and often returning home hours later with a face marred with dried tears. The rest of the day had always tasted bittersweet, the brightly lit birthday candles on the cake never quite managing to dispel the eerie sadness that hung in the air. So, on her 21st birthday, after all the neighbouring families invited to celebrate her coming of age had gone home, she had insisted on knowing the cause behind her mother's subdued mood. Faced with the explosive revelation, Arielle, after recovering from her shock, had finally come to understand not only the reasons for her mother's overly protective behaviour over the years, but also the source of the dull ache she had carried in her own heart ever since she could remember.

An in-depth internet research on the identical twins' phenomenon helped her pinpoint the reasons why she had never felt quite whole, why something always seemed to be missing in her otherwise orderly life. Nothing up to that point, except for the love of the animals in her care, had quite managed to fill the inexplicable void. During the whole course of her adolescence, she had often blamed social and geographical isolation for her inadequacy and inability to truly connect to anyone. With her parents' disclosure, she had suddenly realised that for years she had actually been missing nothing less than a mirror image of herself. Finally confronted with the truth, she had nonetheless remained wary of sharing with anyone the pervasive feelings of loneliness which often engulfed her. Often, she was barely able to control her irrational yet overwhelming guilt at having accidentally strangled her twin in uterus.

It was culpability and angst that had led her to instinctively plunge into action when Obsession's delivery had been compromised: she couldn't have borne the thought of being responsible once again for the death of a twin, regardless of the species. On that August day, she had also made the solemn vow that Obsession would grow up to rival his brother, whatever the personal cost. The two colts were almost undistinguishable now, except for the slight dissimilarity in height and the white coronets on Obsidian's feet. However, she was convinced that with proper nutrition, careful monitoring, targeted exercise and boundless love, her horse would come to fairly compare to his brother by the time they both reached two years of age. If she were successful, no one would be able to tell them apart – on and off the track. In her opinion, that was the least she could do.

Once again, irrational jealousy stabbed at Patrick McCarthy's heart as he surreptitiously watched Arielle kiss her boyfriend goodbye. Hidden in the shadows, thanks to the low roofline of the stables, the former jockey had stopped in his tracks as soon as he had seen the vet's truck ride up on the other side of the fenceline. Just a few metres away from the paddock in which the new broodmare and her two colts were enjoying the early morning sun, he strained to hear their conversation, but a light breeze had spirited their words out of earshot.

Five years prior, the 40-year-old man's career had been dramatically cut short, courtesy of a recalcitrant mount, which had knuckled over at the start of the Tea Rose Stakes at Randwick, throwing him forward in the process and right into the path of a peloton of advancing horses. After weeks of long and painful recovery in hospital to mend broken bones and restore his balance upset by a severe concussion after being trampled, the jockey's career had been all but over. Knocking on doors had come to naught. Guillaume alone had magnanimously offered the desperate man a job.

Ever since coming to Chantilly Farms three years earlier, Patrick had pined after the owner's irresistible daughter, who, infuriatingly, continued to refuse every single one of his advances. Used to being feted and adulated when he was still a successful jockey, Patrick had taken the rejection to heart, coming to spy on her every move and at every opportunity. The night before he had watched her sleep in the stable: if it hadn't been for the agitated mare that had sensed his unrequited presence, he would have tried to seduce her right there and then. With the stables located well away from the house, no one would have heard her scream. The developing romance with the stud farm's vet now seriously interfered with his dream of bedding the beautiful Arielle and consequently hacked into his fantasy to head the famed stables into the next two decades.

Nicknamed by his foes "Pat the Rat", in part due to his devious and much publicised riding style, when he purposefully spooked the competition by scraping paint when riding dangerously close to the inside rail, Patrick was nonetheless a patient man. He was certain that the opportunity would one day present itself for him to make a move. In his view, riding glory had been taken from him unjustly. However, status, fame and fortune could still be his once he seduced Chantilly Farms' only heiress.

It was shortly after seven when Arielle, after pushing open the garden gate, knocked on the front door of Nathan's neat little Victorian cottage. Keen to be forgiven for her earlier forgetfulness, she had taken particular care with her outfit, wearing a cross-heart dress of the softest cashmere in the same blue-green hue as her eyes. The knit draped gracefully on her lean body. She had completed the look with a pair of tight-fitting, high-heeled boots. A simple wide leather belt cinched her small waist. Despite her heels, she nonetheless tiptoed to kiss his close-shaven cheeks.

"You're certainly a sight for sore eyes!" approved Nathan, grabbing the two bags of groceries hanging on her arms, after quickly taking in her svelte figure.

"You're not too bad yourself," replied Arielle playfully, her eyes dancing over his taut body. "I thought you might be starving so I've purchased a whole bunch of tapas. Dinner could be ready in a matter of minutes."

"That's fine," he replied with a lack of enthusiasm, which surprised her since she was sure he would have skipped lunch as usual.

"What a day! Just when I thought a country practice would be drama free! Let's start with some wine," he proposed listlessly. "I badly need to unwind,"

Looking at his fatigue-lined face, Arielle realised there was more to his edgy mood than just a lack of food. She watched him uncork the wine and waited for him to pour.

"Do you want to talk about it?"

"Something isn't quite right at Pandora's," began Nathan, "and it bothers me a great deal. One of their fillies came down with Lyme's disease."

"Which one?" interrupted Arielle, with her curiosity roused.

"Gitane."

"Ouch, that's going to hurt them for the Spring Carnival. Wasn't she due to race at Randwick alongside Silver Bolt?"

"Well, the way it's going, she'll be a scratch at least for the beginning of the season. With a course of antibiotics though I believe we should get on top of it. Fumigation has now been done but a tad too late. Last week's temperatures, more typical of the middle of summer than the end of winter had taken everyone by surprise and they weren't ready. That's not what bothers me though."

Arielle knew better than to press: Nathan wasn't one of those men who responded well to pressure. Unhurriedly, the latter took a sip of his wine.

"There's something not quite right going on at the farm," he repeated.

"You're speaking in riddles. What do you mean?"

"Do you remember the night Obsidian and Obsession were born?" began Nathan.

"How could I forget?" Arielle replied, smiling sweetly.

"Do you remember how I had told you I couldn't wait up with you because I had to put a horse down?"

Arielle's face clouded: putting down a horse was something they both abhorred even though they both knew that in some circumstances it needed to be done.

"I'd been called to Pandora's because Napoleon had suddenly developed laminitis. He was in too much pain not to put him out of his misery."

"Napoleon? As in the famous overseas-bred stud purchased at the beginning of last year and claimed to be of the best lineage ever?"

"One and the same. Except that during his first season none of the mares covered lodged a return."

Arielle's eyes widened. The purchase price of the stud had been highly publicised and she had often heard Guillaume scoff at the excessive fee, regarding the whole affair as just another publicity stunt by Pandora's owners.

"The horse had been tested over and over again but no one could figure out what was wrong. However, oftentimes, as we all know, a change of climate, a different environment and a slew of other factors can impact performance. For the first two weeks of the following season, none of the mares placed in his care were with foal. We were facing a repeat of last season's disaster. Then abruptly Trent dismissed my services. When I was finally allowed to resume my activities and return to check on the mares, all were pregnant."

33

"What are you saying, Nate? That another stud impregnated those mares? But it will show up in the bloodstock. You can't falsify the DNA of those foals. Each will be tested before their ID card can be issued. Could it not be possible that Napoleon finally came to the party and did what the Cavalieri brothers paid for in the first place?"

"I hope so," replied Nathan, his face taut, "otherwise I face a problem of monumental proportions."

Arielle's eyes widened, the implication hardly lost on her.

"Do I understand you correctly? Trent Winnings would have purposefully falsified the bloodstock of the horse? Why on earth would he do that? If the word gets out, he's finished! So is Pandora Estates' reputation for that matter! And since he can't easily falsify the bloodstock of the horse the only thing he could have done..."

Arielle's hand flew to her mouth. She looked at her lover, completely horrified.

Nathan finished her sentence.

"... is use artificial insemination. Napoleon was purchased overseas. Practices abroad aren't covered by the same regulations as they are here: perhaps the previous owner had taken some "insurance". Look, it's not that farfetched: after all, it's Trent Winnings we're talking about. With a man of his antecedents, there is no doubt in my mind he could have stooped so low. He probably saw it as the only way of saving face."

Nathan shook his head, mouth downturned dejectedly, his shoulders slumped. By sharing what had bothered him most for the past three months, robbing him of sleep, he had hoped to feel better. However, the weight hardly seemed to lift. Contrary to popular belief, a problem shared was not necessarily a problem halved.

Arielle's mind reeled at the implications. Nonetheless, she tried to calm him down.

"Nate, sweetheart, think about what you're saying. All the horses sired by Napoleon would be banned from racing forever and Trent's license immediately suspended! I'd suspect he would even face jail time for his deception. Even if the owners claim they didn't know anything about it, Pandora will from now on come under close scrutiny by the authorities of Racing New South Wales, provided they are still allowed to operate. It'd be nothing short of a juicy scandal, that's for sure!"

Nathan sighed and shuddered.

"Unfortunately, it might be only the tip of the iceberg."

This time Arielle's mouth hung open. She could not even formulate a single sound. Nathan pleaded with her.

"You can't tell anyone of this conversation. Perhaps I didn't read the signs correctly. I've been very tired attending to all the foaling everywhere. How's Obsession by the way? Will he survive the evening without you or you without him?"

"Stop chiding me and don't change the subject. What do you mean by "the tip of the iceberg"?" And, by the way, whatever you tell me in confidence remains under lock and key. I'm offended you could think otherwise!"

"I know that, darling. I'm sorry. I probably worry too much but if Trent Winning is capable of this sort of cheating with Napoleon, who can say for sure it hasn't happened before? When Trent first purchased Napoleon two years ago, the stallion was already a proven stud. For God's sake, that's why Pandora paid over $1,000,000 for him! But within three months at the Estates, the horse appeared listless and disinterested. During the first year, I ran through the entire gamut of remedies to renew his famous vigour, but still the mares were without foal. The mares' owners have been furious, forcing Pandora to strike a deal: the mares would be covered for free the following year. And at the very beginning of the season, it certainly did not look as if Pandora would be able to keep its promise. Then, suddenly, by all indicators, Napoleon appears to have finally adapted to his new environment, resuming his career as a stud."

"I can feel a 'but' coming," Arielle said, holding her breath.

"Since Napoleon has now conveniently passed, it's impossible for me at this point to test any of his sperm. I have kept some blood samples though. Maybe those will be enough."

35

"It's rather part of the course that the horses born from those unions should carry some of the traits of both parents. That's why the stud fees for this particular mating is so high," said Arielle, trying to dispel his fears.

"I've no idea whether any test can determine whether the sperm was live or frozen. I don't even know whether the DNA remains the same."

"Do you really believe that Trent would be so criminal as to artificially inseminate the mares in his care just to justify the exorbitant stud fees he charges? Nate, are you sure?"

"I'm not sure, but the timing is extremely suspicious at best. That's what's doing my head in. And if I'm proven right, then my reputation is on the line: I should have raised the alarm a lot earlier. And in order to prove that, in best-case scenario, it was the first and only time we could be required to retest all the horses sired at Pandora Estates for their paternal bloodlines and..." Nathan trailed.

"... Pandora will have to reimburse all the stud fees it has charged for the past few years, and since many horses bred at Pandora Estates have won many races here and abroad, it would put international racing on its head. Oh my God! This can't be happening!"

Arielle had turned a light shade of green. She felt nauseous.

"Arielle, let's not jump to conclusions. I'm conducting my own investigation to see whether a DNA sequence remains the same when using frozen sperm. Until then, there is nothing to do but wait. The foals have been tested and Napoleon so far is unequivocally shown to be the stud. Except, I know in my heart it's not possible. Oh, my God, look at the time. Let's eat! I'm really starving."

It took minutes for them to set the table for two. They savoured the prepared dishes in silence, neither of them in the mood for romance, the earlier conversation playing on both their minds. Nathan worried that if his intuition served him right, he would become a pawn in a scandal which would taint not only his client's reputation but his by the same token, just for failing to come forward any sooner. Arielle, on the other hand, wondered if she should break his confidence and give her father the heads-up.

Pandora Estates had always been Chantilly Farms' biggest competition. She also knew that her father, with his larger-than-life personality, often took great risks when backing his horses. Their horses, however, during the 2011 season, never quite managed to take the first prize in any of the major races, often losing to Pandora's own in major last-minute upsets. On more than one occasion, she had observed the worried look on her mother's face when Guillaume had played up to the press and the punters, as if financial losses weren't worth mentioning. She suspected though that her insider knowledge could inadvertently cause more damage that she could anticipate, and, by the end of dinner, decided that Pandora's woes had nothing to do with her.

However, two years later, when Obsidian would come up against one of the yearlings sired by Napoleon, the conversation would once again come back to haunt her.

CHAPTER III

Sebastian Cavalieri's brooding dark looks could have been mistaken for that of a man constantly exposed to the sun. They were, however, typical of his Sicilian ancestry. Indeed, a week before Mussolini appointed Cesare Mori as the prefect of Palermo in Southern Italy, everyone had known that the fascist leader had declared open war on the Sicilian Mafia. This grand propaganda coup had been designed as the fascist leader's last-ditch effort to exert full control over all Italian life. Under direct orders, the newly minted Palermo prefect had assembled a small army composed of Carabinieri and ruthless militiamen to round up the suspects, town after town. Sebastian's family, unfortunately rumoured to hold ties with the local mafia, had been taken hostage, their land holdings sold for a song. In October 1925, when Sebastian was barely 18, his father, Lucio, thanks to a sympathetic neighbour, had avoided prosecution by fleeing to Argentina, the only one amongst his male relatives to escape imprisonment. The tenacious and solidly built man was never to return.

Working first as a wrangler on the semi-arid pampas of Argentina, Lucio's fortuitous marriage into the influential Fuentes family had finally helped him acquire his own estancias. The plenteous and vivacious Isabel would later bear him three sons. However, when Juan Peron had come to power in 1946 and quickly established his own neo-Nazi ideology, Lucio, having seen it all before, had decided it was time to uproot his family, lest his past caught up with him once again. With plenty of skills and money behind him, Australia had welcomed him with open arms.

With the proceeds of the sale from his Argentinean farm, Lucio had first moved his family to Far North Queensland. There, he had first secured a cattle ranch, where he'd also kept plenty of horses for the muster, training his young sons to ride. After just a few years, the astute Italian had become convinced that horseracing would come to occupy centre stage in Australian sports, its popularity far exceeding that of the polo matches so common in his second home. He had thus made the courageous decision to sell his prosperous cattle ranch and purchase instead a parcel of land in the Hunter Valley.

There he had quickly chosen to dedicate his time and resources to breeding and training horses specifically for the track. With the heat-filled summers reminding him of Sicily, the climate of New South Wales had better suited his temperament anyway. He had also loved the vine-covered hills and olive groves dotting every bend.

Forty years later, having prospered beyond his wildest dreams, what had become known as Pandora Estates was headed by his eldest, Sebastian, now 66 years of age. Stefano, the youngest of the three, worked by his side. However, the middle son, Cesare, had taken up a career as an international polo player, a sport and lifestyle which matched his playboy personality. He was now living in Houston, Texas, with his own brood, having finally settled down at the prime old age of 50 with a woman 20 years his junior. All three men had inherited their father's olive skin, brooding good looks and tenacity, as well as their mother's lustrous jet black hair, fierce intelligence and volatile disposition.

When Sebastian had suffered a stroke three years previously, Stefano had convinced him to finally hire a studmaster to assist with the management of the hugely profitable farm. Trent Winnings' confirmed reputation for a tightly run ship had preceded him. The two brothers had purposefully ignored the rumours regarding his alleged elastic morals and, at first, they had congratulated each other on their decision.

The purchase of Napoleon, an overseas stud of impeccable credentials, had been privately brokered the year before upon Trent Winning's enthusiastic recommendation. He had argued for weeks that the foreign-born stud would further raise the company's profile and uniquely diversify the bloodstock. The quite substantial fees the animal would commend for his stud services would make his $1,000,000 purchase price pay for itself within a few seasons.

The mahogany stud had been sired overseas as part of the stables run by Sheikh Karim bin Zayed Al Nahyan, the crown prince of Abu Dhabi's younger brother, and sold to Sheik Rashid Al Martam, a wealthy entrepreneur, with fingers in many pies, who owned both racing camels and thoroughbreds. Napoleon had thrice won the Dubai Gold Cup. In the United Arab Emirates Derby he had proudly taken his place inside the winner's circle for four years in a row.

In 2009, his seven-year brilliant career had come to an abrupt end when he'd sustained an injury after falling down 300 yards into the two-mile race, throwing the jockey and virtually stopping the race. Humiliated, Sheikh Rashid couldn't wait to get rid of him, but his advisers had recommended he put the horse up for stud instead. For the next two years, Napoleon had amply demonstrated his staying power, yet Sheikh Rashid had still smarted from his earlier public disgrace.

When Trent Winnings had approached him, a deal had quickly been struck. However, travel to Australia and breeding conditions under the tropical climate had seemingly tempered the champion's ardour. He had failed, time after time, to lodge a return. With so much riding on the horse's potential, Sebastian and Stefano had been devastated. Indeed, in order to acquire the fabled stud and meet the required upfront price, they had taken a second mortgage on the farm. Now it appeared that Trent's choice was set to jeopardise Pandora's viability: gossip alone could disseminate them.

What Trent Winnings' resume had cunningly failed to list was the number of times he had been under investigation for perceived anomalies on and off the track. Since he had never been caught, his official record remained untainted. However, it was widely known in horseracing circles that very little ever stood between Trent and his ambition. The Cavalieri brothers, however, hadn't cared about the rumours circulating around their studmaster when they hired him. They had wanted a man who could produce results and until the purchase of Napoleon, Trent had delivered exactly that. However, when the stud had failed to settle for an entire season, they had begun to panic. The stud fees paid so far into a trust account could have already halved the initial purchase price, reducing their loan to bearable levels. As it stood though, they were now facing a return of all fees with penalties, a prospect which sent shivers down their spines. Thus, they had given Trent an ultimatum: either recover their money by returning the stud to its former owner or get the stud to perform at last.

Trent had tried to reason with them, pleading for more time. Returning Napoleon to Sheikh Rashid was out of the question. When he had brokered the deal, he had done so by lining his own pocket through a substantial kickback. A return of the horse would inevitably expose his underhanded financial manipulations and he would be left with little choice but join the ranks of the unemployed. Trent reeled at the thought, but he wasn't a man without a fallback plan.

With a horse purchased from overseas bloodstock, the DNA typing wasn't nearly as stringent as that imposed either by the Australian Jockey Club or the Victorian Racing Club, nor was the practice of freezing sperm for later artificial insemination necessarily forbidden. Trent suspected that some of Napoleon's sperm had been held back by its original owner, just in case. After much pleading and many threats to expose Sheikh Rashid for his shoddy practices, when they had conspired to overvalue the horse and then split the difference, Trent Winnings finally received the parcel he had been waiting for containing the face-saving cryogenic vials of the stud's semen.

Due to Pandora's unblemished reputation over decades, the Australian Stud Book representatives had never seen any reason to physically witness any of Pandora Estates' studs covering the mares during any breeding season. Nor had they had ever requested to be present to monitor the preparations before and afterwards.

Carefully, and one by one, Trent had thawed the vials' content as required, and, under the cover of night, with a purpose-made turkey baster of his own making, had impregnated the mares, one after the other. During the day, as required by law for thoroughbreds, he had gone about the necessary business of recording the movements of the mares within designated paddocks along with their alleged covering on precise dates. In any case, any farmhand would have testified they had seen the distinctive buckskin stallion mounting over and over again the various mares grazing through the paddocks. The fact that he still shot blanks was a secret Trent guarded jealously.

During the particularly critical two-week period, Winnings had nonetheless been careful to postpone Nathan Heather's attendance to the property under various pretexts. Only once he had been certain that the 30 mares in his care would test positive, had he called Nathan back to treat the mares allegedly covered during his absence. The veterinary surgeon's presence was required to lodge the appropriate stallion return. With a stud fee exceeding $20,000 per mare, Napoleon had thus returned more than half his purchase price. In the eyes of the Cavalieri brothers, it had now proved to be a good investment. All they needed was one more season and they would be back on top.

As relieved as Trent had been that his subterfuge had not been discovered, he was nonetheless keen to cover his tracks as rapidly as possible. A couple of weeks past the breeding season proper, he had injected the horse with a chemical mixture designed to inflame and weaken the folds of tissue connecting the horse's pedal bone to the hoof. After waiting days for the horse's condition to deteriorate beyond help, he had urgently called Nathan who had regretfully rendered his diagnostic. Napoleon had been inexplicably affected with Founder's disease: the only humane solution required immediate euthanasia.

The Cavalieri brothers had been devastated by the news but Trent cushioned their loss by reminding them that during his regretfully short time at the farm, the stud had nonetheless repaid at least half of their original outlay. Moreover, in all likelihood, he was bound to have sired future champions, giving them another glimmer of hope. However, Trent had not been quite careful enough, never accounting for Nathan's inner moral compass. Indeed, the latter, dismayed that a horse in his care would develop such a painful disease in such short a time without noticing it first, had taken upon himself to perform a discreet post-mortem. Whilst the tests failed to reveal how the stud had suddenly contracted laminitis, they nonetheless inadvertently confirmed his suspicions that the horse would have been incapable of siring a new generation of runners, regardless of Winning's affirmation to the contrary.

The Haras de la Selle had seen over six generations come and go between its walls. The family motto was that each generation only gave birth to as many children as was required to produce at least one male heir to carry on the family name. It was incumbent for males only to continue the family business and hold on to the ancestral properties. For a family whose ancestry dated back to the 16th century, direct lineage was easy to trace. As chance had it, each generation had produced no more than two children before a boy was born. Guillaume though had been the only child. His entire upbringing had been focused on his future duties as sole heir apparent. His father, Romain de la Selle, had been Duc et Pair de France and upon his death, as per tradition, Guillaume had inherited the title in his place.

His entire childhood had been that of any male child born out of money and privilege. Excellence in academic pursuits and mastery of noble sports had been the sole focus of his primary years. During his entire schooling, Guillaume had come to live with his only aunt in the capital, in a vast apartment located in nearby Rue des Saint Peres. Finally, he had graduated with top marks in his baccalaureate exams from the Lycee Louis-Le-Grand, renowned for turning boys into men through a strict Jesuit education. After a summer back home, filled with parties and pretty girls, the 18-

year-old boy had been shipped to Cambridge to obtain his MBA. A natural in the saddle, he had soon become a proficient polo player, competing in tournaments all over the United Kingdom, proudly wearing the school colours. Falling in love with a blonde beauty of English peerage had also been part of the course. Interestingly enough, during that entire period, he had never had once knowingly crossed paths with Hamdam, who had only been one year ahead of him; nor had he run into any occasion which would have provided an introduction to his college girlfriend's second cousin, Sarah. However, a few years later when the two young men had met at the Domaine de La Selle, where their fathers had discussed business, they had quickly acknowledged how much they had in common. Sharing a passion for polo and racing thoroughbreds had been the icing on the cake, cementing the instant friendship even further.

All over Paris and across many of the provinces, from the time of his graduation forward, Guillaume's name had begun to appear prominently on dowagers' lists. Deemed a most eligible bachelor for their daughters, he had graced many a debutante circuit. Upon his return from England, Guillaume had remained much in demand. It hadn't just been young girls who'd thrown themselves at him due to his sturdy prospects and irresistible good looks, but more mature women as well. Thanks to two of his mother's friends, who had taken upon themselves to perfect his education behind closed doors, Guillaume had learned to be a savvy and patient lover in bed, generous and thoughtful out of it. Once he'd left them, the women who had crossed his path had plenty of regrets. None however, ever called him a cad, his behaviour too gentlemanly to leave behind any traces of bitterness. Moreover, he had already proven that he could take over the reins of the family business and do his family proud. By the age of 28, Guillaume, well-bred and well-educated, had the world at his feet.

After the massacre at the Ecume des Jours, having to give up his title, his name, his reputation, his estate and his future had been too much for the young man to bear. In his adopted country, pride, ego and deep-seated anger nonetheless propelled him over time to rise to the top of his profession once again, paradoxically on his own merits rather than by birth right. Despite his accomplishments, Guillaume had never quite managed to truly overcome the overwhelming loss of his past. He had been ill prepared for his sudden and brutal reversal of fortune.

In his eyes, the now sexagenarian, who had been forced to bury the rightful sense of entitlement he had carried since birth, was nothing less than a self-made man. In his opinion though Australia had only turned him into a nouveau riche, just like so many others. Since he couldn't safely claim his peerage, nor boast of his distinguished ancestry, he wanted, at the very least, his legacy to be remembered. To that end, he had vowed long ago that Chantilly Farms and its owner would become a benchmark in horse breeding and training. His legacy would be known for raising champions and establishing an industry standard to which everyone would aspire. Had he been able to fulfil his destiny at the Haras de la Selle, fame and honours would have been his decades ago. Like always when he dwelled on the subject, bile and resentment churned his stomach. However, he was now certain that he held the jewel in his crown. He certainly had the right jockey for the job: it was time to raise the stakes and make his final mark.

Surf Rider displayed all the right pedigree. Foaled from Symphonie at Chantilly Farms three years prior and sired by Silver Lining, a Triple Crown winner, Surf Rider's style was that of a stalker, rarely making the lead but known to gain momentum to overtake tired front runners. After modest beginnings, he had recently placed at the Caulfield Cup and the Victoria Derby. He ran especially well in the wet, preferring heavy tracks. Luck had been on Guillaume's side when he had been balloted to run for the Melbourne Cup as number three. When his barrier assignment also came in third, close to the inside rail, Guillaume, superstitious like many when it came to racing, knew he couldn't lose. Moreover, weather conditions had been tipped for light rain on the day. The odds on the gelding had nonetheless remained long: since the race exhibited a particularly strong field, Surf Rider was still considered an outsider. Two of the horses, against which he had previously lost, were also due to run against him, further impairing his chances.

However, Guillaume believed that his horse, with Arielle on his back, would form an invincible pair: the horse would not carry more than 58 kilos and thus would not have to load on any additional weight. So convinced was Guillaume that Surf Rider could win that, unbeknownst to his wife and daughter, he placed an unprecedented bet at the 50-1 odds. In case of a win, Guillaume would instantly become a multi-millionaire, taking home not just the $6,000,000 prize money but the proceeds of his risky bet as well. The $500,000 invested, however, could just as well bankrupt him.

★ ★

Arielle, in Chantilly Farms' unmistakable silks of a red background with the French fleur de lys silhouetted in white both on the front and back, repeated by three smaller versions running along both sleeves, paraded along the birdcage with a pretend air of confidence. It was her first time running the Flemington course and she was more nervous than excited. She couldn't help notice that her father looked inexplicably tense. She couldn't imagine why since he was such an old hat when it came to the Cup: in the past he had trained many of the horses whose owners had entered and won that particular race. It was also true that Surf Rider could be at a slight disadvantage since he could be perturbed by running anti-clockwise. On the other hand, her mother, chatting on the rail with one of her friends, looked poised and elegant in her white chiffon dress. A red fascinator held back her ginger hair and matched her red high-heeled shoes. Even from atop Surf Rider she had been hard to miss. Arielle waved at them both. They both returned a thumbs-up sign and a smile of encouragement.

A few minutes later, at a gingerly canter, Surf Rider was brought to his box. The clock had just struck three when it started raining. For the first few hundred metres, Arielle hung back, leaving her horse to run a few lengths behind the leaders,

47

conserving his strength. After the first turn though, Surf Rider, now fully in its element with the track getting wetter by the minute, seemed to grow another leg and raced past the pack, keeping close to the inside rail. However, he became agitated when another horse suddenly drifted in, pushing him dangerously close to the rail. Arielle kept her sang-froid without releasing her grip. She regretted skipping the blinkers she had removed at the last minute, afraid that the rain might impair the horse's vision. The blinkers would have improved his concentration and allowed him not to be spooked by a horse riding too close. Unnerved, Surf Rider nonetheless slowed down, losing precious seconds. Arielle, undaunted, urged him on, maintaining a firm grip, all her senses focused on just one thing: finishing the race as honourably as possible. She had been the only female jockey running that year and everyone had speculated on her chances for weeks. She did not expect to win but she wanted to honour her silks regardless.

She was now within four lengths of the front runner, amidst a pack of six horses all running neck to neck, the thunder of hooves on the heavy track resonating in her ears. As she took the second turn, rain almost obscured her vision, rivulets cascading down on both sides of her helmet. Now, all she could hear was the horse's breath and her own heartbeat. She could only see three horses in the lead and she added pressure for Surf Rider to quickly gain momentum. The grandstand finally came into view. Within seconds, they bypassed a brown gelding which Arielle's mind registered as one of the race's favourites and her heart tightened. The finish line was fast approaching.

She whipped her mount once again, encouraging him loudly over the falling rain, when suddenly an Irish-born champagne mare, aptly called Champagne Dream, seemingly sprouted wings in the last two hundred metres, accelerating in the straight. However, Black Velvet, considered by many the fastest horse of its generation and a Cup winner for the past two consecutive years, already had its foot on the till. It was closely followed by Champagne Dream who claimed second place, merely a length ahead of Surf Rider, who proudly finished third. Arielle was ecstatic. It was her first time on that particular track. Admittedly riding a mud lark but without enough experience, her performance nonetheless swelled her with pride. She couldn't wait to share the moment with her father.

Guillaume was livid. He had literally been taken to the cleaners. From now on, there would be huge financial pressure on him running Chantilly Farms, having lost most of his savings on a single bet. Always a gentleman, he steeled himself to accept the compliments of high-profile punters and owners alike, now milling in the members' enclosure. He agreeably conceded it had been a race well run and that the form of his jockey had been superb. Sarah, detecting something very wrong beneath her husband's socially debonair manner, was immediately worried, her imagination running amok. Both managed to put their worries aside to warmly congratulate Arielle on her performance. Both knew she had given it her all.

In her wildest dreams, Arielle could never have imagined that her very own father would have bet on his own horse. The man she knew wasn't a gambling man, as he knew all too well that the slightest mistake could change the course of a race. He had often mocked the punters who had risked their savings on what they had believed was a dead cert. Over the years, the Melbourne Cup had been known for its upsets, with many favourites finishing dead last. Her surprise thus knew no limits when a man by the name of Roger Cunning, a notorious bookie, approached her father standing by her side in the members' enclosure.

"Hey, Will. You must have really thought that pretty girl of yours had it in the bag, didn't you?" he joked somewhat rudely, his sarcasm inescapable.

"Hello, Roger. My girl ran very well today. I'm proud of her," replied Guillaume icily, trying to maintain his composure.

Everyone knew a punter had a couple of days to settle his bets. This was neither the time nor the place.

"Too bad Surf Rider didn't ride as smoothly," mocked Roger. "I agree with you though," he added offhandedly, "for all instances and purposes, I agree everything appeared to run in his favour –

49

the ballot number, the stall, the heavy track and the lightweight mount."

Arielle didn't care for his tone. How dare the man speak to her father like that?

"Papa, what is he talking about?" she interrupted.

Roger Cunning turned to look at her, his eyes narrowing in an expression of disdain.

"I'd say your father has lost much more than he can afford today. All thanks to you, my love. Will, don't forget our appointment in three days' time." He winked, walking away, leaving Arielle aghast.

"Papa?" questioned Arielle, dumbfounded. "Papa?" she repeated. "Is it true? You placed a large wager on Surf Rider? Why? And why didn't you tell me?"

"Would that have made a difference?" replied Guillaume, his tone both harsh and defiant.

"But the horse had long odds! Did you bet on it to win?" inquired Arielle once again, unable to hide her growing disbelief.

"I did," admitted Guillaume, not daring to look in her eyes.

"But why?" persisted Arielle, incapable of accepting the unbelievable answer at face value.

"It's complicated. We'll talk about it later and it really doesn't concern you," replied Guillaume sternly. "In the meantime, put on a brave face, just as I need to do."

Arielle knew only too well that there were few secrets kept for long at any track. Moreover, Roger Cunning had the reputation of gossiping more than most, nothing ever out of bounds, waiving his client's right to privacy as if it didn't concern him. She wondered how severe the blow to their financial welfare had been.

Basically overnight it became known that Chantilly Farms' owner had lost a considerable amount of money backing his own horse. Guillaume, instead of riding tall as had been his intention, had to deflect riles and mockeries trailing behind his passage. Back in the Hunter, his mood turned sour and foul. He soon came to scrutinise every expense and question every invoice. Moreover, he postponed all non-emergency repairs and scheduled upkeep. The bank helped him out of his conundrum by allowing him to take out a second mortgage on the farm. Despite the loan, his absence at the spring markets was duly noted, fuelling further speculations. Everyone wondered whether the rumours had, in fact, been true. Had Surf Rider really driven Chantilly Farms into the ground? Was Guillaume still financially viable? Was it safe to leave horses in his care? Was he simply too old to train their champions? Had he lost his Midas touch?

For the first time in their marriage, Sarah berated Guillaume for his arrogance, refusing to understand how pride and vanity could have led him to imperil everything they had worked so hard to achieve. After many acrimonious fights, she left the farm to allegedly 'clear her head', and took a holiday abroad to put as much distance as possible between the husband she judged irresponsible and the gossip that plagued them both. Arielle did not see her in six weeks and often wondered whether her parents had reached the end of their road together. Sulkily, after his efforts to reassure other owners that everything was fine and that the race had had little impact on his affairs, Guillaume threw himself back into his work, spending every waking moment training his new protégé – Obsidian. The almost two-year-old gelding was as fast as they came and, session after session, Guillaume's hopes that he was indeed raising another champion rose accordingly. Two seasoned jockeys were primarily assigned to ride him, with Arielle as a convenient alternate. Guillaume was unwilling to take any further chances when it came to a strong hopeful.

While Arielle knew her father had not blamed her for losing at the Flemington racecourse with a horse that had, in her experience, little chance of taking out the first prize, he was certainly nominating her as his preferred jockey less often than in the past, especially when it came to mount and train with Obsidian. By exercising less demands on her time, her father inadvertently left her with more time to dedicate to her own horse – Obsession. She was cautious not to train on the same tracks at the same time. Having had the opportunity to saddle both twins, she had noticed how naturally fast they both were and how equally comfortable they ran on both fast and slow tracks, a versatility that would serve them well in their careers. However, by precaution, whenever she rode Obsession close to the farm, she took to wrap both his forelegs, virtually erasing any markings differentiating him from his brother. For fun, she had also taught him to imitate some of the latter's trademark movements, such as shaking his head side to side before a race, letting his mane fly, and bristling from head to tail whenever a new jockey mounted him. She had been delighted when, on a couple of occasions, she had even fooled her own father when he had unexpectedly come to the track to see her ride, remaining astonished by how flawlessly she had run the course, the horse barely breaking a sweat.

Throughout the late autumn and early winter, Guillaume's mood failed to improve, barely registering his wife's return to the homestead. In his eagerness to gild his faded laurels, everything else had become secondary. He couldn't wait to enter Obsidian in country races and qualify for the Spring Carnival, desperately pinning all his hopes on the spirited gelding. He needed to restore his reputation and, in his now skewed opinion, only a horse winning in spectacular fashion could erase his last public disgrace. By casting his daughter aside as the preferred jockey when it came to some of his favourites, Arielle had been left with little choice but to lend her services to other owners. Thankfully, her own reputation had remained unblemished. Her place at Flemington had only increased her profile as a jockey of considerable worth. Moreover, Arielle had been grateful for any time spent away from her brooding father and despondent mother.

To add to her woes, her boyfriend, Nathan, had proved of little comfort throughout the trying period, preoccupied as he had become with what he now referred to as the "Napoleon conspiracy". By the full moon in June, Arielle had become so weary of the foul-tempered moods which characterised the two men in her life that she decided to take matters into her own hands. Indeed, if she could not help make up for her father's misfortunes, she could at least help her lover solve the riddle left behind by the late Napoleon. She could hardly have guessed though that the overseas phone call that followed would once again turn her life upside down.

CHAPTER IV

For the first five days, Hamdam had left Arielle to recover from jetlag. He noted that the young woman seemed tireless. His fourth wife, Latifah, had taken her mentoring role seriously, taking the Australian everywhere, from camel races in the desert to falconry demonstrations, from dune riding to stargazing. Together, they had visited both the magnificent mosque in Abu Dhabi, the Emirates Palace and the souqs in Deira, in the old part of town. They had even skied on the man-made snow fields in the Mall of the Emirates where Arielle had excelled on the indoor 400-metres black run. He was also aware that Latifah had chosen a gorgeous abaya from Catherina's latest collection and that Arielle had been enchanted to wear it whenever in public, declaring she had become a true princess. The two women had also enjoyed entire days at the ESPA spa, a Moroccan-inspired hammam, located at the One and Only Royal Mirage Hotel. On the sixth day, when Hamdam declared that he would finally like to bring his young guest to his stables, located not far from the Meydan racecourse, Arielle had been relieved, clapping her approval.

Early that morning, donning her usual equestrian gear, she had waited in the hallway of the grand house for Hamdam to send for her. The sexagenarian could not help but notice how the skin-tight outfit revealed her perfectly proportioned figure: he only prayed that her prowess in the saddle would justify such immodest attire in public. As far as he knew there was no road map to follow when it came to proper attire for female jockeys: she was the only one he had ever laid eyes on. Latifah had begged to accompany them but Hamdam had not wished to share with anyone the anticipated emotion he hoped his friend's daughter would provide him.

The stables, located behind Oud Metha Road, formed three sides of a vast compound located a 15-minute ride from Sheikh Zayed Road, known locally as the "strip". Generously proportioned stalls occupied three of the buildings. The fourth housed offices, tack rooms and a reception room, with deep comfortable seats scattered around small coffee tables. An elaborate fountain, composed of four life-size bronze horses rearing on their hind legs, stood in the middle of the courtyard, water spouting from their open mouths. A dozen men stopped in their tracks to stare at Arielle as soon as she stepped out of the four-wheel-drive Porsche. Hamdam addressed a few words in Arabic to the kandura-clad man who came to welcome him and a few minutes later, Arielle was led to the nearest stalls.

"Arielle, pick your horse. Tabassum here," he said, pointing to the man who was shadowing him, "will saddle it for you and then we'll go to the track."

"Where is the track?" asked Arielle, wanting to know.

"It's right behind the compound. It's a three-kilometre track with a couple of bends in it and a long straight of about six-hundred metres," replied Hamdam proudly.

"I can pick any horse?"

"Whichever one strikes your fancy," encouraged Hamdam, curious to see how trained Arielle's eye really was.

Slowly Arielle began to walk past the enclosures where the horses, inquisitive by nature, were peering out, eyeing the small group. A couple of them, quite nosy, came up to nuzzle Arielle who stroked their noses and murmured terms of endearment in return. Finally, after doing the rounds once again, she settled on a chestnut mare with a lightning bolt marking between her eyes.

"May I please ride that one?" asked Arielle, looking straight at Hamdam.

Behind him the man introduced earlier as Tabassum coughed loudly, shook his head vigorously and frowned in a pained expression.

"Excellent choice, my dear," smiled Hamdam, ignoring his manager's reprove. "It's the latest addition to my stable. You have

56

a very good eye. I brought her over from England a few months ago. I've yet to race her but in training she has looked promising."

"Really? Most English horses are more used to the wet. How does she perform on a drier track?"

"The jury isn't out yet. Maybe you'll help me figure out what to do with her," replied Hamdam cautiously but with eyes crinkled with merriment.

He snapped his fingers and the stablemaster gave orders for the horse to be saddled.

Unconsciously, Arielle, under Tabassum's bemused eye, nonetheless verified everything was in order, blissfully unaware of the men's surprise at watching her double-checking their work. Arielle climbed on easily and quickly adjusted her reins and stirrups.

"What's her name?"

"Aazeen. It means beauty in Arabic."

"Didn't you tell me her pedigree is primarily English? Didn't she have another name before that?" questioned Arielle. It was unusual to change a horse's name once it had been registered.

"Beauty. We converted it to Arabic for convenience's sake as most of the Pakistani staff don't speak English."

"Hey there, Aazeen," whispered Arielle softly as she patted the horse's flank, prompting her mount to perk up her ears. "I'm ready," she announced, looking round. Tabassum was already on the back of another horse, motioning for her to follow him.

"I'll follow you by car," said Hamdam. "You'll take the short cut to the track,"

Arielle had difficulties focusing. The track ahead of her seemed to disappear in shimmers of light, sand drifting in and out of her range of vision, compressing and distorting distances. She sensed the impatience in the animal beneath her: the horse wanted to run. Led to the starting block stall by Tabassum, she squinted in the harsh flat light. Hamdam came up beside her.

"Would you like my sunglasses? They are especially made. They will cut down on the glare and prevent the sand from getting into your eyes. I suggest you first take one lap around to judge the lay of the land and then if you'd be ever so gracious, I'd love to time you on the track the second time around."

"Of course, thank you," replied Arielle, bending down to reach the proffered glasses.

"Her poise in the saddle is certainly impressive," reflected Hamdam. None of his jockeys seemed to form one with the horses they raced, especially this one. Moreover, Arielle had asked all the right questions. The horse had underperformed again and again on the often sand-blown track. Furthermore, whenever the wind picked up, the horse would buck and rear, the sand in her nostrils provoking sneezes that racked her whole body, usually overthrowing her mount in the process. Aazeen so far had proved to be a mistake. There was no denying it had been a costly one.

With the lightest pressure of her heels, Arielle was off at a light canter to warm up the horse and assuage her nerves, taking in the landmarks around her to identify them later so as to navigate the track with greater ease. After her first lap, she took place in the box without being asked, waiting for the signal. A warm breeze had picked up and Tabassum looked nervously at Hamdam, who ignored him once again. He counted down to zero and blew the horn.

Arielle was off, the large clock ticking. She had been told to race up to the second post, alive with a large red banner floating at high mast, clearly indicating the 2600 metres mark. Halfway down the course, Hamdam disbelieving, looked at his stopwatch once again: Arielle had already shaved 90 seconds off the horse's best time so far. By the time she finished the course, had it been a real race on this particular track, she would have come in first, a few lengths ahead of the fastest horse in his stable. Hamdam was dumbfounded; not only had Arielle kept Aazeen under control in spite of the light wind but she had obtained the best performance out of the horse to date. The girl was amazing.

As Arielle trotted back to the stands, the few men in attendance cheered. They couldn't wait to tell their friends about this girl, this

Australian jockey who had just blown away any misconception they may have had about a woman racing. Hamdam saw pure greed and joy light up their eyes. Quickly he let Tabassum know that if any details of today's performance escaped the compound walls, everyone's visa would be cancelled immediately and indiscriminately, leaving them with no choice but to return to their country of origin within 24 hours. His manager promised that he had nothing to worry about; he would control his men.

"That was fun," conceded Arielle as she dismounted. "Your horse is a really fine horse. I'd suggest blinkers next time you race her. She won't be spooked by the wind and the sand as much, leaving your jockey with greater control. That's a great track by the way! Whose is it?"

"Mine. I train all my horses here."

Now curious, Arielle questioned him some more.

"Does every Emirati have his own stable and his own private track?"

Hamdam laughed.

"I guess not; like everywhere else, it's the domain of a privileged few. How else would I monitor my horses and check up on my jockeys? Us Bedouins, we have a long history with horses. Like your father, I loved playing polo, and unlike him I love hunting on horseback, but above all I love the thrill of a good race."

"Papa really played polo? I thought you were joking when you first mentioned it. I'd never heard him talk about it," said Arielle, astonished.

Hamdam winced. Polo had been part of Guillaume's former life and he realised too late that he probably had not shared any of it with his daughter.

"It was a long, long time ago when we were both students," he said evasively. Eager to change the subject, he put forward his proposal instead.

"So, Arielle, the season has already started. The Dubai Cup is held at the end of it, in just two months' time. Would you like to race for me?" asked Hamdam, hoping to distract her from his faux pas. Right away he mistook the dubitative look on her face and quickly added, "I'd pay you of course, and above the awards, I promise you. Salaries are higher here than in most parts of the world."

It was Arielle's turn to laugh.

"I'd love to. And I don't need to be paid. I already told you that I'd do anything to repay your generous hospitality. Racing for you is the least I can do and it would be an honour," she added with a bright smile. "When do I begin?"

"Let's go and celebrate first," replied Hamdam, beaming, his black eyes crinkled in merriment. "And for the record, I want you to know how sorry I am I didn't believe you when you first told me you were a professional jockey."

"You didn't believe me?" Arielle blushed. It had never occurred to her that anyone would question her claims. "Ouch! In that case, you must have thought I was an insufferable brat bragging about her abilities. I'm the one who should apologise."

Hamdam looked at her thoughtfully; not only was she talented but she also possessed one of those very rare qualities he most appreciated in a woman – humility. At that very minute, he knew that no matter how much he would push her into the public eye, she was likely to remain steadfast and level-headed. He was now quite certain that his friend Guillaume would never come to regret his decision to entrust her in his care. It was definitely time to celebrate. Allah had once again looked kindly upon him. Arielle was a most unexpected gift.

On their way back home, Hamdam picked up the car phone often, speaking quickly in Arabic. To Arielle's ears it sounded as if he was barking up orders. In fact, Hamdam was making plans for the evening ahead. He wanted his uncle to meet the young woman and for that he needed to secure a plush venue with little room for any outsiders. In-between calls, he suggested Arielle call Latifah and let her know that he wanted her by his side and ready by six o'clock, for an evening of indulgent fun. As an incentive, he also added that the two women would be welcome to kick up their heels afterwards at a nightclub of their choice. Arielle was thrilled: she loved dancing and back home she'd seldom had the occasion to indulge. Life at Chantilly Farms was hardly conducive to late nights of dancing and drinking with people her own age. As soon as they reached the house, Hamdam asked for Arielle to follow him to his office. As he closed the door softly behind her and beckoned her to sit in the deep velvet-lined sofa, Arielle began to feel somewhat nervous.

"Arielle, I would be lying if I said I wasn't impressed by your performance this morning. I'm serious when I say I'd like you to race for me. But you need to realise a few things first," he added slowly.

Arielle watched his face furrow in concentration. Hamdam was trying to find the right words. She wondered what they would be.

"We've never had a woman race on our racecourses," he began. "If you race for me, you'll be the first and, as such, you'll be an overnight sensation."

"I doubt that," interrupted Arielle. "Out there I look like any other small jockey on a horse."

Hamdam raised his eyebrows. Didn't the girl have any idea how beautiful she was and how inherently feminine she was? Her silks would hardly manage to cover that simple fact!

Hamdam cleared his throat.

"You do know that betting is illegal in our country, don't you?"

Arielle nodded.

"So in order to attract an international crowd and compensate in a way for the excitement normally provided by betting, our races carry a substantial purse and lavish pageantry. You'd become the star attraction of the season. Are you ready for that?"

Arielle smiled and shrugged her slim shoulders.

"I think you're putting too much creed in my gender being an anomaly in this particular sport, but if you believe that it will help turn me into a 'sensation' as you put it, and that in doing so I can make you proud, then I'm ready. I also promise not to do anything that would make you regret your decision. The way I see it, it's you who provides me with an opportunity of a lifetime, not the other way around. If by virtue of being a woman, I can offer you more publicity and more clout, then Inch Allah."

Hamdam smiled broadly.

"I see you're improving your Arabic."

Arielle giggled.

"I'll never be as talented a linguist as Latifah, that's for sure! Her English is absolutely remarkable."

The more time Hamdam spent in the company of the young woman, the more he liked her. She was straight forward, thoughtful, intelligent and well-mannered, with a great sense of humour to boot. Moreover, she was blessed with qualities of adaptation he found most endearing. Mentally, he saluted his old friend Guillaume: his daughter was certainly doing him proud.

"Well, my dear, I'm sure Latifah is chomping at the bits to get you ready for tonight's party. You're the guest of honour. Once the oldies retire, you can go and dance the night away."

Arielle used all her restraint not to jump to his neck as she would have her own father's.

"At what time do the festivities start?"

"As soon as the sun goes down. And, Arielle?" he called to her already retreating back, "please go shopping and buy yourself something nice," he added, putting a large roll of dirhams into her hand.

Arielle blushed.

"I can't accept this."

"Yes, you can. Consider it an advance on your salary," replied Hamdam, amused by her refusal. Decidedly, she was a most unusual woman, even refusing money to buy new clothes; in his experience, it was unheard of.

As Arielle stepped into her room, she saw Latifah sprawled on her daybed, munching on stuffed dates, a tall pitcher of icy lemon mint by her side, watching another instalment of the Desperate

Housewives of New York on her television set. She jumped to her feet at her arrival.

"Sorry, I made myself at home," she announced guiltily. "I didn't want to miss you on your return. Tell me everything, and don't leave anything out!" she cried excitedly. "Whatever you've done to Hamdam, you've earned me an entire evening of freedom!"

"Your husband is most generous," replied Arielle, dropping the wad of bills which floated on the marble floor down to Latifah's feet.

"We're supposed to go shopping before tonight. I don't know if I can be bothered. I've plenty of stuff to wear."

"Oh really?" retorted Latifah dubiously, rolling her eyes. "Let's have a look at your closet," she added, skipping to reach the walk-in robe where the contents of Arielle's two suitcases were neatly hanging. She flipped through the half dozen dresses and stopped abruptly, turning to the woman she already considered a friend.

"Is that it? Are you hiding the rest somewhere else?" she questioned, slightly aghast since her own walk-in closet was the size of a small room with over 80 dresses and as many abayas hanging neatly, row after row.

Arielle yawned.

"I've more dresses here that I've had during my entire lifetime!" she said dismissively. "Who needs dresses when you spend your time taking care of horses? Any of those will do, won't they?"

"Are you mad? You can't wear any of these to go to the Buddha Bar and then onward to the very chic Boudoir nightclub! Absolutely not! We can't waste any more time on your silly objections! Let's go now as we'll need time to have our hair and make-up done, and I know you'll want a massage and a nap to be fully refreshed before the evening kicks in," said Latifah in a firm tone which did not expect to be further contradicted. Arielle yawned once again. The idea of a luxurious massage after the morning ride was tempting, but a nap? Was Latifah serious? Did a night on the town really require so many preparations?

63

Arielle sighed loudly and Latifah rolled her eyes.

"Come on, I'll take the Porsche. I promise I won't keep you more than one hour, two at the most. Aisha, my beauty consultant, will be here by 5.30 pm. Come on, let's go," she insisted.

"Let me at least change into something more appropriate than my riding gear," said Arielle, hurrying to the bathroom to change. "I'll be right out."

Even though the young woman thought it was much ado about nothing, she went along, caught up in Latifah's enthusiasm. Less than six hours later, she would forever be thankful for the care she had been forced to take in her appearance.

By the time they returned home, the clock had already struck three. During their shopping escapade, Arielle had told Latifah everything that had happened during the extraordinary morning and Latifah had her repeat some of the details over and over again. She just couldn't imagine her new friend competing as a jockey as part of her husband's stable. She wasn't sure whether the latter was setting her up to fail and she worried: she had come to care about the charge she now regarded as a younger sister. On the other hand, were Arielle to succeed, would she be ready for the media furore sure to surround her?

Since Hamdam had invited his entire entourage to the Buddha Bar, a luxurious bar at the marina described as uber cool for the well-heeled, she was certain there would be some kind of official announcement. Even Catherina, who was in town, had told her earlier she would join in. At first, Latifah had been annoyed at the prospect. Catherina always stole the limelight thanks to her natural elegance and Anglo-Saxon good looks. However, she took consolation in the knowledge that after the party, she'd be left alone to go and dance at the Boudoir where her husband had already reserved for her a black table near the dance floor. For the entire night she'd never want for anything, nor would any of her friends. Perhaps that was compensation enough for Catherina's undesirable presence.

Arielle, her long honey-streaked auburn hair twisted in a bun at the base of her neck, her skin scrubbed and radiant, her make-up light and luminous, donned a short black Dior linen shift dress with a lacy back, a short matching bolero and stunning red patent high-heel peep-toe shoes. Latifah wore one of Catherina's creations, an abaya of the most extraordinary silk with embroideries of reds and oranges along the neck, with long sleeves covering her arms and hands, ending in a point at her index finger. Underneath, she wore a mid-thigh off-the-shoulder dress of the brightest pink, courtesy of Christian Lacroix. In the meantime, her high-heeled shoes of the same pink were blissfully covered by her habit. Her plan was to take off the abaya as soon as they arrived at the Jumeirah's parking lot.

By the time her chauffeur pulled up in front of the Buddha Bar, the sun was setting down beyond the marina. Crowds were pressing on the sidewalks. As she climbed the steps to the bar's entrance, Arielle inhaled the rich floating aroma of toufah and enad shisha drifting in the breeze from the cafés below. The two women walked into the lavishly decorated bar a few minutes past six, admiring on the way through the Asian-laced decor with its deep reds and comfortable seating. As soon as they gave their name to the pretty East European hostess, they were ushered to the terrace where Hamdam had reserved every table, efficiently preventing uninvited guests to step foot in the enclave.

Hamdam was already there, surrounded by a few men, half of whom wore civilian clothing. Arielle heard many languages spoken in a variety of accents. As soon as Hamdam noticed her, he beckoned her over.

"Arielle, I was just bragging about you. I told my friends here how dexterous you are on a horse."

"You're too kind," replied Arielle with a smile, her head slightly bowed in a sign of respect.

"You look beautiful, my dear," admired Hamdam, looking her up and down. "What would you like to drink?" he offered as the waitress hovered.

"A lemon mint, no sugar, would be perfect," replied Arielle after noticing the full pitchers already set on the tables. Hamdam shot her an appreciative glance: she had observed an unspoken rule of etiquette by not ordering alcohol in his presence. In public, it was essential to maintain a certain amount of decorum and as much as he was aware that Arielle knew him to indulge behind closed doors, she had been sensible enough to respect traditions.

"Go and enjoy yourself. I'll send for you when my uncle arrives," he added and Arielle took her cue. The men surrounding Hamdam had basically undressed her with their eyes and she had felt most vulnerable. Why didn't she imitate Latifah by wearing her own abaya? It would have been so much easier! She knew it had not been expected of her but she nonetheless already regretted it.

Latifah introduced Arielle to all the people she knew, giving her explanations as to who they were once the introductions were over with. Food circulated everywhere on stylish platters. Arielle noticed that a number of foreigners, who had demanded access to the terrace, had been firmly turned away and ushered instead to one of the cosy corners inside.

One hour later, there was a perceptible change in atmosphere, and Arielle spun around to see what had prompted it. Sheikh Maktoum had just walked in, immaculate as always, with an entourage of about a dozen men. A handful of women trailed behind. Hamdam stood up to greet his uncle with a firm handshake followed by the customary kiss on both cheeks. They all sat down in a flurry of white robes, exchanging boisterous greetings and compliments. Once again Arielle was called forth.

"My dear uncle," began Hamdam, "this is the young lady I spoke to you about," he announced just as a somewhat nervous Arielle walked up to the table.

Raw power emanated from the tall man with piercing eyes, a boxer's nose and a somewhat crooked smile. His eyes, fixed on her, however, were nothing but kind.

"I hear great things about you," said Sheikh Maktoum, "but are you sure you want to race for my nephew?" he joked, testing her.

"It's a great privilege to have been asked and I can only hope to be worthy," replied Arielle deferentially. "It's the least I can do to repay his generous hospitality," she added, looking down demurely. "I'd even race camels if I knew how."

Sheikh Maktoum laughed throatily, as did his entourage. With his finger, he motioned for her to come closer and gently lifted her chin so she could level her gaze with his.

"Hard to miss the family resemblance," he observed, turning to Hamdam and remembering the discussions he'd had all those years ago with Arielle's grandfather. "What would your father say about this?"

"I believe my father would be thrilled and forever in Hamdam's debt for giving me this chance. The calibre of the races here is known worldwide. I can't wait to prove myself."

"Very well, we'll see you next on the track. Are you enjoying your stay so far?"

"I love everything about it!" exclaimed Arielle, her shyness evaporating. "It's so very different from Australia but so beautiful in so many ways."

"What did you most enjoy so far?"

"Hands down, I loved the grand mosque at Abu Dhabi! It's so majestic in its architecture, so pure in its decor that it can only inspire the deepest of faith. I was blown away. It gave me an insight into Islam like nothing else could," she enthused, "and, of course, the architecture in Dubai is absolutely mind-blowing! Every building is more beautiful than the next! The desert is an ever-changing canvas I could never tire of admiring. And don't start me on the food either; all too delicious."

She stopped abruptly, aware that the assembled men were all staring at her thoughtfully. None had expected such a spontaneous declaration of love for everything they held dearest to their hearts.

67

Since none of them could notice any trace of guile in her face nor detect sarcasm in her tone, they nodded approvingly. Unknowingly, Arielle had won the tacit endorsement of the most powerful men in the city. As Latifah led her away, she congratulated her.

"You couldn't have done better if I had coached you," she beamed.

"What are you talking about? I only spoke the truth!"

"That is why you're so brilliant, my young friend! Now all we have to do is wait for Hamdam's uncle to take his leave and we're free to enjoy the night!"

At that very moment, Arielle's heart arrested. The most beautiful man she had ever seen had approached the table where Hamdam was talking animatedly with his uncle and the handful of men standing around them. He had kissed them ceremoniously and had just lifted his head when his eyes met hers. The impeccable kandura emphasised his height and did little to hide a svelte and athletic physique. With razor-sharp cheekbones, a neat, trimmed beard, thick eyebrows and lashes to match, full rosy lips, a straight nose, and skin the colour of liquid honey, Sheikh Majid Borkan Al Kasimi looked as if he had just stepped out of a fashion magazine cover. Arielle was transfixed by the captivating eyes, her heart beating at an unusual rate.

"Arielle, did you hear a word I said?" repeated Latifah, turning around discreetly to see what had fascinated her friend so. She repressed a giggle.

"I see you're distracted by a much more interesting subject," she teased.

Arielle tore herself away from the sight of the man who had yet to stop staring at her.

"Who is he?" she asked breathlessly.

"Majid is from Sharjah, a neighbouring Emirate state, related by blood to the royal family there. He's a poet and a well-known photographer to boot, having published many books. His latest claim to fame was being expelled from Saudi Arabia three months ago whilst attending the Genadariya festival in Riyadh."

"Why was he expelled?" asked Arielle, taking the bait.

"According to the press, he was asked to leave on grounds of being too good-looking."

Arielle laughed, the spell momentarily broken.

"You're kidding, right?"

"I wouldn't dream of it!" replied Latifah in a mock-indignant tone. "The Commission for the Promotion of Virtue and Prevention of Vice was afraid he may cause women to drop their veil and relinquish their virtue. Consequently, he was escorted out."

"That's very funny! I'm sure it isn't true and you're pulling my leg. I'd love to be introduced though," added Arielle uncertainly.

"I don't think that will be necessary," noted Latifah as Hamdam was making his way to the small group of women resting against the terrace wall, the young man in question following in tow.

"Arielle, this is Sheikh Majid Borkan Al Kasimi," said Hamdam benevolently.

"Majid, this is Arielle LaSalle, my protégée. Majid requested an introduction after I told him of my plans for you. He said he'd love to photograph you on course: some pre-event publicity photos can't hurt and he's the best there is. By the way, you have made an excellent impression on everyone," he added with a smile.

"The pleasure is all mine, asalaam alaikum," said Majid, bending to kiss Arielle's hand in a very European fashion. The young woman blushed deeply, not daring to look at him.

"Walaikum salam," saluted Arielle in return.

"Do you speak Arabic?' he asked, slightly confused.

"No, I don't," replied Arielle, mirth dancing in her voice. "I believe that being polite and knowing how to greet someone isn't akin to knowing a language, now is it?"

"You're absolutely right, of course," answered Majid smiling broadly, with the slightest hint of an accent in his otherwise perfect English. "You're a very interesting young woman. Everyone tells me you're a jockey. Is that true?"

"If everyone says so, it must be true. But I'm surely not nearly as interesting as someone who makes the front page for being too good-looking!"

"Touché!" Majid's laugh was musical. "I'd like to state for the record that I was never expelled by the religious police. I was just confused with someone else. Just let me know when you'd be available for those photographs," he added with a glint in his eyes.

"Surely Hamdam will let you know when. It was nice meeting you." Arielle started to turn away. Majid knew he had been dismissed. Taken aback, he smiled tightly.

"Sheikha Latifah, it was a pleasure seeing you again," he saluted, bowing slightly, turning his attention to the latter.

"I can't wait to see you again," he murmured nonetheless in Arielle's ear as he brushed past, leaving her stunned and speechless.

When, one hour later, an older generation joined in the festivities, the two women were granted permission to finally leave the gathering. All the way up to Jumereiah they never noticed the black Bentley following them. Arielle would soon learn that little stood between an Emirati and the prospect of a new conquest.

Within minutes of parking the car, Latifah emerged from the back seat minus her abaya, her long jet-black hair held up by large tortoiseshell combs draping over one naked shoulder. Arielle took a quick brush to her own hair and distractedly splashed on her wrists and neck a few drops of the liquid oud, which Latifah had insisted the royal perfumer create just for her. She was still troubled by her earlier encounter with the Emirati; in her life so far she'd rarely had the opportunity to meet men outside the racing game or outside her parents' circles. She was still astounded by her primeval response to his physical presence, with sweaty palms, dry lips, knotted stomach and pounding heart giving her away. Until now she had never experienced the telltale symptoms she had read about in the numerous romance novels which populated her evenings at Chantilly Farm. She wondered how much time would pass before she could lay eyes on him again, and whether she would be able to stand it without making a fool of herself. She was no longer in the mood for dancing. In truth, all she wanted now was to go home, open her iPad, search the internet to her heart's content and learn everything she could about the arresting man who, after one look, had just captured her imagination.

Everyone inside the deceivingly small nightclub was dressed to impress. There was not an abaya or a kandura in sight. The crowd was mostly expats, with a sprinkling of fashionably dressed Emirati sporting the latest trends. The loud music pumped urban fever themes from US Top 40 charts amongst an atmosphere of decadent intimacy, with small tables and low cushions jammed against the polished dance floor. Latifah had obviously rallied her troops. Several of her girlfriends waved for them to come and join them in the VIP area where her table had been reserved. It was the first time Arielle had stepped foot in a nightclub and she could not get enough of the sounds and sights that greeted her. A glass of champagne was thrust into her hand and Arielle gulped it down. Shortly afterwards she found herself on the dance floor, moving liberally to the beat. As the music slowed, exhausted and exhilarated she turned around to find herself face-to-face with the man she had met an hour earlier.

"You!" she blurted. "What are you doing here?"

"I couldn't stay away from you," he murmured. "Waiting to see you whenever Hamdam got around to it was just too long."

Arielle remained tongue-tied, unable to express an intelligible thought.

"Please dance with me," he begged, grabbing her by the waist before she could answer.

Unable to resist the pleading eyes, Arielle let him twirl her around the dance floor under the envious look of the other women watching them. With every move, he pressed his hand in the small of her back and despite the heat, Arielle shivered time and time again, not daring to look up at him.

"How did you know I'd be here?" she finally managed after a few minutes.

For a second Majid wondered whether he should lie.

"I waited for you to leave the Buddha Bar and followed you here," he replied simply.

Surprised by his admission, Arielle looked up at him.

"So you're a photographer and a bit of a stalker, are you?" she questioned deadpan.

It was Majid's turn to be caught off guard. Most of the women he courted often failed to reveal the slightest sense of humour.

"What would you do in my shoes if you were confronted with a beautiful, intelligent, witty woman with a promising career in the saddle? Would you let her run away?"

"Does unabashed flattery usually give you what you want?"

"Usually," he admitted, "but what do you think I want?" he taunted her.

Arielle's cheeks turned crimson. She might not be experienced in the flirting game but she wasn't stupid either.

"Oh!" he said, grinning at her discomfort. "You believe I'd want to go to bed with you? You couldn't be more wrong! I'd only want to prime you so you'd give me the best tips for the Dubai World Cup."

"So, you don't want to bed me but you'd like me to betray the oath to my profession by giving you insider's tips for a race for which there is allegedly no betting? Did I understand this correctly?" she bantered.

"I did say you were smart, didn't I? Did I also mention captivating and sexy or did you mock me before I could finish?"

Arielle laughed.

"I need a break. Can we stop for a minute? I'd love a drink please."

"What can I get you?"

"Surprise me. Something exotic and sophisticated with a small paper umbrella, of course."

"Your wish is my command. I'll be right back."

Arielle's eyes followed him to the bar. She wondered how old he was. She wondered if he was married even though she hadn't noticed a wedding band on his finger. She came back to sit down next to Latifah.

"Are you enjoying yourself?" queried Latifah merrily. "He's quite a specimen of a man," she added approvingly, referring to Majid.

"Maybe, but he's probably married with three wives and 10 kids," retorted Arielle.

"Certainly not. That's one man fiercely holding on to his bachelor ways! For a while, his family cut him off for refusing to settle down but since he makes his own money, they soon gave up. He promised solemnly though that he'd wed by the age of 30. I believe his birthday is coming up soon."

"How do you know all that?"

"You only need to read the papers. He's legendary around here. He was always a talented photographer but before working behind the lens he stood in front of it. His face used to be splashed on every billboard in town and his address listed in every woman's Blackberry, wishing to marry her daughters."

"Why would he be interested in me?"

"You're a novelty," stated Latifah bluntly. "You're destined to become famous. His name tied to yours is good for both of your images. Besides, why wouldn't he be? You're young, smart, beautiful, talented and adorable; he'd be crazy not to chance it. But let's see how he moves through the courtship phases first."

"Courtship phases?" Arielle shot her a blank look.

A friend of Latifah, by the name of Maryam, a classic beauty with a curvaceous body, joined in the conversation.

"Emirati are generous people," she explained. "You'll be doused in honeyed compliments about your looks, your intelligence, your wit and your style. You'll receive half a dozen calls a day and three times as many text messages. He'll shower you with gifts, if it's within his means, which, in this case, it would be. He'll force himself somehow into your daily routine until you can't escape him. Everywhere you'll turn, he'll be there waiting for you. He'll make you feel as if there is no other woman on earth."

A pretty Lebanese woman by the name of Delilah, sitting right next to them, jumped in to continue the tale.

"After two weeks, he'll suddenly stop calling. We refer to it as "phase two", and it's now time for you to chase after him..."

"And what happens when you don't?" asked Arielle, dumbfounded.

"Most of the time the man will lose interest. There are just too many fish in the sea!"

They all laughed throatily. Obviously it was a well-known routine and from the looks on their impeccably made-up faces, most of Latifah's friends appeared to have been caught playing it at one time or another.

"Something appears most entertaining," said Majid, returning with Arielle's drink, a bright concoction surmounted by a hibiscus flower.

"We're looking out for our young friend here," replied Maryam. "Making sure that she understands how Emirati men play the game of love."

"Ouch!" smiled Majid. "That must hurt. But are you positive we all play games?" he added, winking at Maryam, a woman he had bedded a few months prior, when her husband had been out of town.

Maryam shifted uncomfortably in her seat but no one noticed.

"It seems that it all starts with a mobile number," quipped Arielle, now looking straight at him, her eyes challenging his. "In my particular case, the so-called chase could only be cut short as I've yet to purchase a local phone!" She laughed and then added, still smiling at him, "Thank you for the drink though. I look forward to seeing you at the track when you come and photograph me."

With those last words, she turned her back on him, engaging immediately in an animated conversation with another one of Latifah's friends sitting on her left. Most of the women had remained stock still: dismissing a man outright was rare; turning your back on one of Dubai's most eligible bachelors was practically criminal. They repressed smiles at Majid's discomfiture who, after staring at Arielle's back for a few seconds, nodded curtly, crossed the dance floor and disappeared out of sight. No sooner had he exited that Latifah clapped loudly and all seven women started talking all at once, analysing what had just happened. Arielle looked from one to the other, uncomprehending.

"What's the big deal?" she asked innocently.

"I don't think poor Majid will ever recover!" laughed Delilah, a Syrian woman in her early thirties and one of Latifah's confidantes.

"That was absolutely priceless! You Australians really call a spade a spade!"

"I don't understand what I've done wrong," repeated Arielle, bewildered.

"You called him at his own game and now he's stuck! That was really too funny," added Maryam, glad that someone else had for once put Majid in his place. After all, they were contemporaries, had grown up together in the same circles and Maryam was not the only one to have witnessed a long trail of broken hearts in his wake.

What none of them had expected though was to see Majid come back half an hour later and walk straight up to Arielle, past her entourage. He held a small box in his hand and thrust it over to her.

"Please open it," he instructed, his intense eyes riveted on hers.

Delicately, Arielle untied the red bow and opened the box. A brand new iPhone 5 lay inside.

"It's charged and ready to go. Now you have a phone. My number has already been programmed and now I've yours. Since all the charming ladies here believe that without a phone, romance can't blossom, I figure that now nothing should stand in the way," he quipped, a touch defiantly.

Everyone nearby turned around to see why the group had dissolved in fits of giggles. Quickly aware that the laughter was not malicious, Majid soon accepted their invitation to sit down and join them. A little while later, some of his friends came along as well. It was well past three in the morning when Latifah decided it was time for them to head home.

Arielle was too excited to fall asleep. After a long hot shower, she lay on her bed with her iPad to look up the fascinating Majid. Delilah had been right: there were pages and pages of newspapers clippings, bios and photos of the young man. She read avidly through every single one of them. She also noted that he had never been photographed with the same woman twice. Although speculations over his love interests abounded, he had never really been associated with anyone for long. Suddenly, she realised she hadn't even looked at her brand new phone: five messages waited to be read. Not surprisingly Majid authored every single one of them.

Well, you took your time opening up your phone read the first one, followed seconds later *by I hope you weren't offended by this gift. You can just consider it a loan if you wish and give it back to me when you return to Australia, whenever that is.*

In spite of what you may have heard began the third one *I'm not in the habit of doing this. I've been tricked by what I think the French call 'coup de foudre'.*

Then, another obviously typed while they were chatting together at the nightclub. *You look so adorable, it's hard for me to take my eyes off you.*

Then finally, sent 20 minutes before, the last message read *Sleep well. I can only hope you'll be dreaming of me as I will be of you.*

Arielle smiled: she could hardly think of anything else. It had been an extraordinary day and an unbelievable night. As she slowly drifted off to sleep, not far from there, Majid wondered why she had not replied to any of his texts. Had she thrown away the phone? Or could it be that she wasn't at all interested? He wasn't quite sure he'd be able to deal with the rejection. The experience was completely new to him and it unsettled him.

CHAPTER V

By the time Arielle woke, the sun was at its zenith. A folded note had been slipped under her door. She opened it slowly. Hamdam requested her presence at the stables by three. Hurriedly, Arielle showered and dressed. In the kitchen she found Latifah in a long floating silk robe drinking Arabic coffee and munching on sweets. They kissed each other good morning in the otherwise empty kitchen.

"How's your hangover?" questioned Latifah.

"Fine," replied Arielle. "How's yours? Feeling a bit under the weather?" she joked, looking at her friend's blotchy skin and red-rimmed eyes.

"Where are you going?" asked Latifah, noticing for the first time that Arielle was fully dressed and ready to go out.

"Your husband sent me a note to be at the stables by three. How do I get there?"

"Oh, I forgot, he left you the keys to a Mini. I think you're supposed to drive."

"Are you crazy? In this city's traffic? With everyone driving as if the four horses of the Apocalypse are chasing after them? I'll get killed!"

"Use your GPS," moaned Latifah, her head in the palms of her hands. "Or if you're really scared, ask one of the staff to give you a lift. I can't possibly go anywhere!"

"I've got to go," stated Arielle, looking at her wristwatch. "I'll see you later."

Out on the driveway, Arielle stared, speechless, at the brand new, shiny blue steel Mini parked by the door. There was a folded note stuck on the windshield.

"This should get you from point A to point B. It's yours. See you soon."

Hamdam's signature was scrawled at the bottom. Arielle turned around. One of the gardeners was watching her curiously. Boldly, Arielle walked up to him.

"Can you drive?" she asked. He nodded shyly.

"Can you drive me to the stables?" she pleaded. The man nodded once again, turned on his heels and walked away briskly. Completely dumbfounded, Arielle remained rooted on the spot, wondering what had just happened when the same young man quickly reappeared, having changed into a butter-cream sherwani jacket with its telltale Nehru collar and matching churidar, the loose trousers fastened at the ankles, an outfit she had come to recognise as the traditional Hindu dress code for men.

"Let's go," he said laconically.

When Arielle saw him take his seat on the left, she thanked her lucky stars for her presence of mind. From her observations so far, driving in the UAE was hair-raising at best; she was convinced that by driving on the right, when she had never done so before, would have had catastrophic consequences. For the 15-minute drive the man at her side said nothing but Arielle nonetheless convinced him to wait for her to take her home later. After a quick phone call, he agreed.

The stable compound was in a flurry of activity, with horses being saddled amongst four-wheel drives whilst men yelled at each other across the massive courtyard. Hamdam was standing in the middle of it all, smoking a cigar whilst intently talking to a dozen men Arielle immediately identified as jockeys. A soon as she approached the group, they fell silent. Hamdam introduced her. They kept watching her with great curiosity but said nothing. Hamdam gave an end to the awkward moment.

"I've gathered them today for a mock race," he explained. "Consider it a trial. You'll ride the same horse as you did yesterday. I want to see how Aazeen performs alongside other horses."

Arielle could not hide her shock. She wasn't used to being given orders and she certainly hadn't expected to be thrown into a race without preamble. Hamdam mistook the look on her face for one of fear.

"Aren't you up to it?" he questioned, his eyebrows noticeably raised in displeasure.

"Not a problem," replied the young woman, keeping her temper in check. "I just wasn't expecting it. I thought I'd be given the courtesy of some warning."

Hamdam shot her a look of surprise.

"I must have misunderstood," he said carefully. "I thought you wanted to race for me," he added gently, knowing that without her his plans to upstage his compatriots would come to naught.

"I did. I do. How many horses do you plan on racing?" she asked, skirting any further discussion on what she considered plainly rude behaviour.

"Twelve."

"At your service," she added, her tone sharp, turning to the horse which had just been brought up to her so that he couldn't see how angry she was. The other jockeys waited for her to mount the horse none of them had been able to master and then climbed on the back of their assigned mounts for the day. Together they filed down the sandy path all the way to the track. Arielle, her eyes misting with tears of frustration, failed to notice the two SUVs parked alongside the track, their darkened windows impenetrable, their motors idling, in prime position to observe the proceedings.

As soon as the signal blared and the gates opened, Arielle's head emptied of all thoughts, concentrating solely on the track ahead. Somehow, sensing her determination, her mount responded well to her unspoken injunctions, the blinkers helping her focus without distraction. For the first few hundred metres, all Arielle could hear was the laboured breath of the horses flanking hers and the crack of whips whizzing past. On what she remembered to be the last bend before the straight, she cut through the pack of four surrounding her, giving Aazeen room to manoeuvre, propelling her forward. The filly, now unencumbered, ran at the head of the field, leaving the other contestants well behind. By the time she galloped through the finish line six full lengths in front of the closest horse, the cacophony of car horns welcoming her across the line was deafening. Arielle slowed down and patted the horse in appreciation of her unexpected performance. She didn't have a stopwatch but by experience, she knew her time to have been good, very good in fact.

Arielle took off her helmet and, with the back of her hand, wiped her face crusted with sand. A stablehand had come to take the lead and calm down the horse dripping in sweat. Past the makeshift grandstand, she saluted Hamdam stiffly and kept walking back to the stables. She was brushing down her horse when he came to join her.

"That was magnificent!"

"It would have been better if I'd had time to prepare," replied Arielle crossly.

"I don't understand," said Hamdam, looking at her quizzically. He now gathered the young woman was upset but he still couldn't fathom why.

"Normally a jockey, at least in my part of the world, has time to mentally prepare for a race; time to saddle her own mount; to check track conditions and a host of other things to give her or his best performance on the day. You thrust this upon me without warning," she replied petulantly. "I said I'd race for you but I'm not sure the conditions are right if that's the way it's going to be. I'm in your debt for your generous hospitality but I won't risk my life for your pleasure."

Arielle was close to tears.

Dumbfounded by her outburst, Hamdam put a reassuring hand on her shoulder.

"Calm down," he said in a conciliatory tone. "I had no idea, Arielle. I'm used to people doing my bidding without question. Of course, it won't happen again. My uncle was most impatient in having a look at you. I could hardly refuse."

"Your uncle?"

"He watched the race from the back of his car, and he is most impressed. As I am. You were right about the blinkers. It was the fastest time by any of my horses on this track. You've done me proud."

"I'm glad," said Arielle, her anger subsiding. "I believe I've been rude for not thanking you right away for the gift of the car. Please forgive me. I'm curious though; did you really think I could get here on my own?"

"What do you mean? Can't you drive?" queried Hamdam, surprised.

"Not on the right side of the road, I can't!"

"Oh, I had forgotten! Of course! I'll assign a chauffeur to take you where you want to go, whenever you want to go anywhere. Did you like the car though?"

Arielle repressed a smile.

"It's certainly the right size for me and deceivingly big on the inside. It's most generous of you but it wasn't necessary. And since you agree to assign me a chauffeur, could I rely on the young man who brought me here? Not a great conversationalist I'm afraid but a very good driver."

"Consider it done. Now can we talk about your schedule? The Dubai World Cup is six weeks from now."

"Don't I need to qualify first?"

"You just did."

The pair spent the rest of the afternoon running through her training program. Arielle had over 10 unopened text messages on her new phone.

'What is wrong with this girl?' wondered Majid for the umpteenth time. He had already left her a dozen messages. It was time for the evening call to prayers and he had yet to hear back from her. 'Surely I haven't imagined the mutual attraction? Has Maryam spread nasty rumours about me? Or has Arielle been promised to someone back home?'

He soon dismissed the nagging thought. Maryam would keep her mouth shut less she'd incriminate herself and damage her own reputation. And he would have sensed somehow if there had been someone else. So why wasn't Arielle replying? It was simply driving him to distraction. Most women he had come across in the past decade had fallen over themselves whenever he'd lavished them with any attention. This particular one eluded him completely. As infuriating as it was, it made it also all the more titillating.

After her lengthy meeting with Hamdam and the stablemaster, Arielle was free to go. The young man who had driven her to the stables was still there waiting for her. She found out his name was Ata, which meant 'gift' in his language. He'd been born and raised in the north of India, near Jaipur, in a small village close to the Thar Desert. He had been in Hamdam's employ for just under a year. He was 19 years old. He had been thrilled to know his duties had been unexpectedly changed to that of chauffeuring the enigmatic foreigner and on the way home he told her so.

"Your English is quite good," complimented Arielle, seduced by the tilt of his accent.

"It isn't so but I'm very happy you asked for me. Tending to the garden all the time gets a bit boring. Did you know you left your phone in the car? It hasn't stopped beeping all afternoon."

"Oh! My phone! I'm not used to having one," admitted Arielle. "So it's not glued to my side yet!"

They both laughed easily as Arielle scrolled down the messages and frowned.

"Something wrong?"

"No, not really," smiled Arielle distractedly. "This guy I met last night has left many messages for me. He doesn't seem pleased I haven't replied."

"An Emirati?" questioned Ata shyly.

"Yes he is. Why do you ask?"

"Emirati men aren't very respectful towards white women or any women who aren't their own," elaborated Ata, shooting her a sideways glance to gauge her reaction.

"How can you say that? This particular one was nothing but charming and polite."

"Of course," said the young Hindu knowledgeably, "until you allow him to make love to you. And then he'll disappear in the desert sands."

"That's a very cynical view of the world," observed Arielle.

"But it's so very true. But don't worry; they treat Indian, Pakistani, Thai and black women even worse."

Arielle frowned, displeased. The turn of the conversation was making her uncomfortable. She wasn't yet in the mood to have her dream shattered.

"Watch where you're going!" she admonished. Ata, astute enough to know that the subject was now off limits and the conversation over, kept his eyes firmly on the road while Arielle busily scrolled down her messages.

I'm sorry she replied to the last text, *I've been quite busy. May I make it up to you? I'm free for lunch tomorrow.*

The answer came back almost immediately.

How about I pick you up at two?

A tad late for lunch, isn't it? I'll be at the track all morning and be starving by then. Perhaps better postpone it.

The girl didn't make it easy on him yet he was loath thinking she might be playing games.

What would suit you better?

Dinner might be best. Then there is no pressure on your schedule or mine.

Majid sensed that if he told her he didn't eat dinner until 10.30 in the evening, he'd lose the opportunity once again.

I'll pick you up at eight. Is there anything you don't eat?

I'm easy.

'If only that were true,' reflected Majid.

The hours until the following night would stretch interminably but apparently he had no other choice but to wait.

You've been on my mind declared the following text.

The reply took a few minutes.

Likewise. See you tomorrow.

Once again she had cut short any further conversation.

Majid stared at his small screen, extremely frustrated. On impulse he called Hamdam.

"Hamdam, I was wondering if I could come by the track tomorrow and begin to take a few photos. The more publicity you manage to build up around the girl, the better, isn't it? I could leak them to the press. I'm sure they'll bite in a minute."

"What a fantastic idea, but I believe we'll need to follow it through quickly with some glamour shots."

"How about this weekend?" suggested Majid, unwilling to let any opportunity to see Arielle pass him by. "We could leave on Thursday and be home by sunset on Saturday. I can just picture it: the deserts of Oman, the rock formations, the turquoise wadis and your new jockey in a series of evening gowns? Perhaps even modelling a few pieces from Catherina's new collection?"

"Excellent idea, but obviously she can't travel alone with you so I'll have Latifah and a couple of her girlfriends come along as chaperones. I'll book a hotel and set it all up. All you'll have left to do is take the most amazing photos."

"Sounds perfect," agreed Majid, a tad disappointed by the idea of chaperones. Even though he had known he wouldn't be able to be entirely alone with Arielle, regardless of the scenario, he had hoped for a miracle nonetheless.

"I'll be at the stables by nine. Will I have the pleasure of seeing you there?"

"Perhaps later in the day. Have a good evening. Ma'asallama, Majid."

For the next two mornings, Majid came by the stables, taking many shots of Arielle on both occasions. Neither time did she pay him much attention, entirely focused on the job at hand, although she had graciously accepted to strike a pose here and there, whenever he had requested her to do so. Her offhandedness troubled him more than he cared to admit. He had been certain that his unique good looks and exuberant charm would work their magic on her, as they had done on every other female he had come across until now. She hadn't seem immune to the voltage of his smile a few days before but nor had she gone out of her way to seek his approval. On a couple of shots he had even snapped her rolling her eyes at the artificiality of the poses he had asked her to strike for him. She had even gone so far as sticking her tongue out at the camera in mock protest. Majid had been baffled: used to immortalise women on film who were also keen to capture his heart in return, he had never experienced the polite and playful indifference Arielle bestowed upon him. Unfortunately, the more time he spent in her presence, the more inescapable his daydreams had become. He could think of virtually nothing else. She had even managed to cancel their dinner plans at the very last minute due to what she had called an unbearable headache. Majid had come to a point where he dreaded the weekend away as much as he yearned for it. What would happen if she continued to treat him like a pesky stalker? He was quite certain than neither his ego nor his heart would survive the ordeal.

Arielle had been flustered to see Majid come by the stables on the next morning, armed with impressive camera equipment. She had been thankful that for most of his visit she had stayed on top of the horses she had exercised around the course so as not to share the same levelled ground as him. She dreaded looking at him directly less her eyes betrayed her longing. She engineered many tricks to stay as far away from him as possible under the circumstances, well aware that Hamdam wanted many publicity shots for the paper's social pages. For theatricality, she had even reared her horse while taking off her helmet as she had seen done in so many western movies, but Majid had been taken back by the sudden move and forgot to press the shutter on the camera, missing the shot completely. After shaking her head and rolling her eyes at his ineptitude, she had stuck her tongue out as if to say "you deserved it".

His presence alone flustered her to the point that she decided to cancel their dinner plans, unable to imagine sitting across the table from him, making small talk when just the scent of him made her weak at the knees. She had heard disappointment and anger in his voice when she had hidden behind a migraine to cancel at the last minute but Majid had recovered quickly, wishing her well and telling her he looked forward to spending more time with her at the weekend. Arielle's anxiety rose every time anyone mentioned the week-end ahead. She hoped that her thunderous crush would not lead her to do or say anything amazingly stupid in public. Latifah, in whom she had confided, had tried to reassure her; in her opinion Majid was as enchanted with her as she was with him. According to her, in these situations no one really had the upper hand.

It took Hamdam less than an hour to make plans for his wife, her friends and Arielle to travel to the Sultanate of Oman. The small group would take the one-hour late afternoon Wednesday flight to Muscat where they would spend the night in a private villa at the Chedi Muscat Hotel located on the Gulf beachfront. He had organised for two Jeeps to drive the small group late on the following afternoon across the desert to reach the luxury Bedouin-style camp in the Wahiba sand dunes. He knew it would take the desert monkeys, his affectionate term for the four-wheel-drive Jeeps, approximately two hours to reach their destination. His itinerary would allow for Majid to take photos on the beach in Muscat at sunset, when the Gulf waters mirrored the mountain range behind, followed the next morning by photos in the nearby gorges carved by thousands of years of erosion, with their impressive vertical cliffs and waterfalls cascading down into intensely turquoise waterholes. The chosen locations couldn't fail to provide the ultimate backdrops for glamour shots. The desert, of course, with its rippling honey-dipped sand dunes, which turned paprika at dusk, would be the ultimate canvas. In order to turn Arielle into a sensation and thus make his stables the talk of the town he needed to lay down proper groundwork. He wanted Arielle to be perceived as delicate, fragile and unattainable – an angel riding his horse to victory. Her diminutive stature, her untouched natural beauty and Majid's vision were sure to cement his mental picture of the campaign.

Latifah beamed with delight when her husband told her of his plans for Arielle's future. Chaperoning the young woman had so far proved a much appreciated break in her routine. She had volunteered to select and manage Arielle's wardrobe. For the three days preceding the unexpected trip, she had kept busy, borrowing gowns all over town, selecting dresses for their cut and colour, determined to make the most of Arielle's fair colouring, mane of auburn hair and light-green eyes. She relished the idea of a weekend away with her best friends and without the permanent scrutiny for appropriate behaviour.

The short Thursday flight proved uneventful and the four women eagerly settled in their rooms, planning to reconvene for supper after freshening up. Wisely, Hamdam had purposefully reserved a room for Majid on what he thought was the opposite side of the hotel. However, chance intervened when due to the horseshoe-shaped complex, the young man's room ended up being located directly opposite Arielle's, separated only by a short stroll through the palm-fringed gardens. Smoking on her rear terrace after a refreshing shower, she noticed him straightaway and waved at him. Majid took it as an invitation to cross over and come and see her, his heart beating excitedly against his chest. Indeed, last time he had spoken with her was when she had cancelled their dinner plans. In his living memory, he couldn't recall when a woman had forfeited the opportunity to be seen with him. He knew that it was conceited of him to think he was irresistible but nothing in his past had prepared him for any manner of rejection. In Arielle's case the signals were confusing and for the first time he had come to doubt his power over the fair sex.

"How was your trip?" inquired Arielle as he stepped onto her bougainvillea-framed private terrace.

"As uneventful as yours, I'm sure," he replied, somewhat guarded. "I took an earlier flight to firm up some locations for tomorrow's shoot. Are you averse to waking at dawn?"

"Undoubtedly when light is at its best?" said Arielle, her eyes teasing him.

'Why can't I think of a clever reply?' wondered Majid, shifting his weight from one foot to the other and replying instead, "The light is softer then. The beach will be empty. It will also be low tide so I can take a few shots of you running on the beach. The mountain tops will crest the waves so with a little chance on my side, I'll be able to create quite a surrealistic image."

"Are you sure you need a subject to ruin it all?" challenged Arielle.

This time he smiled, sure she had baited him.

"It's the subject that will make it work, otherwise it's just another landscape," he replied flirtatiously.

"Oh, the subject will be fine. Latifah is a beautiful woman. Didn't Hamdam inform you about his change of heart? Apparently, she has been complaining I steal the limelight and since he wants to make her happy and you were already here, he thought it would be best for all involved," she told him with a straight face, watching his reaction closely.

Majid spat out the glass of cold pomegranate juice she had just offered him.

"Are you all right?" she asked, laughing at his stricken face. "Gosh! You're so gullible! I'm only joking! You do take yourself very seriously, don't you?"

"I used to," replied Majid softly, wiping his mouth with the sleeve of his immaculate white shirt. "Although when you're around, I don't seem to know who I am anymore," looking up at her face now flushed pink. She looked so fragile and adorable that he couldn't help himself and dared touching her cheek.

Unexpectedly, Arielle pressed his palm hard against her skin and inhaled deeply, his scent filling her lungs. Then, just as fiercely, she removed his hand, stepping back to look at him squarely.

"You scare me," she announced bluntly. "You're older, wiser, with a great deal of experience about life and... women," she added, her tone dropping so low that Majid, hanging on her every breath, bent forward to hear her. "... and I'm just an innocent young girl from the country," she finished, her voice a mere whisper.

"Innocent?" Majid asked, raising a sceptical eyebrow.

In his opinion she had so far manipulated his feelings and played at his heart strings like no other woman had ever done and many had been well versed in the games of seduction.

"Don't you find me harmless?" she questioned, surprised.

"Not in the least! You're as dangerous as they come..." he added, his voice trembling.

"I've never been with a man; that's what I meant by innocent," insisted Arielle, looking down at her bare feet. "You'd know just by kissing me how inexperienced I was and I'd undoubtedly disappoint you. And since that's all I can think about, I don't quite know how to act around you," she pursued, her words tumbling rapidly.

Shocked by her candid admission, so obviously stripped of all artifice, Majid impulsively took her into his arms and lifted her head so his eyes could silently request permission. Arielle shuddered involuntarily, staring back at him wordlessly and then parted her lips in acquiescence. Their soulful kiss was interrupted by the doorbell followed by a familiar voice yelling out, "Arielle, are you ready? We're going down to the pool bar. There's a barbecue on the beach tonight. Are you game?"

"Be right out!" Arielle yelled back, her cheeks crimson, her body trembling and her breath short.

Reluctantly, Majid released her but not without exerting the promise that he could pick up where he'd left off later that evening. He quickly disappeared, a lithe shadow moving rapidly through the theatrically lit gardens.

91

Having discarded traditional clothing in favour of elegant evening resort wear, Latifah's friends were in the mood to party. The exquisitely clad group made quite an entrance at the pool bar where cocktail hour was already in full swing. They soon revelled in the attention of a group of five American men, likewise in their early thirties, who had chosen the hotel as their headquarters to gather all their travel necessities before going camping in the desert for the following fortnight. Arielle's accent had been the ice breaker; the four women were invited to join them for a drink and later share their meal on the beach where a Bedouin barbecue and seating were being set up by hotel staff. Far enough away from home, the women dropped their usual guard and the conversation turned lively and fun, the Americans only too happy to meet real locals in the flesh, alcohol breaking everyone's customary reserve.

At first Majid hadn't been pleased by the turn of events, loathe to share Arielle's attention with the Anglo-Saxon men who unabashedly competed for her attention. However, it soon became obvious to everyone that Arielle only had eyes for the infuriatingly handsome Arab man. Majid had taken advantage of the informal seating arrangement to sit as close to Arielle as possible, their feverish fingers meeting in the dark behind their backs. The excellent meal of slow-cooked spitfire lamb, grilled vegetables and salads, copiously doused with white burgundies and Californian chardonnays, contributed to the joyous atmosphere. They danced under the stars to the sound of flutes and guitars intermingled with the gentle lapping of the waves breaking on the beach. However, by one o'clock it was time to retire as everyone had early plans for the next day. Nonetheless and to everyone's delight, the Americans promised to stop by and visit with their newfound friends at their desert camp the following night. Flirting with ruggedly handsome foreigners was not a pastime any of them had the opportunity to indulge in often and they all agreed it would be fun.

Returning to their rooms, Majid and Arielle lagged behind the others, neither wanting the evening to end.

"Come by my room in one hour," whispered Arielle in the dark.

"Are you sure? We need to be at the beach by six," replied Majid in the same tone.

"Who needs sleep?"

'How can I resist?' thought Majid. "I'll be there," he said, giving her hand a brief squeeze.

Outside the doors of their respective rooms the women bade each other goodnight. Latifah was careful to mention that she had ordered the hotel staff to lay out in Arielle's room the outfits she would need in the morning. Kissing her young friend goodnight, she also told her that it was highly unlikely that she would come and watch the photo shoot. Arielle knew only too well she abhorred early mornings. She was also certain that her chaperone would likely suffer from a hangover. It did not cross her mind that Latifah had wanted to give her privacy.

"Don't worry, I'll be fine. Sleep well and thank you for a wonderful night."

"I'm sure you will," replied Latifah, winking at her and disappearing quickly in a rush of silks.

Barely one hour later, Majid tapped lightly at her window and she let him in discreetly. Minutes later, their hastily removed clothes dotted the cool mosaic floors. Majid reined his impatience at possessing her, in awe at the gift of a virginity he wasn't sure he deserved. He didn't feign his tenderness when he covered her with kisses and caresses from head to toe, leaving not a single inch of her body untouched by his tongue or his hands until she begged for a release she didn't know she could want so badly. She watched him curiously when he unwrapped a condom and stifled a scream when he entered her. Pain quickly turned into pleasure and Majid put his hand over her mouth to stifle her moans, his explosion more intense than he could last remember. Arielle's post-coitus alarm at seeing so much blood was tempered by his laughter. He assured her he would tip the chambermaid well and that no one would be the wiser. He thanked her many times for her gift, his generous mouth quivering with emotion. For the next four hours, they made love over and over again, their discovery of the other melting away their tiredness. When dawn finally broke, they sprung from the bed and Majid once again disappeared out of sight, telling her to come to the beach as soon as she had taken a shower and washed their lust off her skin.

The glow of passion ensured Arielle needed no make-up, and her freshly washed hair cascaded freely over her shoulders. She walked onto the beach in the palest honey-coloured djellaba. In the morning light, the dress made her look entirely nude. Renewed desire caught in Majid's throat as soon as he saw her. Despite his lack of concentration, he called out a few poses, alternatively requesting her to twirl in the breaking light and lay on the sand with her back arched, arms over her head, the gentle waves tickling her feet. The azure waters reflected in her eyes while the mountain range beyond was mirrored in the sea. There was no hint of fatigue from a sleepless night on her flawless face and her eyes smiled at the camera with a dreamy, faraway look which made her seem both unattainable and goddess-like. In that instant she could have shamed many international models. Majid knew instantly he had clicked onto award-winning photographs.

Later that morning they drove to the nearby gorges and took another series of photographs amongst the impressive boulders and rock formations. After an hour or so, they could no longer resist the temptation to take off their clothes and plunge headfirst into the intense turquoise waters of the natural pools. At this time of the day Majid was certain they ran little risk of running into anyone else.

By the time they returned to the hotel, a little after 1 pm, they were both absolutely famished. Their companions were already sitting around a table, picking at their food, drinking copious amounts of sweet cardamom-spiced coffee, their mood rather subdued. Large dark shades perched on every nose did their utmost to hide the aftermath of the night before. By contrast, Arielle was the portrait of youthful vigour, seemingly unaffected by the events of the previous night. Even though Latifah noticed her protégée's unusual appetite, she didn't mention it. There would be plenty of time later to interrogate her about the morning's events, although she admitted out loud not to hold any regrets for skipping the dawn photo shoot.

A little after two, a pair of matching four-wheel-drive Jeeps stood at the hotel entrance, ready for the short drive through the sand dunes to take them to their ultimate destination – a group of 30 luxuriously appointed tents pitched in the middle of the Wahiba Desert, like so many white seashells randomly dotting a stretch of beach.

The temperatures seemed to rise as soon as they skirted the highway to manoeuvre the shifting hills, and Arielle was surprised to see how difficult the driving actually was and how skilled their drivers turned out to be. When, after a two-hour, white-knuckle drive, they came upon a hill which looked down on cream canvas roofs sitting on top of huts like so many pointed hats, they knew they had arrived at the luxury hotel designed to look like a Bedouin encampment without any of the hardships of desert living. Just as they began their descent, and almost on cue, a camel train rode over the opposite hill, perfectly silhouetted against the hard blue sky. Arielle's eyes widened at the sight and she clapped her hands in puerile delight.

"Oh my God! It's just so picture perfect!" she marvelled in awe. Latifah laughed.

"Bless Allah for all his creations," chorused Latifah.

"Oh, I'm so glad to be here with you!" exclaimed Arielle, impulsively hugging her friend sitting next to her on the back seat.

"And with Majid," joked Latifah, throwing her friend a sideways glance to check whether the young man had been on her mind.

"That too!" thrilled Arielle, flushing ever so slightly, a blush which did not escape Latifah's astute sense of observation.

"I'll be cursed," cried out Latifah, suddenly piecing together Arielle's unusual appetite that morning, her unbridled enthusiasm despite the rough ride over and the pervasive glow of her skin which made her look positively tired and old by comparison.

"What happened during the shoot this morning?" she questioned suspiciously.

"Nothing happened," replied Arielle firmly. "He took some pictures. I posed."

"Really?" pursued Latifah, unwilling to be put off.

Slowly Arielle turned to confront her.

"You're asking the wrong question."

And then, unable to contain her happiness and her secret any longer, she blurted out, "He's the most wonderful man I've ever met!"

"Oh, Arielle, don't tell me he seduced you! Hamdam would kill me! I'm supposed to look after your welfare. This is a disaster!"

"Don't fret, Lati," replied Arielle, using the woman's nickname. "And don't scold me. It was wonderful. I've no regrets. It was exactly as I always imagined it would be. Be happy for me!"

Latifah moaned; in her view she had just fallen short in her duty of care. What would she say to Hamdam now? Could she count on the notorious playboy to be discreet? Wouldn't he boast about his latest conquest and ruin Arielle's reputation in the process? Would it sully her husband's plans?

She shook her head and was about to speak when Arielle silenced her.

"I'm old enough. It was about time I stopped dragging around my virginity like a noose. Majid was an extraordinarily patient and solicitous lover. Not that I have much to compare it to, but it was beautiful." She sighed contentedly.

"I'm finally a woman and I'm happy. I'm sorry it happened on your watch but you're not responsible for my actions. You don't have to tell anyone anything. You won't, will you?" she added nervously.

Latifah shrugged her shoulders and tutted.

"You can't be seen with him in public, you do know that, don't you? Are you planning to see him again? How do you think you're going to manage?"

"I'm sorry, Lati, but even though I'm a guest in your house, I'm neither an Emirati nor a Muslim woman. I do what I wish with my body. I won't embarrass you or Hamdam or your family name in any way but I'm pretty sure I've the right to see whomever I want. And you, of all people, I'd have thought would be in my corner. Am I wrong?"

"As long as you're both extremely discreet, you have my blessing... So I guess his reputation is well deserved?"

Arielle laughed happily, relief flooding her features.

"It was absolutely magical, but I'm thoroughly exhausted. I hope a long siesta is on the menu for this afternoon."

★ ★

From the middle of the pitched-roof ceiling of each tent, silky fabrics with ton-sur-ton laced overlays were festooned back on the walls so as to drape down graciously onto the floor. Bejewelled oil lamps of varying shapes and sizes hung everywhere, projecting geometric patterns on the white-washed walls through their intricate lattice work. Authentic cashmere carpets woven in Iran and Pakistan covered the floors, overlapping in thick layers. One third of the room was devoted to a round marble tub large enough to accommodate two people comfortably. On one side of the tent, glass sliding doors opened up onto a suspended small wooden deck and the desert beyond. As soon as she stepped into the room, the luxurious and exotic surroundings enveloped Arielle like a cocoon. She whistled softly, entranced by the sights but, overcome with fatigue, she soon collapsed, fully dressed, onto the king-sized bed which dominated the space.

It was close to sundown when she finally awoke from her dreamless slumber. She took a quick shower, lathered her body with scented oils and donned a light-orange caftan with pale embroideries of gold and yellow along the open neckline and hems. As she walked towards the centre of the encampment, she noticed some of the guests sitting around large communal tables, nibbling on dates and nuts, while others lounged on comfortable, oversized cushions thrown over carpets floating directly on the sand. Her companions, sipping cool drinks, were apparently waiting for her. Arielle apologised profusely for sleeping so long, not daring to look at Majid, who devoured her with his eyes.

The latter quickly announced that with his model finally awake they would take advantage of the late afternoon light to take more photos. As the sun slowly dipped over the horizon, the honey-coloured sand dunes had begun to tinge paprika red. In her outfit, Arielle blended effortlessly with the landscape, her simple shift reflecting the waning light. With the changing winds, the dunes around them constantly shifted shapes. A roll of film and three outfit changes later, Majid declared himself satisfied that he had captured both Arielle's soul and the country's nomadic spirit.

Arielle had rarely observed such brightly lit configurations of stars. The jet-ink sky stood above her like a diamond-speckled dome. The hotel staff had lit an open camp fire upon which their meal would be cooked. Bedouins from neighbouring settlements had filtered into the camp, coming along to cook thin salty breads which they offered to the guests. Heavily veiled women proposed traditional henna tattoos for their hands and feet and Arielle couldn't resist the finely traced arabesques one of them drew on her right foot. True to their word, the Americans they had met the night before came to join them for dinner and the evening dissolved once again in rambunctious laughter, animated conversations and flirtatious banter.

Arielle didn't doubt for a second that if the threat of impropriety hadn't weighed so heavily on Latifah's friends, they would have certainly entertained a few hours of uninhibited sex with the well-built and charming strangers. Indeed, all of them, just like Latifah, had married men at least twice their age, ranking as third or fourth wife in the household to which they belonged. They had all been virgins when they had married and Arielle thought it was more than natural that they would fantasise of uninhibited intercourse with men their own age. For her part, she could hardly wait for the moment they would all drift back towards their tents so that she could be alone with Majid.

It was well past midnight when the two insatiable lovers met in private once again. Majid had so longed for her all day, unable to sleep or eat, that, when he finally held her, he just couldn't let go, thunderstruck that he had fallen so hard for the wispy girl he had metamorphosed into a woman just a few hours earlier. Up to that point, Arielle hadn't known what pure bliss really meant.

Dawn surprised their sleeping bodies intertwined on the dishevelled bed, a dreamy smile still dancing on their lips. Suddenly alerted by the sounds of the camp stirring, Majid made a hurried exit under the cover of the early morning fog, saluting sheepishly on his way out one of the American men sneaking out likewise from one of the tents he had known to be Maryam's. At least he wouldn't be the only one holding onto a secret.

After a light breakfast of fruits, nuts and honey yogurt, the group set out on a camel ride across the shape-shifting sands, a last opportunity to take a few more picturesque photos. Late that morning Arielle even tried her hand at sand boarding down a steep dune, her hair and face soon prickled with dusty sand, her eyes shining bright with excitement. Majid, watching her, already missed the freedom from prying eyes the last 24 hours had afforded them. He wondered unhappily what would become of them once they returned to Dubai that evening. Maryam's mood matched his own. Arielle, on the other hand, revelled in every minute of what she knew would remain an unforgettable experience, one that had transformed her young life forever. The trip back home lacked lustre, but Majid found solace in the fact that Latifah had manoeuvred it so that he could sit next to Arielle on the plane ride back. At this point, it was evident to all the women present that they were clearly infatuated with each other.

None intended to stand in the way of a blossoming romance, even though, privately, the small group acknowledged it was doomed to failure. It was a given that Arielle, in the end, would have little to show for it besides a broken heart. None would have guessed their predictions would prove so fallible.

CHAPTER VI

Three weeks later, there wasn't a magazine or a tabloid in town that did not carry, in some form or another, glamour shots of Arielle, courtesy of Majid's lens. From the popular Masala to Dar Al-Sada, from Ahlan! to OK! and from Grazie Bahrain to Emirates Woman, Arielle either graced the cover or filled the inside spread. A&E magazine, which Arielle understood later stood for Adam and Eve, as well as Millionaire, had featured lengthy articles. She was the novelty no one seemed to tire from, so unimaginable it was for most people that a woman so pretty, young and sexy could have devoted her life to horseracing as a professional jockey. It defied all accepted conventions. On the other hand, Hamdam couldn't have wished for better publicity for the races ahead. Racing tickets, customarily always at a premium, had now been sold out weeks ahead of time.

Bemused reporters sneaked up to the track to watch Arielle train. A senior feature reporter for the Friday Magazine's supplement to the Gulf News had even interviewed Hamdam at length to question him on his unconventional choice for a jockey. Trying to assess how the Crown Prince's nephew had come across the young woman, since it was admittedly her first visit to the country, had been a challenge. Indeed, Hamdam had been quick to sidestep the question by answering that he was always on the lookout for new talent wherever it might hide. Arielle had flagged his radar while perusing Australian newspapers online. He only mentioned in passing that he had come across her father once during a business deal brokered by his own father decades earlier. Likewise, mindful of Arielle's safety, he had coached her to remain as vague as possible about her father's origins when asked to delve into her family background for the profile article. The latter assured him that her father spoke little of his life prior to immigrating to Australia. Chantilly Farms was the only truth she knew.

Sheik Maktoum had warmly congratulated his nephew on a number of occasions, agreeing that their plan to make the annual race the most coveted event of the year had worked beyond their wildest dreams. UAE-owned horses were already fetching good odds on international betting exchanges. Hotels posted full capacity, as were rentals, booked for the entire month. Moreover, since the Prince's new focus had been to launch the city as a medical tourist destination, availing itself of all the latest technologies and boasting world-class accommodation, first-rate doctors and a ratio of healthcare workers to patients the envy of the civilised world, media attention had played right into his hands. Indeed, the first plastic surgery state-of-the-art medical complex of its kind in the world was due to open merely two weeks prior to the big race. Newspapers articles openly suggested that, while men met at the track, their wives, daughters or girlfriends could enjoy treatments that would show them off at their best on Cup Day. Arielle had been the charismatic hook to increase publicity for the carefully planned rollout and all eyes were on the small Emirate.

However, Hamdam was a man wise enough to understand the enormous pressure put on the young girl. He knew that his star jockey should be kept content if he wished for her to remain focused. A healthy balance of work and play was mandatory to achieve his aims. Experienced in the way of women, he had recognised the magical qualities suffusing Majid's photographs, currently splashed on every newsstand across the Emirates. Each and every one carried the ineffable stamp of passion-filled eyes tracking its prey through the uncompromising lens. From Arielle's own body language, it was clear to him that if the muse was kept apart from the artist for too long, her assiduousness may falter and her enthusiasm wane. Neither would further his aims.

To date, he had done his best to offset the young woman's professional activities with social occasions where the two young people could meet innocuously. However, he knew that it was high time to offer her a real break, away from the overwhelming publicity. The tabloids had already hinted of a romance between the two. For the first time, and to everyone's surprise, Majid had done little to dispel them. In fact, he was proud to be seen shadowing Arielle at every event, eager as he was to spend whatever time her schedule afforded her. His sought-after photographs had brought a healthy injection of cash to his bank accounts but it frustrated him greatly never to have the chance to splash any of it on her. He spent most of his waking hours trying to figure out how to be alone with her. However, there wasn't really anyone he could draw into his confidence, and so he unhappily bade his time.

Barely a week after her first appearance in the local press, Arielle, riding Paprika Sands, a sorrel gelding owned by the Prince of Dubai himself, won the first of the lead-up races to the Carnival. When she repeated her feat the following weekend on the back of Oil Princess, a dark bay filly belonging to the Sheikh of Abu Dhabi, her reputation was all but anchored. In an astute political move, Hamdam had magnanimously offered her to ride for the two rulers, happily holding back Aazeen for the big reveal. As days sped by, he became increasingly convinced that his already twice-winning jockey could bring his untested mare across the finish line, hopefully in the lead. He had craved international recognition and honours since he'd started collecting racehorses over 15 years ago. Somehow he had always missed the top spot. With Arielle riding his most expensive purchase to date, he was now sure that the much-deserved laurels were finally in sight. He could taste victory and thought of nothing else. However, he increasingly worried about Arielle losing her focus, having caught her daydreaming more than once.

After consulting both Catherina and Latifah, he decided that a short break in Paris would be just the antidote to Arielle's blues.

Publicly he'd claim Arielle needed a new wardrobe for the races' after-parties. Privately, he hoped that Majid would steal the opportunity to spend time with her in utter privacy. Latifah, once again, was ordered to accompany her charge, purely for window-dressing. Maryam was invited to join them once again. When Majid opened an anonymous email on the very same afternoon, revealing Arielle's flight details and hotel reservations, he had jumped for joy, never questioning the origin of his tooth fairy. He wasted no time in booking a seat on the same flight, requesting adjoining rooms at the Plaza Athenee. He decided to surprise Arielle and divulged nothing of his plans until they ran into each other in the Emirates VIP lounge. He hoped this trip would be his chance to tell her how he really felt. The City of Lights was, in his opinion, the perfect showcase.

In late February, they landed in a city so blanketed with snow as to be virtually unrecognisable. If it weren't for the iconic monuments peppering the metropolis, they could have landed in a snowfield anywhere in the world. It had inexplicably snowed for three days straight. The fast-falling shower of fluffy flakes, which usually melted as soon as it hit the asphalt, had instead steadily accumulated. Fresh snow softened the cornice of every building, thickly coating the branches of every naked tree, covering the top of bushes and erasing the pavements, burying park benches and topping street lights with dazed conical hats. At four in the afternoon, the light was virtually opaque, the sky melting into a rich grey heavily laced with white. Arielle was enchanted. She rarely witnessed the effects of heavy snowfall back home. Seeing Paris for the first time as a pure winter wonderland brought tears of delight to her eyes.

As soon as they exited Customs, she minded neither the cold wind which whipped them, nor the slowness of the drive from the airport due to the poor weather forecast. Thanks to the treacherous road conditions, traffic was sparse. As they neared their final destination, she observed, through the hire car's quasi-fogged windows, a multitude of children playing in the snow, building snowmen in the parks and throwing snowballs at each other on the streets. Parents had swapped their strollers for sleighs. Teenagers had taken to the boulevards with their skis, while a few determined passers-by had taken the opportunity to show off the latest runway fur coats. Likewise, Arielle looked adorable in Latifah's generous loan of a sable coat and matching hat. On the trip over, she had chatted non-stop with Majid, holding hands and stealing kisses whenever they thought no one had been watching them. Now she was lost in contemplation, hardly believing her good fortune.

After checking in, Majid – a consummate gentleman – diplomatically proposed the four of them share their first dinner in Paris. However, Latifah would have none of it. She claimed exhaustion after the seven-hour flight, wanting nothing else but a hot bath and room service, a plan to which Maryam enthusiastically subscribed. With adjoining rooms and just an internal door to separate their quarters, it took minutes for the two lovers to unlock their side of the door and jump into each other's arms. The last month had been torture on both of them. Yet so much had happened that somehow they had managed to live through the forced separation: now they unequivocally intended to make up for lost time. They readily agreed that a long bubble bath together, followed by an early dinner in front of the lit fireplace, was the only possible way to spend their first night alone. As far as they were concerned, there was always tomorrow, and the day after that, to visit the sights and experience a slice of the French capital.

No sooner had Arielle shed her clothes than Majid requested she stand in front of the huge mirror hanging above the fireplace and close her eyes. Intrigued, she did as she was told. Something cold and hard was slipped around her neck. When she opened her eyes, a diamond necklace sparkled at her throat.

"There is a diamond for every day since I first laid eyes on you," said Majid proudly. "I hope you like it."

"I can't accept this," replied Arielle, astounded by the unexpectedly lavish gift.

"I would slide a diamond ring on your finger if I could," he added wistfully. "I may as well tell you that I've fallen head over heels in love with you and wish for nothing else but to share your life."

His face was taut, his features drawn, words sticking in his throat.

Slowly, Arielle turned around to face him.

"And I love you too," she said simply, caressing his cheek, "but we both know it can never be. My life isn't in the Middle East. I can't expect you to follow me to Australia and I would never forgive myself for forcing your hand. I'm a jockey, born and bred. It'd break my parents' hearts if I was never to return home. Converting to Islam would be difficult enough, but eventually sharing you as per your customs is something I could never endure. Let's enjoy this for what it is. You've made me a very happy woman by telling me you'd wish you could marry me: it shows me I wasn't just a roll in the hay or another notch on your bedpost."

"How could you ever think that?" replied Majid indignantly, colour rising in his sculpted cheeks.

"I was more than forewarned about Arab men and their courtship of foreigners. "No strings attached" is the word on the street. And speaking of which, according to rumours, you seemed to have made quite a career of it," she teased, her tone purposely light and playful.

"That was before I met you," he admitted sheepishly.

"That's what they all say," joked Arielle. "Now enough banter. Let's see if you're still as good as I remember."

And, without leaving him the chance to reply, she ran to the bathroom where the tub threatened to overflow with liquid-amber scented oils. By the time Majid jumped in with her he could barely see the crown of her head. Just under the waterline, the choker of scintillating diamonds at her throat threw luminous sparks across the mirrored walls.

The following three days were pure bliss. As Hamdam had predicted, the couple saw little of Maryam and Latifah, who were delighted to shop to their hearts' content and dine nightly at upscale restaurants. The two lovers quickly fell into a routine that suited them both. They woke early and visited museums in the mornings, with the Louvre, the Musée d'Orsay and, upon Arielle's suggestion, the Musée des Arts Premiers on their must-do list. They ate hearty lunches in obscure but cosy brasseries, ran back to the hotel after lunch to make love all afternoon and then ventured out for dinner. Firstly, Majid reserved a table at the Tour d'Argent and then, on the following night, at Alain Ducasse's famous Jules Verne restaurant located on the second floor of the Eiffel Tower, with its breathtaking views of Paris. On their last night, they dined at the Bar a Huitres on the Boulevard du Montparnasse and enjoyed the most wonderful seafood Arielle had ever tasted. Even though she had claimed beforehand she'd be hard to please since she had been spoiled for choice, quality and freshness back home, she delighted in the fare. Everywhere they went staff fawned over the good-looking and elegant couple who left generous tips.

Time to return to Dubai came all too quickly and Arielle spilled many tears on the flight back, remaining as inconsolable as her lover. However, Latifah managed in the end to reason with them: Arielle had to concentrate until the Cup was over. After that, she promised to plot it just so they could find time to be together again, shielded from wagging tongues and publicity flashes.

For the next two weeks, they hardly saw each other, but the big day was finally upon them. Cup Day had been scheduled for 30th March. The horses were paraded in front of a full house, the Meydan racecourse packed to the rafters. A sea of dishdash and kanduras sparkled in the sunlight, boldly peppered by the many ex-pats' brightly coloured outfits. Arielle proudly wore Hamdam's silks. On Aazeen's back, she looked incredibly small and almost frail, yet the giant TV screens caressed her resolute visage. Every spectator trained their binoculars to take a good look at her. Hamdam knew the competition would be fierce. Since his mare had yet to prove she could run in an international race on his turf, her odds were a long shot. His jockey, on the other hand, had already won the public's heart. Paprika Sands and Oil Princess also took their barriers next to Arielle's. The majority of the other contenders were overseas horses with impressive records.

The thunder out of the gates was deafening, the crowd already on its feet. Ears perked with determination, nostrils flaring, Aazeen was not intimidated in the slightest, straining at the bit and taking position in the forward peloton in the first 100 metres. Arielle subtly held the mare back, knowing that her best performance would be attained after the last bend in the last straight. As she came up to the lead, and for the next few seconds, she wanted to be sure she wouldn't be caught wide. Only two other horses ran ahead of her. Paprika Sands was one of them; the other she recognised as Prior Estimate, a gelding owned by the Queen of England and the first royal horse to have won at Ascot the previous season.

She pushed forward and her mare sprouted wings, squeezing through the narrow space left by the two horses ahead of her, eager to leave in the dust the other three which were breathing down her neck. For a few breath-holding seconds, the three horses ran neck to neck. Bookies the world over cursed under their breath, tearing their hair apart, just as Arielle let go of her mount which slid past like a bullet, in the nick of time, to cross the finish line a full length ahead of the Queen's Prior Estimate and Paprika Sands, who took third place. The crowd cheered. Cars honked on the streets beyond, the cacophony only exacerbated by the loud speakers spelling out the order of the winning horses.

So overwhelmed was Hamdam with emotion that Catherina, at his side as usual on this very public of occasions, feared he would succumb to a heart attack right in the middle of the VIP stand. She quickly signalled a waiter for some cold water, loosened the neck of his kandura, and fanned him with the pocket fan she always carried in her purse, her menopause often prompting hot flushes at the most incongruous of times. By the time Arielle had been paraded in front of the grandstand, he had moderately recovered, his face nonetheless still flushed with pride and excitement. Moments later, he held high above his head the much-coveted trophy. Tonight he would be the toast of the town and the envy of all his compatriots. The fact that he was now a few million dollars richer was just icing on the cake. There were tears in his eyes when he congratulated his jockey. It was certainly Arielle's first win of international stature. Winning a race most considered one of the most prestigious races on the racing calendar clocked as her biggest achievement to date. Back home, her parents, watching the race on the internet, had jumped for joy: never had Guillaume been so proud of his daughter. He only wished he could have been there to share the magic with her.

The after-party kicked on until the wee hours of the morning. For most of the night Arielle remained dutifully glued to Hamdam's side. He had insisted on introducing her to all the dignitaries from neighbouring states who had come to offer their congratulations. Behind his back, some were so bold as to offer her lucrative contracts to ride for them, offers she declined gently but firmly. Indeed, on that most extraordinary of days, she wished for only two things: for Majid and her parents to be at her side. Sadly neither was possible even though they had both sent many a congratulatory text.

When she finally returned home at dawn, her room was filled with lavish bouquets from admirers she didn't know she had. After stripping off, she was just about to welcome the heavenly feel of the crisp white linen sheets, when she noticed on her pillow a small bag tied at the handles by a ribbon with the word 'Cartier' scrawled across it. Underneath the bow, she detected a folded note she almost didn't find the strength to open, exhausted as she was.

My darling, you were magnificent, it said. *Please accept this as a fitting souvenir of this most extraordinary day. With all my love, M.*

From inside the small red leather box, she lifted out a delicately fashioned diamond-encrusted miniature horse hanging on a fine gold chain. Stunned by the thoughtful gift, she admired for a few minutes the exquisite details of the workmanship, and clasped it in her hand and against her heart. She was still holding it tight when she woke up at midday the following day, her phone softly beeping by her side.

Despite their repeated pleadings, neither Hamdam nor his wives could convince Arielle to remain as a guest a minute longer. Arielle had won enough money in her own right to secure her own accommodation. She longed before all else for a lack of restrictions from a social and religious etiquette which weren't her own, and finally to come and go as she pleased. In fact, above all else, she yearned for the freedom to frequent Majid whenever she wanted. She was more than ready to sacrifice the lavish lifestyle of Hamdam's household for a few unhurried hours in her lover's arms. During her previous chats with other ex-pat women, she had discovered that many had chosen to live in the part of town known as Emirates Hills, and she made her intentions to live in the same enclave clear to her host. In the end, Hamdam had little choice but to relent.

Since it was a condition of the lease for her rent to be paid 12 months ahead of time, Hamdam generously took over the payment for the spacious and conveniently located three-bedroom house she had chosen in Spring One. Hamdam had nonetheless regarded the dwelling as far too modest for her station. On the other hand, he had reluctantly agreed it was a fairly secure location. After some heated discussions with the landlord, he took it upon himself to make some improvements before Arielle moved in, replacing the standard white tiles with travertine marble throughout and upgrading the open-plan kitchen with all the latest appliances. Magnanimously he also offered her to keep the young Indian boy, Ata, exclusively in her employ as her jack-of-all-trades, to tend to her garden, her security, and her driving, as well as all household chores in-between. They had both been delighted by the arrangement. Latifah had helped shop for furniture and everything else Arielle had needed to decorate the house and the two women promised to continue socialising with each other as frequently as possible.

Ata alone knew that Majid had taken a second residence just a block away in the same gated estate. Suspicious at first of the man's intentions towards the woman he had come to feel so protective towards, in the end, he had nonetheless succumbed to Majid's charm and easy-going manner.

For the next 18 months, the two lovers lived within a short stroll of each other's residence. Since their high garden walls opened up onto a busy street, it was easy for either one of them to enter each other's house through the back door without raising any suspicions from their neighbours. Whenever she wasn't training or racing for Hamdam, they spent most of their time together. They also attended university, both enrolling in business management courses.

Arielle took the opportunity to learn the basics in Arabic, a language she already guessed would take her a lifetime to master. Her attempts to converse put her in good stead with the other jockeys and, most importantly, with the stablehands. Majid, of course, volunteered to tutor her after classes. Amongst her peers, Latifah was the only one to share in Arielle's well-kept secret. As surprised as she was that Majid had, in effect, abandoned his legendary playboy ways, effectively withdrawing from the social circuit to date Arielle exclusively, she continued to worry about what would happen next. Regardless of her misgivings, for the next few blissful months, her fears remained unfounded.

The following year Arielle again won four out of six starts during the Dubai World Cup festival but on Cup Day only ranked second, losing to the favourite, an American-owned horse competing on the day. With most of her expenses paid, by the time Arielle was due to return home, she had saved a sizeable amount of money along with her trophies. Her going-away party was a lavish affair attended by several rulers of the neighbouring Emirates states.

Catherina had organised the festivities, and like everything else she did, it had been impeccably set. As usual, it turned out to be one of those parties guests spoke about for years afterwards, while those skipped from the guest list kept lamenting they had missed it.

It was with a heavy heart that Arielle bade goodbye to the friends she had made, Latifah in particular. To Ata she gifted her Mini: in his gratitude, the now 22-year-old had forgone all etiquette, hugging and kissing her, letting her know he would never forget her.

On the other hand, so broken-hearted and sad were the two lovers that, on the night before her departure, holding each other tight and crying for their loss was all they managed to do. At the departure gate, Majid could hardly bear to watch her go, holding onto Latifah for support. He was convinced he would never hear from her again; he couldn't have been more wrong. However, it would take well over a decade.

CHAPTER VII

After a few laps in his 20-metre pool, Majid lay on his bed, still trying to cool down. Once again the weather had been unbearably hot, temperatures soaring well into the fifties, sapping most of his energy despite the freezing air conditioning working overtime. He had almost fallen asleep when his phone rang. He quickly glanced at the display: the number was blocked. He wondered whether he should answer it, fearing it was none other than his editor-in-chief wanting to discuss the next issue of Arabian Nights. He had launched the popular magazine just a few years back: it had proved to be an appealing mixture of in-depth background articles on the movers and shakers of the UAE, both Emirati and ex-pats, combined with the latest fashion trends and social circuit gossip. Since its maiden issue, the magazine had become a favourite of the European and American expatriate community. Within months it was distributed overseas as well, foreigners loving the informative tips it gave them when it came to living in that particular region of the Middle East. Mildly irritated by the interruption, Majid took the phone to his ear.

"Majid?"

He recognised the voice instantly and his heart jumped to his throat.

"Arielle? Is that truly you?"

"Am I catching you at a bad time? Perhaps in the embrace of one of your many wives?" teased Arielle, her voice warm and friendly.

Shocked to hear her voice after a decade of silence, Majid thought better of answering the question.

"Has something happened?" he questioned immediately, alarmed. Only the most unusual of circumstances could have prompted her to call him after shutting him out for so long.

"You may say that," replied Arielle enigmatically. "You're the only person I could think of who could help me. I'm in a jam."

"Shoot."

For one hour straight Arielle told him the whole story of her father's public disgrace and her suspicion that rival breeders could have falsified bloodstock by using frozen sperm. In recounting the tale, she was careful to omit that it was her current boyfriend's obsession with what she referred to as the 'Napoleon conspiracy' which had prompted the unexpected call. Listening to her, Majid wasn't quite sure why the sperm provenance was of such crucial importance but since it seemed so obviously vital, he promised to look into it and discreetly approach the horse's previous owners. Unbeknown to Arielle, it would be a rather easy task since he had married the man's daughter seven years ago.

"Are you still wearing your necklace?" he asked finally, his tone light but his heart painfully hammering against his chest.

"Which one? The diamond necklace you gifted me in Paris or the horse you surprised me with after my first win?"

"Either."

"I wear your horse around my neck every day. As for the diamond necklace it remains more acquainted with my safe than the paddocks in which I spend most of my time."

"Are you married?" he asked almost shyly for a man who had just celebrated his 40th birthday weeks earlier.

"Unlike you, I'm not," she replied lightly, "and before you ask me how I know, I subscribe to Arabian Nights. Congratulations by the way. It's a beautiful magazine."

"Why aren't you married?" he insisted, his mouth dry and his ears ringing.

"I fell so deeply in love once that I've never seemed to manage to recapture those feelings since," replied Arielle candidly. "I've a boyfriend but marriage isn't on the cards yet. At least not for me," she added pensively. An unexpected jealousy pang stabbed at

Majid's heart but he didn't wish to question her further, memories of her rapidly flooding his brain.

"Give me your number. I'll call you back as soon as I've found something out."

"I'm glad you haven't changed your number. I'd have been stuck. Reception here isn't always reliable. I'll text you my email address. Majid, I've got to go. It's wonderful to hear your voice again."

Majid did not mistake the hint of wistfulness in her voice.

"As it was for me. We'll speak again soon."

Within minutes, Majid was dressed in one of the forty snow-white kanduras filling his closet. If he were to speak to her again soon, he'd better have concrete information to give her.

Minutes later he had fixed his father-in-law an appointment, inviting him for later that afternoon to smoke apple shisha and drink mint tea in one of the open-air cafés alongside the marina. The meeting had been scheduled for early evening, once the sun had set and the temperatures taken the scorch of the day out of the equation. Meanwhile he would spend his time doing some research since he knew almost nothing of his father-in-law's stables. He held little regard for either the man or his businesses and thus so far had never bothered. Now he couldn't wait to gather as much information as possible. He dialled Hamdam's number first of all to gain the type of information he would not gain by surfing the net. Indeed, after Arielle's departure and for the past decade, the two men had remained quite friendly, enjoying each other's wit and company. The conversation proved most enlightening.

When the mares allegedly covered by Napoleon gave birth to two dozen foals between them, Nathan Heathers, true to his word, had stored blood samples from each one of them before their rightful owners had come to take them home. The Cavalieri brothers had kept just one of the foals, since the brooding mare had been theirs. Not without a sense of humour, they had named her Josephine: the pedigree legend of the blood bay filly was very promising. When Nathan had verified her DNA prior to registration for the records maintained by the Australian Stud books, there had been no doubt as to her sire's line or her dam's. Likewise, no obvious foul play had been detected in any of the other foals birthed that particular year. However, Nathan had been adamant that something remained amiss: in his analysis the stallion's DNA sequence did not seem to be exactly the same for every tested horse, an anomaly he had never run across until then despite his years of experience.

Puzzled by his findings, he had begun contacting geneticists and biologists to understand the possible source of those particular mutations. As a result, he spent most of his free time researching the subject and conversing with experts, unwittingly casting Arielle aside in the process.

With her call for help to her former lover, Arielle believed she had solely aimed at either dispelling or confirming Nathan's suspicions that something was amiss with Napoleon's progeny. It had been her last-ditch attempt at regaining some semblance of a normal relationship with the young veterinarian. Indeed, Nathan had basically devoted the last 12 months uncovering what was wrong with Pandora Estates' foreign stud. What she had not anticipated was to feel her passion for her first love so unexpectedly rekindled after one simple phone call. It had taken her months and months of sheer willpower not to contact Majid when she first returned home. She had cried for him every night, for weeks on end, but she had been convinced that their relationship was doomed from the start and she had seen no point in putting on hold both of their lives. In her mind, her silence had set him free.

Now after hanging up the phone, she realised she was shaking with emotions of such force it left her bereft. It had taken her years to get over her ill-fated affair. In the last decade, Nathan had been the only man capable of shaking Majid's hold on her heart. From her physical, almost nauseous reaction to the sound of his voice, apparently the old bond still held, an unwelcome phoenix rising from the ashes of her past. She questioned her motives for calling him after all these years but soon convinced herself that he had been the only person she intrinsically trusted to discreetly find the answers she sought.

Initially, Hamdam had rated as her first choice. However, ever since her first win, he had become a very public figure in the racing world, rising in stature with every passing year. Casting suspicion on Napoleon would undoubtedly arouse Hamdam's curiosity. Further explanations as to the reasons behind her line of inquiry would lead him to react and she couldn't vouch for his reaction. An unchecked rumour could take a life of its own and become prejudicial for all involved, casting clouds on the outcome of international races. In his position, Hamdam would be duty-bound to act on what he knew. After Arielle's departure, Hamdam, buoyed by his success, had often taken to race his horses abroad, often threatening to come and try the Australian turf. After the young woman's lengthy but safe stay in Dubai and in spite of the media furore or perhaps because of it, Guillaume and Hamdam had seen no harm in reconnecting. Thus, they communicated often, mostly via Skype and emails. Hamdam was well aware of Guillaume's explosive loss but diplomatically, during their fortnightly conversations, he never mentioned it. From the other side of the world, he nonetheless continued to monitor his friend's moves on the racing circuit, albeit from afar.

During his conversation with Majid, Hamdam, cautiously at first, but soon warming up to his subject, had revealed that Sheikh Rashid, Majid's father-in-law, bore a reputation for shady deals with foreigners. According to him, the Emirati businessman had made a career of showing his disdain towards non-believers by fleecing them whenever he could. He had brokered such unorthodox deals that the businessmen he had run across always came to regret crossing his path. Persuasive and clever, however, he had always managed leaving his opponents feeling foolish rather than outraged: most of the men he had cheated had been too embarrassed to report any of his dealings to the authorities, and, so far he had gotten away with it. After listening to Hamdam's scathing portrayal, Majid knew beyond a shadow of a doubt that Arielle had been right. All he needed was confirmation. He hoped that during the ensuing discussion with his father-in-law he would finally come to hold the bargaining chip he sorely needed to re-establish a connection with Arielle. Moreover, he had secretly despised the man since marrying his daughter, Assa, a shy beauty six years his junior. A chance at humiliating the infuriatingly arrogant man lifted his spirits.

After seven years of marriage, Sheikh Rashid's youngest daughter had failed to bear him an heir. So far, Majid had not repudiated his wife, knowing only too well how miserable her life would become. Every time the subject was broached during family gatherings, her father had threatened to ruin his reputation and bankrupt Arabian Nights, which he had cleverly backed at its very beginnings, if he decided to do anything about it. The marriage had been brokered according to ancient traditions and Assa had come with a handsome dowry and her father's resources. Despite his best efforts, Majid held no feelings for his wife other than respect and a type of benevolent tolerance for her barren state. His heart, however, had firmly remained out of her reach. Without children to cement the union, Majid had wondered more than once why he carried forth in a tolerable but loveless marriage. He had no desire to marry more than one wife either, repelling his own family's pressures to marry again.

When he had heard Arielle breathing down the phone once again, after a decade-long silence, he had remembered why. He had been certain that Arielle's refusal to contemplate a future with him had had more to do with their respective traditions than with incompatibility of religion or her career for that matter. He had been sure that the matter of religious conversion had been only one of the facets in her decision to separate. On the other hand, the prospect of potentially sharing him with other women had been a deal breaker.

When Majid came to sit on the terrace on the seaside promenade, Rashid customarily kissed his son-in-law on both cheeks. Two sishas had already been lit and various small dishes of hummus, grilled haloumi, labne, kibbeh and shawarma had been placed between them. They sat opposite each other, resting comfortably on Arabic-style banquettes set with thick pillows. In Majid's opinion, Rashid was as corpulent as he was smarmy, sweat dripping from his wide, pock-marked forehead. Despite the late hour and the cool breeze rising off the water, the temperatures were still in the high thirties. It took a few lungfuls of sisha and a few mouthfuls of the delicious nibbles before Majid could bring the conversation round to the subject that preoccupied him.

Rashid knew his son-in-law to be generally well informed on a variety of subjects. Therefore, he never questioned his knowledge of the deal he had brokered three years ago with an Australian breeder when he had sold him the famous stallion for stud. He boasted repetitively about the exorbitant sale price he had obtained for the horse in question and delved at length into the venality of the foreign stablemaster. It took another hour and subtle probing before Rashid finally confided that he had split the kickback with the studmaster when the horse was sold well above reserve, having skilfully rigged the auction. He also admitted to always taking out some form of insurance whenever dealing with foreigners, whom, in his opinion, could never be trusted. To that end, he had simply frozen Napoleon's sperm before shipping him out, and had believed himself most clever for doing so.

Mistaking Majid's quizzical look for one of implied criticism, Rashid was quick to explain away his unconscionable actions. In Napoleon's case, he insisted that his foresight alone had come to save the day. Indeed, the stallion had proven infertile by the time he had reached Australian shores. The matter could have proved highly embarrassing for all concerned if it had come to light and led to an expensive settlement for breach of contract. Moreover, it could have threatened to expose Rashid's fraud in the process. However, he argued that, thanks to the few precautionary cryogenic vials stored in his purposefully-built safe, he had been able to swiftly repair the breach. He had even joked that due to his immeasurable cunning no one, as far as he knew, had guessed at the subterfuge. His sense of self-importance and fatuity made Majid squirm, yet he did his best to remain impassable, carefully hiding his growing contempt for the man. When they finally parted ways, Majid was jubilant: he had extracted everything he needed to call Arielle back on the very same day. He now held the irrefutable proof of the man's culpability.

Rashid, for his part, was glad to have apparently once again dodged the bullet in regards to his daughter's fecundity or rather lack of it. It had been a rather embarrassing state of affairs which had unnervingly kept tongues wagging for far too long. Talking about horses had certainly been a much easier topic than discussing Majid's lack of progeny.

★ ★

Apart from Josephine, a quarter of the yearlings sired by Napoleon had proved noteworthy as racing thoroughbreds. When, a few hours later, Arielle confirmed that Trent Winnings had used frozen sperm to impregnate the mares allegedly covered by the stud, Nathan had remained dubious. Arielle had refused to name her source, attesting only that it was highly reliable, but he had insisted that without it, the information was simply worthless. Baffled by his reticence, Arielle nonetheless argued that exposing the deleterious DNA sequence, and thanks to the quick degeneration of frozen sperm, should be proof enough. Majid's revelations had corroborated their suspicions: in her opinion, little else was required to make his case. They were definitely on the right track. Once the DNA configurations were analysed specifically to point out the permutations, the scam would be exposed once and for all. They did not need to implicate anyone else and certainly not her overseas source.

After further discussion, they reluctantly agreed that the manner in which they brought Trent to the attention of the authorities was now their only dilemma. Indeed, out of the two dozen horses born that year, half a dozen had gone to win several important races and were now contenders for major Group I races. Refuting the legitimacy of the racers would imply previous wins become scratched and tally enormous losses for the industry. Inquiries and lawsuits were liable to bring the entire sport into disrepute. With Arielle's confirmation that forbidden sperm had been used, Nathan had felt intellectually vindicated. His conscience, on the other hand, gave him little respite. In his book, Winnings should be arrested for his duplicity regardless of the cost. The catastrophic ramifications, however, did not escape him. In the end, he remained convinced that without the original seller's own confession on record, it was likely to come down to his word against Winnings' in any inquiry. Arielle had continued to infuriate him by refusing to expose her source; on the other hand, he admitted she had done her best to help him regain his sanity by proving his suspicions had been well founded. At this point, he could not go and blow the lid on the whole story without dragging her along. His sense of fairness would not allow her to stand through an inquiry.

After three hours of heated debate, weighing the pros and cons of divulging their knowledge of foul play and confirming Nathan's earlier hypothesis, the couple decided that the best course of action was to scare the culprit into a confession. They would draft an anonymous note which would let him know that the world had not been blind to his machinations; that he had been found out and that he was being watched. Naively they hoped that the fear of public exposure would prompt him to quit his job and quickly leave town. The idea of blackmailing the scoundrel into resigning his position and disappearing from the racing world was the most appealing solution to them both. They wished to destabilise him to the point where he was left with no other choice but make it stop. In the end,

Arielle left it up to Nathan to decide the manner in which the message would be delivered.

In her opinion, Arielle had done everything in her power to squelch what she regarded as Nathan's unhealthy obsession. During their discussions it had become abundantly clear that, if on the one hand she had given Nathan peace of mind in regards to his sanity, it certainly had not put an end to his ruminations. Apparently the battle would not be over until Trent Winnings was run out of town. She wanted no part of it. It wasn't her fight. What was her fight, however, was that Josephine, Trafalgar, Walkabout and Bittersweet had all qualified for the same races in which her father had entered some of his horses, Obsidian, his protégé in particular. If it ever came to a close call, she knew she wouldn't hesitate to have the other horses disqualified by casting doubts on their questionable lineage. She was ready to deal with the ensuing scandal if it meant protecting her father. Meanwhile, she'll remain alert, shelving the burning secret in the recesses of her memory, but not before putting pen to paper first, recording the whole saga on a file in her computer.

Since the beginning of the season, Obsidian had clocked an impressive number of wins, gilding his laurels from the previous year, when, as a two-year-old, he had taken the purse at the Chipping Norton Stakes at Warwick Farms in March, followed by two wins out of three starts during the Golden Slipper Stakes at Rosehill. He ranked second, both at the AJC Australian Derby and the Australian Guineas. Now Guillaume had his eyes firmly set on the Melbourne Cup. Well over the qualifying threshold win in prizes, Obsidian had enhanced his Cup ambitions by qualifying for the Caulfield Cup, the final instalment in the three days of the Caulfield Racing Carnival, part of the wider Melbourne spring carnival. The reputed trainer, Mel Walters, had requested Arielle jockey her horse for the same race. Guillaume had not objected and betting exchanges reflected to the upside public's sentiment.

Guillaume's luck, however, held firm when Obsidian sprinted through the finish line by a length, automatically qualifying for the Melbourne Cup. Arielle's ridden horse had come in third. Obsidian, having consistently displayed great form, came to the attention of savvy punters who increasingly kept a close eye on him. When the horse had finally qualified as part of the field of 24 to run the race, Guillaume's spirits had soared. Josephine, Pandora Estates' hopeful, had also earned a spot. To Arielle's dismay so had Walkabout who was fast becoming a favourite amongst pedigree buffs. Deciding whether he would name Arielle as his jockey for the ultimate race plagued Guillaume for days. Fate, however took the decision right out of his hands.

When, in the very last days of October, Obsidian, boarding at Green Acres Farm while racing in Victoria, began to lose his appetite, Patrick, in whose care the thoroughbred had been entrusted while interstate, at first had not overly worried. It wasn't unusual for a horse to go off his feed for a day or two. However, when the very next day he noticed the horse's flared nostrils, inexplicable shaking and overall nervousness he had called Nathan immediately, believing it might be a badly timed colic, due to a change in diet. By late morning, when Nathan finally arrived to check out the animal and attempted to lead him out his stall, he observed the horse's reticence in moving forward, the animal reflecting a tendency to lean back as if he wished to put pressure off his hoofs. After detecting a palpable increase in pulse in the hooves, Nathan, thoroughly alarmed, diagnosed a sudden onset of Founders' disease. In racing circles, acute laminitis was considered life-threatening. In the best case scenario, the horse could be cured over time with appropriate medication but he certainly couldn't run either in the short nor the medium term. In the worst case scenario, the inflammation would spread and the horse would have to be put down to avoid further pain.

Guillaume was utterly devastated by the diagnosis. Obsidian to date had done much to restore his sullied reputation. Indeed, on the back of his proven success and unable to forget his earlier humiliation, he had once again decided to back his own horse to the hilt. A compelling win would not only shut up his detractors once and for all, but put Chantilly Farms back on top. He could not fathom losing face twice. Guillaume was sitting in his office, gathering the last necessary bits of paperwork prior to his afternoon flight to Melbourne when, at the news, he clutched his heart and let out a painful howl, fearing a heart attack. Arielle, loitering nearby, barged in to see what the matter was. She found her father slumped forward on his desk, with his head in his hands, weeping softly, a sight she had never formerly witnessed.

"Papa, Papa, my God, what's wrong? What happened?" she cried out in alarm, rushing to his side.

"Obsidian. Founders," was all he managed to utter.

Arielle's hand flew to her mouth, her eyes wide with shock. Nathan had alerted her that morning that he needed to fly to Melbourne ahead of schedule, with Patrick worrying about the horse's inexplicable behaviour. She had thought nothing of it.

"Has Nate called you?"

"He can't run. He may have to be put down. I'm finished," wailed her father, who suddenly looked old and frail.

"What do you mean you're through? It's most unfortunate, I agree since Obsidian was so promising but there will be other Cups and other colts," argued Arielle reassuringly.

Despondently, Guillaume shook his head, unable to look at her. Slow understanding crept in Arielle's voice.

"No, Papa, no! Tell me you haven't done it again! What is it about winning the Melbourne Cup that makes you lose all reason? Tell me why you'd back your own horse once again? It has taken three years for Chantilly Farms to recover financially and become viable again! You almost bankrupted us the first time! Why would you risk it again? How many times do you think you can start over?"

Guillaume finally lifted his head to look her in the eye. Tears streaked his handsome face.

"Mark my words, Obsidian is the best horse I've ever trained in my entire career. I know I would have won this, especially with you riding him."

"When were you going to inform me?"

"Tonight, on the flight down. I made the decision a few days ago: the Stewarts have already been informed. I waited to see if you were going to ride one of Walter's horses. Walkabout has been deemed the favourite and I wanted you to have that chance."

Arielle smiled sadly at her father: didn't he know that there were never any other horses she'd rather ride than his, regardless of their chances?

"What do we do now? Do I dare ask how much you've bet?"

"Chantilly Farms would change hands. I'd retire in disgrace," replied Guillaume, his voice so low Arielle had to stoop to hear him.

"I can't let that happen," replied Arielle immediately, trying to control both her horror at the situation and her anger at her father.

"You have as much choice in the matter as I do," replied Guillaume dejectedly.

"My choice would be to cancel our flight immediately and get on the road as quickly as possible with Obsession in the float. Papa, Obsession is much faster than his twin!"

"You're joking, right?" replied Guillaume, unsure if at that very moment he was questioning the feasibility of a substitution or his daughter's assertion that her untried horse was faster than the one he had so assiduously trained for the past 36 months.

"Papa, if you're bound to lose it all, at the very least don't you go abdicating without a fight! Even you can't tell the difference between the two horses! Do you know how many times you've timed me around the track, believing I was riding Obsidian when it was Obsession I was pushing? I had you fooled by bandaging his forelegs to hide his coronets, the only visible difference between them. We run very little risk that the stewards would want to blood type out of the blue a horse that has allegedly already been fully vetted. No one besides Nate and Patrick know Obsidian has been born a twin. I'm sure they could keep a secret if it meant keeping their jobs. I can assure you Nate won't breathe a word; I vouch for his silence. In Patrick's case, I'm sure it's a question of naming a number. This will be the Cotton Affair the way it should have been pulled off," she added, her laughter hollow.

"And if we are caught?"

"I'll be the end of both our careers. We'll play chess from adjoining cells. But we won't," assured Arielle with a great deal more confidence than she felt. If they were caught it would mean public disgrace, a scandal of monumental proportions, heavy fines, license suspensions and banishment from racing for a number of years or even a lifetime. Basically, it would break her father's business and end her career. Apparently, her father's business, as she knew it, could be finished either way. Thus, in Arielle's mind it was a risk worth taking for both of them. Moreover, without racing in her life, Majid would have nothing left to compete against. She had chosen her career over him 10 years ago; maybe this time she could finally choose him without any regrets. She would be free to go and do as she pleased. From his daily emails, it had been easy to read between the lines: he had no more forgotten her than she had him. Guillaume stared at his determined daughter and reluctantly agreed to the scheme. They'd leave the farm as soon as Obsession was readied for the eight-hour ride. Meanwhile, he'd call Nate and then Patrick: they were still a vital part of the plan if the unfathomable conspiracy was to succeed.

They took turns driving the truck. They had agreed that Arielle would speak to Nate first, while Guillaume would try to sway Patrick. In the end neither man had required much convincing. Patrick had promptly stopped Guillaume from embarrassing himself: as soon as he had heard they were both on their way down with Obsession in the back, he had understood right away what his boss had had in mind. As far as he was concerned Guillaume had saved his life and the indignity of collecting unemployment for the rest of his life. After his accident, Guillaume alone had lent him a hand: he had been magnanimous and kind. Over the years he had shown him nothing but respect. When no one else would have anything more to do with a jockey who could no longer perform, Guillaume had offered him full employment: he owed him. The idea of thumbing the establishment who had so cruelly dismissed him was an added bonus. If Obsession was to win, the bribe of 10% of the purse was just icing on the cake.

Likewise, Nathan had understood both Guillaume's predicament and Arielle's fierce determination to protect her father's reputation. With Napoleon's illegal progeny running against her and owned by the biggest names in town, he felt that the proposed substitution was the lesser of two evils and would even out the field. At least Obsession's pedigree was clean. Guillaume had always been fair and treated him like an equal. Moreover, he was in love with his daughter. Why wouldn't he help them? The pair had likewise sweetened the deal by offering him the same cut they had Patrick. What both father and daughter did not mention was that besides the prize money, an enormous personal bet was riding on the outcome. In the case of defeat, they would be all on the street regardless.

As they waited for the float to arrive, Patrick and Nate had done their best to keep the thoroughbred comfortable and away from prying eyes. To the overly curious, Nate had mentioned a case of mild indigestion due to the slight alteration in food. All day they took turns fielding questions and barring access. Forced to rely on another trainer's stables for the duration of the carnival, Patrick was well aware that privacy was always challenging. However, he had also counted on everyone's understanding of the unspoken rule of giving interstate trainers and their charge a wide berth as a matter of common courtesy. He had even come up with an ingenious way to further bridge the disparity between the two colts. He took advantage of his time alone nursing the sick horse by bleaching his forelegs to imitate Obsession's coronets. The result, though slightly yellowish in tint, would pass muster for any casual observer. Following the same line of reasoning, he had sent Nathan to purchase hair dye so they could obliterate Obsession's characteristic socks as soon as the horse arrived. When on race day the steward in attendance would request for the bandages to be taken off and check the horse's legs, there would be no obvious telltale sign, especially if no one was looking for it.

The four co-conspirators had all agreed that the truck would pull up well after dark, and the horses exchanged rapidly. Patrick would then drive the float back to Chantilly Farms immediately thereafter and return with a rental car the following day. Two one-way tickets, both originating from Sydney to land in Melbourne on two consecutive days, would appear damning during an inquiry if there was ever to be one. Of course, if anyone was to look for a rental car, it would mean they were already neck high into an investigation: they all hoped it wouldn't come to that. However, taking basic precautions was, in their view, absolutely necessary and hardly a waste of time. Around half past eight, under the cover of darkness, the float finally pulled in. Thinking ahead, the night before Patrick had rendered inoperative the two security cameras covering the yard. First he had disabled the one trained on the entrance to the property and then the one specifically aimed at the horses' stalls where Obsidian was berthed. He knew for a fact that no one looked at the recordings unless they had reason to do so.

By midnight, the switch had been made, with everything going according to plan, without a hitch or a wrinkle. Neither security nor the night watchman had heard or seen the truck arrive or depart, too busy watching a semi-final rugby league match between their home state and Queensland. By the time the match had finished, Patrick was already driving back to the Hunter Valley with Obsidian lying in the back, drugs keeping him semi-conscious and without pain. By the early morning hours of Thursday, Obsidian, now Obsession, was declared fit to run and thus Arielle spent the last three days before the race preparing him for the track. Bookies and punters loitering around the course nodded their approval at the horse's solid form. Then the big day was finally upon them.

When Arielle was led from the birdcage to her assigned barrier, fourth from the inside rail, she breathed in deeply and exhaled slowly, all nervousness rapidly evaporating. Until that very moment she had kept misinterpreting every look, every nod, and every lingering hand flattering her horse, her paranoia at discovery in full swing. As the two dozen horses settled noisily, tensely awaiting the start, it began to rain. Arielle smiled happily: Obsession was a mud lark and the heavy track would only spur him on whereas it could potentially disadvantage some of her competition, reducing the odds. The gates opened to a thunder of hoofs. Within the first two furlongs, Obsession settled fourth on the fence and stayed inside, off the bend, until the field suddenly cleared in front of him. Arielle yelled into the wind, "Now, Obsession. Now fly, little one!"

The horse sprouted wings despite the worsening weather, the rain now coming down hard, obscuring the field, the course rapidly degrading. The grandstand was on its feet. Nathan nervously chewed his bottom lip. Patrick clenched his fists. Guillaume closed his eyes in a short prayer. When he snapped them open, Arielle was clearly in the lead, Walkabout dangerously on her heels, with Josephine trailing just a half-length behind. With one last effort, Obsession shook them off.

When he greeted the judge, after piloting the field in the last 50 metres, the three men standing in the enclosure, regardless of the deluge, jumped loudly for joy, hugging each other and slapping each other's backs like teenagers after a high-school football match home-run win. In their mind, genetics, training, skeletal soundness combined with the skills of the jockey and their collaborative quick thinking had combined to win the day: Arielle had been right. Her protégé was a racehorse through and through. He had run faster and better than his twin could have ever done. At three minutes and seventeen seconds exactly, Arielle had run within a breath of Kingston Rule's celebrated win, back in 1990.

Guillaume's risky Trifecta win had just netted him over $3,200,000 dollars. Added to the prize money, it had been a very profitable afternoon indeed. He was back on top, his name on every lip. Likewise, Patrick and Nathan had added a significant bonus to their earnings. All accepted congratulations from the gallery with beaming smiles and not a single afterthought. In that exhilarating moment, they had almost come to forget their earlier duplicity: it was getting easier to rationalise their actions by the hour. After all, they had taken care of both colts since their birth. Perhaps Nathan and Guillaume had been too quick to call Obsession unfit to run all those years ago, but for all intents and purposes it was easy to pretend they were now just one and the same. Meanwhile, Arielle had shown to be not only the best jockey of the season, but also a great trainer too. Guillaume wondered more than once if the pupil had not come to surpass the teacher. Who could have thought than an untried horse could come to win the famous Cup?

Under the VIP Emirates tent, Majid had watched the race with great trepidation and a nervousness that surprised even him. He had not set eyes on Arielle since he had watched her disappear down the slim corridor that had led her to her plane almost 10 years ago to the day. His binoculars had been trained on her ever since he had glimpsed her before the race, proudly displaying her family's silks in the members' enclosure. During their long and frequent email chats, she had refused to turn on the webcam and he had ached to see with his own eyes what she had become. It hadn't been too difficult to figure out precisely where she would be on the afternoon of that first Tuesday of November.

He had flown in Hamdam's private jet just the day before. After 30 years, the old man had been just as keen to surprise Guillaume: after a few drinks the week before, both had decided, on the spur of the moment, how great it would be to attend the fabled race. While Hamdam's social prominence could be assessed by the sheer number of people forming his immediate entourage, there was only a handful of men he could call friends. Travelling with Majid suited him fine. Checking out firsthand whether it would be worth racing a couple of his horses Down Under the following year was an opportunity he couldn't miss. Both had cheered at Arielle's spectacular win: in their eyes a climate of celebration was the ideal backdrop for a reunion. Had Arielle lost, the moment could have proved awkward.

As soon as Guillaume and Arielle arrived under the Emirates VIP marquee to celebrate their win, they came nose to nose with their past: there were no words to describe the stunned silence which descended upon them. Like a child, Arielle rubbed her eyes to ascertain it wasn't a mirage. Then, quickly recovering from her shock and forgetting all matters of propriety, she shrieked unceremoniously and jumped at Majid, who collected her in his arms. Likewise, Guillaume could not let go of his old friend, both men caught in an emotional embrace. Had either Patrick or Nathan seen Arielle's face at the very moment she laid eyes upon her former lover, and the unmistakable spark in her eyes, any hope they could have secretly harboured to share her life for the long run would have evaporated on the spot. Undoubtedly, they'd also have instantly regretted the pact that now bounded them to father and daughter alike.

Both Emirati shared a suite at the Crown Towers, since their last-minute decision had left them with little choice, Melbourne hotels booked months in advance for the Spring Carnival. After some inconsiderable arm twisting, the hotel had liberated a villa, a decision made somewhat easier when Hamdam had wired them a sizeable sum, expressing the wish to gamble during his stay in the high rollers' private gaming rooms. The inclement weather having cut short the endless on-course celebrations at Flemington, the two men invited both Hamdam and Arielle back to their hotel so that they could – in Hamdam's own words – finally pop a decent vintage bottle of French champagne. Father and daughter had happily acquiesced: it was a perfect end to a perfect day and they just had so much to talk about. Guillaume needed to touch base with Sarah first: after their last public disgrace, his wife had obstinately refused to set foot again in Melbourne, regardless of the reason. Like the rest of the nation, she had watched it on television and had been terribly proud of her daughter and very excited for her husband. When she heard that Hamdam had surprised her husband by showing up at the races, she extended an invitation for him and his guest to come and spend some time with them the following weekend. Guillaume promised to relay the invitation, kissed her goodnight and returned to his host. It did not take long for Majid to manoeuvre Arielle away from the two old friends and onto the enclosed terrace from which they could view the shimmering river beneath them and the cityscape across it. As the pyrotechnic fires below belched into the air, the couple gazed tenderly into each other's eyes, all the lies, the years and the compromises suddenly forgotten.

CHAPTER VIII

Father and daughter remained in Melbourne for another two days, availing themselves to the press that hounded them for interviews. The photo of Arielle kissing her horse on the nose when officials handed down the cup to her father standing next to her had made every newspaper's front page across the country the following morning. A horse sired at Chantilly Farms, trained by the owner and ridden by the owner's daughter, at the longest odds possible, was a story many could run with: headlines told the world that in the case of Chantilly Farms it was all kept in the family, outsiders unrequited. Experts predicted that it would not be the last public sighting of the magnificent horse. They were all convinced that thanks to his meteoric rise to fame, Obsidian was more than likely to repeat his performance in the years to come. The additional two days reminded the two men – now well past their prime – how much they valued their friendship and how much they had missed each other. Likewise, the two former lovers agreed that a whole life still lay ahead of them: every minute not spent with the media had been spent with each other.

By late Friday night, the whole family was back at Chantilly Farms, Hamdam and Majid in tow. Sarah had slaved over dinner, eager to impress her guests with her culinary expertise. Dinner was delicious and the conversation animated, lubricated by excellent cellar wines. The frequent looks of longing passing between her daughter and the beautiful man sitting on her left, however, did not escape her maternal attention. She wondered how Nathan would take the inevitable news and whether Majid had been all along the reason why her daughter had not yet married. During the post-dinner drinks, Guillaume discussed his proposed purchase of the land that separated him from his closest rival. Sarah was in favour of renovating Chantilly Farms and increasing its standing instead. Guillaume wished to expand his land holdings, and Hamdam naturally remained fairly neutral, even though, in his opinion, one never owned too much real estate. Arielle, revelling in Majid's presence under her parents' roof, remained non-committal, refusing to let the debate spoil her happiness. When the older generation finally took their leave, they stayed behind, nursing a late harvest wine, holding hands and looking deeply into each other's eyes, their former passion fully rekindled. They were so lost in the contemplation of each other that neither noticed the furtive silhouette running past the living room windows.

Indeed, Guillaume's windfall could not have come at a better time: his closest neighbours, the Mooneys, had contacted him a few weeks prior to check whether he would be in the market to purchase a few more parcels of land in order to expand his activities. The proposed land in question was all that separated Chantilly Farms' paddocks from those at Pandora Estates. After a few decades tending their commercial orchards, the owners wanted to retire to North Queensland, having found the house of their dreams near Port Douglas. Since their brood had made it clear that working the land would never figure in their future, they saw no point in hanging on to either the business or the land. Guillaume, however, was not the sole contender. The eager farmers had put forward the same proposition to the Cavalieri brothers. It had come as little surprise that both interested parties had wished to postpone further discussions until after the Melbourne Cup, the outcome vital for them both.

With Guillaume's fortuitous winnings, Chantilly Farms was now in a position to purchase Apple Legends, the orchards next door, leaving him still with plenty left over to gild his laurels. The business meeting was set for early on Saturday morning, Dave

Mooney impatient to seal the deal and snare a buyer regardless of who it was. By losing on Cup Day, he was well aware that the Cavalieri brothers would most likely opt out of the option. If Guillaume escaped his net, his whole plan for a retirement in the sun would need to be postponed indefinitely. After 40 years of backbreaking work, husband and wife were more than keen to enjoy warm lazy days and balmy evenings year round, and Dave was determined to win over one of his two closest neighbours.

Soon after breakfast Guillaume set off to his appointment, while Hamdam lingered on, regaling Sarah with many stories of his home country and memories of Arielle's visit a decade ago. Arielle and Majid had skipped breakfast, saddling at dawn to take a ride out onto the property, happy to be alone, away from everyone. Patrick, still spying on Arielle's every move whenever he had a chance, watched them canter away, his instincts telling him clearly that the foreigner was trouble.

When later that morning he ran into Nathan checking up on Obsidian's dismal progress, he casually asked him if he knew the identity of the guests staying at the house, insinuating adroitly that Arielle seemed particularly friendly with the younger of the two men; he hadn't seen her so happy in ages. In his opinion they acted like old friends, but his tone alluded to a great deal more than friendship. Listening to him, Nathan' eyes narrowed in a pained expression, his face clouding instantly. He waited as long as he possibly could to catch a glimpse of her but they still hadn't returned well after lunch had come and gone. Eventually, he gave up and returned to his cottage.

Back in Melbourne, Arielle had agreed to spend the evening with him on that Saturday night to quietly celebrate their successful switch in front of the entire world. In spite of Patrick's suggestions, he knew she would come by as promised, and he occupied the time by cooking for her. When at half past eight she still hadn't shown and when his increasingly frantic calls had remained unanswered, he'd decided to go past the house. The same scene Patrick had witnessed the night before, when he had furtively crept by the French door windows to take a good look at Chantilly Farms' unexpected visitors, greeted him: watching Arielle languidly kiss another man had been more than he could bear. Nathan had fled into the night.

Nathan was not by definition an introspective man. As far as he was concerned, his relationship with Arielle had been a given. They were single, healthy, and available. More to the point, they appreciated each other's company. Nothing else needed to be said. He had never spoken of marriage since in his mind, it was the only natural outcome as to where their relationship was heading. Now, back in his cottage alone, he wondered whether he should not have discussed it earlier. Arielle had never mentioned falling for anyone else but he suddenly realised he had never asked about former lovers. As far as he was concerned, living in the present was all that mattered to him and thus it had seemed completely irrelevant to revisit the past. He also knew that on top of her equestrian success, Arielle's natural beauty and easy-going manner earned her many admirers. Yet he had seen her keep her distance, remaining reserved and somewhat distant, usually rebuffing potential suitors with a dismissive smile and a flippant joke. He had witnessed many times the look of disbelief painted on the men's faces when they had realised they had been dismissed without a second thought, like a lame horse overlooked at the markets. Humiliated, none had come back for more.

Surely the man he had seen kissing her had not turned her head in the last 72 hours: it was simply impossible. He knew how long it had taken him to win her trust and for her to become comfortable around him. He also clearly remembered how many more weeks had gone by before he'd been able to coax her into his bed. Until now he had never experienced jealousy towards anyone. His mother had taught him well: as far as he was concerned, women were free to come and go and, when it was time for them to leave, he did not pursue them and wished them well. Even though he wasn't adverse to the chase, until now, he never had to compete for any female attention, knowing he embodied most of the qualities which made an able man a desirable catch. His physical attributes could hardly be denied. Moreover, he was a professional man with a flourishing career who earned a decent living. He also presented a laid-back facade of honesty, sincerity and stability doused with a good sense of humour. However, what Nathan could never admit to himself was that, in his pursuit of what he believed was right, he was often single-minded to the point of fixation. For months now, Trent Winnings' deception had been his primary focus to the detriment of everything else. It had never occurred to him until now that Arielle could have grown tired of playing second fiddle to his obsession.

Trusting he would be alone in the negotiating seat, Guillaume, visibly annoyed to be sitting across the table from Stefano Cavalieri, nonetheless let Dave Mooney go through the motions of his proposal. The latter opened the discussion by proposing to let go of the 20 hectares of land for bare market value, provided the deal could be struck by week's end. According to his bluff, he had already registered interest from other parties, but had given them first right of refusal for the sake of neighbourly courtesy. He likewise warned them that he would put the land up for auction if they couldn't reach an agreement. Obviously, it was neither in Stefano's nor Guillaume's interest to see the land abutting their properties to fall into the hands of yet another breeder, who would by default increase competition in terms of services. The cunning Dave Mooney suspected Stefano might be short on cash. On the other hand, Guillaume was arguably solvent, thanks to his performance of late. By placing the two rivals in the same room, Dave banked on the fact that the Italian would fight his competitor tooth and nail on the price, making sure that Guillaume did not obtain the property for a song. He had not been wrong: the heated negotiations raged all morning long, with Guillaume and Stefano trying to outwit each other. By lunch time, they all reluctantly agreed to table any further discussions until the following Friday morning when they would both put in their final offer in a sealed envelope. Dave Mooney would have until five o'clock that evening to accept one of them.

Chantilly Farms had always been Stefano's Achilles heel. From the very beginning he had resented Guillaume's formidable personality, and his propensity to turn most of the horses in his care into winners. Moreover, he had envied his ability to fray with the rich and powerful with utmost ease, proof of a breeding he could never call upon, even though Guillaume had never spoken of his antecedents to anyone. In the past, overwhelmed by jealousy and resentment, Stefano had made discreet inquiries to uncover his rival's past, but to his surprise, he had come up empty. Prior to his arrival in Australia, Guillaume's slate had evidently been wiped clean, something which had always struck him as strange. Whether he came from a lack of records was always a red flag. His instincts told him that if he was able to somehow figure out who the man he only knew as Will LaSalle had been prior to immigrating to Australia, he was sure to uncover an unsavoury past which he could use against him, forcing him to back out of the current real-estate deal. The purchase of the land was not only vital to his plans for the further expansion of Pandora Estates but also essential in containing Chantilly Farms' own. Indeed, the acquisition of Apple Legends would help double Chantilly Farms' capacity and turn Pandora Estates into a second-rate option for those owners wishing to breed and train their horses. It had been bad enough to lose to Guillaume on the racetrack: he had no intention of losing on a real-estate deal as well. He had long ago pinpointed Guillaume's accent as uniquely European. It was now time to go back to the drawing board. Time was running out.

After three days at Chantilly Farms, Hamdam and Majid were due to leave. Arielle offered to drive them back to Sydney International Airport. The prospect of losing Majid a second time was heartbreaking and their goodbyes as poignant as they had been a decade earlier, when she had left the UAE to return home. This time, however, they promised each other it was only a matter of time before they would be together again. Before they could be reunited, they needed first and foremost to take care of personal business so as to be completely free of any impediment. Majid would need to instigate a divorce as soon as he returned to Dubai and Arielle decided she would publicly announce her retirement and leave her career behind. Both knew their sudden decision would meet with disapproval from all involved parties, but neither of them really cared. They were financially secure in their own right and at their age, neither needed their families' consent. Since Majid, at first, wouldn't be able to live in Dubai with his lover until they were truly married and because there was little point in Arielle staying in the Hunter Valley once she left the world of racing behind, they had both agreed to go and plan for their future in Paris.

When Arielle returned the following day, after spending the night in Sydney, she shared her plans with her parents. Guillaume was livid. However, he wasn't nearly as resentful as Patrick would turn out to be, nor as angry as Nathan. In one felled swoop she had unknowingly shattered all their dreams.

"I've heard from Nathan you're quitting racing. Is that true?" questioned Patrick late the following afternoon when she came back to the stables after riding Obsession for a couple of hours.

"I see good news travel fast," replied Arielle, unconcerned, kissing her horse on the nose and murmuring terms of endearment into his ears. "Overseas, here I come."

"What are you talking about?" pursued Patrick through clenched teeth.

"I've decided to live abroad for a while."

"To escape justice?" retorted Patrick malevolently.

Stunned by his aggressive tone, Arielle turned around to confront him.

"We haven't been caught. The whole matter is now water under the bridge," she replied calmly.

"It is, unless someone alerts the authorities. You wouldn't want that, would you?" he hissed nastily.

Arielle's eyes narrowed. Sensing his mistress's tenseness, Obsession's ears pricked up.

"And what would you gain by that? It's my understanding that you've been paid mightily for your role in it," said Arielle haughtily. "You'd be investigated as much as I would, and, if my memory serves me right your past isn't exactly lily white. You'd have to prove it. With Obsidian on death row, it'd be a matter of your word against ours."

Patrick blanched.

"It's that Arab isn't it?"

"I've no idea who you're referring to," replied Arielle, trying to keep her emotions under control. How dare he blackmail her?

"I've seen you with him! You can't deny you're lovers!" he barked, jealousy strangling his last words.

"Have you been spying on me?" she asked, surprised.

"Wait until I tell Nathan you're nothing but a cheating whore!"

Arielle's shock at the vehemence of his words rendered her speechless. Patrick mistook her silence for fear and pressed on.

"Did you really think that you could get away with it? I won't have it! Mark my words!" he added, rage darkening the throbbing veins in his neck.

"How does my relationship with Nate have anything to do with you? How does anything I do concern you?"

"Well, when your father needed me he had no problem enlisting my help, did he? I couldn't care less about your relationship with Nate!" he replied with a tone that implied everything to the contrary.

Arielle looked at him closely. From where he was now standing, a few metres away from her, his legs spread apart and his arms crossed over his chest, she could detect the pungent smell of alcohol on his breath.

"You're drunk, Patrick and you're acting like a thwarted lover!" accused Arielle incredulously."Why don't you tell me what's really going on?" she added as calmly as possible in the face of his incomprehensible attack.

Patrick stared her down. If she left the country, his dreams to one day bed her and inherit Chantilly Farms would all come to naught. Until now, he had bidden his time. Now time was running out. He needed to act quickly: the alcohol cursing through his veins helped him throw caution to the wind.

"You're jealous!" reiterated Arielle, now laughing at him. "Unbelievable! What planet are you on? Did you really think I could ever go for a man like you? You must be joking!" she added, her eyes dancing with barely controlled merriment.

Her cruel laughter was more than Patrick could bear. Swiftly he bridged the gap between them, and with the back of his hand struck her hard across the face, catching Arielle unaware. She tripped over the feed bucket she had brought up to Obsession, lost her balance and hit her head on the jam of the door stall, momentarily blacking out. Seizing the opportunity, Patrick quickly opened the door to the next empty stall and dragged her body inside. By the time Arielle recovered her senses, she realised he was on top of her, with her arms roughly tied with a horse's lead over her head, his knees on either side of her, her shirt already unbuttoned. Patrick was panting heavily.

When Stefano's father had fled Italy under Mussolini, it had been no secret that his family had been targeted by the dictator's war on what was referred to as Cosa Nostra. Directly in the line of fire, Lucio had managed to escape to Argentina thanks to his numerous contacts, finally settling in Australia after Juan Peron seized power. During his two decades abroad, first as a wrangler and then as proud owner of the large estancia located a couple hours south of Buenos Aires, he had come across many of his former compatriots. Indeed, under Mussolini's regime, anyone who had been perceived as meddling in politics, bullying voters into voting for candidates they favoured, intimidating witnesses when it came to prosecution, counterfeiting, racketeering or drug dealing had been a marked man. Most had fled for similar reasons, eager to avoid the Carabinieri's payback of old moral debts, when the mafia had been truly in charge and the police had to do their bidding in order to keep their jobs and kiss their children goodnight. Those same acquaintances had looked him up when they came to settle in Australia after the Second World War. Stefano remembered meeting some of the old men when they had come to visit his father, talking about the old country and drinking grappa late into the night. Those same men, he knew, had kept their tentacles in Sydney's underworld. By rifling through his late father's files he was sure he could locate those men's sons and persuade them to make inquiries into Guillaume's past. He desperately needed to find something to hurt Guillaume's chances at acquiring Apple Orchards.

It took over a dozen phone calls for Stefano to hear back from a man who introduced himself as Dante Alberti. During their amicable conversation, they both established their grandfathers had come from the same Sicilian village, west of Palermo. Both elders had helped their oldest son gain freedom and flee their birth country before it was too late. It didn't take long for Stefano to form the opinion that the man he was talking to had most probably kept in the same line of work as the generations which had come before him. A few minutes later, they came to an understanding. In exchange for a well-timed tip next time Josephine ran a Group I race, Dante would happily dig into Guillaume's past. He still had many connections abroad, not all above board. What he found astounded them both: for the first 48 hours neither knew how to use the information to their best advantage.

As a child of merely 13, Joe Guarini vividly remembered visiting his father and three uncles at Les Baumettes prison in the port city of Marseille. They had finally been transferred there from the infamous Fresnes jail, located in the Val-de-Marne near Paris, where they had first been imprisoned while awaiting trial. After the lengthy and very public court case, the four men had received five consecutive life sentences for the killing of 14 innocent bystanders at the Ecume des Jours restaurant, unavoidable collateral damage in their planned assassination of Marcel Francisco. Thirty years later, Joe could still recall each and every one of his monthly visits: how he had shuddered at the sight of the well-fed rats running along the walls, the exposed electrical wires and the constantly leaking roofs. He could also vividly remember how often he had retched due to the pervasive smell of rot and mould that had assailed him on every occasion.

Two of his uncles had managed to survive the inhuman prison conditions for nearly 15 years before being knifed to death during a particularly savage inmate brawl. The youngest of his uncles had contracted pneumonia a couple of years later, dying alone in the infirmary, the prevailing unsanitary conditions hastening his demise. The Guarini brothers had, in fact, spent a lifetime collecting enemies in and outside prison walls. Once Joe's father was finally left on his own, sensing a brutal end, and without his brothers to protect him, he had committed a much publicised suicide. Inconsolable, Joe had spent nearly a decade trying to avenge his father's death. Locating the sole survivor of the massacre at the Ecume des Jours – the illusive man who had so definitively put an end to his family name by identifying all perpetrators – had been his sole mission. Yet, shortly after the trial, the man he knew as Guillaume de La Selle had simply vanished. After countless searches he had finally given up.

In the early sixties, the busy Marseilles port was a privileged route for drug trafficking and many of those caught in the police net ended up at the notorious Les Baumettes prison. Dante Alberti's father had been amongst those men, serving a 60-year sentence. Alberti Senior had stayed alive by remaining indispensable to the hordes of illiterate men who had passed through the same walls. As a semi-educated man, he had spent most of his jail sentence writing letters on everyone's behalf. After his father's capture, Dante, with his life in danger, had been forced to immigrate as far away as possible from the drug cartels reigning over the south of France. Up until the old man died Dante had received a letter a week. The Guarini brothers and the crimes which had landed them in the same overcrowded cell had figured predominantly in the old man's letters. Dante Alberti Senior at first had spoken little French, communicating with his cell mates mainly thanks to the language similarities between his mother tongue and Corsican dialect. In his letters and due to his mispronunciation, he had come to describe the only witness to the Guarini brothers' murders as a boy simply referred to as LaSelle, his father allegedly known throughout Europe for his racing success.

When Stefano Cavalieri had begun his inquiries about Guillaume's past, the name LaSelle had rung a familiar bell. After checking his late father's letters, Dante had made the call. The Guarini brothers, until their last breath, had, according to his father, helped keep him safe in prison. Now the son was presented with the opportunity to repay posthumously a debt of honour: it was his duty first and foremost. It took him less than a day to locate Joe Guarini. It took less than 36 hours for the latter to land in Sydney.

CHAPTER IX

At first Joe Guarini had listened cautiously to Dante's tale but the salient facts had matched his own recollections. There was no doubt in his mind he had found the man he had been looking for his entire life. The man Dante had described as Will LaSalle was undoubtedly the right age and had obviously pursued a career Down Under in the only field he knew well. It didn't bear any stretch of the imagination to figure out that he had changed his name from Guillaume de La Selle to Will LaSalle, the names sufficiently similar to always remember the alias without ever forgetting the past. During what he had found to be an extraordinarily long flight, he had spent most of his time alternating between flirting with the pretty hostesses and catching up with his prey's movements over the past 30 years. Thankfully the latter were fairly well documented. Aware that the racing season was now over, he was certain he could easily locate Guillaume back home at Chantilly Farms.

As previously agreed, Dante met Joe Guarini in the parking lot of McDonalds located near the airport, on a sideway exit street. After the long flight, Guarini didn't mind the short walk. Moreover he was not encumbered by any luggage, except for a modest carry-on. By meeting outside the airport, they were thus sure to avoid the surveillance cameras recording the comings and goings in the airport loading and pick-up bays.

Once in the car, Dante handed the Frenchman a paper bag with the untraceable handgun requested over the phone. Paid in cash, the hired car had been leased in Dante's name to prevent anyone from connecting them if things turned ugly. When the car would finally be returned to Budget Car Hire, Joe would already be safely out of the country. He promised to park it exactly where Dante picked him up: the latter would then return it as if nothing had happened. Outside of banalities, the two men exchanged few words. Once they reached Mascot, Dante got out of the car under an overpass and handed Joe the keys. In exchange, the latter remitted him a thick padded envelope with enough cash to cover his expenses in relation to the illegal gun, the car rental and, of course, the information. They shook hands, never intending to see each other again. As far as Dante was concerned, he had now played his part and absolved his moral debt.

As arranged, Joe found a map in the glove compartment, with directions to the Hunter Valley and Chantilly Farms' location clearly highlighted. Beyond confronting the man who had deprived him of his entire childhood and led him to grow up without a family, Joe didn't have a set plan. He figured he didn't really need one. From his understanding the farms were isolated from each other, and Guillaume lived with only two other people under his roof – his daughter and his wife. Joe was certain he would easily find the occasion to isolate the man he had hated for most of his adult life and spare his family: blood shedding of the innocent wasn't really his style. Depending on the tenor of the conversation he might also lean towards blackmail: wasn't financial compensation for emotional torts the outcome of most court judgments anyway? Guillaume was undoubtedly rich. In fact, extorting a sizeable amount of money could alter his customary motto of "a life for a life". During the two-hour drive, Joe Guarini's focus oscillated between the many possible scenarios. What he never expected was to suffer a blown tire on the way out of town after hitting a particularly deep pothole. By the time he was back on the road, it was already dark.

The rental car didn't come equipped with a GPS – an optional extra – and Joe soon became hopelessly lost, each property poorly signposted, the roads twisting and turning and often ending nowhere. Reaching the crossroads near Apple Legends, he finally saw the small wooden sign indicating the way to Chantilly Farms. However, fate had intervened that very morning when a delivery truck, speeding out of the orchards with a full load, had gone off the road and knocked over the sign which now pointed straight at Pandora Estates. In the dark, Joe followed the bumpy road until the impressive homestead came into view. The old Queenslander-type dwelling, with its wraparound porch, was flanked on the right inside by a row of low-roofed, dimly lit buildings, which Joe presumed would be no other than the stables. Paddocks loomed on the other side. When he finally came to the entrance to a private road indicated by an impressive wrought-iron gate without a padlock, he parked his car under a huge eucalyptus tree and continued on foot, guided by the light ahead, his revolver securely tucked in his belt.

Dishevelled, unrepentant, and yet already scared by the consequences of his unconscionable actions, Patrick fled Chantilly Farms, careening out of the property in his battered old ute. On the way out he placed a quick call to his friend, Trent, announcing his impromptu visit. Trent Winnings had been his only friend since coming to work at Chantilly Farms. The two men had recognised in each other the same indomitable will to survive everything that had befallen them in the course of their lives. Moreover, they shared much in common, holding similar positions for their respective employers. Hearing the anxiety in his voice, the latter told him he could be found in his office at the far end of the stables: a bottle of old malt whiskey would be waiting for him on arrival. It took Patrick merely 15 minutes to reach Pandora's gates, and in his haste he did not notice the car parked incongruously on the side of the road, a few metres away from the entrance.

Joe Guarini cautiously approached the rows of barns, a single light burning bright at the far end of the first building as his sole guide. Through the mud-caked window panes, he observed two men sitting across from each other, huddled in intense conversation, one with a large cigar dangling from his lips, the other gesticulating empathically, a bottle of scotch between them. From the newspaper photograph he had memorised earlier neither seemed to resemble the man he was looking for. Close to nine o'clock at night, he hadn't expected to find anyone still on the property apart from Guillaume and his immediate family. Therefore, he came nearer to try and catch some of what sounded like a heated exchange. Hopefully the discussion at hand would help him understand who the two men were and where they fit in the grand scheme of things.

The snippets of conversation proved most enlightening: apparently both men had been involved in different deceptions, ranting and confessing all to each other over steady drinks. One of the men in particular appeared to have been involved in a rape. Guarini wrinkled his nose in distaste: in his book, raping a woman was a sign of weakness. He disliked the man instantly. However, he intuited that if he came even closer he would be party to secrets he'd be able to use later. He slithered past the pens and crouched underneath the open office window, hiding in the shadows. He had done so just in time.

A truck was riding up through the fields at what appeared to be full speed. It stopped short a few metres off the building. With the high beams of the truck behind him, a rather tall man exited and stood still, silhouetted against the jet ink sky. The car engine was left running.

"Bloody hell!" exclaimed one of the voices as soon as they had heard the approaching truck. "It must be Will! Must have gone the back way, through the paddocks! He's going to kill you! I reckon he won't take his daughter's assault too lightly. What are you going to say?"

"I can't see how he'd do anything! He can't touch me! I've too much hanging over his head!"

Joe smiled in the dark. The newcomer at the scene was certainly of the right height and stature to be his prey. The voices had just confirmed the man he had been hunting for over 40 years was finally within arms' reach. He cocked his gun just as the two men exited the small field office, standing in front of the door, their combined girth blocking the narrow entrance. They waited side by side for the new arrival on the scene to make the first move.

"Will, I can explain!" shouted Patrick, shielding his eyes from the intense light, his voice now trembling with fear. The tall man in the Akubra hat still did not move.

"Come on, let's talk about this. I didn't mean to hurt her. Don't you understand? I love her. I can explain!" shouted Patrick, increasingly unnerved by the confronting silence.

"Come inside," invited Trent, yelling likewise. "We can all talk about this like gentlemen."

"Like gentlemen?" The voice was harsh and filled with repressed anger. "Pat, you're finished."

Patrick, puzzled, squinted into the light. He'd be darned: it wasn't Will's voice but Nathan's. He breathed a sigh of relief.

"Mate, it's not what it looks like, I swear! I just wanted to teach her a lesson. It just got out of hand. I'm sorry. I'm sure she'd agree! It was all her fault anyway. She was going to leave us for that Arab."

"I don't believe you," came back the sober reply.

"Come on over here where I can see you," insisted Patrick. "I can explain, I swear!"

Before he could add anything, a man jumped out of the shadows, his gun drawn. The gun pointed squarely at Nathan's head.

"And who the hell are you?" barked Trent, taking measure of the intruder and instinctively retreating into the doorway to grab his shotgun leaning against the door frame.

"You two stay still," replied the commanding voice with a thick foreign accent. "I've no bones to pick with you. Stay put and you'll live. I've come here to kill this man," he said, gesturing toward Nathan, "and I've waited 40 years for the pleasure."

Dumbfounded, Nathan looked straight at the man he failed to recognise. Forty years? He hadn't even been born then. What was he talking about? He stepped forward and out of the beam of light which had prevented the three other men from identifying him readily.

"Not another step!" warned Joe shrilly. At that exact moment, Trent, who had just managed to wrap his fingers around the barrel of his gun, inched it towards him until it rested firmly against his leg.

"Hands over your head," instructed the foreigner, "right where I can see them."

Nathan stopped dead in his tracks and did what he was told, the rim of his Akubra hat still obscuring his features.

"You're LaSalle, no?" demanded Joe, his chin pointing in Nathan's direction.

"Who wants to know?" replied Nathan calmly.

"Joe Guarini. Name rings a bell, doesn't it? You thought you could hide, didn't you? Well, now your past has caught up with you. Thanks to you, my entire family was disseminated. They all perished in jail, one way or another, because of you. I watched my mother die of a broken heart. I grew up without a father and I owe it all to you!" screeched Joe, with jet lag and years of resentment turning his tone into pure venom. "Now you're going to pay for it!"

Uncomprehending of the unfolding drama, the three men stood shock still. A lone owl pierced the eerie silence. Startled, Joe Guarini levelled his gun and cocked the trigger, aiming directly at Nate rooted to the spot. The latter was still trying to gauge the situation when Trent swiftly retrieved his shotgun and shot the trespasser with a bullet straight through the chest. However, at the very last minute, Joe, who had sensed conspicuous movement to his left, just where the other two men stood near the stable office door, had already turned to the side. Just as he was hit, he reflexively emptied the already cocked gun in his hand. With an expression of utter surprise, eyes wide with shock, Patrick fell backwards, a bloody hole widening on his forehead. In the chaos, Trent inadvertently dropped at his feet the smouldering cigar still dangling at the corner of his mouth. The overtly dry hay instantly caught fire. As flames quickly leaped up the wooden stalls and smoke began to swirl around them, the distressed horses began to neigh and bristle in their pens, desperately kicking their enclosures.

"Free the horses," yelled Nathan, who was already frantically pulling the pins from the pen doors and chasing the horses away from the fire which was rapidly gaining momentum. Coughing through the dense smoke, Trent moved into action, likewise helping to chase the horses away to safety. In the distance they could already hear the sound of sirens. Suddenly, in a deafening whoosh, the central beam broke off the roof now engulfed in flames, falling straight across Trent's legs and torso, pinning the heavy-set man to the floor.

"Nate, Nate," he screamed loudly to be heard over the thunderous crackling of the structure. "Help me. I'm stuck."

Nate looked at the few metres of inferno that separated him from the man he had loathed for so long. For a fleeting second he wondered whether it wouldn't be a fitting death. As far as he was concerned, the man could burn in hell for what he had done. He lunged nonetheless towards the man and managed to take hold of his wrists, pulling him slowly out of the burning wreckage and away to safety. With Trent out of harm's way, there was nothing more he could do. He certainly had no intention of sticking around waiting for the police to show up and explain what had happened.

"Trent, I was never here. Do you hear me?" he screamed to the man covered in black soot and spluttering on the ground, his charred and mangled left leg dangling at an awkward angle, his chest painfully crushed, his broken ribs making breathing laboured and difficult. "I've just saved your life and in my book, yours didn't deserve to be spared. I know what you did with Napoleon. I've all the proof I need."

"What about Napoleon?" blustered Trent, trying to focus, smoke and shock obscuring his vision.

"Should I mention the words 'artificial insemination' or the use of frozen sperm? Aren't both practices perfectly illegal? At least in this country? You're nothing but a cheat and a despicable man with low moral standards. Your career's over. I want you out of

151

the game forever. By your actions you have mocked everything I stand for," shouted Nathan, now shaking with anger, adrenalin coursing through his entire body.

After staring at the young man standing over him with his closed fists on his hips, yelling over the inferno, Trent shrugged his shoulders dismissively and shook his head.

"Can't we discuss this later? Surely you're not going to leave me like this? I know you've secrets too," cried Trent, his voice starting to weaken from shock and massive loss of blood, charred pieces of wood sticking through his thigh, his knee a bloody mess.

"Fire trucks and ambulances are on their way. Can't you hear them? If you live through this, take the opportunity to resign your post or I'll come after you with a vengeance. Consider yourself forewarned. Goodbye and good luck. I don't expect to ever see you around."

Without giving Trent a second look, Nathan pivoted on his heels and ran to his truck, taking off across the paddocks along the same road he had taken driving in, his lights switched off, relying for guidance solely on the faint moon and his memory, while fire trucks, ambulances and police cars sped up the drive on the opposite side.

When Arielle still hadn't made any attempt to contact him after dropping her guests off at the airport, Nathan, after waiting all day for her to call him, had finally screwed up the courage to drive to the house and confront her. On the way up the long shaded drive, he passed Patrick's truck speeding away in the opposite direction. As they passed each other, amidst the billowing dust, the two men exchanged a look through their open windows. Patrick looked ashen and Nathan fleetingly wondered what had him so spooked. Past the stables, noticing the main doors to two of the pens flapping in the wind, he stopped his truck to go and close them. In the stalls beyond, the horses seemed unusually agitated and instinctively Nathan went in to investigate.

With no other sounds around but the rustling of the animals in their stalls, he heard a muffled cry. It took him less than a minute to discover Arielle lying on the ground, her hands still tied above her head, blood running from her nose, her left eye contused and shut, a dirty rag stuffed in her mouth, bruises already darkening across her naked thighs, and her tattered clothing discarded nearby. A primeval scream escaped Nathan's lips. He rushed to her side, took out the rag, unfastened the rope and cradled her head. Her eyes slowly opened and she smiled wanly with an unfocused gaze. Nathan quickly grabbed one of the horse's blankets, covered her naked body, lifted her up and carried her to the front door of the house, all the while yelling for help.

Alerted by the commotion, Guillaume and Sarah, who had already retired for the evening, rushed downstairs to the living room, just as Nathan dropped Arielle's slack body on one of the deep leather couches.

"I just found her in the barn, in the stall next to Obsession's. She was tied up and gagged," Nathan explained haltingly, tears in his eyes.

"I'll call the police," Guillaume said, livid.

"Don't," Arielle begged, her voice a mere whisper.

"What are you saying, darling?" Sarah asked, confused. "You need a doctor. It's obvious you've been assaulted. We need to alert the police. Did you see your attacker?"

"Pat," Arielle replied, her eyes closed shut.

Taken aback by the revelation, Guillaume began pacing in front of the couch. If Patrick was indeed the culprit, he could already guess where this was going. If they fingered him on assault charges, his stablemaster would undoubtedly play his trump card.

"Sarah, take care of her," Guillaume instructed. "She's right, we can't call the police. Are you sure it was Pat?" he asked, looking at his daughter's bloody face, bile souring his stomach.

"Papa, I'm sure!"

"Will, it makes sense: I saw his truck leaving a few minutes before I got here. He looked like a man in a hurry to get the hell out," Nathan concurred.

"What happened?" Guillaume asked.

"For some reason, the news tipped him over," Arielle replied, breathing hard through her broken nose and cracked lips. "We had an altercation and then he hit me."

"What news?" Nathan questioned, flabbergasted. "What are you talking about?"

"I'm quitting racing, Nate," Arielle said gently, each word a monumental effort. "I'm done," she repeated, exhausted.

"Are you done with me too?" he asked, completely taken aback. Her silence gave him his answer. His jaw tightened but he pursued nonetheless.

"What does it all have to do with Pat anyway?"

"Nothing, except that he claimed to have always fancied me. In his mind I was always destined to be his and apparently he's terribly jealous: he didn't want me to go," Arielle whispered. "Nate, he hit me and then he raped me," she repeated, unable to repress the onslaught of tears.

Before either Guillaume or Sarah could stop him, Nathan went out the door. They heard the door to his truck slam hard and the vehicle speed away.

When Nathan returned to the house 45 minutes later, Arielle, wearing a loose nightgown and a mohair shawl tightly draped across her shoulders, was slowly drinking from a cup, her head carefully bandaged, the blood on her face gently washed away thanks to her mother's attentive first aid. She looked up as he opened the door.

"Pat's been taken care of," announced Nathan bluntly. Both Guillaume and Sarah looked at him intently, their eyes wide, the meaning hardly lost on either of them. Without a word, Guillaume went to the bar, poured two fingers of scotch into a crystal tumbler and handed it to him.

"What have you done, son?" he asked quietly.

"Let's say there has been an accident. Look out your window," he added calmly, pointing to the room's east-facing bay windows. In the distance, a fire raged, lighting up the sky.

"Pandora Estates," murmured Guillaume, mesmerised. "Should I ask?"

"As far as we're all concerned, I was here all evening. I mean, once I discovered Arielle's body in the barn, I stayed here to help you take care of her. I never left. Do we all agree?"

The LaSalles looked at each other and nodded. They knew the exact details of what happened would soon filter through anyway. In the meantime, the less they knew, the more effective the lies.

"Why didn't we call the police when you first found Arielle?" asked Sarah, always pragmatic.

"There is no timeframe on when I found her. You should probably call them now."

Guillaume smiled in the face of the young man's assertiveness. Nathan was definitely controlling the proceedings. Sarah went to the phone and dialled 000.

"So if you're no longer racing, what are you going to do?" questioned Nathan gently, taking hold of Arielle's feverish hand in his.

"I'm moving overseas," said Arielle in a feeble voice, not daring to look at him.

"When were you going to tell me?"

"I was trying to find just the right time."

"It's because of that man, isn't it? The one who came to visit last weekend."

Arielle's face gave her away. Nathan stared at her, dumbfounded. His world had just crashed. When he finally found his voice, he murmured, "Pat was right in the end." And then, fearing his emotions would betray him, he stood up and turned away from her to stare through the windows, seeing nothing but a red glow lighting the sky. Police sirens filled the night.

★ ★

Alerted by the continuous barking of his two mastiffs, Stefano Cavalieri switched off his television set to check out what had provoked their unrest. As he opened his front door, he immediately realised the lower barn was on fire, flames already leaping to the other nearby structures. Yelling for his wife to call emergencies, get dressed and get out of the house immediately, he ran down the gravelled drive towards the burning barn. Relief flooded him when he came across his horses huddling at the far end of the paddock abutting the gardens to the house. At first glance, at least, he had lost none of his thoroughbreds. As he approached the fire, he noticed the flames quickly closing in on a motionless shape lying on the ground a few metres away from the fire-swept barn. With his hand over his mouth to avoid choking on the thick smoke, he cautiously neared. Instantly he recognised his studmaster, Trent Winnings. Just as quickly he noticed the mangled leg, a large piece of metal sticking through it and the blood pooling underneath. The man appeared unconscious. He dragged the limp body a few metres away still.

"Don't move," he admonished, cradling the man who slowly opened his eyes. "The ambulance is on its way. Can you hear it? Hang in there. It won't be long now."

Trent, summoning the last of his strength, unceremoniously grabbed his boss by the collar of his shirt, his eyes wide and bloodshot, and his words haltingly raw.

"I'm sorry, mate. Napoleon. I tried my best. I don't know what happened."

"What about Napoleon?" asked Stefano, believing the man delirious with fever. "It's okay. It happens. It was unfortunate he had to be put down but such is life. Don't beat yourself up about it."

"Listen to me, "he implored. "Napoleon was a dud. I impregnated the mares," elaborated Trent, his words now coming in short staccato.

"You did what?"

Stefano almost let go of the man's head he had kept cradled on his knees.

"I'm sorry," repeated Trent, his eyes now completely unfocused.

"Who knows about this?"

"Nate found out. If I don't make it though, take a close look at Obsidian..."

Trent's voice was now no more than a whisper, but before Stefano could question him further, his eyes rolled back in their sockets, his mouth slackened, and his head rolled to the side. Stefano immediately took two fingers to his throat to check for his pulse: there was none. Trent had died with the most explosive revelation still on his lips. Stefano crossed himself, closed the man's eyes and dropped his head in his hands.

Less than five minutes later, a gloved hand touched his shoulder.

"Mate, don't worry. We've got it under control here."

Stefano opened his eyes and looked up at the voice; a dozen other firefighters were already dousing the flames. Several uniformed policemen now stood next to the man who had first addressed him.

"Sorry, mate. We've done all we can. We've saved all the other buildings but with the barometer in the late thirties for the past three weeks, the smallest spark would have done it," continued the burly man.

One of the officers cleared his throat and motioned for two of his colleagues standing slightly back to approach with a body bag. It was obvious Stefano was in shock. Gently they requested he stand up so they could take Trent's body away. Numb and exhausted, Stefano did as he was told. A man in a dark suit approached him.

"I'm Detective Tom Derek," began the policeman, introducing himself. "Can you tell me what happened here?"

"My dogs were barking non-stop, which is fairly unusual, so I came out to check what was wrong and immediately saw the barn on fire. I asked my wife to call you guys and ran down here. The blaze made it difficult to see anything but then I heard screams of agony and saw Trent lying there. His leg was all twisted and burned. There was a lot of blood too and flames were fast closing in, so I pulled him here. He died in my arms."

"Who's the man in relation to you?"

"Sorry, officer, I'm Stefano Cavalieri, the owner of this property. Trent Winnings is... was my studmaster. I did my best."

"He didn't have much of a chance with his injuries, loss of blood and smoke inhalation," replied the uniformed officer sympathetically. "Do you have any idea how the fire started?"

"Not a clue. I don't even know what Trent was still doing here at this hour. Normally he goes home by sundown, unless it's foaling season."

"Hey, boss," yelled one of the policemen, who had followed three of the Rural Fire Service firemen into the now extinguished but still smouldering building. "We've got two stiffs here!"

Sergeant Tom Derek, who had been questioning Stefano, excused himself and sprinted away. He returned minutes later.

"Who else was here?" he asked, his tone suddenly turned professional and crisp.

"I've no idea!" Stefano shook his head. This was really too much: he now had three bodies on his property and one charred building. He felt a serious headache coming on. Having never forgotten the police confrontations of his childhood, he feared what was coming. Regardless of what the police discovered, he would be in the thick of it and the mere thought made him noxious. When seconds later the police recovered both a hand gun and a shot gun, Pandora Estates burned-down barn was cordoned off and declared a crime scene. Stefano let out a long painful sigh: from here on, the night would stretch interminably.

At the same moment Inspector Derek was securing the crime scene at Pandora Estates, a white police Toyota Land Cruiser 4WD had stopped in front of Chantilly Farms. At the front door, Guillaume was waiting for them. He instantly recognised one of the policemen, Senior Detective Sergeant Zack Summers, whom he had met on several prior occasions during community meetings down in Maitland. They shook hands and Zack Summers introduced him to his constable.

"Sorry to see you, mate, under the circumstances," said the detective sympathetically. "How's Arielle?"

Obviously the detective had already been briefed by the operator who had taken the emergency call.

"Holding up, but barely," replied Guillaume, his face taut, his eyes filled with worry. "Please, come on in."

The two uniforms were led to the house's vast living room where Arielle still lay on the couch, burrowed under a soft blanket, her eyes rimmed red, the bruises on her face already turning a light shade of purple. Introductions were made all around.

"Arielle, I know this is rather difficult," began Senior Detective Sergeant Summers, 'but can you tell me what happened in your own words?"

"I'd just come back from a run on Obse..." she stopped, closed her eyes and corrected herself, "on Obsidian and was brushing him down when Pat walked in and confronted me."

"Who's Pat?" asked the constable in charge of taking notes.

"Our stable manager," replied Guillaume without hesitation.

"From the smell of his breath, Pat was quite inebriated and seemed upset and quite belligerent for some reason. We had a few words, an altercation of sorts, and then, out of nowhere, he hit me. In my surprise, I tripped backwards over the feed bucket. I must have hit my head because when I came to, he was on top of me and my hands had been tied over my head." Tears now coursed freely down her cheeks at the recollection, but she bravely continued on. "I tried to scream as he ripped open my shirt. He stuffed a rag in my mouth then took off my jeans and then..." Arielle faltered, "and then he raped me. He must have hit me once again or I blacked out on my own, I can't remember, because the next thing I remember is hearing Nate's voice." She lay back and closed her eyes, her heart-wrenching sobs muffled by the pillows beneath her head.

Zack Summers motioned for the others to step away and give Arielle some breathing room. He turned to Nathan.

"How did you happen to find her?" queried the detective. "Is it usual for you to come by so late in the evening? Was there a veterinary emergency on the premises?"

"I needed to speak to Arielle and she wasn't answering her phone. I decided to come by and speak to her face to face."

"Isn't it a tad late for a social call?" insisted the detective.

With many years experience to his credit, Zack Summers knew when the people he interviewed were holding back.

"We've been dating for a while. She hadn't called me when she returned to town after dropping off some guests in Sydney and I was worried."

Zack Summers sensed he'd need to get back to that piece of information later: for the time being he filed it away.

"So you came to speak with her. So why wouldn't you walk straight to the house, considering the time?"

"Usually, when Arielle does not pick up, it means she is still in the barns. So I decided to go there first."

"Then what happened?" pursued Summers, jotting down notes.

"I saw that a couple of gates had been left open and I went to close them. As I approached the barn in question, the horses seemed particularly agitated so I went in to investigate and calm them down. The stall next to Obsidian's was wide open. They're usually locked at night, regardless of whether they're occupied or not. That's when I saw Arielle lying on the ground, unconscious, bound and gagged. She wasn't moving and from her condition, it was clear she had been assaulted."

"What did you do next?"

"I went down on my knees, checked her pulse, took the gag out of her mouth, cut the binds, covered her with a horse blanket and brought her up to the house."

"What time would you say it was?"

"About eight-thirty, nine o 'clock."

"Mrs LaSalle, the call to the station came almost one hour later. Why wait that long?"

"We wanted to assess the situation first," volunteered Sarah. "It seemed more important to check that my daughter was physically safe and sound than report a crime had been committed," she added a touch defensively. "Moreover there was no urgency in finding the culprit. We already knew who it was and he wouldn't have far to run anyway."

"How are you feeling?' asked Detective Summers, turning his attention once again to the victim.

"Disorientated, embarrassed, powerless and vulnerable," replied Arielle, looking up. "I can't believe he attacked me like that. I've known him for years and he's never shown any violence towards me."

"You said he'd been drinking though?"

Arielle nodded her assent.

"Do you have any idea why he assaulted you?"

Arielle looked away, trying to think of a tactful reply but Sarah jumped in.

"The bastard was completely infatuated with my daughter! Everyone knew it! She turned down his advances and he couldn't take the rejection!" she added vehemently.

"Did he often make inappropriate advances?" queried the detective.

"I know he was watching me all the time. Deflecting his advances hasn't been a problem. Until now, I thought he was pretty much harmless."

"So why would he attack you now when he's had presumably plenty of opportunities beforehand?"

"I've no idea," replied Arielle, looking away, fixing an imaginary point on the wall behind him. Summers' instincts told him once again that something was amiss but he knew that with time the truth would eventually surface and thus he didn't press her.

"Will, do you know where your stablemaster is right this instant?"

"I saw him drive out of the property like a bat out of hell just as I was driving in," replied Nathan right away.

"Must have gone home," ventured Guillaume slyly, knowing that Pat had gone straight to Pandora Estates. "Or to a bar. Obviously he hasn't turned himself in."

"Thank you for your time," said Zack, after rapidly checking over the notes taken by his constable. "Arielle, do you want to make a formal complaint at this time? If you intend to do so, I'd need you to go and see a health sexual counsellor as soon as possible in order to gather the necessary forensic medical evidence so we can proceed with criminal action. We'd also need you down at the station to provide us with a formal statement."

Arielle vehemently shook her head.

"I'm not sure I want to do that. I just never want to see him around anymore. I want him arrested, of course, but I don't want to go to court and have to humiliate myself all over again by reliving the story for judge and jury. I just want him gone from my life!" Arielle started to sob once again and the two policemen decided it was time to take their leave. It would be only a matter of time before they located Winnings and interrogated him anyway. For the time being, there was nothing else they could do, especially if the victim refused to cooperate.

"I'm sorry, Will, for what happened to your daughter. She should seek medical attention tomorrow to check everything is okay. I understand she might not want to take this to court but don't worry, it'll be my pleasure to find the guy and make his life hell. Call me if she changes her mind."

"Thanks, Zack. Will do. By the way, what happened at Pandora Estates? Do you know? Is everyone safe?"

The sky was no longer glowing red but evidence of a major fire was still floating in the light wind.

"We'll stop by on our way back to the station to see if we can lend a hand. From the radio dispatcher, a barn or two caught fire. Busy night! Well, Will, take care of your family. You know where to find me if you need anything," he added, handing him his business card.

Guillaume nodded. At least the crime had been reported. Arielle was now on record for not wanting to pursue it and no motive other than jealousy and rejection had been alluded to for committing the crime in the first place. Hopefully, Nathan was also in the clear. However, in Guillaume's opinion, the police hadn't asked nearly enough questions about what could have triggered Patrick to assault Arielle so suddenly on that particular night. Neither had they delved into Nathan's relationship with both the victim and the offender. In his experience, it was certainly not the last time he would see his friend Zack in relation to the accident. He very much doubted that the tone would be as congenial next time around.

CHAPTER X

As the 4WD drove out of the property, the radio broadcasted a call for immediate back-up at Pandora Estates. Since they had intended to stop by and check it out anyway on their way back to the station, Detective Summers radioed in that he would attend the scene along with his constable. As they came to the crossroads, Zack Summers, who was by nature a particularly observant man, noticed that the sign to the property was askew and had spun around, placing Pandora Estates in the complete opposite direction. He made a note to let the owner know. At the gate to the property, he also wondered why a car was parked off the road. The drive to the homestead and the stables was at least a couple of kilometres long. He couldn't imagine what would prompt anyone to park that far back, unless, of course, they weren't familiar with the lay of the land, assuming that entry gates meant the buildings were straight ahead.

It took the two men mere minutes to find themselves in the heart of the action: the two ambulances on the scene were pulling away just as they parked alongside the other two police cars and fire trucks already on the scene.

"Hey, Summers, thanks for coming along," hailed Tom Derek. The two men knew each other well, working out of the same station, albeit often on different shifts, and socialising on occasions. In the past five years, serving together, they had come to respect each other's integrity and Derek immediately bowed to Summers' seniority.

"No worries. Was on my way back from Chantilly Farms."

"Problem?"

"Assault and rape. And you, besides the fire?"

"Three stiffs."

Summers whistled softly: the Hunter Valley wasn't exactly known as a hotbed for crime.

"Foul play?"

"You'll be the judge but from what I've seen, it sure smells like it."

"Do we have IDs?"

"One of them was pronounced dead at the scene when we arrived due to massive blood loss thanks to severe injuries combined with fatal smoke inhalation. The coroner will tell us exactly what happened. However, the other two bodies are almost burned beyond recognition. Both are males. I'd say in their forties. I called for back-up because we also found a handgun and a shotgun at the scene and both victims exhibited bullet wounds: one through the chest, the other through the head."

"Any witnesses?"

"Presumably the third dead guy; the owner didn't hear any shots. He only came down to see his stables on fire after the dogs alerted him to something being amiss."

"The owner of this property is Stefano Cavalieri, isn't it?" asked Summers, who prided himself on remembering the names of everyone worthy of mention living in the county.

"Right over there," said Derek, pointing to Stefano sitting on a log, his face still buried in his hands."We've already taken a statement."

Summers walked over to where Stefano was still sitting on a sawn-off trunk, staring vacuously into the night.

"Mr Cavalieri," said Zack, approaching Stefano. "I'm Detective Zack Summers. You've had quite a shocker tonight," he stated sympathetically. "My colleague has already taken your statement, so for now I won't ask you to repeat it. Do you have any idea who the two bodies just found at the scene could be?"

Stefano looked up at the man who spoke to him and levelled his gaze at the tall, broad-shouldered man standing in front of him. Clean shaven, with a bald head, a strong square face and piercing eyes, the man exuded power and intelligence.

"The two vehicles parked in the yard are Trent's and Pat's. The shotgun belonged to Trent. Trent was just taken to the morgue so one of the bodies must be Pat's. As far as the other one is concerned, your guess is as good as mine."

"Whose car is parked at the entrance to the property a couple of metres past the gates?"

"What car are you talking about? I've no idea. It certainly isn't mine or my wife's. Both our vehicles are parked close to the front of the house."

"Were you expecting any visitors?"

"No," answered Stefano laconically.

"When you say the other utility vehicle belongs to "Pat", are you referring to Patrick McCarthy, the stud manager for Chantilly Farms?"

"One and the same."

Zack Summers did not believe in coincidences. Patrick McCarthy had allegedly assaulted Arielle. Two hours later, he was found dead at Pandora Estates with a bullet through his head. Surely the two incidents were related, even if he couldn't grasp the connection as of yet. However, without eyewitnesses, figuring out exactly what had happened would take time. Moreover, the mystery of the third man's identity still remained.

"Were Patrick and Trent friends? Was it usual for them to visit one another?"

"They knew each other well. I can't tell you if their relationship was anything more than a friendship of convenience but I'd imagine they'd share some sort of a bond. After all, they held similar positions. I believe they socialised on a more or less regular basis."

"From what I read in the local press, Chantilly Farms and Pandora Estates are more foes than friends?"

"Our horses often compete against one another in major races but that doesn't make us enemies," replied Cavalieri carefully.

"Thank you for your time, Mr Cavalieri. Would it be possible for you to come down to the station tomorrow to make an official statement?"

167

"I don't really have a choice in the matter, now do I?" grumbled Stefano. "Are we finished here?"

"We need to gather as much forensic evidence as possible but your presence is no longer necessary. You can go home now."

"Thank you. Good night, Detective."

As Stefano rose to leave, Zack Summers stopped him.

"One more thing; do you carry insurance?"

"With priceless thoroughbreds under my care? It'd be irresponsible not to! Why do you ask?"

"Just a routine question," Zack answered glibly: indeed he couldn't dismiss outright the possibility that the fire might have been purposefully set, motivated by financial gain. The double murder and the fire were definitely related, with one either the unfortunate consequence of the other, or deliberately lit after the fact to cover the homicides. Only careful police work could unravel the mystery. In the meantime, while the tracks were still fresh, Zack had to consider every angle.

Stefano walked slowly back towards the house, having aged 10 years in the last hour. He knew his insurance would cover the cost of rebuilding the damaged structures, but it would take weeks, if not months. Moreover, he had now lost his studmaster and would need to fill the position quickly before summer was upon him or he'd miss out on the entire season. As far as he was concerned, the most shocking event of the night was Trent's dying revelations that he had artificially inseminated the mares in his care with Napoleon's frozen sperm. The admission that the local veterinarian knew all about it was considerably adding to his headaches. He wondered if Joe Guarini would keep his promise. His losses for one single evening were already staggering. He certainly did not want to lose to Guillaume as well. More than ever he needed the extra land the purchase of Apple Legends would guarantee. However, he was highly aware that, without some fast action, in three days' time the deal would be sealed with or without him.

The police worked tirelessly all night, gathering clues and photographing ever inch of the area which had been designated as the primary crime scene. The car found abandoned under the thick canopy of trees at the bottom of the hill had been a rental car. Zack's constable soon uncovered that the car found at the bottom of the hill near the entrance had been rented at Sydney Airport on the morning of the shootings. It was due back the following day. The lease had been issued to a man by the name of Dante Alberti, a Potts Point resident. When the police woke him at six o'clock in the morning, Dante, at first, hadn't known what to make of the call but soon gathered that things had gone terribly wrong for Joe Guarini. He quickly admitted he had indeed rented a car since his own was booked in for a service. However, he insisted that the car was parked on the street, not far from his unit. When the police asked him to go and check its whereabouts, Dante acted surprised that it was no longer parked where he had left it, intimating that it must have been stolen during the night by some joy riders. Facetiously, he asked whether he should now report it stolen. The police told him they would alert the rental company and keep the car as evidence until further notice. They confirmed it was now related to a murder investigation. Dante didn't care to ask any more questions, availing himself to the police instead, in case they wished to contact him at a later date.

After hanging up with the police, Dante quickly took his BMW to a smash repairer belonging to a man he knew, forcing him to falsify the date in his log book, attesting that the car had been dropped off the night before, right upon closing, when the rest of his mechanics had already gone home for the day. The small garage owner had had previous dealings with Dante and feared the man's reputation. He would do as asked to stay out of trouble; Dante's protection had served him well in the past. He would be foolish to jeopardise it.

Once bullets had been recovered at the scene and their trajectory carefully analysed, the police were able to reconstruct part of the crime scene: the John Doe, whose identity still remained a mystery, as any identification paper had burned in the fire, had pulled the trigger that killed Patrick McCarthy. The gun had been found clutched in his right hand. Who had killed the intruder was unclear since the bullet recovered under the second victim had been fired by the shotgun belonging to Trent. The latter's skin had been too burned to check for residue. When the police had initially arrived, Trent had just died in Stefano's arms, a few metres away from where the shooting had taken place. It didn't make any sense. As far as the rental car was concerned, Zack Summers would need to double check the lessee's alibi but right now he saw no reason not to believe the man. Many cars were stolen in King Cross during an average week. Rental cars were no exception.

Moreover, thanks to the farm's isolation, it would have been impossible to reach it without a vehicle. He was certain their John Doe was the car's thief. Why had he come to Pandora Estates in the middle of the night? Cavalieri has been adamant he hadn't expected any visitors. Trent had remained on the property after hours and for no apparent reason: perhaps he had been the one expecting the John Doe? In any case, Zack Summers was certain that after his assault on Arielle, Patrick had gone straight down to Pandora to confide in his friend, probably to boast about his sexual prowess. In all likelihood, Pat's version of the events would have seen him testify that the girl had received just what she deserved and had asked for it. Summers had seen it way too often. During their heart-to-heart, the two men had then been surprised by an intruder and a confrontation had followed. Pat had been killed. Trent had died shortly afterwards as a result of his injuries. From the position of the bodies and the trajectory of the bullets, the John Doe and Pat hadn't faced each other. Had something spooked them? The police so far had recovered only one shell case from each weapon: only one shot had been fired and it had been fatal. Both guns had been fired to kill. Zack was certain that both Patrick and Trent would have been proficient with firearms; most people working on farms were. But it also implied that the intruder had been just as skilled: they would need to wait for the ballistic report to see if they could get a trace on the gun. Zack feared it was unlikely. The next step now was to cast a broader net and re-interview everyone connected to both farms. Patrick so far was the only visible link between both crime scenes. Surely it meant something.

After the police finally departed in the early-morning hours, Stefano attempted to reassign the 20 displaced horses to other pens but available space remained a problem. Nathan called in to lend a hand and suggested he board the four unallocated horses to Chantilly Farms but Stefano firmly put him in his place.

"Why would I want that man to keep my horses?' spat Stefano. "In his care, something is bound to happen to them, one way or another," he muttered under his breath.

"Stefano, you're being irrational. Chantilly Farms is a stone's throw away. Until the barn is rebuilt, it's an easy commute to keep them training daily. Sure, it's somewhat of an inconvenience, but not nearly as problematic as returning the horses to their original owners. Or receive training while they are kept elsewhere. It's a much better alternative than anything else I can think of," countered Nathan at his most conciliatory.

Stefano wavered. Nathan was right: it was the best solution but he was certain that after the stunt he had pulled with the proposed purchase of Apple Legends when he'd vied to wrestle it away from Will, the latter might not be as amenable to lending him a hand as the veterinarian seemed to think.

"Can't see Will helping out," he finally said chewing his lower lip.

"I'll speak to Arielle. I'm sure it will be fine," replied Nathan with confidence.

"Arielle?"

"Don't worry, it'll work out."

"Why would you speak with Arielle and not directly with Will?" questioned Stefano. Understanding suddenly dawned on him but he needed his suspicions to be confirmed out loud.

"Are you two an item?" he repeated.

"Not that it's any of your business," replied Nathan, smiling wryly, thereby confirming the old man's worst fears. "I assure you she'll talk to her father on our behalf. Will isn't an unreasonable man and around here everyone helps each other out in cases such as this."

Stefano stared at him open-mouthed; if Nathan and Arielle were lovers, the chances were that they would have discussed Napoleon. With Arielle aware that the famous stud had been unable to settle since its purchase, in all likelihood so would her father. Stefano felt sick.

"Are you all right, Stefano?" inquired Nathan solicitously when he noticed the blood draining from his face.

"I'm feeling a bit queasy. Haven't digested my brekkie," replied Stefano haltingly. "It'll pass, don't worry."

He sat down heavily on one of the charred beams left behind by the fire.

"Make the call, Nate," he said dejectedly, knowing it was by far the most sensible solution to his immediate problems.

★ ★

When faced with a natural disaster, most country folk came together and Guillaume was no exception. As soon as he heard of Stefano's plight, he was more than willing to host some of his horses until a more permanent solution could be found. In his mind, the request could only mean the hatchets were buried: the meeting to settle on Apple Legends was only 48 hours away. Hopefully Stefano would now withdraw his bid, leaving him to negotiate alone. However, the accidental fire had only served to increase Stefano's resolve to add more land to his current holdings to build additional facilities. The accident had highlighted how close he ran to the wire, rubbing his nose in the weaknesses of his operations already bursting at the seams.

After writing his initial report, Senior Detective Zack Summers began the painstaking task of ripping his known victims' lives apart to figure out what could have possibly designed them as targets. Meanwhile he waited for a phone call from the forensic lab: his John Doe wore a corrective dental device called Invisalign, made in California. Miraculously, the hard plastic shield hadn't melted: each transparent impression mould had been stamped with a serial number. He soon learned that each serial number related back to a registered patient. As soon as the overseas lab opened, he would get his answer. He was certain that the man's identity was key to figuring out the reason for his presence at Pandora Estates the night before.

When the response came back, he had not expected to find a foreign national: the dental work had been done in France, in the city of Marseilles. He was quickly able to determine that his John Doe, a man by the name of Joe Guarini, 44 years of age, had flown in the morning of the murders, arriving on a Thai Airlines flight after transferring in Bangkok. Armed with his photograph, he had immediately contacted the car rental agency. The employee on duty confirmed she had never set eyes on the man. Yet the car had been in his possession. Since the shotgun had belonged to Trent and Patrick didn't own a registered gun, he assumed the handgun found in Guarini's hand had belonged to the latter, eliminating the possibility of a struggle. However, the man couldn't have gone through four sets of airport security without the firearm being detected. Thus, the gun would have been obtained on arrival in Australia. In view of the timeframe, Guarini would have needed the right contacts. Obviously the man had flown into the country with the intent to kill. His return ticket issued for the following day indicated premeditation. By anyone's standards, it was too short of a stay to construct any other argument.

Zack was surprised the inbound passenger wouldn't have been questioned at the airport in regards to his suspiciously short overnight stay, but perhaps nothing about his demeanour or his luggage had flagged Customs and he had slipped through the net. The gun, which had come back from ballistics early afternoon, had been wiped clean: the forensic team couldn't find any serial numbers and the gun, prior to the murders at Pandora Estates, as far as anyone knew, had never been fired. The shell casing and the bullet could not provide further clues either, nor could they be tied to any other ongoing or past investigations. The detective had just hit a brick wall. On a hunch, he decided to call Interpol to check whether his victim had had previous run-ins with the law. What he found out proved to be fascinating, layering his case with yet more questions.

After carefully reading the report emailed by his overseas colleagues, Detective Zack Summers wasn't any better off at figuring out why a descendant of one of Corsica's most notorious mob family would come to Australia to execute what had now all the earmarks of a professional hit. According to the timeframe, Guarini must have driven to the Hunter Valley shortly after arriving in town. Obviously he had made a stop in Kings Cross to steal the car and presumably to purchase the gun and, without accomplices on the ground, it would have proved extremely difficult. A copy of his passport had shown it had been his first-time flying to the southern hemisphere. Summers suspected there was now more to the theft of the car than previously assumed. He teamed up with Kings Cross police so they could harass their local informants to find out who could have provided Guarini with an untraceable gun. He also knew firsthand that the mid-week drive to the Hunter Valley would have been an easy one, taking no more than two solid hours. Since the murders had taken place between eight and nine o'clock in the evening, a few hours remained unaccounted for between Guarini's early morning arrival flight and his subsequent demise at Pandora Estates. He had already requested the footage from the Roads and Traffic Authorities. The rental car would have been flashed going through the numerous tolls. Hopefully, the recorded footage would give him a useful explanation for the time lapse.

Two hours later, he held the full explanation. The Holden Commodore had been snapped driving through the usual tolls until it hit the F3 freeway heading north towards Newcastle. The car had also been identified on CCTV cameras at a truck stop where Guarini had apparently taken his time over lunch. One hour later it had been caught speeding by a camera 40 kilometres out of Cessnock. Immediately thereafter a call had been recorded from of the emergency booths, requesting assistance for a blown tyre. The local NRMA truck called to the scene had taken over two hours to respond as it had been a very busy day. The driver had confirmed that it was well past six when he'd finally replaced the tyre and waved the car on its way. When the photograph of the suspect had been emailed to the smash repair office, it had been promptly identified by the tow truck driver. There was no doubt that Guarini had been the driver of the vehicle on that fated day.

By the time the vehicle had been back on the road, the sun would have already set behind the tree line, framing the horizon. The detective knew better than most how treacherous the roads could be for anyone unfamiliar with the territory. It wasn't a stretch of the imagination to surmise that the driver had become hopelessly lost. The map found in the glove compartment of the car had shown the road highlighted from the freeway exit all the way to Guillaume's stud farm. It was safe to assume that Guarini, in all likelihood, had come to Pandora Estates by mistake, Chantilly Farms being his ultimate destination. Summers suddenly recalled seeing the sign to the property knocked around and pointing in the opposite direction. Armed with this new information, which slanted the investigation in a completely new direction, Summers decided it was high time to return to the homestead and have another chat with Will.

Through the entire Customs clearance and embarkation process, Hamdam had unhappily watched his younger friend struggle to keep his emotions in check. Hamdam knew all too well what it felt like to be passionately in love. He remembered clearly the first time he had seen Catherina stride across the campus lawn towards him on the morning after the inter-collegiate dance where they had been introduced to each other. The young woman hadn't just been beautiful, she'd radiated from the inside out and he hadn't been able to take his eyes off her. They had quickly become inseparable and all too soon planned for the future. At first it had been very difficult for Catherina to accept that in this day and age, a man like Hamdam wasn't free to do as he wished and she had long pestered and rebelled against his traditions and his religion. Losing him, however, was unthinkable. After a few short months, she had converted to Islam and patiently waited for Hamdam to come back and ask for her. She had already accepted to wait for him to fulfil first his family's expectations. To his first wife, Hamdam had shown nothing but kindness: she had fully understood her role and performed her duties according to the letter of the Qur'an. When Hamdam had made it clear two years after their nuptials that he would marry again, she hadn't objected. By then she was already pregnant with their second son.

At first she had welcomed Catherina into their home with open arms. But it had soon become evident to them both that they had too little in common to become friends. On the other hand, they had co-habited easily with little interaction, their rapport courteous and civil. Both had happily fallen into their respective roles. For six years, blinded by the fuel of passion, Hamdam had waited for children to bless his new union. Allah, however, hadn't smiled upon him. They had both been devastated. When he had finally announced his desire to marry again to increase his brood, he had faced Catherina's tears and recriminations for well over a month.

His third wife, just like the first had provided him with healthy heirs.

His choice to marry once again, however, had alienated the love of his life for the most part of a year. He had stood powerless as she began to spend more and more time overseas. It had taken well over a decade for her to forgive him. In the end, their bond had been too strong to ever contemplate a divorce. After all, Catherina had walked into the marriage with her eyes wide open. His wedding to Latifah had been an old man's indulgence. By then Catherina had blossomed into her own person and their relationship had fallen into one of friendship. In fact, when Hamdam was honest with himself, he knew he loved them all, albeit in very different ways. In his circles, polygamy had been a way of life and an undeniable proof of financial success. He would have been loath to relinquish any of his wives. Through the years, his generosity of heart and spirit had helped keep the fragile equilibrium. He was, nonetheless, well aware that his lifestyle wasn't suitable for everyone. To relieve his friend's burden he felt compelled to address the issue.

As soon as the plane reached cruising altitude and drinks placed in front of them both, he swiftly invited Majid to share what was on his mind.

"A penny for your thoughts," he said jovially, inviting his companion to open up.

"Hamdam, I am at a loss," replied Majid thoughtfully. "I never expected to feel so strongly about Arielle after all this time. What am I going to do? I know now that I should never have let her return home all those years ago. I've wasted the past decade. I can no longer contemplate a future without her."

"Will she convert to Islam?" queried Hamdam, delving straight into the heart of the matter.

"We have discussed it. She believes in God. She believes in an all-knowledgeable Supreme Being. It is her belief that this benevolent Supreme Being goes by many names, including Allah. I don't believe a matter of religion would stand in her way. Our customs and practices though are non-negotiable: she would never accept to share her household with other wives."

"Catherina did."

"She isn't Catherina. Are you really sure that if the situation presented itself today, 30 years later, Catherina would make the same choice? No offense, Hamdam, but it was another era. If I wish to spend my life with Arielle, I need to divorce and promise never to marry anyone else."

"Islam disapproves of divorce most of all," Hamdam reminded him gently.

"Marriage is a gift of God to lead a happy and enjoyable life and continue lineage," replied Majid likewise quoting the scriptures. "My wife is barren. I've the upmost respect for her and hold her in great affection, but I'm not in love with her. I'd like to provide my ageing parents with grandchildren to light up their golden years. I feel very sad to come to such a wretched decision, but losing Arielle is out of the question."

"I understand," Hamdam assured him softly. "I don't envy you, my young friend. Talaq isn't to be entered in lightly and Sheikh Rashid will hit the roof!" he added with mirth in his voice. He profoundly disliked the man he had run across on a number of occasions. He was also certain the man wouldn't enjoy welcoming his daughter back under his roof and be responsible for her welfare once again.

"I don't wish to hurt my wife's feelings but I don't know what else to do."

"Allah is all knowing. Pray and He will help you make the right decision. If you can't hold it together on equitable terms, separate with kindness."

"Hamdam, thank you for listening. I'm grateful for the advice and the sympathetic ear."

"It's nothing, my friend. Even an old man such as me needs to bow to what stares him in the face. You'd have to be blind not to notice how much you and Arielle care for one another. You should try and get some rest; you look exhausted. You'll have enough to deal with on your return."

Majid didn't wait to be told twice.

"How was your flight?" queried Assa as soon as Majid pushed open the front door to their spacious and comfortable home. "Welcome home," she added with a smile. "I'm very glad you're back. This house feels empty without you." Her large guileless eyes rested upon him, waiting for a comment. Majid looked at his wife: he noted immediately she had bought a new outfit for his return and guilt stabbed at his heart.

"The flight was fine. I slept most of the way over," he replied, his face impassable, his words clipped.

Assa, astute and perceptive by nature, sensed from his tone that all wasn't right and she stepped back.

"I'm sure you feel jet lagged though. Perhaps you'd like me to pour you a bath and wash you? I could then follow it up with a massage to relieve the tension from your back and shoulders?"

Majid winced. Assa was being more agreeable than usual: a cold or even indifferent welcome would have made the conversation he couldn't wait to hold a great deal easier.

"How was Hamdam?" she continued lightly, despite her heart arresting when she watched malevolent shadows fleet across his handsome features. "Did he enjoy the races? Will he take his horses there next season? Did you enjoy Australia? Is it as beautiful and wild as everyone says it is?" she babbled, keen to fill the deepening silence which crept over them both.

"Assa, darling, we need to talk," said Majid gently, his eyes avoiding hers. "Let's go into the living room, please."

Assa's entire body tensed: his tone sounded ominous.

"Sure," she replied, quietly. "I'll be right in. Let me fetch you a tall glass of mint tea first."

Majid's face broke into a tense smile and he walked into the light-filled living room, bearing the weight of the world on his shoulders. Out of sight, Assa inhaled deeply, bracing herself for what was to come. She wasn't sure what it was he had to talk to her about so urgently but her instincts assured her the conversation would be far from pleasant.

"Was everything all right during my absence?" began Majid as soon as Assa walked back in, carrying a tray of mint tea and delicate sweets.

"Everything was as usual," replied Assa, coming to sit across from him to pour the tea.

"What did the doctor have to say?" questioned Majid, referring to Assa's last visit to the fertility specialist.

Assa lowered her gaze in shame, tears already threatening.

"Allah has forsaken me," she replied, her voice barely audible. "We'll never have children, Majid. I'm so sorry. My womb is apparently barren. He confirmed there is nothing we can do. This time he alluded to a possible genetic defect of my fallopian tubes, which would make it very difficult to fall pregnant regardless. It seems the story changes every time I consult with him."

She began to weep silently. Majid steeled himself; he knew how painful the entire ordeal had been for her. To date, they had already submitted to 10 rounds of IVF without success.

"Sometimes," he began slowly, "it's not the woman's fault. The chemistry between two people just doesn't work, and Allah, in his infinite wisdom, prevents a child to be born from that union."

Confused, Assa looked up at her husband.

"I don't understand what you're trying to say."

"I mean that you and I aren't meant to have children together, but it doesn't mean that you can't have children with someone else, someone more compatible."

Assa's eyes widened. What was he trying to say exactly? The doctor had never introduced the possibility of incompatibility. He had been adamant in letting her carry the burden alone. She remained silent, wishing for him to explain further.

"Assa, do you believe I'm in love with you?" asked Majid, looking away.

"You've always treated me with equanimity and respect. I've never had anything to complain about. You've proved to be a fair and compassionate husband through all this," she added slowly, her voice now trembling, her hands pointing to her flat stomach. "I love you enough for both of us," she added. "Don't worry."

"Assa, I don't know how to tell you this as there is no right way. You've been a model wife to me. You've been a good friend and you've kept my house in wonderful order. However, I need passion in my life. I could have overlooked not giving my parents the grandchildren they are seeking, but..." Majid explained, looking as her face faltered.

"It's that Australian woman, that jockey, isn't it?" yelled a distraught Assa, with an anger Majid hadn't thought her capable of. "I wondered time and time again if she was the reason you had suddenly decided to accompany Hamdam to Melbourne. I saw her on television when she won the race. I admit she is very beautiful, but she isn't one of us!" she cried out.

"Listen to me, Assa," implored Majid. "Don't make this any harder, please. I met Arielle a long time before I met you. She has always had a very special place in my heart. I'd never been able to quite forget her, even though I've tried, believe me! When I saw her again I knew I had made a mistake to let her go. Assa, I'm so sorry, I can't live without her. Why do you think I married so late? Why do you think I let our families talk me into marriage?"

"I always thought I was the luckiest woman in the world," replied Assa through her sobs, remembering how stunned she had been at his proposal. "Every woman in Dubai and beyond wanted to be married to you, but then you chose me. I never understood why, but who am I to question Allah? I wondered for a while whether it was the generous dowry bestowed upon you but, in all these years, you've never shown to be that interested in money, so I just counted my blessings."

Majid walked over to where his wife had dissolved into a puddle on the floor, sliding down from the couch until she had felt the cold marble floor through her robes. He helped her up and sat her on his knees, caressing her hair.

"Assa, darling, you've been good to me, but I love another. I can't help where my heart lies. Trust me, I wish I could. Hurting you is the last thing I want," he added in a strangled voice.

Before he could continue, Assa briskly interrupted him.

"So take her as your second wife," she said defiantly.

"I would if I could. It's the nature of our ways which was responsible for us parting the first time around. Now I've a chance to get her back. Please understand, Assa, if there was any other way, I'd happily take it. I don't wish you any harm. Talaq is the only way."

Assa dropped her head on his shoulders, sobs racking her frame. By pronouncing the dreaded word "talaq", Majid had initiated the divorce proceedings: she was now at his mercy.

"What will happen to me now? My father will be furious. What will you do if he withdraws his investment in Arabian Nights?"

"Let me worry about it," replied Majid, knowing full well that her father was unlikely to challenge an investment which not only had been quite profitable to date but had also considerably helped raise his profile in the community.

Seeing her approach had drawn a blank, Assa quickly changed tack.

"He'll blame the breakdown of our union on my inability to give you children: he'll make my life a living hell. He'll never understand that it has little to do with it, that you're simply in love with a foreigner too narrow-minded to accept polygamist customs in place for centuries."

"You're close to your cousin, Abida, and her husband, Daris," replied Majid, deflecting the accusations. "You could go and live with them instead. Their house is large enough. I'll speak to them. You won't be living at their expense. I'll restitute your entire dowry so you'll be financially independent. You're beautiful and intelligent and kind. I'm certain that Allah in his wisdom will provide a more suitable husband for you than I could ever be."

"When do you plan on announcing this?" asked Assa, defeated, knowing she had exhausted all possible arguments.

"We'll need to get our families together in the next week or so. I'll respect tradition and all matters of waiting periods. During that time, you'll have a chance to adjust."

Assa shook her head vehemently. Majid had just struck her a terrible blow. How could she ever adjust to being repudiated like this, just like a possession which had past its use-by date? On the other hand, she knew in her heart that the man she had married would remain generous and kind until the third and last irrevocable talaq was finally pronounced.

Devastated, Assa looked at her soon-to-be ex-husband and said quietly, "Majid, I hope this woman, Arielle, will make you happy. You deserve to be happy. I only wish you could have walked along the road to happiness without walking across my grave."

With her last words still hanging in the air, she left the room. Consumed with guilt, Majid stared at her retreating back. He exhaled heavily, his emotions now irretrievably laced with overwhelming jetlag. With his head swimming and his vision blurred, he lay down on the inviting couch, the full length of his body sinking into the plush cushions. Within minutes he was asleep, galloping through open fields, Arielle laughing in the wind beside him, the leaves of the trees whispering Assa's pain as they ran past.

CHAPTER XI

Three days later, Guillaume watched as the white Toyota Land Cruiser drove up to his front door once again. Detective Zack Summers' face was a blank canvas.

"Hi, Will. I hope this isn't inconvenient. I need to run a few things past you. How's Arielle faring?"

"Good morning, Zack. Arielle is still bruised and battered but recovering nicely from her injuries. Her mental state is more worrisome. Care for a cup of coffee? Let's go to my office where we won't be interrupted, shall we?"

The two men walked into Guillaume's office and Guillaume turned to the credenza where he lit up his Nespresso machine to brew two espressos. Meanwhile, Zack looked around at the impressive floor-to-ceiling library filled with every imaginable book on racing and breeding in many different languages. He whistled admiringly at the neatly stacked leather-bound covers.

"Quite an impressive collection!" he stated as Guillaume handed him his coffee, gesturing for him to sit in one of the club armchairs.

"I'm sure I don't owe your visit to my book collection," replied Guillaume, his face expressionless. "Have you found where my former stablemaster has been hiding?" he continued more sternly.

"I have. Perhaps what I'm going to tell you will help in Arielle's recovery. Patrick McCarthy has been found dead at Pandora Estates."

In his surprise, Guillaume almost burned the roof of his mouth on the scalding coffee, gulping it too quickly.

"I don't understand."

"You remember the other night seeing a fire at Pandora Estates, don't you?"

"Of course!, Stefano subsequently asked me to house some of his horses. I gather that an entire barn burned down. But what does that have to do with Pat?"

"Pat was found dead at the scene with a bullet through his head."

"Unbelievable!" exclaimed Guillaume, quite taken aback by the pronouncement. Zack watched his reaction closely. Guillaume noticed the scrutiny.

"Come on, Zack, how in hell could I have been at the farm before you reached it? You'd think I'd avenge my daughter's honour by killing a man?"

"Would you?"

"Yep, probably," admitted Guillaume, "but in this case, I'm sure your facts tell you I wasn't there."

"How about Nathan?"

Guillaume kept his sang-froid, answering the detective by looking him straight in the eye.

"Nathan stayed here with us all night. You saw him. He slept in the guest room. What happened exactly?"

For the next 20 minutes, Zack depicted the scene which had confronted him when he arrived at Pandora Estates.

"My God, so Stefano lost his stablemaster as well on the same night? How weird is that? What are the chances?"

Guillaume was baffled. Zack let his guard down: from Guillaume's candid reaction, it was obvious the man had had no part in what had happened on the other side of the valley that particular night.

"To top it all though we found another body," Zack added.

"Another body?"

Guillaume's astonishment was genuine.

"You found three dead men on the grounds? That's unbelievable! That should cover our little town's quota for the year!"

"What's most disturbing is that we discovered the third man was a contract killer," continued Zack, ignoring the interruption. "I suspect that neither Trent nor Pat were the intended victims."

"You're speaking in riddles," said Guillaume, the hair on his back inexplicably rising.

"The post signs around Apple Legends had been knocked about and were pointing in the wrong direction. I believe the man intended to come here instead but got lost. The map found in his car with Chantilly Farms circled in red confirmed it," continued Zack.

"What are you saying, Zack? That someone had come upon Pandora Estates by mistake and was meant to come here?"

"Does the name Joe Guarini mean anything to you?"

Guillaume's colour drained from his face, yet he tried to keep his composure. He remained silent.

"I discovered that this Joe Guarini, a man in his late forties, had landed in Sydney on the morning of the murders," pursued Detective Summers, watching Guillaume closely. "Apparently he's related to one of the most powerful mafia families from Corsica. You flinched when I mentioned the name: I can only assume it's familiar. Would you care to tell me why?"

"I've never heard of him," denied Guillaume stonily, his hands involuntarily shaking.

"I don't believe that. It's written all over your face, mate," stated Zack, matter-of-fact. "However, I admit I can't see the connection."

"Neither can I," reiterated Guillaume.

"Where exactly were you born, Will?"

"Would you like to see my passport or my birth certificate? I was born in Switzerland," replied Guillaume defensively.

"Don't get offended, Will. It's part of my job. So you have no idea what a Corsican Mafioso would want with Chantilly Farms? Could Arielle have run into him while abroad? Could he have been looking for your guests?"

"What guests?" asked Guillaume, now confused by the rapid questions.

"Nathan told me the other day," replied Zack, looking down at his notes, "that he'd come by to speak with Arielle since she hadn't returned his calls after dropping your guests off at the airport."

Guillaume quickly recovered.

"My guests were from Dubai. Arielle stayed with them when she sojourned there a decade ago. They came for the Melbourne Cup. And I offered for them to come down here for the weekend afterwards."

"You sent Arielle to sojourn in Dubai? How old was she at the time? Barely 21? You must have formed quite a friendship with these Middle Eastern men to entrust your only child in their care," questioned Zack, disbelief clearly painted on his face.

"I'm not sure what you're trying to insinuate. I've known Sheikh Hamdam from way back when he came to my father's estate with his uncle to discuss horseracing…"

Guillaume realised too late he had revealed too much and brusquely stood up to cut the interview short. "Listen, Zack, I've lots on my plate. Is there anything else I can assist you with? I must go back to work, if you don't mind."

Zack Summers knew he had hit a nerve. However, he wasn't sure where. He decided nothing more would be gained by pressing Guillaume at this time. He'd come back another time once he had dug further into Guillaume's past. At the door he thanked Guillaume for his hospitality and added one more question.

"Let me know if something comes to mind, Will. I'm sure this Guarini came here to settle a score. Perhaps he had a bone to pick with Pat? This whole thing has me rather puzzled. Good day."

As the 4WD sped away, Guillaume was left shaking on his front doorsteps.

Joe Guarini? He knew the name only too well. If Zack was right about his age, he was either the son or the grandson of the man who had shot his parents. Long ago, his testimony had put the whole Corsican clan behind bars. Had the man come to seek revenge? How did he find him? Guillaume had spent a lifetime burying his tracks: how could he have uncovered them? Had Hamdam's unexpected visit anything to do with it? Could his friend be unwittingly responsible for bringing the killer to his door? Guillaume re-entered his study and sat down heavily behind his desk. He wondered if Joe Guarini had shared his travel plans with others. Had he shared his intentions of confronting the man responsible for his relatives' incarceration? Would anyone else come looking for him in his wake? Were there other men's sons also seeking revenge? Guillaume couldn't remember all the faces nor could he recall the exact age of the men he had helped send to jail. At the time, he had been told that his compelling recount of the events on that day had wiped out an entire family by sending all the male relatives to maximum-security prisons. After the much-publicised trial, he had fled the country to avoid reprisals from other gang members. Until now, it had never occurred to him that those men may have had young sons or daughters, who could wish, out of a twisted sense of filial duty, to silence the man who had deprived them of their childhood. Guillaume, for the first time in decades, wondered if the prosecutor was still alive, if he could make inquiries as to the descendants of those men who had indiscriminately killed everyone present at the Ecume des Jours on that fatal day. Surely the past was meant to stay in the past. Guillaume shivered in spite of the heat, wondering what he should do next. He locked his office door and lifted from his safe a dossier he had not opened in years.

★ ★

Zack Summers contacted the Australian Federal Police, requesting he be put in touch with the Interpol officer most likely to give him background information about a Corsican Mafia family by the name of Guarini. The information was needed as part of a criminal investigation taking place in the Hunter Valley in Australia, in the State of New South Wales, involving a victim of the same name. It was nearly six o'clock when the phone rang.

"Officer Marc Cartel here, may I speak with Detective Summers please?"

The accent was undoubtedly French.

"Speaking."

"I've received a request from my superiors to help you with an investigation in the death of a French national by the name of Joe Guarini. What do you need to know?"

The officer's voice was even and professional, his English quite fluent.

"Thank you for calling me back so quickly. I'm investigating a triple murder. One of the victims was identified as Joe Guarini thanks to dental records. He arrived in Australia on the morning of the murders in question. However, from the evidence found so far, the victim came with the intent to kill. The other two men found dead at the scene were apparently not the intended victims."

"Sounds complicated," sympathised the Frenchman, "but, when-ever the Corsican Mafia is involved, nothing is ever simple. Here it is. Joe Guarini is the only male survivor to the legendary Guarini family. The entire clan, along with all known associates, 10 men in all, were indicted after a vicious shooting back in 1967 in the middle of the worst territorial war between two of the most powerful Corsican mafia families," he read, looking down at his files.

"How did an entire clan come to be behind bars in one fell swoop?" questioned Zack, now intrigued.

"There was one single and compelling eyewitness, who survived the attacks: a young man by the name of Guillaume de La Selle. Guillaume de La Selle belonged to a prominent horseracing family. Both parents were killed during the shooting. He had no siblings."

"What happened to this eyewitness?" asked Zack, his heart racing, knowing he was now holding the first vital clue.

"Witness protection: from all accounts, he left the country."

"Do we know where he went?"

"Sorry, the records are sealed."

"Can you find out?"

"It may take some time. The prosecutor at the time is now deceased. Is it relevant to your case?"

"I can't move forward without that information."

"Okay, I'll get back to you. Give me at least 24 hours."

"Thank you, Marc. Here is my mobile number. You can call me on that number day or night."

"Nice talking to you. I hope I can find the answers you're after."

Zack Summers stared at the phone. Horseracing family? Really? When his colleague said "De La Selle" had he meant "LaSalle"? How many men and women in witness protection had blown their cover over the years by going back to what they knew best, thereby leaving an unfathomable trail? Granted, back in the sixties, Australia would have been heralded as the Holy Grail, the furthest, and, in all likelihood, the safest nation possible to disappear to, in order to avoid retribution. Since the UN had not recognised Interpol as an intergovernmental organisation until 1971, and their headquarters had not moved to Lyons, France, until the late eighties, databases hadn't been accessible until a decade after that. Only in the past 20 years could those sent to witness protection fear to be located. Before then, most traces of their lives had disappeared into a web of paperwork, none of it easily accessible. Locating a witness 30 years after the fact was mostly due to sheer luck. Indeed, even the worst war criminals had been discovered accidentally 40 years after their heinous crimes, often thanks to someone's infallible memory of an inimitable tick or a diehard habit, which time and distance couldn't break.

In his heart, Zack Summers was now certain that Will LaSalle had been the intended victim; all he had to do was prove it. In his long experience as a homicide detective, he knew revenge to be a powerful motive. It still wouldn't unravel what had happened at Pandora Estates, but it would at least explain Joe Guarini's armed presence in the Hunter Valley. Zack worried above all else that if the man had been capable of travelling that far across the globe, three decades after the fact, then someone else had also connected the dots. Once he figured out who that third party was, and the motive behind that third party's actions, he would be able to establish what had really happened on the night. The detective grabbed his coat and on impulse decided to drive back to Chantilly Farms. Perhaps his friend would, this time around, be more forthcoming.

"Papa!" yelled Arielle, who had ambled down to the stables to check up on Obsession. Due to a slight leg injury, the horse hadn't been ridden in over a week and showed signs of impatience.

"What is it, darling?" replied Guillaume, who was nearby, checking that Stefano's horses were adapting to their new temporary environment.

"Summer's car is coming up the drive again."

"Again?" muttered Guillaume under his breath. "What on earth did he want now? "Don't worry, cherie," he said out loud. "I'll meet him. How's our star doing?" he asked, intentionally changing the subject.

"I'll take him for a quick ride. He hates being cooped up. Don't worry, I won't be long," Arielle yelled back, happy that the detective's inopportune visit would prevent her father from talking her out of it.

"Be careful."

Arielle shrugged. She longed for a canter. She hoped it would help lift her mood and she felt sufficiently recovered to enjoy the ride. Majid had called her many times, but she didn't know what to say to him. She had let her mother take the calls and explain that she'd been sick. She wasn't yet ready to tell him what had befallen her, afraid that he might push her away in disgust. The rape had left her ashamed. She felt dirty and sullied, and she couldn't imagine he'd feel any different. She had just finished saddling up the horse when the 4WD came to a screeching halt beside her.

She waved to the detective, but since he didn't get out of the car, she turned around to continue saddling her horse, ignoring him. Zack, in fact, had just received a voice message. The number was blocked. He dialled into his voicemail. It was from Marc.

"Guillaume de la Selle's testimony," it began, "was traded for an Australian passport. He has never set foot back in France since. Call me if you need anything else. Au revoir."

As he hung up the phone, Guillaume was rapping on his window.

"Come on up, Zack. I need to clean up first. You know your way to the library, don't you? I'll be with you shortly."

Summers exited his car and the two men shook hands. They walked up to the house in silence, each preoccupied by his own thoughts. Beyond the front door, Guillaume indicated the way and went up the stairs to his rooms. Left alone in the library, Zack perused the shelves, his attention suddenly drawn to a thick bottle-green leather spine with two dates stencilled in gold: 1946-1976. It stuck out slightly compared to the other neatly ordered tomes. Intrigued, he pulled it out. It was a photo album with old-fashioned vellum leaves separating the pages. The first few black and white photographs showed an impressive villa, which immediately reminded him of the very one he was standing in, with magnificent gardens extending past the living room. Each photo had been carefully labelled in a neat and legible calligraphy, all in French. He recognised Guillaume as a young child, sitting proudly on a horse followed by many more, showing the adolescent playing polo, riding horses, sitting at family dinners and enjoying exotic holidays. After his 21st birthday, Guillaume was snapped at racecourses all over Europe next to an equally tall man. Due to the strong resemblance, Zack surmised the man would be no other that Guillaume's father. His mother had been a handsome woman by all standards. Several shots, in colour, and more recently, according to the dates beside them, showed Guillaume posing next to men clad in kandura. The last photo was that of a single imposing tombstone etched with his parents' full names, followed by dates on either side. The last date corresponded to the day of the massacre at the Ecume des Jours. Pages after that had been left blank, with yellowing newspaper clippings caught between the vellum, still waiting to be slotted in.

Absorbed by his discovery, Detective Zack Summers did not hear his host enter the study. Guillaume was standing right behind him when he put the album back in its place.

"Found anything of interest?" he questioned coolly.

"Let's say it confirms everything I was just told by Marc Cartel, a detective with Interpol," replied Summers, nonplussed, placing the heavy tome back where he had found it. Pivoting on his heels to face Guillaume, he calmly repeated his conversation with the French homologue.

"So what?" replied Guillaume defensively, after listening to Zack's recount. "Let's say you're right and Guarini came here with the intention of confronting me and settling a score three decades later. So what? Was he not found dead at Pandora Estates? Obviously he never came here. As far as I'm concerned: case closed."

"Will? Should I continue calling you Will or would you prefer I call you Guillaume?" replied Zack. "I'm rather surprised a man like you can't see the big picture! Let's assume that Guarini spent the first 20 years of his life hating you and plotting his revenge, and another 10 years trying to locate you. Why would he have found you now, unless he's been alerted by someone as to your whereabouts? Someone else knows who you are and that someone has something to gain by alerting Joe Guarini. That person knew Guarini would be compelled to do something about it. The way I see it, whoever that individual is, he won't stop there. He has brought Guarini to your door with murder on his mind. Since, by all evidence, you're still standing upright, it's unlikely to stop there. So what enemies have you made, Will? Who'd want you dead? What other secrets are you harbouring?"

The two men sat on deep leather chairs across from each other, staring hard at each other's face. Abruptly, Guillaume stood to pour them both a scotch.

"Zack, it hadn't occurred to me but you're right. My secret has been safe for 30 years so why now? I can't answer that. As far as I know I made no enemies in my former life. I didn't think I had any now either. But you're right, someone else must know. Someone else must have figured it out."

"Your Arab friends?" suggested Zack.

"Hamdam has known all along. During his visit he told me he had purchased most of our champions when the Brittany horse breeding farm went up for sale. He long suspected that Will LaSalle from Australia might be the same Guillaume de la Selle he'd spent so much time with when we were young. When I sent Arielle overseas 10 years ago, his suspicions were confirmed. He's a most private man. I trust him with my life, literally. Hell, I trusted no one else with my daughter. He'd have absolutely nothing to gain by getting me killed. You're definitely barking up the wrong tree there."

"Have you pissed someone off in your racing circles then? Perhaps your spectacular Melbourne Cup win ruffled a few feathers? You were a long shot: some punters must have lost a fortune."

"I'm sure that's true," replied Guillaume tightly, "but such is the name of the game. I couldn't imagine upsetting anyone badly enough to want me dead, at least in the literal sense of the word!" emphasised Guillaume, his mind now on Stefano. "Stefano has lost the most by the two favourites losing to Obsession, but surely there can't be any connection, or is there?"

"Will, please keep an eye out and remain on your guard. This isn't over: I can feel it. At least it confirms why Guarini was here. In my opinion, he went to Pandora by mistake, surprised Trent and Pat in conversation; a confrontation followed where Pat was mistakenly shot by Guarini and Trent probably reacted, shooting the intruder. Have you told your family yet?"

"Do I need to?"

"For their safety, I would. Sorry to have bothered you once again, but please let me know right away if you notice anything suspicious anywhere."

"Thanks, mate. Your forthrightness is much appreciated. I'll inform Sarah and Arielle. Years ago when I came here, I stopped looking over my shoulder: I'm not relishing doing it once again."

"We'll get to the bottom of this, don't worry. Good night, Will."

On the ride out of the property Zack intuited that Patrick had more to do with the incident than just being in the wrong place at the wrong time. Two crimes had been committed on the same night: rape and murder. The only common denominator to both was Pat. It was now time to dig into the deceased's background and unearth the skeletons he had buried with him.

Dinner at Chantilly Farms that night was a tense affair. Guillaume had intended to delve into the subject slowly and carefully, but Arielle pre-empted him as soon as they sat down.

"Papa, why would Zack come back to see you three times in a row?" she asked innocently enough, chewing on a piece of sourdough bread lathered with homemade butter.

"Zack came back three times?" repeated Sarah, unnerved by the news.

"He wanted to speak to me about the events at Pandora's," began Guillaume, not really knowing where to start.

"What does it have to do with us, except for Pat being there at the time?"

"Well, everything it seems," sighed Guillaume. "If you could both stop interrupting me for a minute, I'll tell you what happened."

With his wife and daughter hanging on every word, Guillaume recounted the murders at Pandora's farms and the ongoing police investigation, revealing that Pat had accidentally been killed in the crossfire between Trent and a man named Joe Guarini.

Then, deciding there was no turning back, he narrated for them the events that had taken place in France 50 years prior, events which had led him to come and settle in Australia. It was the very first time he had spoken about the massacre at the Ecume des Jours in over half a century. Spinning the tale, in all its horrid details, left him both breathless and immensely relieved to share his burden at last. Finally, he told them why Zack had insisted he tell them the whole saga right away. According to the detective, the dangers he believed buried when he had left Europe behind had now come knocking at his door once again. During the painful confession, the meal had remained untouched. The women though had filled their glasses on a couple of occasions, simultaneously entranced and sickened by the tale, both looking at Guillaume as if they were seeing him for the very first time.

"So, Papa," queried Arielle, when she was certain he was finished, "who do you think knows who you are? And why would they want you dead?"

"In the past few hours, I have thought of nothing else. In my opinion, the only person with anything to gain would be Stefano Cavalieri," replied Guillaume pensively. "With Obsession's win, he would have lost a fortune. I imagine he wasn't thrilled. With his burned-down barns, he'd be losing clients, and having his horses in our care would certainly add insult to injury. Moreover, we're locked in a battle for the acquisition of Apple Legends. By eliminating me, he'd eliminate his toughest competition on and off the track, and would obtain the now much-needed land for below-market value as there would be no opposition to his bid."

"I didn't know he was the other contender for that purchase?" said Sarah, surprised by the pronouncement. "Why didn't you tell me?"

"Sorry, darling, it must have slipped my mind. The final meeting is tomorrow though, if you'd like to come and lend your support. In truth, I hadn't expected Stefano to be there in the first place. I'd no idea the Mooneys were playing both sides of the fence, but I should have guessed. It was rather naïve of me. But to get back to Cavalieri, I can't imagine how he would have come across Joe Guarini. That's what puzzles me most. In any case, we'll need to be careful. Guarini's undesirable presence might just be the tip of the iceberg. If Stefano is behind this, and desperate enough to contract a killer, now that his earlier plan has been foiled, he might still wish to come back for more."

"We'll be on our guard," assured Sarah, baffled by the avalanche of revelations. "I can't believe you've never told me any of this until now. I'm not sure I know who you are anymore," she added shaking her head, her eyes shiny with tears.

"Come on, darling. Surely you can understand that my primary concern has always been your safety. I saw no point in bringing up a painful past. Nothing I could have done or said would have changed any of it. The less you knew, the safer you were," replied Guillaume, pulling her close. "I've no more secrets, I swear. That's all of it."

Sarah returned his embrace and smiled into his eyes, her admiration for his courage boundless.

In her growing excitement, Arielle interrupted the bonding moment.

"Papa, have you kept anything from your past? Do you have photos of my grandparents? Photos of the house you grew up in?" asked Arielle, incredulous as she was that the father she thought she knew so well had lived a completely different life, one fraught with danger and laced with murder.

"At the time, I was requested by the prosecution to leave everything behind, but I couldn't let everything vanish without a trace. Come to the library. Bring your drinks since you haven't touched your food."

For the next two hours, huddled together, Guillaume commented on each page of the photo album Zack had accidentally retrieved only hours earlier. When Arielle saw Hamdam as a young man she fleetingly wondered if he had divulged to Majid who his friend really was. Perhaps the policeman had been right all along: perhaps it was their Middle East connection that had inadvertently brought danger to their door.

CHAPTER XII

After subpoenaing copies of Patrick's financial records, Detective Zack Summers began the tedious task of reading through them page by page, looking for anomalies. It didn't take long for him to discover that three days after the Flemington race, $396,000 exactly had been deposited into his account. The cheque had been issued by Chantilly Farms. Zack wondered whether Guillaume was just plain mad or insanely generous. It was exactly 10% of the prize money, an amount he deemed incredibly high as a bonus for Guillaume's stable manager. However, Guillaume might have a different way of dealing with staff than what he was used to. Armed with the knowledge, he decided to pursue the angle and have a quick chat with the local Commonwealth Bank branch manager, one of his wife's cousins: by experience, in any investigation, following the money trail invariably led to new answers and usually unearthed brand-new leads. Often it also revealed powerful financial motives besides.

Merely one hour later, Dean Wiseman, manager of the bank located in Elgin Street in Maitland, confirmed that Guillaume himself had deposited the prize money in full after the race. Once the cheque had cleared, he had been instructed to transfer identical sums to both his manager and to Nathan Heathers, the local veterinary surgeon. After vague promises to catch up soon for a family barbecue, Zack thanked him for his time.

He walked out onto the street slightly light-headed, puzzling over the reasons that would compel Guillaume to be so generous towards his employees. In his mind, the reward was still disproportionate to any service they could have possibly rendered in the course of their trade. He had already confirmed the fact that both men had gone to Melbourne to assist Guillaume during the pre- and post-race periods, both attending to his thoroughbred's special needs. Perhaps it was just part and parcel of Guillaume's flamboyant nature and a way to ensure their unerring loyalty by handsomely rewarding them for their long-term services. Perhaps, just by force of habit and professional bias, his mind was unnecessarily suspicious. Nonetheless, he made a note to question Nathan at the very first opportunity with regards to the money and ensure that it had been nothing more than a munificent gesture.

If Dave Mooney was surprised to welcome Sarah alongside her husband, he didn't show it. Stefano Cavalieri shook their hands limply, trying immediately to unhinge the couple by letting it slip that he had come by quite a bit earlier to iron out some details in the proposed purchase. Guillaume remained impassable while Dave Mooney fidgeted, unhappy with Stefano's allusions, not wanting to put Guillaume offside so early on in the discussion.

"So, gentlemen, have you come up with an offer I can't possibly refuse?" the fruit farmer asked with as much joviality as he could muster.

"I've already given you mine," replied Stefano right away, his face inscrutable.

Mooney cleared his throat.

"With all due respect, Stefano, you've only indicated a possible range. I'm after a firm offer. The papers are ready to be signed. They have been vetted through my lawyers. However, the exact sum still remains blank."

"So what's your offer?" challenged Stefano, looking directly at Will.

"I can't really come up with a number at this point," replied the Frenchman. "I have been waiting for Dave to give away his reserve to evaluate whether it's reasonable or not."

"I'd walk away for around the $3,000,000 mark and not a penny less," announced Dave with more aplomb than he felt.

"So you're basically after three times the market price for land you know neither of us intends to continue developing as orchards. From my research, it has come to my attention that you've proposed the farm and business for sale for the past three years with absolutely no takers, isn't that right? You've also returned a marginal profit only once in the same time period. Correct me if I'm wrong," counter-acted Guillaume quickly, with Stefano hanging on his every word.

Dave Mooney had turned a light shade of purple, the veins in his neck throbbing, his eyes narrowing to pinpricks: the conversation was heading in the wrong direction.

"How the hell would you know that?" he barked, his voice strangled by rage, having dropped all pretence at affability. "My tax returns aren't public knowledge!"

"In my book it's called due diligence. You don't really think I'd buy this property simply for its convenience, do you? I'm after a fair market value, as is Cavalieri, I'm sure."

Stefano's head bobbed up and down in acquiescence. What game was Will playing?

"We can conclude this right now for $1,200,000. In this economy, you'd be lucky to get that from anyone else. I'd bet any current valuation would come in the same ballpark. As you've seen, no one is rushing into farmland, except perhaps the Chinese. But you've struck out already with potential overseas buyers, haven't you?" added Guillaume, with ice in his tone.

"That's ridiculously low," whimpered Mooney. "In fact, it's downright insulting!"

"Well, maybe Stefano can better the offer?" replied Guillaume with an exaggerated shrug of the shoulders, turning to Stefano. The latter had become increasingly uncomfortable, tugging at his shirt collar. He knew something wasn't quite right but he couldn't put his finger on it. Why would Will talk down the property when they both knew how vital the land was to both of them? The shoe dropped seconds later.

"By the way, Cavalieri," said Guillaume, now addressing his opponent, "I haven't had time to offer you my condolences for

Winnings' passing. Please accept them now: you've had quite a shocking time of late, haven't you? Have the police yet revealed the identity of the third man found dead on your property?"

It was Stefano's turn to swallow his bile. Baffled by the complete volte-face in the conversation, Mooney looked back and forth from one man to the other. Feeling somehow his chances slipping away, he tried to pinpoint the origin of the hostility he heard in Guillaume's tone.

"The police found three bodies on your property?" he interrupted, annoyed to be so clearly out of the loop.

"Yes," continued Guillaume, enjoying the men's discomfort. "Surely, you remember when, just last week, Stefano had his barns burn down? There was also a shooting on the very same night. I lost Patrick McCarthy and he lost Trent Winnings: an incredible coincidence indeed. Apparently there was a third party, an intruder, who also turned up dead."

"I didn't hear anything about that," mumbled Mooney, wondering why he had been left in the dark.

"The police are still investigating," piped up Sarah, who had let the conversation run its course until then. "It's all hush-hush. It's rumoured the intruder was a contract killer, can you believe it?" She rolled her eyes for emphasis.

Stefano Cavalieri had always known when to call it quits. The couple's insinuations indicated they knew the identity of the intruder. It was time for him to fold, lest he wanted to unleash Guillaume's wrath: part of his reputation had certainly been built on a refusal to back down in most confrontations. It certainly would not take long for his rival to figure out that he was the one who had given the assassin all the information he needed to see him dead.

"It was unbelievable!" repeated Stefano, ill-at-ease, avoiding Sarah's hard stare. "What has the world come to? Contract killers in our fields. It sounds like a late night episode of CSI," he added, trying to keep the tremor out of his voice. "Let's get back to the business at hand though. I'll top Will's offer by $100,000," he said, pretending he still cared about the deal, when all he wanted to do was leave the meeting as quickly as possible.

"Let's make it an even $1,500,000. That's $200,000 more than my first offer and $100,000 above his," countered Guillaume, watching Stefano closely. "Unless, of course, Cavalieri wants to up the ante once again?" he added, the challenge unmistakable.

"Too rich for my blood unless..." said Stefano immediately, "unless, Dave, you're willing to wait until the insurance money comes in.'

"When would that be?" asked Mooney feebly.

"According to the insurers, another three or four months, I reckon."

"How much more would you offer then?" ventured Mooney.

"I'd be able to offer you close to what the land is worth under the best circumstances. Probably another $100,000," replied Stefano half-heartedly. He hoped Mooney wouldn't take him up on his offer, since it would have been too dear a price to pay anyway.

Sensing Dave's hesitation, Guillaume rose from his seat, immediately followed by Sarah.

"Where are you going?" questioned Mooney, panicked.

"One bird in the hand..." began Guillaume.

"Done, I accept your offer," said Dave quickly, wiping the sweat off his forehead with the back of his hand. "At that price, it's an absolute steal, Will and you know it. But I promised my wife a deal would be struck today. Sorry, Stefano, I can't wait another few months. Retirement is calling."

As Guillaume and his wife sat back down, Stefano stood up.

"Well played," he whispered in Guillaume's ear. "You haven't seen the last of me though."

"That's what Guarini thought too," Guillaume murmured back.

The ashen look on Stefano's face told him everything he needed to know. The Italian jumped back as if he had just been hit. He slammed the door on his way out.

"Hello, Nate! Sorry to come by like this unannounced," apologised Summers, walking up to the stable where Nathan was checking out the champion mare, Josephine. "Do you have a minute? I've a couple more questions."

"Arielle refuses to press charges," replied Nathan dismissively while opening the mare's mouth wide to check out her teeth.

"I agree that putting herself through a trial when the perpetrator is already deceased would only reopen her wounds. No, my question in fact, is in regards to Will."

Nathan, his senses on alert, let go of the horse, who shook her mane eloquently. Dental examinations weren't her favourite pastime.

"What about Will?"

"To your knowledge does he have any enemies?"

"Not that I can think of," replied Nathan, confused. "Why do you ask?"

"You heard about what happened here the night of the fire, haven't you?"

"Rumours abound," Nate replied carefully.

"We found a third unidentified body at the scene, just a few metres in fact from where you're standing. We also found a rental car parked at the bottom of the property. The man had driven from Sydney after landing at Kingsford Smith International that very morning. We have it on good authority that he'd come here to kill Will."

'That explains a lot,' thought Nathan. 'That's why the stranger mistook me for Will.'

"Are you telling me that a foreigner flew in from overseas and came all the way here in the middle of the night to murder Will? But he ended up here at Pandora Estates instead?"

"That's exactly what I'm saying."

"Frankly, I'd have no idea. Chantilly Farms isn't boarding any foreign horses at this time, nor is it in the planning as far as I know. The only hint of a foreign connection was the weekend before last when the LaSalles opened their home to a couple of foreign visitors. So in response to your question, no, I'd have no idea who'd want Will dead."

"Who did he upset most by winning the Melbourne Cup?"

A shiver coursed through Nathan's back, his hair standing at the nape of his neck.

"I'd imagine more than one person. Obsidian was short-changed by betting exchanges and, according to the majority of punters, had little chance of winning."

"Stefano had some of his horses running too, didn't he?"

"You're looking at one of them."

"So did you have to make a choice on whose horses you'd attend to during the festival?"

"Stefano didn't ask. Will did."

"Was there anything wrong with the horse prior to the race which would require your attention?"

"A simple case of indigestion but after treatment, it cleared up the day before."

"I suppose Will was very grateful. That's probably why he was so generous..." trailed Zack.

"What are you talking about?" stalled Nathan, feeling uneasy by the line of questioning. "Obviously the detective was fishing for information but did he really suspect anything in regards to the substitution? It was unlikely. Who could have talked? He certainly hadn't and he couldn't imagine Arielle or Will doing so either. The only man susceptible to betrayal was Pat and Pat was dead. What exactly was the cop insinuating?

"When I went through Patrick's bank records it seems that close to $400,000 had been wired to his account after the race, courtesy of Chantilly Farms. Coincidentally, it was the exact same amount which had been wired to your account. It's rather difficult to accept that anyone would have given away 20% of the purse just as a thank you..." continued Zack, his eyes boring into Nathan.

"Will LaSalle isn't just anyone," said Nathan defensively. "It was his first Melbourne Cup win. If you recall last time he didn't come out nearly as lucky. Chantilly Farms did quite well: Arielle was the jockey and Will was both trainer and owner. They combined purses. He told us before the race that if his horse won, he'd give us 10% of the prize money. He's a man of his word and both Pat and I have worked pretty hard," added Nathan, hoping his face didn't betray his inner turmoil.

"I bet you have!" replied the detective, a touch sarcastically. "You both earned what? Three or four times your annual salary in one go?"

"You'd have netted twice that if you had bet on the horse!" retorted Nathan.

"That's true," admitted Zack. "Well, thank you for clearing up the matter of the money. Meanwhile, keep your ears to the ground, Nate. It worries me that the man we found intended to come after Will. Please let me know if you notice anything suspicious around here. Have a good day."

The detective touched the brim of his hat and Nathan watched him walk away towards the homestead. He was left with no illusion that Stefano Cavalieri was next in the firing line.

Stefano Cavalieri's day was getting progressively worse with Detective Zack Summers approaching his front door. It had already been a bad morning, with Will wresting the coveted land holdings. Moreover, since Trent's dying confession, he had wondered how to approach the vet with regards to the artificial insemination. In fact, he had been quite surprised that Nate had not yet alluded to it in any way, shape or form. Was his silence an indication of disinterest or a calculated move? At the moment, wherever he turned, the future looked bleak. Losing the Melbourne Cup had been a blow to his finances and his pride: he dearly regretted his much-publicised quips to the press beforehand, when he had mercilessly diced the competition. The traumatic loss of his stables, barely a week later, had added to his financial woes. Just a few hours before, he had also squandered the opportunity to increase his land holdings. To top it all, his studmaster was now dead. Unfortunately, his secret hadn't died with him. The artificial insemination tort was certain to rear its ugly head at some point in the future. It went without saying that bringing Joe Guarini to Australia had proved a disaster. Now it seemed that he had to face the police once again. He was ready to bet that Zack had already pieced it all together and was only knocking on his door to confirm his hunches: his reputation as a fine detective preceded him. In any case, since Stefano by nature distrusted the police and their methods, the conversation was unlikely to be pleasant.

"Good day, Mr Cavalieri," said Detective Summers as soon as the front door opened. "I hope this isn't inconvenient. Unfortunately, I need to ask you a few more questions regarding the shooting from the other night."

"Please come in, Detective. Let's sit under the porch on the other side. It's a fine day. We won't be disturbed. Maria," he yelled, "can you bring us some coffee please?"

In the cavernous house, Zack heard heavy footsteps and the distinctive sound of cupboards opening and closing. He followed his host out to the shielded verandah, facing north to the open fields where horses grazed peacefully. The day was clear, without a cloud to mar the deep blue sky.

"What can I help you with, Detective?"

"After the ballistic report, we figured out that the intruder shot Patrick McCarthy and that Trent shot the intruder," began Zack, watching Stefano's face. "From our investigation, we also put a name to our John Doe, a man by the name of Joe Guarini."

Stefano's brows furrowed and a muscle twitched in his lower jaw. Neither escaped the detective's scrutiny.

"We discovered that this Joe Guarini was a French national, his family reputed to be part of the Corsican mafia. From the evidence found at the scene, it has come to light that this Guarini character had come to Pandora by mistake," he continued.

"By mistake?"

"He had come armed with the intent to kill. However, his victim wasn't any of the men present on your property that night. It appears that the intended victim was Will LaSalle."

"Will LaSalle? Really?" replied Stefano, swallowing hard and trying his best to appear surprised, his shirt already sticking to his back.

"When I spoke to Will yesterday, he recognised the name and he told me that the man had probably borne a grudge due to something that happened back in Europe decades ago. Thus, we hypothesise the motive to be revenge, but you already know all about that, don't you Mr Cavalieri?"

"I'm sorry," stammered Stefano, "but I've no idea what you're insinuating. I don't know anyone by that name. Are you accusing me of something, Detective?"

Zack changed tack.

"The story goes that your father came to settle in Australia to avoid persecution when Mussolini went after the mafia, is that right?"

"For argument's sake and to cut a long story short, let's agree on the basic premises," replied Stefano gruffly.

"And would you confirm that your father maintained ties to the old country?" questioned Zack, unfazed.

Maria chose that very moment to step onto the verandah, carrying a tray laden with coffee and cake. She had overheard the last question.

"The old Italian guard used to come here all the time," she confirmed, laughing. "They'd talk of the old country and their mafia ways for hours on end. I was a young spouse then but I remember it quite well," she added merrily, ignoring her husband's seething looks.

"Thanks, Maria. Please leave us now," said Stefano curtly, trying his best to control his temper. Maria shrugged her shoulders and left the tray on a coffee table. Her husband had been in a foul mood ever since that dreadful fire and she had learned long ago to ignore his temperamental bouts.

"So could we assume that through your contacts or your father's former contacts, you could have come across Joe Guarini?"

"No, you can't," replied Stefano firmly. "You do know that the Italian Mafia and the Corsican Mafia have very little in common, right? So why would I know anything about this Guarini character you keep referring to? How would I know he had it in for Will? From what you've told me, whatever happened between them happened decades ago. I don't even know where Will comes from, for Christ's sake! And what reasons would I have to want to hurt him, or do you have a theory for that too? Or are you forgetting that I've placed a half dozen of my horses under his care?"

"Oh, I've several theories," replied Zack, ignoring the outburst. "Ask anyone in town and they'd tell you there is no love lost between the two of you. You lost to his horse at Flemington and that must have hurt. Especially after your rants to the press that it had absolutely no chance in hell of winning, and I quote. You lost your studmaster in the fire and half of your boarding facilities. Now your horses are at his place. I can't imagine that was an easy decision for you either."

"All too true but I still can't see any motive to conspire to kill. Nor have you established beyond a reasonable doubt that I know this Joe Guarini, or have you left something out, Detective?"

"What about Apple Legends?"

Stefano's shoulders dropped.

"I had to drop the bid. Mooney was after way too much money."

"I'm not sure I understand," questioned Zack, who had meant to imply something completely different by the question.

"Everyone knows that adding the Mooney's property to either Will's or my land would have given us a great advantage over the competition and over each other," explained Stefano. "However, this morning, Will beat me fair and square in the negotiations. It's over. And I certainly wouldn't have killed him over it. It's just business."

Zack looked straight at Stefano but didn't say anything. The two men were rivals over property too? It certainly did not help Stefano's case.

"Did Trent say anything to you before he died?" continued Zack, leaving the matter of property aside.

Stefano closed his eyes. He needed the police to get off his back. Moreover, he hadn't really understood what Trent had meant. Sending the detective on a wild goose chase though would give him time to breathe and gather his thoughts. He embellished.

"His dying words were that I should "have a close look at Obsidian" and I quote. I've no idea what he meant by that."

"Was he referring to Will's champion?"

"Do you know any other horse by that name?"

"Did he say anything else?"

Once again Stefano screwed his eyes shut, the scene still vivid in his mind.

"He said he was sorry."

"Sorry for what?"

"He didn't have a chance to elucidate. Obsidian was the last word on his lips," repeated Stefano for emphasis. "Then he took his last breath."

"All right, Mr Cavalieri, that will be all for today. I apologise for the interruption to your day. These investigations take time, especially when we're dealing with multiple murders without a single reliable eyewitness."

"I understand, Detective. Any time," said a relieved Stefano, incredulous at dodging the bullet so easily.

"Oh, one more thing..." said Zack. "Do you have a mobile phone? Could I call you if anything else comes up?"

"Sure."

Stefano dictated the number and Zack punched it into his phone. All he had to do now was request from Telstra the list of all in-coming and outgoing calls for the week or so preceding the murders at Pandora Estates. He was hopeful something would turn up.

The call flashed on her phone and absentmindedly Arielle picked it up. It was three o'clock in the afternoon, nine in the morning in Dubai.

"Finally!' exclaimed the voice she knew so well. "If I didn't know any better I'd think you've been avoiding me! Are you feeling better?" questioned Majid, relieved.

"Oh! My darling! It's so good to hear your voice! I've missed you so terribly," replied Arielle, tears catching in her throat. "So much has happened since you left. I've been completely overwhelmed."

"I can hear it in your voice. I'd thought you'd forgotten about me," he replied tenderly. "Are you all right?"

"I don't know where to start but this little heart-to-heart will have to wait because…"

Before she could finish her sentence Majid interrupted her.

"For the past six days, I've had no news from you except through your mother and you want me to wait? I can't accept that!" replied Majid, his usually gentle tone rising in displeasure.

"I'm not putting you off. I'm in the yard cleaning up Obsession's stable. It isn't the most comfortable or conducive of environments for a private chat. Can I call you back in 15 minutes? I'll give me time to walk up to the house and close the door to my bedroom."

Majid relented.

"Fifteen minutes and not a minute more or I'll start harassing you," he teased.

"Don't worry. I'm leaving the stables now," said Arielle reassuringly.

After pouring a tall glass of iced tea, Majid walked out into his shaded garden and waited. The temperature was already in the mid-thirties. He hoped she wouldn't be too long. He had so much to tell her: the past week had been emotionally difficult and he longed to share it with her. He had also been extremely worried.

After initiating talaq with his wife, Majid had needed to confront her family. He hadn't looked forward to the meeting. Following his initial conversation with Assa, it had been scheduled for lunch on Saturday. She had left early that morning to go and see her mother and explain there was no turning back. Since Majid had returned and made his intentions clear, she had gone through her entire albeit limited repertoire of seduction, to get him to renounce his divorce plans. Majid had remained immune to the attention she had lavished upon him, day after night, spending most of his time away from the house, locked up inside Arabian Nights' offices. Now the dreaded day to make her humiliation public was upon him. Majid had done his best to try and mentally prepare for the uncomfortable meeting, fearing Sheik Rashid's explosive reaction. He certainly hadn't expected what confronted him on that particular afternoon.

As soon as Majid walked into his in-laws' house, the whispered conversations ceased immediately and all of eyes focused on him at once. He counted over 16 people in all. He took the only vacant seat, with Assa seating directly opposite him. Rashid's every feature denoted how angry he was. His wife, on the other hand, displayed a tear-stricken face, her heavily kohl-rimmed eyes a blur. Majid took centre stage and explained his decision as gently as possible, pronouncing talaq for the second time. Tearfully but firmly he begged the family to acknowledge that Assa's failure to produce children had little to do with his decision. He had simply fallen head over heels in love with another woman, with whom he wanted to build a new life. Unfortunately, her origins made polygamy unacceptable. As soon as he was finished, Rashid menaced to withdraw his support for Arabian Nights, but when he realised Majid wasn't the slightest bit phased by the empty threat, he abandoned that particular line of attack. The magazine had been very profitable and over the years had gone a long way to improve his social standing in the community. He would be loath to let it go. He nonetheless hoped that his posturing showed the assembled family that he was prepared to go to any length to protect his daughter's future. When he fell silent, everyone in turn attempted to dissuade Majid, alternatively quoting the Qur'an and playing at his heartstrings, begging him to reconcile. Majid remained immune to the heart-wrenching pleas.

After the assembled group had exhausted their supplications, Majid reiterated his promise to return Assa's dowry in full, insuring her future financial freedom. True to his earlier word, he beseeched her cousins to take her in, once the divorce proceedings were over, enticing them with a generous monetary gift. In the end, they relented. Despite her pain, Assa was proud of her soon-to-be ex-husband's generosity and the kindness he had shown her throughout the course of the afternoon.

Two hours later, however, aware that Majid had made up his mind and nothing anyone could say would sway his decision, Rashid requested a one-on-one conversation with his son-in-law. He had already intimated that unless Majid reconsider and try to work it out, he had much damaging evidence against the woman he proposed to wed. Adjourning to another living room, Majid waited nervously for the man he so despised to reveal his hand.

Over the last few months, Rashid's first wife, Baysan, had often voiced her mounting fears that their daughter, Assa, might one day be repudiated due to her inability to conceive. She had increasingly fretted over what she had described as a cooling of marital rapports. At first Rashid had downplayed her worries, but when the lamenting didn't cease, he began to look for alternatives. Indeed, at this juncture in his life, he had no intention to carry his daughter financially once again. Moreover, her return under his roof would shame him unnecessarily. Thus, when Majid had accompanied Hamdam to Melbourne, Rashid had wondered why. Anyone in Hamdam's entourage would have happily made the trip if the old man had required company. In his opinion, the much younger Majid had been a curious choice; intuition told him that besides the famed races something else may have played a part in enticing his son-in-law to make the long journey. Employing the services of a private investigator, it hadn't taken him long to discover his previous dalliance with Arielle and, by the same token, Hamdam's friendship with Guillaume. The latter had struck him as strange: indeed careful research demonstrated that, as far as anyone knew, in the last four decades, the two men had never been on the same continent at the same time, nor had they ever attended the same events. A friendship allegedly spanning half a century was thus highly unlikely. Unless, of course, one of them wasn't who he said he was.

Since Hamdam's every move could be easily traced back to his birth, Will LaSalle and his daughter had become the object of Rashid's obsession. Apparently though, the man had no past until 30 years before, when he had emerged as one of the most astute and successful thoroughbred breeders and trainers in Australia, his horses gracing many turfs. It was by a stroke of sheer luck that during a charity fundraiser dinner officiated by the ruling Prince of Dubai, the conversation had turned to racing. It wasn't long before Rashid discovered that current industry racing practices respected throughout the UAE had been made possible thanks to the Prince's father's unique friendship with a man by the name of Romain de La Selle. Intrigued, Rashid had followed the crumbs until he'd come across the stack of articles relating to the circumstances surrounding the Frenchman's violent death. There had been only one survivor to the slaughter that day. After that, locating Guillaume's university records and matching them against Hamdam had been child's play. The septuagenarians had indeed known each other for decades, except that Guillaume de la Selle had become Will LaSalle in the interim. It was hardly a stretch of the imagination to conclude that the change of identity had been prompted by fear of reprisal: messing around with the Corsican mafia was indeed dangerous.

For two days Rashid pondered the best way to use that information to the man's detriment. The solution suddenly blinded him: to save his daughter's marriage, all he had to do was eliminate the competition. If something was to happen to the LaSalle family at the other end of the world, it could never be traced back to him. Moreover, the authorities would eventually come to the same conclusions: Guillaume's past had unfortunately

214

finally caught up with him. By the time Rashid's investigators had come across Joe Guarini's name, he was stunned to learn the man was already on a plane bound for Sydney. Someone had beaten him to the punch. When, a few days after Majid's return, the news filtered through that the same man had been found dead on a property in Chantilly Farms' vicinity along with two others, he had been baffled.

Thanks to his wife, Baysan, he was well aware that it was immediately upon his return that Majid had requested a divorce. She had been adamant that without the other woman's existence, Majid had confirmed that he'd have happily continued the arrangement, eventually taking on a second wife to bear him children. After all, he was a kind man and wished her daughter no harm. Rashid knew that according to their laws, Majid would respect the traditional three months' delay: he soon convinced himself that before the time elapsed, Arielle needed to disappear. He wondered whether Majid knew anything about Arielle's family's past. It was time to ask. It might prove to give him the best course of action yet. The young man might inadvertently give him just the type of information he could use. When, after the family gathering, Majid was summoned for a tête-à-tête chat, the young man assumed it was Rashid's last desperate attempt to bring him to reason. The conversation, however, took him by surprise.

As far as he was concerned, Rashid's disclosure of Arielle's father's past did little to change his mind and he told him as much. The tale only explained how she had come to be under Hamdam's roof all those years ago. Rashid's insinuations that she'd been less than honest with him were rejected outright. However, the insinuation that her life might be in danger unnerved him. It made him all the more uneasy in light of their lack of communication over the past week. He was determined more than ever to warn her as soon as possible about the potential danger surrounding her father. It never occurred to him that the man she had most to fear from at that very minute was calmly standing in front of him, smoking a thin cigar. When Rashid finally exhausted his plea, Majid thanked his father-in-law for a most enlightening conversation and took his leave. Privately he wondered why the man had bothered: was he that obtuse as to think that Guillaume's sad antecedents would lead him to love his daughter less? However, he accepted that pride and prejudice knew few boundaries. Rashid certainly wasn't the type of man who'd stop at threats to get his own way.

Full of irrational hope, Assa had stood on the other side of the door, awaiting the outcome of the meeting. As he exited, Majid refused to meet her eyes and behind him, her father shook his head and shrugged his shoulders. As Majid walked away, Rashid came out to the landing and hugged his daughter in a rare display of affection.

"Don't worry. I'll fix it. It's not over yet. Have faith. Go home and pray. Allah will not abandon you in your time of need."

Assa lowered her head obediently and followed her husband home.

Meanwhile, Rashid made a few calls. Something Majid had said nagged at the edges of his brain. They had spoken of his stay in Australia; how he had only reconnected with Arielle when she'd walked in under the Emirates VIP tent. He had mentioned how irrationally proud he had been of her victory, one which had been all the more surprising that no one had seen it coming. By all accounts, Guillaume's champion had been good enough. Yet, in all the races which had helped him qualify beforehand, none had displayed a heavy track. It had rained on that day in Melbourne; expert opinions had believed his chances slim at best. The horse had nonetheless won by a comfortable margin. In Rashid's experience, it had been an upset the likes of which were not often seen. His instincts told him there was more to the story than met the eye.

"It's me," said Arielle breathlessly, calling Majid back as promised. "How are you, my love?"

"Missing you terribly but it won't be long now until we're together, forever under the gaze of Allah."

"What do you mean, darling?" she asked softly, his beloved face floating in front of her as he spoke.

"I've asked my wife for a divorce," he began. Laying face down, her eyes closed so as to feel the caress of his voice, holding the phone over the edge of the bed, Arielle flipped over and sat up quickly, holding her breath, her heart pounding against her chest. "Our custom is that I need to wait three months," he continued. "I can remarry immediately after that."

"You're too fast for me," stammered Arielle, completely taken aback by the swiftness of his actions. "Isn't your wife sure to contest the divorce? Isn't there a long settlement period?"

Majid's laugh rang hollow.

"Don't worry about that. She can't contest it or oppose it. It isn't how it's done. I've given her back her dowry so she'll be financially comfortable."

"I didn't ask for that," said Arielle, miserable. How could her happiness be predicated on someone else's misery? Majid had never said anything negative about his wife: from all accounts, she had been the perfect spouse. She did not care for the home-wrecker label but now that's exactly what she was.

Majid misunderstood her sadness.

"Arielle, don't you want us to be together anymore?" he asked anxiously.

"Of course I do, but I can't help feel sorry for her."

"Would you have ever considered being a second wife?"

"You know what the answer is," replied Arielle softly.

"So, there is no other way. Now I can properly court you and do things right."

"What do you mean, Majid?"

"You can't possibly think that I'd ask you to marry me over the phone, do you? You'll know when the time's right."

"Before you say anything else, and once I've told you what I've to tell you, maybe that time will never come," Arielle said, hesitating. She knew he loved her, but would he understand?

217

"Darling, your father's past has nothing to do with us. I don't care," interrupted Majid quickly.

Arielle, completely thrown, sat stock still, gripping the phone tightly, her mind a blank. Half a dozen kookaburras, laughing on the property fences, stood as a preamble to dusk. Simultaneously, a pandemonium of rainbow lorikeets squawked overhead in their flight to nearby trees. For a full minute, the familiar noises obliterated all other sounds, preventing conversation.

"Arielle, are you still there?" repeated Majid, fearing the connection had been lost.

"What do you know about my father?" demanded Arielle in a strangled voice as soon as the noisy birds had flown past.

"It appears my father-in-law has taken it upon himself to investigate your family and has managed to piece it together. Somehow, he thought it'd be a deterrent; that I couldn't possibly think of marriage with someone who had been less than truthful with me."

"Majid, listen to me. Papa only told me his story 24 hours ago! How extraordinary that you'd bring it up so shortly after that!! He's never spoken of his childhood or his past prior to arriving on Australian shores. Mum and I knew he'd lost his parents in a tragic accident but we never knew how. Since it was obviously too painful to talk about, we've never pressed him."

"So why did he choose to tell you now after all the years of silence?" asked Majid, curious.

"That's what I needed to talk to you about," said Arielle, closing her eyes, trying to find the right words.

During her recount of the entire saga, Majid remained silent, his heart aching at everything she had gone through. During her slow and hesitant recount of her rape, he had clenched his fists involuntarily, livid with anger. When she told him of the police's suspicions that a man had come to murder her father, he wondered more than once if Rashid had anything to do with it.

"I wish I could be there right now, next to you, holding you in my arms. Honey, my heart bleeds for you. I can't imagine everything you've gone through. I'm so very sorry. You deserve none of this," said Majid emphatically, his melodious voice filled with sadness and empathy.

"Maybe I deserved it," replied Arielle slowly, her voice barely audible. Perhaps it's my karma."

"How could you ever think that?" counteracted Majid forcefully. "Rape is an act of violence, not a display of lust or love for that matter!"

"Perhaps it was God's way to make me pay for what I'd done." Her tone was wistful and filled with tears.

"Darling, you're not making any sense!" said Majid, mistaking her words. "Our meeting was blessed by Allah, I've no doubt about that. With any divorce there is unfortunate collateral damage, but I assure you, you're not to blame. It was my decision after all."

"I wasn't talking about that. I cheated. Everything that has happened to me is none other than my rightful punishment for cheating."

Majid was at a loss for words. What was she talking about? Being raped was not cheating: was she too distraught to see things clearly? Surely she did not mean she cheated on him with another man? He had assumed she'd stop seeing the veterinary surgeon she had told him about when they'd resumed their relationship, but it's true he hadn't asked for confirmation. Was that it? What was really going on? Her words confused him. Before he could find anything to say, she continued.

"We won the Melbourne Cup by cheating," she elaborated, every word clear and final. It was the first time she had voiced it loud and by sharing the immense burden, she felt suddenly lighter.

"Slow down, princess. What in Allah's name are you talking about?"

For the second time in less than a few minutes, Majid, shaken, listened to the second instalment of the extraordinary tale. By the time Arielle fell silent, the sun had disappeared behind the palm trees lining his garden, refusing to take the heat of the day away with it. Majid felt feverish, emotions sticking to his bronzed skin.

"Now that you know everything, am I still the type of woman you'd want to share your life with?"

Majid did not hesitate. "You've shown me to be the type of woman who'd do anything to save her family's honour. My ancestors were nomads and warriors. Confronted with a moral dilemma you elected family over society's rules. In my book, it's to be respected even though I know what you've conspired to do is perfectly illegal. In your shoes, I'd have done the same thing. You didn't really have a choice, did you?"

Arielle remained still but Majid, relieved that her secrets hadn't denoted a change of heart as far as he was concerned, unexpectedly laughed.

"You've fooled the whole world! At least you don't do things by half! I'd have been upset if you'd confessed to some petty larceny. If the truth ever surfaces, it'd be the biggest scandal to ever hit racing!"

"Do I turn myself in, now that I've spilled all?" asked Arielle, her voice raw with emotion.

"To what purpose exactly?" replied Majid, secretly amused by the half-hearted suggestion. "You've already announced your plans to stop racing. You've accepted to come and live here or anywhere in Europe which strikes our fancy. I've no intention of derailing our plans by letting you pass through the door of a police station. Perhaps Hamdam would be shocked, but I'm sure there are plenty of skeletons in his closet and he knows your father better than most. I'm not losing you over this! However, I'm now worried about your safety more than ever. Are you sure Pat didn't tell anyone? Will Nathan talk? He's accepted to be part of this fraud because he's in love with you. He now knows you won't be spending your life with him. Could he blackmail you just like this despicable Patrick character has tried to do?"

"And implicate himself? And risk prison? And lose his business and his license? No, I don't think so, but then after the past week, I'm no longer certain of anything."

Arielle gave a defeated sigh, which the miles did little to hide.

"Sweetheart, can you hold on for a few more weeks? Can you just promise me to look over your shoulder and make sure you look twice before putting you foot down anywhere? I've to stay here until the last talaq is pronounced. After that, I'll be on the next flight over to ask your father for your hand in marriage. Where he comes from, that'd be expected and I wouldn't have it any other way. May I suggest something though?"

"Go ahead," invited Arielle, a smile slowly spreading across her tension-lined features. Not only had he not rejected her after hearing of the rape, but he hadn't judged her for what she had conspired to do. She was a very lucky woman and, as far as she was concerned nothing could stand in her way anymore. Majid was her destiny and she was going to do everything in her power to seize it with both hands.

"I know you're not going to want to hear this, but something terrible and unfortunate should happen to Obsession lest the subterfuge somehow comes to the fore. I don't want you and your family buried under the weight of an unprecedented scandal, nor do I plan to bring you dates and oranges behind bars for the next decade."

"Majid, what you're proposing is a mighty high price to pay!" retorted Arielle, horrified by the suggestion.

"It's the only thing that makes sense. Your champion is the only physical evidence left. At least promise me you'll give it some thought."

"For you, I'll do anything and you know that. I'll discuss it with Papa. Majid?"

"Yes?"

"Thank you for not judging me or treating me like the criminal I am."

"You're my shining star in the moonless night and the dream which turns sleep into a blessing. I love you too. We'll speak soon. Arielle?"

"Yes?"

"Thanks for trusting me. I wouldn't want to build our future on secrets and lies. Please hang in there. I'll be there soon. And never forget how much I love you. I made a mistake once. I've now been given a second chance. I won't mess it up this time around!"

They hung up the phone at the same time, both staring dejectedly at the handset, alive seconds earlier with their lover's voice. For Arielle it had been the most difficult conversation of her adult life. If he had ever needed one, it had been for Majid the last proof that Arielle was the only woman for him. It never occurred to him that Assa, hidden in the coolness of their house behind the partially closed Persian shutters, had listened to every single word of it.

CHAPTER XIII

Arielle tossed and turned throughout the night, unable to chase away the feeling of impending doom which had shadowed her every thought since her declaration of guilt to Majid. Even though she was convinced that her lover wouldn't betray her, she questioned the wisdom to have confessed all in a moment of weakness. After all, the subterfuge had not engaged her alone: it implicated Nathan and her father as well. If it ever came to light, she knew it would inflict untold damage upon the sport and potentially impact the multitude of people who derived their income from it, either directly or indirectly. By daybreak, she had come to see the wisdom in Majid's suggestion: to keep her family safe, all traces of her former deceit needed to disappear. However, the abhorrent idea of harming her most cherished horse made her feel nauseous.

When she came down for breakfast, both her parents couldn't help but notice the dark circles under her eyes, the matted hair and the bilious tinge to her skin.

"Are you all right, cherie?" asked Guillaume with great concern as soon as he laid eyes on her. "Did you have a bad night?"

"Did something happen during your call to your friend Majid last night?" questioned Sarah, equally alarmed by her dishevelled state.

Ignoring them both, Arielle poured herself a cup of coffee, trying to compose herself. She came to sit directly across from her father and levelled her gaze at him. He further lowered his newspaper, trying to read her thoughts.

"You're not worried about everything I told you the other night, are you?" asked Guillaume anxiously. "Guarini is dead. I'm sure it's the end of it. The police are just being cautious," he added reassuringly, reaching across the table to pat her hand.

"Maman," inquired Arielle, looking now at her mother, "do you know what happened at the Melbourne Cup?"

Sarah's face instantly clouded over and she shot a sideways glance at her husband who remained impassable.

"I'm not sure what you mean, darling?" she delayed.

Guillaume, waiting for the drama to unfold, sat in the sunlit kitchen, the air now pregnant with untold secrets.

"Do you know what happened with Obsidian?" repeated Arielle doggedly.

"I've told her," interrupted Guillaume softly, relieving his wife from her conundrum. "After the other night, there was no point in keeping anymore secrets from each other."

"I was already suspicious," confirmed Sarah. "That morning, on my way out of town to go shopping, I noticed Obsession's absence from the far-eastern paddock. I'd heard some commotion during the night, but had been too tired to go and investigate. The lorry was gone when I woke up. I put two and two together."

Arielle exhaled loudly and flashed her father a grateful smile.

"Since we're now all on the same page, I've something to propose and, trust me, this decision hasn't been taken lightly."

With her parents' attention now focused on her, Arielle continued bravely.

"With this Guarini character showing up on the scene 40 years later to exact revenge, it has confirmed my belief that you can't get away with murder, in a matter of speaking, of course. What I mean is that we got away switching one horse for another, as the entire world watched and cheered us on. Thanks to Obsession's victory, Papa, you recouped all your former losses and regilded your laurels. On top of it, it allowed you to restore your reputation here and abroad. You're now regarded as the best trainer in the country. All of this though was accomplished solely by cheating, None of us can deny it, or can we?"

Guillaume's face hardened: where was her little sermon heading exactly? He did not care to be lectured on his shortcomings and the means he took to achieve his end. His daughter was perilously close to crossing the line of his tolerance.

"I don't want to get caught," continued Arielle, looking down at her steaming cup of coffee, her eyes rimmed red, a muscle twitching in her right cheek, "and in order to avoid getting caught, ever, not now or 30 years from now, the only solution is to erase any party to our fraud."

Wide-eyed, mouth open in protest, Sarah interrupted her soliloquy.

"You can't possibly be suggesting that something happen to Nate?" cried Sarah, clearly alarmed by the implications.

"Not to Nate, Maman," smiled Arielle wryly, shaking her head, her heart now ripping apart as she uttered the last few words, "but to my horse, Obsession..."

Completely taken aback, both Guillaume and Sarah stared at their only daughter who had started to cry, unable to look at them in the face. For a full minute, Guillaume, robbed of speech, shook his head vehemently, resolutely refusing to hear the wisdom beneath her words. It was Sarah who first displayed her inner turmoil, her voice shaking.

"But honey, you love that horse! That's absurd! We'd never ask you to do that! What has gotten into you?"

Arielle ignored her well-meaning interruption, directing her plea to her father. "Papa: you've seen firsthand that no matter how hard you've tried to bury your past and let bygones be bygones, your past has come looking for you regardless. I guarantee you that the oppressive secret we share between us will surface at some point: not today, maybe not tomorrow, but one day for sure. The horse itself is the only material proof that we've manipulated the system beyond anyone's intendment. Even though premeditation was brief and brought on merely by circumstances, we nonetheless took the time to analyse all the possibilities, consider all the options and weigh in all the probabilities. In the end, the four of us used our considerable combined knowledge to beat the system. Look at the scandals plaguing banks claimed too big to fail, JP Morgan to name just one; the Madoff's Ponzi scheme or the collapse of Lehman Brothers. You recall Walmart's dirty bribes in Mexico or even the Vioxx drug case, don't you? They all believed they had gotten away with it, at least for a while. Everyone involved lined their pockets and accumulated untold riches, but then the house of cards came tumbling down. All it takes is one fanatical whistle blower, one enthusiastic journalist, one disgruntled former employee or a single suspicious punter, who has lost more than he can afford, just about anything. I can't see any of us starting from scratch, never being able to hold our heads high ever again. If Nathan talks, he might be convincing enough to trigger a follow-up inquiry. However, without any living proof to back up his story, the investigation won't go anywhere. That's what I think."

Spent by her impassioned exposé, Arielle stopped abruptly, looking from one parent to the other, searching their respective faces for answers.

"It's a sacrifice I can't ask you to make," replied Guillaume stonily.

"Arielle's right though," admitted Sarah. "Chance intervened when Patrick was shot dead, and I consider him by far the weakest link. We may never get a second chance. Will, you should mull it over."

Thinly, Arielle smiled at her mother. Sarah could always be counted on as the voice of reason.

"The horse still has plenty left in him," resisted Guillaume, unable to process the proposed solution. He had dreamed of Obsession winning many more races. The stallion bore all the hallmarks of becoming another Black Caviar legend. In his mind, the horse was the pot of gold at the end of the rainbow, the champion most trainers dreamed about their entire life. Indeed, Arielle's former assessment had been right: Obsession had turned out a much stronger runner than his twin.

"But, at the end of the day, it's my horse. You both know how I love that horse, more than I've loved anything else in my life, but I love us more. It's time for me to act like a responsible adult, and I've responsibilities towards this family. The trick will be for something to happen which Nathan won't be able to do anything about," she added pensively.

"Have you thought that through as well?" questioned Guillaume uneasily, mesmerised by his daughter's unexpected resolve.

"Not yet but my instinct tells me that it needs to happen sooner rather than later and no matter what, they will be my actions alone."

"I feel incredibly guilty," said Guillaume. "Because of me, you're ready to sacrifice something very important to you. If it hadn't been for the Corsican Mafia showing up at our door, it would have been business as usual."

"To every cloud there is always a silver lining. We may find out that without this Guarini character threatening our lives, we may have fallen into a false sense of complacency. We wouldn't be taking the steps we're now willing to take to save ourselves and it could have spelt disaster in the long run," replied Arielle philosophically.

As Arielle stood up, both her parents came to hug her. The trio remained in a tight embrace for a long minute, comforted as they were by the sole sound of each other's beating heart.

Arielle, who, by her own admission, had just articulated the unthinkable, needed to clear her head the only way she knew how. She dressed and saddled her horse, intent on a long run, away from the property and away from her thoughts. She had been around horses for too long not to know the horrors often inflicted on the noble animals when financial desperation or naked greed came to dominate the owners' thoughts. Regardless of the reasons, lucrative life-insurance policies could turn their very own thoroughbreds into targets of opportunity. She had indeed heard plenty of stories on how a certain type of unscrupulous man could be hired to destroy expensive horses by breaking one of its legs, causing trauma so severe that a veterinarian would have no other choice but to euthanise the animal with a lethal injection. She knew it was possible to rig wires and slice the extension cord down the middle into two strands of wire and attach a pair of alligator clips to the bare end of each wire and then secure the clips to the horse, one in one ear and the other to the rectum and then plug it in to a standard wall socket, after which the electrocuted horse would drop down instantly. Often the horses were simply injected with parasitic blood worms which would bring on a case of thrombo-embolic colic, an illness known to be fatal. Suffocating a horse by jamming ping pong balls up the animal's nostrils or alternatively putting a garbage bag over its head were other common methods. Ramming a rusty nail into the soft tissue of its foot to provoke an infection was another well-known technique. None, however, simply beat shooting the animal right between the eyes, four fingers down from the base of the forelock, with a .38 calibre handgun equipped with a hollow-point bullet. She particularly detested the idea of contaminating the grass clippings with blackberry nightshade, which left the horse to be slowly and painfully poisoned. All true-and-tried methods were distasteful but applied to her situation, they were downright unthinkable.

As Arielle galloped on Obsession's back, with the hum of the wind whizzing past her ears, feeling the familiar heat of the animal between her legs, and the warmth of the early morning sun on her neck and shoulders, the macabre thoughts scrambled her stomach and dizzied her. How could she ever entertain harming the animal that formed one with her every time they rode together, the communion between mount and rider so undeniable, the unquestioning trust built over months and months of riding together? Surely the solution lay elsewhere: she just had to rethink the problem at hand. After all, Nathan was the other weak link. As soon as the thought popped into her head, bile rose in her throat. Momentarily distracted by a wave of nausea she could not repress, Arielle let go of the reins, just as the sure-footed horse readied to jump over a narrow creek, on the opposite bank of which he was used to stopping, knowing Arielle would dismount and leave him to drink while she smoked a cigarette. Unclear as to why his rider would abandon her grip, the horse hesitated at the last minute, his hooves inadvertently slipping on the large mossy pebbles that lined the riverbed. Losing his balance, he knuckled over, throwing his mount forward in the process. Arielle landed on the muddy grass of the creek's embankment, slightly stunned by the fall. Obsession, who had immediately righted himself, nonetheless neighed loudly with a high-pitched, panicky scream. Dazed by her fall, her eyes still unfocused, Arielle took a moment to notice blood running along one of the horse's forelegs, right along the weight-bearing long bone. She stood up unsteadily, cautiously stepping back down into the creek to take hold of the reins, slowly guiding the horse onto firm ground. By force of habit, she touched the animal's muzzle: its nose was ice cold. She could also hear the horse's rapid heartbeat. She knew both to be tale-tell signs of shock. As soon as she managed to move the horse onto the embankment, Obsession lay down on his flank, confirming her diagnosis. Panicked, she retrieved her mobile phone from her back pocket and instantly dialled Nathan's number. His smiling face flashed on her screen.

"Nate," she said rapidly as soon as his voice came on. "I just met with an accident. Can you come quickly?"

"Where are you?" Nathan asked, sensing the distress in her voice, and dispensing with needless questions.

"Along Bushwater's Creek; a few hundred metres down from the crossing, about 10 kilometres out from Chantilly Farms, past the roos' paddock," she explained, referring to one of their paddocks in which mobs of kangaroos were often found grazing alongside their rag of colts, both competing for the same fresh grass.

"Were you riding Obsession?" queried Nathan. "Is he all right?"

"He lost his footing, knuckled down and hurt his foreleg. There's lots of blood and exposed bone. Hurry, Nate, he's in pain!"

"Are you hurt?"

"It's secondary, I assure you. Please hurry!"

"I'll be right there. Keep him comfortable."

Nathan who, for once, had been enjoying a peaceful morning at home catching up on paperwork, ran to his pharmacy to fill his bag with a hypodermic syringe already filled with an anaesthetic solution, along with a second one filled with the barbiturates he hoped he wouldn't have to use. As an additional precaution he also took his .38 calibre handgun. In his ute he raced along the quiet country road until it veered onto a dirt road running alongside the paddock Arielle had mentioned. The creek was just a few hundred metres ahead, shaded by large eucalyptus trees. Once past the cattle crossing, Nathan slowed down, trying to locate Arielle and her horse. They came into view a couple of minutes later, both lying on the ground, the huge horse's head nearly dwarfing Arielle's body. Dispensing with the usual civilities, not wishing to waste precious time, Nathan meticulously examined the open fracture. Arielle's eyes were awash with tears. After a few minutes, Nathan looked up and met hers. He shook his head slowly: words were superfluous. Arielle kissed her horse's nose and murmured endearments in the animal's ear while Nathan took his syringe out of his battered leather satchel and with skill and expertise administered the first vial, plunging the needle straight into Obsession's heart. Within seconds the horse's heartbeat began to slow, his head further drooping on Arielle's lap until his whole body shook, racked by one long shudder. He took his last breath looking up at Arielle with his large black eyes, just as he had taken his first, nearly three years prior.

Devastated, and covered with mud and blood, Arielle eased herself from under the horse's head and Nathan helped her to her feet.

"It's my fault entirely," she said disconsolately. "I suffered a moment's inattention and Obsession lost his footing on the slippery stones. I was thrown. When he got up again I didn't think he'd injured himself and then I saw his leg…"

"Arielle, I'm so sorry," said Nathan sympathetically, hugging her tightly. "I know how much Obsession meant to you. You know this was the only humane thing to do and he didn't suffer. The leg would never have mended. The bone was protruding. He would never have been fit to run anymore and each step would have caused him unbearable pain. I'll take you home now. I'll arrange for the body to be taken away early afternoon and incinerated right away. I'll fill out the necessary paperwork for Obsidian's name to be scratched from the Australian Stud Book. His DNA will burn with it. I know how distressing this it for you, but, in a way, it's the best thing that could ever happen to us."

Incredulous, Arielle listened to Nathan wrapping up the awful accident. Had he really entertained the same conclusion she had reached hours earlier? Gently she pushed him away from her to check whether she had understood him correctly, and hadn't read in his words the echo to her thoughts.

"I'm not sure what you mean," she whispered, searching his face.

"Come on, Arielle, I know you're distraught and this is the worst possible outcome, but let's face it, Pat tried to blackmail you. Hopefully he didn't confide in anyone, but he may have talked; we'll never know. Whatever allegations may now surface, there won't be any proof to find: now we're all truly safe. I'll return Obsidian's ID card to the Association since Obsession was never registered. Your father and I have held onto to it for obvious reasons. No post-mortem will be necessary since the cause of death by euthanasia due to a fatal injury is clear cut," he added firmly.

Nathan, suddenly noticing how badly Arielle was trembling, gallantly took off his jacket and draped it over her shoulders.

In fact, Arielle couldn't shake the ominous feeling that she might have subconsciously caused the horse's fall. Indeed, she had become distracted while inwardly debating the best way of ending its life in order to eliminate their threat of exposure in the process. It was all too spooky.

"Let's go back and let me take care of everything," Nathan offered gently.

"Why are you doing this?" asked Arielle, her voice weak.

"Arielle, I've accepted to be part of this from the very beginning. I also accepted the money. I've already spent most of it upgrading my practice and paying off my mortgage and other sundry debts. In this conspiracy, I'm as guilty as they come.

Granted, it didn't even occur to me to challenge your solution to the problem when Obsidian was too sick to run. I just complied. At the beginning I kept telling myself that I only did it because I loved you and it's what you wanted, but the reality is slightly more complicated than that. I think that before anything else I didn't want the horses illegally sired by Napoleon to win, Josephine in particular, and she was always going to be Obsidian's fiercest competitor. What Winnings did is in my book ultimate cheating. His actions are likely to still influence the outcome of the sport for a few years to come. If his horses, with their disreputable DNA, had won and he hadn't accidentally died, he would have continued profiting from it. For me that was particularly abhorrent and I couldn't stand for it. Switching one highly capable horse for its twin was certainly the lesser of two evils, and, as an untested horse, its chances were remote, we all knew it."

As Arielle continued to stare at him, her eyes wide, her face pale and drawn, he stopped abruptly.

"I'm sorry, Arielle."

Without a word she climbed into the front seat of his truck, her mind reeling with too many emotions to make sense of any of them. She'd left home that morning to clear her head, shuddering at the painful alternatives of getting rid of the incriminating evidence. She was returning home hours later with the only physical evidence finally dealt with, yet she felt nothing but hollow and empty of all feelings. On the ride back, she wondered whether Obsession, with his last breath, hadn't taken her soul away with him.

★ ★

Standing in the front yard, imprinting a new colt, Guillaume saw Nathan's truck speeding up the drive, perplexed as to why Arielle sat next to him. As soon as she got out, her dishevelled state and muddy clothing made his heart beat faster. Where on earth was Obsession? He was certain that right after their discussion, he had seen her leave the farm. Riding with abandon was always how his daughter had handled conflicting situations ever since she had been old enough to saddle her own mount.

"Is everything all right?" he asked with concern when the truck parked next to him.

Incapable of speech, Arielle looked at him and shook her head. Nathan answered for her.

"There's been an accident. I had no other choice but to terminate Obsession's life. I'll need your help to go and get him."

Guillaume paled visibly. He slowly looked from one to the other, his eyes boring into Arielle's.

"What happened exactly?" he reiterated, angling for details.

"When Arielle attempted to cross Bushwater's Creek, the horse slipped and fell. He broke the weight-bearing bone of his foreleg; the internal bone joint components were exposed," explained Nathan, knowing that Guillaume would know exactly what the injury implied.

"It was an accident?" repeated Guillaume, still focusing on his daughter's ravaged face.

"I was deep in thought. I got distracted and let go of the reins just as he prepared to jump," answered Arielle feebly.

"Best outcome then…" muttered Guillaume unhappily.

Distraught, leaning against the truck, Arielle began to cry. Both men stared at her, not knowing what to say. Guillaume was first to break the awkward moment.

"Are you hurt?"

Arielle shook her head in denial.

"Then I suggest you go and get cleaned up. I'll go and take care of things with Nate. Can you take the colt back to his pen?" he added, handing her the lead. Arielle nodded and took the lead, leaving the two men to attend to the business at hand. She listened as the lorry exited the property heading for the hills. As she walked past Obsession's stall on her way out of the stables, she crumbled, sliding against the door until she came to rest in the dirt, burrowing her face in her hands, uncontrollable sobs racking her whole body.

"Father, may I have a word with you in private?" requested Assa over the phone.

Annoyed with the idea of further dealing with his daughter's emotional baggage, Rashid hesitated.

"Assa, he won't change his mind. I've tried everything," he sighed.

Assa wouldn't be deterred.

"Father, do you agree though that if the Australian woman he plans to marry was out of the picture, Majid would see no reason to divorce?"

"It looks that way," replied Rashid, non-committal, his eyes narrowing, further creasing the fleshy crater between his brows.

"I've just overheard a conversation that could help us both," said Assa, well aware that her father cared more about his reputation and social standing than her personal welfare.

Rashid's ears pricked up.

"Since walls have ears, why don't we continue this conversation later? Is your husband home? I could come by the house," offered Rashid, intrigued. He could not remember the last time his daughter had requested a private audience.

"It's Saturday, Father. He's at work. He's always at work lately," stated Assa flatly.

"Give me 20 minutes."

True to his word, a quarter of an hour later, Rashid pulled up in front of his daughter's double garage doors. He rang the doorbell.

Dressed in a vibrant abaya, she welcomed him in. Rashid could not recall the last time he had come to her house; in all her years of marriage, he had seldom stepped foot inside the marital home. He observed how well kept it was, smelling of jasmine and slow-roasted vegetables. The furniture was comfortable and stylish, devoid of the ostentation which characterised his own palace. The walls were covered with a mixture of contemporary art and traditional artefacts.

"I don't recall your home being so lovely," he said, looking around.

Assa blushed at the compliment.

"Let's go sit on the verandah," she suggested. "The overhead fans keep it cool and the afternoon breeze makes it most pleasant."

They sat across from each other, a pitcher of lemon mint and a bowl of freshly picked dates between them. Rashid, somewhat uneasy in finding himself alone with his daughter – an occurrence he could count on the fingers of one hand since her birth – urged her to say what was on her mind. The faster the conversation was over, the quicker he could leave.

"Last night, Majid sat exactly where you're sitting now. He was on the phone to his girlfriend," she began, distaste wrinkling her nose. "I was hiding behind the Persian windows."

"You were eavesdropping on your husband?" tooted Rashid, bemused.

"Father, let me finish, please. I know my English is rudimentary but in 10 years of marriage, I've learned enough to understand what transpired. Granted, I only heard one side of the conversation but from what I understood, it appears that…" Assa could barely pronounce the name of the woman who had shattered her happiness, "… Arielle has ridden another horse to victory," she finished, not daring to look at her father.

"I'm not sure I understand."

"The conversation lasted well over an hour. Majid told her he knew all about her father and that it didn't matter. Then she wanted to talk about her last race. It seemed she confessed that at the last minute she rode another horse because the one she was scheduled to mount had been taken ill."

"That would explain why the horse won in spite of the experts' opinions that it couldn't finish in the top three!" reflected Rashid, his hands tapping on his thighs.

Yet if Assa was right, where would they have found such a horse at short notice? The horse has obviously not arisen any suspicion. How could it be so similar as to fool the stewards?' It was a very juicy piece of information indeed and one prone to destroy Guillaume de la Selle and his daughter, but it was an explanation that invited just as many questions.

"I'd have expected better of you than to spy on your husband," replied Rashid severely. "You must have misunderstood. It's impossible to switch horse at the last minute in such a prestigious race. All horses have to qualify well in advance and they are all vetted and tested right before the race. What you're suggesting is preposterous!"

"So why would she make such a big deal out of it?" cried Assa defensively, upset that what she had believed to be her trump card had proved to be so inconsequential.

"Darling, I understand you'll try anything to save your marriage but spreading vicious rumours like these would only make you appear foolish and vindictive. You've got to stop this and accept your fate," admonished Rashid, rising from his chair, having left his drink untouched. "I'm glad you came to me first with these wild allegations," he added, his tone gentler. "Please know that if I can figure out a way to make Majid back down before he pronounces the last talaq, I will. And spying on your husband, regardless of the circumstances, is unbecoming. No daughter of mine should ever admit to such base activity."

Properly chastised, Assa lowered her gaze and her father kissed her on the forehead.

"I need to run now. You look quite pretty still. Perhaps we'll find another husband for you yet. Allah, in his infinite wisdom, will provide for you. I'm sure of it."

Assa chased away the tears in her eyes with the back of her hand.

"Thank you, Father, for coming to see me at such short notice. Be assured, it won't happen again. There is no excuse for what I've done; please forgive me. I won't breathe a word of it to anyone."

"That would be most sensible. And there is nothing to forgive, my child. But I'm sure you've much to prepare for your life with your cousins. Devote your energy to that."

With these parting words, Rashid was gone. After softly closing the door behind him, Assa, feeling sick, went up to her bedroom and cried herself to sleep.

When Majid returned home late that night, he found her curled in a foetal position, her face streaked with runaway make-up. Gently he woke her up and demanded to know what had upset her so. But after her father's earlier remonstrations, Assa kept silent. Majid did his best to console her but since she would not share her burden, after a while he left her alone.

You must have a sixth sense as far as I'm concerned, Arielle texted back. After her rather traumatic day, unable to sleep, she had replied to Majid's message immediately. He called her back seconds after that.

"I wish you were here," she sighed heavily.

"Had a hard day?" queried Majid. "Did you give my proposal any further thought?"

"I thought of nothing else, and now it's all sorted," announced Arielle sadly. Something in her tone made Majid flinch involuntarily.

"What do you mean, darling?"

"If there's an inquiry at any point, the authorities won't be able to come up with any proof," stated Arielle flatly.

"Surely, you're not insinuating that twin colts' DNA is so similar as to prevent telling them apart?"

"Provided that the horses are still alive," replied Arielle miserably.

"What are you saying?" queried Majid, slightly confused.

"When Obsidian came back from Melbourne, his colic became progressively worse and the horse had to be put down. As far as anyone on the property was concerned, it was my pet horse, Obsession, who died. Earlier today, I met with an accident."

"Are you all right?" interrupted Majid, immediately concerned.

237

"Let me finish, darling. Obsession's fall earlier today produced injuries so severe that the horse would never have walked again. He had to be put down." Arielle's voice was a mere whisper.

"I'm so sorry," said Majid, wondering nonetheless whether she had orchestrated his death as he had suggested the day before, or if it has been truly a fluke. As if reading his mind, Arielle was quick to add that it had been a most unfortunate accident, with the stallion slipping as they'd jumped a creek, resulting in a broken foreleg.

"So now there is no evidence left at all..." murmured Majid.

"There isn't, except in the memories of those involved and those they shared it with," concurred Arielle sadly.

"I know this must be very painful for you, honey, losing your best friend in such a manner, but I'm sure you can see how it's the best outcome of all."

"That's what I'm told. It feels wrong though. The whole thing is wrong. I'm just so tired."

"I can see how upsetting the day was. Try to get some sleep, darling. At least nothing can come lurking out of the shadows. It's over and I'll soon be by your side," he said reassuringly.

"I can't wait."

"Sleep well."

"I'll be dreaming of you."

Majid hung up the phone, deeply worried. Arielle had sounded not only tired but dejected as if her spirit had been crushed. He hoped it hadn't been buried in that faraway creek alongside her horse.

CHAPTER XIV

Frustrated by his lack of progress, Detective Zack Summers decided to go back to the very beginning of the investigation. Small details kept him up at night and he knew from experience that sometimes overlooking those question marks proved to be the downfall of successful forensics. With Stefano's mobile number in hand, the police had requested from Telstra a list of all incoming and outgoing calls for the two weeks preceding the murders at Pandora Estates. It took a few hours of careful checking to eliminate most calls. However, he soon discovered two calls, made two days apart to a name that sounded familiar. Going though his report, he was only mildly surprised to discover that the other party was none other than Dante Alberti. Checking the latter's rap sheet didn't take long. Even though, thanks to fancy legal tap dancing, Dante Alberti had never done a stint in jail due to lack of concrete evidence in a number of cases involving prostitution rings, drug running and weapons possession, the man's résumé clearly showed his involvement with the various gangs running Kings Cross' underworld. In order to debunk the man's earlier excuse that the car he had rented had been stolen on the street while his own car was in the shop for service, Zack sent his constables around to every smash repairer within a 10-kilometre radius from Alberti's address. Within hours, auto mechanic, Gigi Vollo, admitted he had owed Dante a favour, and that there had been nothing wrong with the BMW he had been requested to warehouse for a 24-hour period.

Dante had not expected the police to come back and further probe his alibi: his moral debt had been repaid. Until he saw Zack knocking on his door, he hadn't yet connected the previous week's headlines at Pandora Estates with Joe Guarini. After all, he had left the man with a detailed map to find his way to Chantilly Farms. He had not heard from him since, a clear indication, in his mind, that all had gone to plan. When the police had initially found the car, they hadn't volunteered anything about Guarini's whereabouts. Dante had presumed the man had just ditched the car after his confrontation with Will LaSalle, a move he had thought judicious at the time, since he would have done exactly the same thing.

"Detective," he said with as much joviality as he could muster, opening his door. "Have you found out who stole the rental car? Not that it matters really as my insurance covered it."

"We did," confirmed Zack, not elaborating. "What has me confused though is why you would have lied to us."

"Lied about what?" queried Dante, calmly knowing that volunteering anything to the police was akin to signing your own arrest warrant.

"The car was found in the possession of a man by the name of Joe Guarini," said Zack, showing him the CCTV camera shot of Guarini driving the car to the Hunter Valley.

"I've no idea who this Guarini character is. Should I?" bluffed Dante, glancing quickly at the photograph and inwardly pestering at the stupidity of the man for not even attempting to disguise his identity: surely they had CCTV cameras in Corsica!

"Unfortunately for your little cover story," pursued Zack, undeterred, "we also unearthed phone records that show you made a long-distance call to this same Joe Guarini approximately 10 days ago."

Dante shrugged.

"Moreover, that particular phone call followed another call you received from a man by the name of Stefano Cavalieri. I wonder what the conversation was all about."

"Stefano Cavalieri, you said? Oh yes, I vaguely recall a chat about the old country. Apparently our fathers had come from the same village back in Italy. He'd come across my name in his late father's belongings. He wanted to know if I had met the old man."

"Why would he be interested in that?"

"I've no idea. You'd need to ask him. I've never met the man or his father. Perhaps he's putting together some autobiography," he suggested. "I didn't ask. For one, I'm not really fussed about the past. I don't usually reminisce; most things are better left alone."

"Why would you then call this Joe Guarini whom you pretend to have never met?"

"Pure coincidence, I'm afraid," replied Dante quickly. "A cousin of mine met a man by that name last summer when holidaying in the South of France. They sympathised. Joe wanted to come and visit. He was scheduled to fly in last month. Unfortunately, my cousin is currently a guest of the state. Last time I paid him a visit at Silverwater Correctional Facility he asked me as a favour to call his friend, Joe, and let him know he'd be unavailable for a while. That's all."

"So that's your story? You received a call from a man you've never met. Coincidentally, but shortly thereafter, you placed a long-distance phone call to yet another man you've never met, who, regardless of the contents of that particular conversation, flies nonetheless to Australia two days later, no longer with the intent to vacation, but with murder in mind. It's again pure coincidence that he drives to the Hunter Valley in a stolen car, which happened to have been rented by you the day before his arrival in the country. Did I get that right?"

Dante thought it more prudent not to reply.

"You do know we recovered a gun at the shooting site, don't you?" continued Zack.

"Again, Detective, I ask you, what does it have to do with me?"

"I wonder how long it'd take us to compare the ballistic report to other crimes."

"Detective, you look like a smart man. If you could tie the gun found at the scene to former crimes and pin those crimes on me, I'd already be in handcuffs. My guess is that the gun was clean and you can't trace it back to me, or to anyone else for that matter, as much as you'd like to do so," said Dante, an ironic smile floating on his thin lips.

"I'm sure that you supplied Guarini with the gun, along with the car and the local map."

"If you could prove it, you wouldn't be here. It sounds to me like you don't have any proof and your theories are nothing but blow flies buzzing in the wind. Now, if you don't mind, Detective, I've things to do."

Frustrated, Zack knew there was nothing much else he could do for the time being. He'd always trusted his gut feeling and his instincts told him that Guarini had found his way to LaSalle's door thanks to Dante acting as an intermediary. However, lest he found footage that showed Guarini and Dante together at any point during that morning, without direct admission of guilt, this particular line of inquiry had just hit a dead end.

"Don't leave town. I'll be back."

"Doesn't sound quite as threatening a line as Schwarzenegger's, but don't worry, Detective, my conscience is clear. I'm not going anywhere. Good day."

On his drive back to the Hunter Valley, Zack Summers reviewed the facts at hand. He no longer had any lingering doubt that Stefano Cavalieri was responsible for bringing Joe Guarini to Australia thanks to Dante Alberti's connections abroad. Joe Guarini was the instrument through whom he had intended the elimination of his fiercest competition. Guillaume and Stefano, however, had been neighbours and rivals for over three decades. Why would the latter all of a sudden decide he could no longer tolerate Guillaume in his backyard? Zack didn't believe their fight over the purchase of Apple Orchards enough a motivation, even though he understood the vital need for adding further real estate to their current holdings. Indisputably, and at the very core, what the two men had in common were racehorses. The entire saga only made sense if Guillaume knew something so incredibly sensitive about Stefano's business as to have the capacity to compromise the latter's operations. There was no other explanation to anyone's actions but the necessity to protect a secret. Obviously, it was a secret worth killing for.

Regardless of his friendship with Guillaume, Zack knew the man would never talk unless he forced his hand. However, Stefano had intimated that Trent Winning's last words referred to Guillaume's champion. Outside of winning the Melbourne Cup, Zack couldn't imagine what else could make the horse so exceptional as to become a man's dying words. Since he had no other leads, he was left with little choice than go back to Chantilly Farms and examine the horse in question. He hoped he wouldn't have to go to the stewards to check whether anyone had noticed anything abnormal about the thoroughbred. He doubted that if doping of any kind had been involved, there would be any trace left in the animal's system two weeks later. Stefano had banked on his Melbourne win to purchase Apple Orchards. His plans had come to naught ahead of the barn fire. He would have put the blame squarely on his studmaster who would have cast doubts on Obsidian's ability to win. Blame shifting was nothing new. Perhaps speaking the horse's name in his dying breath had just been remorse over losing the fabled race. Both trainer and owner had been quite vocal over Josephine's chances. It was hard to tell. Moreover, he did not put it past Stefano to send him on another wild-goose chase. However, in order to close the case and make sure that Guillaume's life was no longer threatened, no stone could be left unturned.

★ ★

After Majid's phone call, Arielle had little choice but to share his revelations with her father. She briskly walked into his office where Guillaume was busy issuing the week's pay slips.

"Papa, sorry to bother you but we need to talk."

"Can't this wait? I'm in the middle of payroll."

"I don't believe it can," replied Arielle, sitting down across his desk, littered with paperwork.

Resigned, Guillaume put down his pen and looked up at his daughter. For the next 10 minutes he listened to what had just transpired between Majid and his father-in-law.

"Throughout history, the bravest of men have come undone when love interferes," he said philosophically, his shoulders crumpling under the weight of the disclosure.

"I agree," said Arielle, defending her actions. "If Majid hadn't asked for a divorce in order to be with me, his father-in-law wouldn't have tried to destroy us. Except that we hold the trump card, not him. That's what I came in to talk to you about."

"I don't follow you," replied Guillaume, bewildered.

"You do remember a few weeks back that Nate didn't seem to come around as much and when he did, he always appeared fretful and preoccupied?"

"I thought nothing of it. I thought it was just a lovers' quarrel and since it was none of my business, I didn't ask."

"We didn't have a fight," explained Arielle. "Nate had become obsessed with Napoleon's pedigree and could talk of nothing else. I had become rather bored by it."

"Surely he didn't question his bloodline?" queried Guillaume, suddenly interested.

"No, he didn't, but he did question that of his progeny."

"What about it?"

"Surely you'd heard the rumours that the fabled stud had unsuccessfully settled during the entire first season?"

"It often happens. Animals, like humans, need time to adapt to new environments and that's particularly true of overseas horses. However, he clearly demonstrated in the following year that there was nothing wrong with him."

"Except that Nate was able to prove that the horse was shooting blanks. To make a long story short, Nate discovered that Trent Winnings had artificially inseminated the mares himself under the cover of night and…"

Guillaume interrupted her.

"But all the yearlings were tested, their bloodlines confirmed and subsequently registered. Surely you're mistaken."

"Trent used frozen sperm. Unless the laws have changed, it's illegal in our country. He had the frozen sperm shipped in from the original buyer to cover his tracks."

Understanding illuminated Guillaume's features and he finished her sentence for her. "... and the original seller of the horse was Sheikh Rashid!" he exclaimed.

"I asked Majid to try and figure out what had happened and he confirmed it. Rashid admitted that as a matter of policy he always froze some of his stud's sperm as insurance. He also boasted that in connivance with Trent, they had jacked up the initial purchase price of Napoleon and pocketed the difference. In all likelihood, when Trent realised the stud wouldn't settle, he must have panicked and asked his former accomplice for help. It wouldn't have been good for either party if the word got out that one of the most expensive studs ever purchased couldn't reproduce, and Rashid simply shipped him the required sperm. After the second season, when the stud, as we know, sired a great many colts and fillies that have turned out to be promising runners, his performance compensated for his original outlay. After the foaling season, Trent brought about the horse's demise so his treachery could never be discovered. It was by accident when Nate carried out the autopsy that he noticed something not quite right with the DNA sequence. To my understanding, using frozen sperm provokes slight changes in the composition of the helix," finished Arielle haltingly.

"And you never thought to share this information with me?" queried Guillaume, both baffled by the explanation and irritated that Arielle had kept it a secret.

"In my book, what Trent was up to was none of my business," shrugged Arielle. "I may have leaked it to the stewards if by chance we had lost against one of the horses sired by Napoleon, provided that the loss had catastrophically impacted on our financial health."

"But at the Melbourne Cup you ran against Josephine, Walkabout and a handful of others!"

"True and it's exactly why Nate agreed to the substitution in the first place. According to his moral compass, the subterfuge was the lesser of two evils. Messing with a horse's DNA and provenance are in his book the worst type of cheating possible."

Guillaume nodded. "I guess I'd agree with him," he added pensively. "So now we have a quid-pro-quo. Rashid knows who I am and there is no doubt he'd want to use it as leverage for you to back out of your marriage to Majid. As far as we can ascertain, he does not know about Melbourne and he does not suspect we know about Napoleon. All isn't lost after all."

Guillaume absent-mindedly tapped his fingers on his desk, looking out the window, forgetting his daughter's presence until she called him back to reality.

"What's on your mind, Papa?"

"I was just wondering if Stefano knows about it," he elucidated. "Perhaps that's why he didn't fight harder to get Apple Orchards. He might have been scared that if I were pushed too far, I would expose him as a fraud."

Alarmed, Arielle voiced out loud her father's real worries.

"Do you think that Stefano is the one who hired Joe Guarini? That he did so in order to silence you? If he was aware of what his studmaster was up to, and Trent revealed that Nate knew all about it, he would have concluded Nate spoke to me and in turn I would have shared it with you."

Horrified, Arielle closed her eyes. They both agreed that it was certainly a very good motive to conspire to kill. Father and daughter were about to elaborate on their theories when Sarah knocked on the door. Without waiting for a reply she opened it slightly, announcing that Zack Summers was standing in the foyer, waiting to speak with them. As far as the pair were concerned, his timing couldn't have been worse. Guillaume nonetheless indicated to his wife that the detective should be let in.

"It's becoming a habit," said Guillaume, firmly shaking Zack's hand. Arielle smiled sweetly at the detective and beckoned him to take a seat on the leather lounge across from the glass coffee table.

"I wanted to share with you my latest findings," explained Zack. "I hope I didn't catch you at a bad time?" he questioned, looking from daughter to father.

"Just discussing business matters," replied Guillaume evasively.

246

"This morning, I had an interesting chat with a man down in Sydney. The car Guarini used was rented in his name. He had reported it stolen. However, his story was inconsistent with the facts. Indeed, he had rented the car from the airport the night before Guarini landed, allegedly because his own car was in for repairs. Yet the garage owner admitted he had warehoused the car just as a matter of courtesy since it didn't need any work. With his line of work, Dante isn't someone you easily say no to. Requisitioned CCTV cameras footage at the airport though couldn't provide anything helpful. Dante was the only passenger in the car when he left the parking lot. We have also subpoenaed Dante's phone records and there is clear evidence that he called Guarini overseas and had a long conversation with Stefano beforehand. Which I guess brings me to the purpose of my visit."

Arielle and Guillaume held their breath, their eyes riveted on the detective.

"It appears that Stefano is directly responsible for bringing Joe Guarini here. What I can't understand is why he'd want you dead. In my last interview with him he also shared Trent Winnings' alleged dying words to him."

Zack looked down at his notes in order to quote accurately.

"According to him, Trent's last words were that Stefano should have a "close look at Obsidian"."

Arielle winced. Guillaume forced his face into a blank, unreadable mask. Zack didn't notice either change of expression.

"Now," continued the detective, looking up from his pad, "I can't think of why a dying man would say something like that unless there was something not quite kosher with the horse in question. Was there?"

"I'm not sure what you're getting at and I don't care for the insinuations," replied Guillaume, his eyes cold. "Zack, I'm sure you realise that all the horses are checked before a race, don't you?"

"Would the stewards check the horses for any doping?" pursued Zack without looking Guillaume in the eye.

"They do, especially if they have reason to."

"And if they don't?"

"Doped up horses behave differently. They are always tell-tale signs," replied Guillaume icily.

"So you'd have no idea why Trent Winnings told his boss to look closely at your horse?"

"Absolutely none. Now if you would excuse us, we need to get back to work," replied Guillaume dismissively.

"You won't mind if I go and check Obsidian out for myself, do you?" insisted the detective.

"As a matter of fact, I do. The horse is no longer part of my stable."

Completely taken aback, Zack stared at Guillaume. It was the last thing he had expected.

"We had to put him down," explained Guillaume patiently. "Arielle had an accident yesterday whilst riding. The horse broke his foreleg. And I'll spare you the details, but Nate had to be called in. The animal was in agony and in the case of open wounds due to protruding bones, not only would the horse have never raced again, but it would have never mended either."

Zack looked from Guillaume to Arielle. A tear shone in the latter's eyes.

"I'm sorry," he stammered, still under shock.

"So are we," concluded Guillaume. "It was the most promising thoroughbred I've had the honour to train in a very long while. It's a devastating loss for Chantilly Farms and the world of racing in general," he added somewhat pompously. "Had you come by two days earlier, you could have checked him out to your heart's content. I have a question before you go though. Why would Stefano want me dead after all these years? He could have done it at any time."

"It's the same question I've asked myself over and over again," replied Zack candidly. "I'm fairly certain Stefano is behind all of this. Perhaps your Melbourne Cup win was the icing on a cake of resentment and jealousy built up over a long period of time. We know his finances were stretched thin and he needed that race to make a bid for Apple Orchards. Unless, of course, you have another theory you'd care to share with me?"

"Perhaps," replied Guillaume mysteriously, "but the timing isn't quite right as of yet. So what's going to happen to Stefano now? Do you have enough proof? Will he be arrested for conspiring to commit murder?"

"We're getting close. I'll let you know. Don't let your guard down until he's behind bars. Good day. And I'm truly sorry for your loss: it was a great horse indeed."

The detective nodded to both of them and left the room. Father and daughter breathed a long sigh of relief.

"So, Papa, you really do have a theory?" questioned Arielle in jest once the detective's car billowed out of the driveway.

"Well, Zack's visit confirmed a few things. What I believe may have happened is that Stefano believed I knew about Trent's falsification of the blood stock. He was afraid I'd talk at some point or another. Stefano is the type of man who keeps his hands clean. He must have learned in childhood that it's always best to leave other men to do his dirty work so nothing can ever be traced back to him. Somehow he got to Guarini. He tapped into the man's insatiable desire for revenge. However, it all went pear-shape. When Zack confronted him with the phone evidence, he tried to divert attention back to me with Obsidian..."

"The only way he'd have known anything about Obsidian and the subterfuge would be if Pat divulged the secret to his friend, Trent. In my opinion he could have only done so on the night of the rape." Her eyes clouded at the recollection but bravely she continued on. "It'd make sense that he presented it as an excuse for his unconscionable actions: in his mind, I must have owed him for his part in our little charade. In a sort of macho-male-bonding reciprocity moment, Trent may have confessed in return what he did with Napoleon. After the shootings, in his last breath and with nothing to lose, to redeem himself and even out the field, he gave Stefano the secret he had learned minutes before."

Guillaume tugged at his chin, deep in thought.

"It makes perfect sense. However, if you're right and that's the way it played out, the timing is still off. When Stefano contacted Guarini he didn't know any of this. He didn't yet know his studmaster had cheated the system, nor could he have known how we won the race. Guarini was already here when both Trent and Patrick died, after spilling their secrets to each other. So I'd now have to agree with Zack. Stefano wanted me eliminated well before he could even play at blackmail. I had no idea he hated me so deeply. It's rather disturbing."

"It's true that with you out of the way, by default, Pandora Estates undoubtedly becomes the best breeding farm in New South Wales. Without you as one of the most successful and reputed trainers around, he takes his place on the podium. You can't eliminate jealousy and envy as powerful motives. His purchase of Napoleon was well beyond his means: everyone knows it. It was a matter of pride. He lost face when the stud didn't settle for the entire first season. He was probably at the end of his tether. You know what a cornered man is capable of doing. Guarini was probably the answer to his prayers."

"I'd buy your version of events as well. I'm rather proud to have such a level-headed daughter capable of such sensible analysis! Now, we'll just have to wait and see how it plays out with Stefano on one side, and Rashid on the other. I hope we can survive this, literally. I hope that a truce can be reached, however tainted, for the sake of the sport. The scandal would place the sport in complete disrepute and I can't deny we've played a large part in that."

"Rashid will make his move soon. It's only a matter of a few short weeks before his daughter's divorce is final; he'll play his hand before that."

"God have mercy on our souls."

It didn't take long for their ghosts to come looking for them.

CHAPTER XV

Rashid knew that information was power and that he could leverage secrets to his advantage. For two days he pondered how to best use his daughter's revelations against Guillaume, whom he held responsible for her current situation, and by extension his future social disgrace. As Hamdam's contemporary, but with none of his breeding, Rashid had always regarded the man as a rival: the latter apparently excelled in all the fields men like them were judged by. Hamdam had been blessed with successful marriages: his first wife bore him the sons to continue his lineage; the second was not only a beauty who continued to turn heads wherever she went but her fashion label was now reputed worldwide. The third had added to his brood, and the fourth, with her uncanny aptitude for languages, had proved to be an infallible business ally, filling his golden years with youth and merriment beside. Hamdam's ancestral ties with the ruling class had paved the way to a blissful, strife-free life. His home was regarded as one of the most beautiful in Dubai. His numerous real-estate holdings abroad were often featured in architectural magazines, cited for their daring undertakings. His stable was heralded as one of the best in the world. Even his camels were profitable. By tarnishing Guillaume's reputation and letting his 40-year-strong friendship to Hamdam slip to the tabloids, he could finally hurt him by association. It would be a pleasure to watch him squirm. He'd make sure to recall Arielle's stint in the UAE, when she had raced for him as the first female jockey to run their courses, hopefully tainting Hamdam's former accomplishments. To expose father and daughter as world-class cheats would undoubtedly cast a net of malevolent gossip around the man he had never managed to beat at anything. Revenge would be sweet. He rubbed his hands in delight.

For 10 days straight, Rashid called in every favour from everyone he knew to turn up any kind of impropriety which could have incurred during the Melbourne Cup. Yet every report had come back negative. There had not been a hint of suspicion, a whiff of scandal or a rumour he could build upon. Well aware that his daughter's disclosure was hearsay at best, he bemoaned the possibility that in her eagerness to discredit her rival she could have misunderstood. Frustrated, Rashid finally came to the conclusion that facing Guillaume, man to man, was the only option. In less than a fortnight, Majid would pronounce the third and last talaq. Within hours the whole of Dubai would know what had occurred: he couldn't bear the public disgrace.

After debating exactly what he would say to the man he had never met but whose daughter was upsetting his carefully manicured image, Rashid picked up the phone and dialled the overseas number. Chantilly Farms' number was a matter of public record. It rang interminably and Rashid, annoyed by the contretemps, was about to hang up when a halting voice came to the phone.

"Hello?"

"May I speak to Guillaume de la Selle?" requested the heavily accented Middle-Eastern voice.

Guillaume held his breath. The man had called him by his real name. The voice knew who he was. The man must be somehow connected to Joe Guarini and from his accent was undoubtedly a foreigner. Zack had warned him it wasn't yet over. Guillaume tried to bluff.

"There is no Guillaume here. You must have dialled this number in error."

"No, I'm fairly certain I have the correct number. The man I wish to speak to hides behind the name of Will LaSalle," he repeated, undeterred.

"Speaking," replied Guillaume in an assured voice, abruptly ending the cat-and-mouse game.

"You don't know me, but let's say that we have common interests," continued Rashid unhurriedly, sure to hold all the cards.

"What could those possibly be?" queried Guillaume, his tone frosty.

"We both have daughters. I'm sure we both want what's best for our daughters. I'm sure you wouldn't want to see yours in jail, for example, the same as I wouldn't want to watch mine die of a broken heart."

"I'm not following you," replied Guillaume through clenched teeth, sweat moistening his eyebrows, his fist wrapped tight around the handset.

"Oh yes you do!" quipped the man. "You're playing at being obtuse. And by the way, congratulations on your Melbourne Cup win! What a masterful play!"

"Now you've lost me," said Guillaume, anger unwittingly rising in his tone. "Since you haven't identified yourself nor yet stated the purpose for this inane call, I will terminate this conversation. Goodbye!"

"No, you won't!" The voice was sharp and commanding. "I know you switched horses. I don't know how you did it but you did it. I can make a great deal of trouble for you and your daughter, regardless, just by launching accusations. She'll come under investigation and will most likely end up in jail. Your reputation will be shot. You'll both lose your license," intimated the man.

"What do you want? Who are you?"

"That's the real question, isn't it?' said Rashid, enjoying the other man's discomfort. "I see you can't even be bothered denying my allegations!"

"It's so preposterous that I won't dignify them with an answer nor bother to refute them. What's the use? You make allegations, you threaten me, but still I don't know who you are and what it is you want."

Guillaume's tone was now so calm and so controlled that Rashid, not expecting him to recover so quickly, vacillated in his certitudes.

253

"My name is Sheik Rashid Al …… I've done my research and hold it on good authority that you were once known as Guillaume de la Selle."

"I've nothing to hide," interrupted Guillaume. "And why should your name mean anything to me?"

"Majid is my son-in-law."

"Hamdam's young friend, of course!"

The penny had just dropped and Guillaume, relieved, broke into a fit of laughter. Thrown by the unexpected reaction, Rashid hesitated.

"So let me recall the situation here," said Guillaume as soon as he could talk. "You call me out of the blue. You call me by a name which I haven't heard spoken in decades. You accuse me of cheating in one of the most scrutinised races in the world, by switching horses no less, and you threaten to expose me. Then you finish by telling me you're Majid's father-in-law, as if it would constitute an explanation on its own. So what is this? A shakedown to order my daughter to stop seeing your daughter's husband?" jeered Guillaume. "Did I understand this correctly?"

Rashid was shaken. It wasn't at all how he had envisioned the conversation evolving. The man on the other end of the phone did not sound like a man easily bullied. His tone mocked him like a man without blight on his conscience. Had Assa, in her fear and jealousy, fabricated the entire conversation between her husband and his lover? Her English after all was less than stellar, but did she really have the intellect to formulate such an elaborate lie?

"Your daughter has no business marrying an Arab," retorted Rashid, unable to think of a clever reply to Guillaume's diatribe.

"It's her life. In this country, women do as they please," replied Guillaume, giving nothing away.

"Majid is divorcing my daughter to marry yours."

"I'm sorry Sheik… I'm afraid I didn't catch your name properly. Rashid was it? It might be a problem for you but I assure you, it's no concern of mine."

"I'm warning you. Keep her away from him. Even if you deny you rigged the race, I don't have to prove it. I only have to start rumours. And you know how nefarious those can be!" exploded Rashid.

"You can't do that," muttered Guillaume, his temper at boiling point.

"So we have an understanding?"

"Let me think it over," said Guillaume in an apparent volte-face. "Where can I contact you?"

Rashid, immensely relieved, rattled off his number without thinking.

"Give me a few days," insisted Guillaume.

"You have until Friday week at sundown," replied Rashid, now in control again.

After hanging up the phone, he rubbed his hands in satisfaction. On the other side of the world, Guillaume looked pensively across the eucalypt-peppered lawn. So Rashid somehow knew who he was and what he had done, except the man apparently didn't know his knowledge of Napoleon's record. Guillaume was still left with room to manoeuvre. Arielle's interruption was timely.

"How would Rashid know who I am?" queried Guillaume as soon as she entered his office, the door closing softly behind her.

"Rashid? As in Napoleon's seller?" asked Arielle, astonished.

"As in Majid's father-in-law."

"What?" asked Arielle, incredulous. "You've got to be kidding!"

"I'm afraid not. Was Majid your overseas source when you tried to help Nathan figure out what was wrong with Josephine's DNA?"

Arielle's cheeks coloured.

"I didn't know who else to ask. He knows absolutely everyone. I was sure he could ferret out something useful, but he never mentioned he knew the seller so intimately. No wonder he came back with answers so quickly!"

"What else did you discuss with him?" asked Guillaume, plainly irritated.

"I don't have any secrets from him."

"Really, Arielle? How could you be so naïve? Majid knows everything? It wasn't yours to share! It implicates all of us!" Guillaume's irritation had turned to anger. "Does he know who I am and what happened on Melbourne Cup Day?"

Visibly shaken by the verbal assault, Arielle looked down at her feet.

"Let me explain," she said.

"How old are you, really? Why would you be so eager to share secrets with your lover, secrets which could disseminate us? Unbelievable!" barked Guillaume.

"I didn't want to build our life on lies. Rashid had already told Majid he knew who you were. He'd had you investigated. Majid wanted me to know he didn't care about your past. It seemed like a good time to tell him everything. But I'm sure he wouldn't have told a soul. It would be counterproductive to his aim."

"Which is what?"

"Haven't you been listening, Papa? He wants to marry me and I him."

"I did listen, but until he has formally proposed, I don't know a thing. Meanwhile, could he have told his wife?"

"To what purpose? To rubbish the woman he intends to spend his life with? It makes no sense at all!" cried Arielle.

"From where I stand though, that's exactly what happened. And his wife went on to tell her father. The loop is complete," added Guillaume, resigned.

"What happened exactly?"

Guillaume recounted his earlier conversation and Rashid's ultimatum. Arielle paled and her legs buckled. She leaned on her father's bureau for support. She fished her phone out of her blazer's pocket.

"I'll call him now."

Right in front of her father, Arielle exposed her dilemma.

"I'll get to the bottom of it," said Majid, livid after listening to his lover's story.

Minutes later he knocked on his wife's bedroom door.

256

"Assa, may I speak with you?" he asked through the panelled door, waiting for her reply.

After days of watching her husband shy away from her, Assa was eager to invite him in.

"What can I do for you?" she asked sweetly with a beaming smile.

"Do you listen to all my conversations?" questioned Majid crossly.

"I don't know what you're talking about," stammered Assa, taken aback by his aggressive tone.

"But you'd do anything to save our so-called marriage, wouldn't you?" accused Majid. Assa lowered her gaze, her cheeks burning.

"I don't know what you're referring to," repeated Assa shamefully.

"You listened in during my private conversations with Arielle and somehow felt it was appropriate to repeat what you heard to your father," accused Majid.

Tears began rolling down her cheeks. During their entire union, Majid had never raised his voice at her, not even once.

"I'm sorry," she murmured through her tears.

"Did you think that somehow by repeating overheard conversations you could make me back out of my decision?"

Sniffles answered him.

"What did you tell him exactly?"

"That Arielle won the race by cheating."

"Can you repeat that in English?"

As hard as she tried, Assa couldn't find the words.

"I repeat then. Are you sure this is what you heard?"

Distraught, Assa shook her head vehemently from side to side. Looking down at his wife, sitting on the floor, Majid shrugged his disgust and said, with pity and disdain evident in his eyes, "You're destroying lives by spreading lies. I didn't think you could ever stoop so low. Your actions disgust me. You've disappointed me for the first time in our lives together. I'm sorry it has come to this but I've nothing left to say to you."

With these parting words, Majid slammed the bedroom door, leaving Assa inconsolable. The fear of an uncertain future had led her to actions she had not thought she could be capable of, turning against her the only man who had ever treated her with kindness and respect. They couldn't part on that note. She could never live with herself. She wondered what her father had done with the information. Obviously he had already used it against Majid. She had to make things right, but for the time being the solution escaped her.

Soon thereafter, Arielle received Majid's text message, confirming that Guillaume's suspicions had been right. Assa had hidden behind closed doors to listen in on his conversations, and had repeated to her father what she had so indiscreetly overheard. Arielle immediately confronted her father with the unfathomable truth.

"You have less than a week to call Rashid back. What are you going to do?" she asked sheepishly. "I can't build my happiness on the demise of my family. I'll break up with Majid," she added, her voice breaking as she said it. She continued bravely nonetheless. "Rashid has no reason to make good on his threat if Majid doesn't go ahead with the divorce. He'll stay with her if I disappear from the picture. He has no reason to divorce his wife otherwise."

Guillaume interrupted her somewhat rudely. "So you're now willing to cast yourself as a martyr, is that it?"

"Martyr? No, why?" asked Arielle, surprised by the question.

"You jeopardised your future by helping me with Obsidian when he was not deemed fit to run. You sacrificed your horse to destroy evidence and now you offer to throw away your life to prevent me from losing my reputation? What kind of a man do you think I am? What type of father would I be if I let you consider this for a minute longer? I'm sure there is a solution somewhere and, trust me, we'll find it. As a matter of fact, I've six days to do so."

Grateful, Arielle looked up at her father, her eyes brimming with love. "Will you let me know when you do? I'd like to help. If you don't succeed, I'll lose either way."

"Not all is lost, at least not until the fat lady sings," stated Guillaume. "Now leave me alone. I need to think."

After blowing him a kiss, Arielle exited silently. She couldn't blame Assa for what she had done and understood her motivations. In similar circumstances she wouldn't have acted very differently.

Eighteen months prior, during a three-day stint in a private Clinique in London, well away from prying eyes, the battery of medical tests revealed that Hamdam had developed a tumour near his spine. Unbeknown to his wives and children, under the guise of lengthy overseas business matters, he had been operated on. The tumour had been malignant. Despite the best treatment and further radiation, the tumour had come back, soon followed by another. Only 12 months later, the cancer had metastasised in most of his bones.

After the catastrophic diagnosis, Hamdam had spent the first three months divesting his assets as quietly as possible. The medical findings had been all the more surprising that he had not suffered from any palpable symptoms except for an overwhelming sense of fatigue and a lumbar pain which stabbed him at the most incongruous of times. Quietly, he had converted his massive overseas portfolio of real estate and investments into cash. He had engineered for his assets to be equally split between his four wives and for his eight children to receive a healthy trust fund. He had no intention of his family quibbling over money or being burdened unravelling his complicated holdings. Furthermore, he had no wish for them to live in his shadow once he was gone. With a cash inheritance, they wouldn't have to hold on to the past and could move on to fulfil their own destinies. He had been the happiest of men and he was determined for his legacy to be one without encumbrance.

He had shared his predicament with Guillaume alone. Part of his last wishes had been to travel to Australia and see his friend one more time before he was too ill to make the long journey. The Frenchman had been devastated by the news and the two men had discussed the future. Sensing his friend's end near and without anything to lose, Guillaume finally disclosed the events of the past few weeks, leaving nothing out. While Hamdam's moral compass had prevented him from ever engaging in such duplicity, he had been the first to admit that in his business deals he had often been uncompromising and used everything in his power to reach the end goal. It was not up to him to judge the Frenchman's actions: it would be a matter between him and his God. The spectre of financial ruin was one he'd never had to contemplate and he understood Guillaume's position. On the other hand, he knew Rashid's to be unconscionable at best.

"Inch Allah. How extraordinary that you should call me when I was poised to dial your number," stated Guillaume. "How are you? How is the pain?"

"As good as can be expected," replied Hamdam softly, "but you, my friend, are in trouble."

Guillaume frowned.

"What have you heard?" he questioned.

"That Rashid is intent on blackmail," replied Hamdam, uncharacteristically coming to the point.

Guillaume's voice dropped to a mere whisper.

"Bad news travels as fast as the desert sands. Rashid asked me minutes ago to choose between his daughter and mine."

"I see," said Hamdam pensively.

"There is something he doesn't know though."

Hamdam was all ears. For the next 15 minutes, Guillaume told the Arab everything that had transpired regarding Napoleon's sale and his lack of performance.

Hamdam did not let him finish. "Then we have a solution to your problem," he stated enthusiastically. Guillaume listened attentively. After exposing his plan, Hamdam concluded happily, "I love Arielle like a daughter and Majid like a son. In his infinite wisdom, Allah has provided the path for them to be reunited, even if that path involved treachery."

"I'm so sorry, my friend. I never wanted to be in the position of disappointing you. Trust me, I had no other option."

"I'm certain you didn't believe there was another choice. You don't need my forgiveness. It isn't for me to judge: it's between you and your conscience. Meanwhile, I have every reason to believe our little plan has every chance of succeeding."

"You don't have to do this," choked Guillaume, his words filled with gratitude.

"My days are counted. My sole wish is to part from this world knowing I've done everything in my power to help those who mean something to me. Promise me one thing, though?"

"Anything!"

"When this is over, we'll never speak of it again. You'll never compromise the sport of kings, ever. Regardless of the circumstances."

"It goes without saying," replied Guillaume humbly. "I'll better that: I swear never to bet on my own horses."

"It always seems to get you in trouble, my friend. You're not a betting man. You're an exceptional trainer and an excellent breeder. That should have been enough."

Guillaume assented.

"On another note, when Allah calls me to his side, please ask Latifah to give Arielle my wedding gift."

"Wedding?" interrupted Guillaume.

Hamdam laughed heartily. "Mark my words, my friend, Dubai will soon become your second home."

"I would have opposed it 10 years ago, but now I know better than to stand in her way!" said Guillaume with a smile.

"And one day, you'll become old and wise, just like me." Knowing their birthdays were celebrated in the same month of the same year, both men laughed, all tensions evaporated.

Stefano's headaches seemed to worsen by the minute. The detective had come back twice, each time with more questions, and, each time, those were getting closer and closer to the truth. He wondered what type of pressure had been applied to Dante Alberti to make him flip when Zack had not bought the story that they'd only previously discussed their fathers and the old country. Moreover, since the barn had apparently been destroyed in the course of criminal activity, his insurers had indefinitely postponed payment. Until the police concluded their investigation, all matters of compensation would be withheld. Finding a new studmaster had also proved quite difficult, with none of the applicants demonstrating nearly the same depth of experience as Trent had displayed. After three weeks of an Australia-wide search, he had finally coaxed a man with the right credentials to move down from the Northern Territories. Yet after the same man had spent his first Saturday night at the local pub and listened to the stories of how people were found inexplicably murdered on Stefano's farm, he had packed his bags and left without notice, running from the ongoing investigation. To add to his woes, Walkabout had underperformed in the Queensland races, going off his feed as soon as he had arrived. When his jockey, Rich Little, had been taken ill, hospitalised with kidney stones, Stefano had been ready to throw in the towel. His substitute jockey to run on Josephine's back at Eagle Farm had also proved a poor choice. Lastly, with Napoleon gone, he no longer had a champion to propose for stud for the mares in his care for the following season. Times were bleak.

The registered letter with the offer to purchase Josephine could not have come at a more fortuitous juncture. The offer was twice what he would have expected for the mare after a winning season. The overseas buyer though had requested anonymity and stated forcefully that time was of the essence: thus the horse wouldn't be able to participate in the Queensland races to the end of the season.

For the inconvenience, the buyer had offered a premium. Stefano had less than 24 hours to consider the bona fide offer. A wire transfer would seal the purchase and the horse would be shipped overseas shortly after that: the buyer's agent would come and collect the animal as soon as the transaction was approved. The final destination was not stated but Stefano was assured that the horse would no longer race and be used as a broodmare only. In his current circumstances, Stefano felt he had little choice, even though the unusual secrecy and unparalleled speed made him slightly nervous and somewhat suspicious. However, the mare's purchase would allow him to regain much-needed financial breathing room.

Since Majid remained part of Hamdam's intimate entourage, Assa, after her marriage, had been launched into Dubai's upper social circles, and come to befriend Latifah. Her own father would never have dreamed of introducing her to the same milieu, since in his conservative view a woman had no place being seen outside her home. Latifah, older by seven years, enjoyed the younger woman's unfettered beauty, her naive enthusiasm, her friendly and inconspicuous manners and her equanimity in most situations. They had first met at the launch of Majid's Arabian Nights and had immediately sympathised. Over a long lunch, followed by an afternoon at the spa, they had become fast friends. Over time, Assa had looked to Latifah for guidance and the latter had promptly adopted an older sister persona. She had been at Assa's side every time another round of IVF had failed, and dried her tears of despair. She had known her marriage to be in trouble since their customs required for her to produce children to cement the union, yet Majid had seemed relatively unconcerned. With Latifah's support, Assa had done her best to remain as relevant as possible in her husband's eyes, but there was no need. Majid had obviously enjoyed his wife's perfect manners, unassuming beauty, spendthrift habits, compassionate ways, culinary expertise, impeccable taste and easy lovemaking. When Majid had pronounced the first talaq Assa had naturally turned to Latifah for advice. The latter had listened empathetically to the sad recount, but her spirits had lifted when her friend had fingered Arielle as the "other" woman. She had done her best to hide her joy that the two lovers had finally worked out after all those years that they were indeed meant for each other. As sorry as she felt for her friend's disarray, she also knew that Assa wouldn't be able to save her marriage. No one could interfere with destiny, however painful it turned out to be.

After their last meeting, filled with regret when she observed in Majid's eyes the distance she had created, Assa had once again come sobbing on her friend's shoulder. They were both lying on Latifah's oversized day bed, across from each other. The older woman remained aghast at the unfolding drama. During the recount of her tale, Assa's eyes remained deliberately downcast, lest she saw the same look of disappointment she had witnessed on her husband's face hours earlier. When she finished, Latifah remained silent for a minute or two.

"How is your relationship with your father?" she finally asked.

"My father tolerates me. I believe the happiest day of his life was when he was finally rid of me when I married Majid. Growing up, he was harsh, controlling and demeaning, treating all women in his household with disdain. I came to hate his supercilious and arrogant manner. Until I met Majid, I thought all men of similar stature behaved likewise, only to realise I had been brought up by a chauvinistic bully who hid behind his religion to justify his actions."

The eloquent and quite accurate portrait rendered Latifah speechless. She cleared her throat.

"So darling, why did you go to him?"

"Because he is the only man I know vile enough to bury someone to save his social status," she admitted, tears rolling freely down her cheeks and silently absorbed by the soft cloth of the hijab casually draped over her neck and shoulders.

"Did you think that by besmirching Arielle's reputation you'd gain back Majid's heart?" Latifah was curious.

"I thought that if she was exposed as a liar and a cheat, Majid would reconsider..." she hesitated and Latifah finished her thought.

"... but you soon discovered that nothing you could do would change his mind. You fought for what was yours with the means at your disposal, and I can't blame you for it. I would have done the same. Majid is a special person. But so is Arielle."

It was Assa's turn to be astonished.

"Do you know her personally?" she queried, dumbfounded. It had not even occurred to her that her friend could have known her nemesis.

"I met Arielle years ago. As a matter of fact, she lived under our roof for a while. She is an extraordinary woman. I know you'll think me crazy for saying so, but you'd actually like her. You're very different from each other but you already have one thing in common: Majid. They were madly in love once."

Before she could further elaborate, Assa interrupted her softly.

"I know."

"You know?"

"A few years ago, while cleaning Majid's office, I came upon a leather-bound folder containing hundreds of poems which were never published. They spoke of star-crossed lovers. They spoke of a beautiful foreigner obsessed with horses. The purity of the love he described through his sonnets is something we never shared. Since it never came up in the interim years, I lived with my secret. When he flew back from Australia, I saw in his eyes that this greater love had come knocking once again. It's the will of Allah," she said in a voice so low, so filled with anguish and sadness Latifah had to lean over to hear her. "I now bow to it and I've resigned myself to accept it, even though it tears me apart. I have not come here for your pity though. I have come here to make things right," she added courageously. "And I need your help."

"How so?" queried Latifah, intrigued and admiring her friend for her resilience.

"It's my understanding that your husband knows Arielle's father quite well," she explained.

"For over 50 years."

"Then could you speak to him and explain my dilemma? I'm sure my father has probably already used the information I gave him so we might be too late to warn them. But perhaps there is something we can do to prevent him from inflicting more damage?"

"I'll speak to him."

"Thank you for not judging me a terrible person for what I've done. I love Majid with all my might, but it's clear his heart belongs to another. I can't stand in the way. I want him to be happy and not look down at me as the person who betrayed him. We had a happy marriage: that's what I want him to remember instead of the jealous wife who stabbed him in the back." She sniffled, her eyes clouding once again.

Latifah patted her friend on the shoulders and assured her everything would fall back into place. They hugged tightly and bade each other goodbye. Assa felt slightly more hopeful that she would now be able to right a terrible wrong. However, Latifah wondered whether Hamdam would listen: discovering his closest friend had betrayed the sport he held most dear might not incline him to help. She knew that, regardless of his feelings, he would warn Guillaume.

Reclining on their pillows later that night after making love, she told him the entire saga. Hamdam listened attentively, only asking for precisions from time to time. He did not otherwise comment.

The moon was already high when he placed the call. Asleep next to him, Latifah did not stir.

CHAPTER XVI

Hamdam's agent confirmed the next day that Stefano had accepted the deal. He'd be ready to pick up the mare the following morning and had already arranged for the horse to be transported from Sydney Airport to Dubai on the early afternoon flight. Stefano was shocked at the expediency of the whole transaction: no sooner had the money hit his account than John Delaney rung him to announce he would be at Pandora's gates no later than 10 that morning to pick up the horse. He required all the paperwork be also ready by then. As a favour he inquired whether he could also lay eyes on the famous stud Napoleon when he arrived at the property, but was informed the horse had been put down a few weeks prior after developing acute laminitis. When John had expressed his astonishment, Stefano had brushed off any further questions into the matter, answering gruffly that he had expected to get a lot more out of the stud than a mere two years, but that such was his lot. John was quick to relay the information to Josephine's buyer, thereby confirming what Hamdam already knew. There was no evidence left of Rashid and Trent's treachery except for a dozen offspring.

Following protocol, Nathan was there to assist with the horse's smooth transfer. The bill of sale would become nil and void if there was anything wrong with the horse prior to shipping it out. As the primary veterinary surgeon for the property, Nathan was required to sign all the necessary health certificates. He remitted them all under Stefano's watchful eye. What Stefano never noticed, however, was the additional envelope he had slipped inside the official documents folder. Nathan had taken it upon himself to warn whoever had bought the mare. In his opinion, they deserved to know that the horse had been the result of artificial insemination. Depending on its ultimate use abroad, hiding such facts from authorities could easily be construed as fraud. Anyone would be in their right mind to assume the primary vet would have been privy to the practice. That is why he had decided to include all the research he had conducted earlier, even though he had not reached any irrefutable conclusion. The envelope had been sealed and marked "Private: for your eyes only." Sotto voce, he quickly explained to the agent that the sealed documents were to be remitted directly to the new owner and should not, in any circumstances, be mixed up with the AQIS certificates. John did not raise an eyebrow and assured Nathan it would reach the intended recipient.

Less than 48 hours later, Josephine cantered in Hamdam's paddocks, adjusting to the sand-filled heat and the sticky humidity. She had travelled well and had sailed through the blood works performed on arrival. In possession of Nathan's research, which he had read attentively, Hamdam had subsequently contacted a London-based laboratory which had been regarded as the best in the field of genetic manipulation. While waiting for the mare to arrive at destination, he had also purchased two other horses previously sired by Napoleon, both under bona fide live coverage conditions. After subjecting them to similar tests as Josephine, he had dispatched the whole lot to England. The vials had been imprinted with numbers only. Napoleon's DNA was a matter of public record. He had requested the lots be compared to the stallion's genetic markers to ascertain whether they had all been sired under similar circumstances. He had demanded the results be faxed to him in the briefest delay, his cheque book insuring the analysis be fast tracked.

While waiting for the diagnostic which he hoped would cancel Rashid's attempt at blackmail once and for all, Hamdam summoned Majid to his side. To his younger friend he explained at length the plan concocted with Guillaume. Majid had been moved to tears.

"Let me get this straight. My soon-to-be ex-wife confided in yours. In itself that's quite extraordinary and, in my mind, goes a long way in absolving her for her earlier treason. But you, instead of loathing Guillaume and Arielle for what they have done, decided to help instead? I'm absolutely dumbfounded! I've always known you to be a man of great generosity, and this little plan of yours couldn't have come cheap, but I've also known you to be a man of principles. You've spent a great deal of your life fighting corruption in all its forms. I'd have thought you would have distanced yourself from this sordid affair as fast as the falcon flies."

Hamdam watched him attentively.

"Your words flatter me on many levels. Yet there is one thing you seem to forget. And it is the most important of all."

"I'm all ears."

"I'm also a sentimental man. I place friendship and love above all else. My friendship with Guillaume is irreplaceable. I don't condone what he has done, far from it. But those were his choices, not mine. After all, he hasn't killed anyone. He cheated at sport, like so many before him. It's despicable but it isn't for me to judge. If the situation was reversed, I know I could count on him. Moreover, no one would have enlisted my help if you hadn't been thrown into the mix. My friendship with you is as important to me as Arielle's happiness. Without her, I doubt I'd have achieved the same prominence in horseracing circles. She gave me my "start", so to speak. I owe it to her, and you and Guillaume."

His large eyes misting, his voice choked by emotion, Majid remained silent.

"But my reasons are not all together altruistic," pursued Hamdam, moved by Majid's intense display of emotions. "I also loathe men like your father-in-law. I apologise for my bluntness, Majid, but that is the honest truth. I agree with the Australian veterinary surgeon who trusted me with his research to date: men of Rashid's ilk, capable of perverting a horse's lineage by underhanded tactics, are a worst scourge on the sport than any other. He's well aware that frozen sperm is banned in many countries. He kept it for insurance and future financial gain. He hijacked the prize of the stud to begin with and collected a kickback. I abhor this sort of comportment in business beyond all else. Foreigners are wary of dealing with Middle Eastern men because of men like him who taint everything they touch. We need foreign investments to keep Dubai as the financial hub of our region. I consider burying men like him my civic duty, no less." Hamdam smiled contentedly, mischievousness deepening the crinkling around his eyes. Spontaneously Majid knelt at his feet and kissed his hands, embarrassing Hamdam, who had not expected it.

"There is no need for your display of gratitude, my son," said Hamdam. "I'm having fun."

"When should you receive confirmation of Josephine's tests?"

"Hopefully in a few hours. I hope the results will be ground-breaking. If we can actually determine beyond reasonable doubt that the DNA helix is actually damaged when frozen sperm is used, I'll use my influence to broadcast the results everywhere. Another loophole for unscrupulous breeders will be closed forever. That will be my contribution to the sport. Either that or it will be Guillaume's redemption. In any case, the scandal will finish Rashid."

Majid sighed.

"Something on your mind?"

"I only wish it could have come before Friday which is the deadline my father-in-law gave Guillaume."

"I'm well aware of the tight window. This is why I requested everything to be rushed, regardless of the cost. However, with the scientific world, always expect delays. If I were you I'd do everything in my power to postpone that deadline, just in case."

"My powers seem limited," replied Majid despondently.

"What Rashid fears most is for his daughter to be divorced and consequently for him to become the victim of public rumours. Assa has just shown her devotion to you when she asked Latifah to speak with me. Assa is the key. Either you'll manipulate her into thinking you will no longer pronounce the last talaq because you have had second thoughts, or you'll work together in making her father think he no longer has anything to fear because you're reconciling. But you need to buy time, just in case."

"I agree," said Majid. "I'll speak with Assa. We need a few more days for the truth to rise to the surface and be effective. Thank you for everything, Hamdam. You're like a father to me, but of much better counsel than my own," added Majid, his tone wistful. As the youngest son of a large brood, with his mother as the youngest of four wives, Majid had seen little of his own father over the years. Nearing Hamdam's age, the latter was now in poor health, voiding any hope Majid ever had of a close relationship with the man. Majid bowed his head deferentially, and exited quickly, leaving Hamdam sitting on the oversized chair behind his desk, his thoughtful gaze following him out.

Having left Hamdam's house, Majid drove to the beach where he sat at the wheel of his car, contemplating the rays of the incandescent sun bouncing off the barely rippling waters. Deceiving Assa repulsed him but his choices were limited. From his conversation with Hamdam it seemed unlikely that the London-based labs would have the results in time to stop Rashid in his tracks regarding the blackmail. He wondered how good of an actor he would manage to be. After one hour of inner debate, he finally drove home, very determined to obtain a few days' reprieve.

★ ★

"Assa, darling, are you home?" he yelled out as soon as he pushed open the door. Rosewood oud floated through the rooms while soft ballads drifted from the speakers. Stacks of boxes were neatly lined against the walls of his entry. He found Assa in their living room, humming to herself, carefully wrapping small objects which she was then placing in a trunk. Startled by her husband's incongruous presence at a time where he was usually still in his office, she turned around quickly, almost dropping the crystal figurine held in her hands.

"Is something wrong?" she questioned with alarm in her voice.

"I need to talk to you. Will you please sit down?" invited Majid.

Obediently, Assa sat on one of the large sofas and her husband came to sit next to her. He could sense the tension emanating from her whole body.

"You can stop packing. Since we last talked I've had a great deal of time to think about my decisions," he began.

Assa's eyes grew wide and her mouth quivered.

"I'm 40 years old. I thought I was ready to start all over again. I have come to realise though that doing so means that I'd have to live elsewhere like a refugee. Dubai is my home. I've also tried to figure out how I could run Arabian Nights whilst residing elsewhere, and I know it'd be nearly impossible. I'd have to sell the magazine and without it, what would I have?"

"You don't need the income," counteracted Assa softly. "You'd be able to do anything you want. You could start publishing again by devoting time to your poetry and above all else, you'd be with the woman you've loved for the best part of your adult life." Uttering the words left her mouth dry; she could almost taste blood.

"That's just it," replied Majid without looking at her, his voice marred with an undercurrent of despair impossible to ignore. "I'm sure Arielle would rapidly grow bored. She claims she is happy giving up her career, but I know that after a few months, she'll miss it and she'll miss her home. We come from different worlds. As much as I've tried to ignore it and convince myself that it could work, I'm sure it would only last a while." He sighed deeply.

"Oh, Majid!" exclaimed Assa, visibly shaken by his misery. "You've waited for her all your life! Surely you couldn't give her up so easily without even trying? I'm sure she'd adjust to living abroad."

Majid shot her a surprised look. Could Assa really have changed her tune so quickly?

"Listen to me. Nothing is that easy. Seeing her again brought back so many memories. But it was such a long time ago: she was still a child and I certainly was a different man than the one I am today. You've been a good wife to me. I don't see the point in changing that. In fact, I don't really see what choice I have. I need to turn my back on Arielle. It's the only reasonable and adult thing to do. Reason guided me 10 years ago. I don't see why it would fail me now." Disconsolately, he dropped his head in his hands. Assa came closer and put a reassuring arm around his shoulders.

"You could keep her as a mistress," she suggested quietly.

"For a while, perhaps, until she realises that marriage isn't on the cards and then she'll return home. It'd be incredibly selfish of me to string her along. No matter how tempting it might be to play her to satisfy my needs, at the end of the day, I know I'm not that type of man."

They both fell silent. Assa alone heard the distinctive click of the back door closing.

Abruptly she stood up and hurried to the kitchen. It was empty, the smells of fragrant rice still floating in the air. Quickly she returned to the living room where Majid still sat, lost in thought.

"Very well played," stated Assa calmly, smiling at her husband.

Majid looked at her quizzically.

"Did you know my mother was here?"

"I thought I recognised her driver smoking a cigarette on the sidewalk as I pulled in, but my mind was elsewhere and I didn't pay it too much attention," admitted Majid. "Where is your mother?" he questioned, slightly puzzled by what she had just said.

"I hope she's bought it," continued Assa easily.

"You've lost me," replied Majid sincerely.

"I hope she bought your little charade," repeated Assa. "Anyone eavesdropping would be convinced you've had a complete change of heart and that you will no longer pronounce the last talaq."

"But you didn't?" Majid was stunned and could hardly hide his disbelief. What was going on? He had come in the hope of convincing his wife he would renounce the divorce, at least for the immediate future. Now she inferred that she had not been duped by his declarations. Had Assa just played along? It was all the more surprising that he had been actually quite sincere in voicing his doubts out loud over his future. In lieu of a reply, Assa disappeared once again. She came back minutes later with a thick leather-bound folder Majid recognised at once. He blanched.

"Where did you find that?" he asked in a strangled voice, his heart beating faster.

"Shortly after our nuptials, while spring cleaning your office," confessed Assa. "These poems don't lie. You love this woman beyond all reason and you always have. It's the will of Allah. Such strong feelings can't be denied."

"You've known all along?" reiterated Majid, utterly thrown by her revelation.

"I prayed daily for the woman who inspired those poems to never come back into your life. And for a while Allah smiled upon me. But in the end what was written in the heavens has come to pass. She has come back as she was always meant to do. Moreover, the interim years have apparently neither dimmed your enthusiasm nor hers. I can't measure up to that. Allah is my witness. I've tried."

"What are you saying?"

"I love you. I'm sure I will only ever love you. But this unrequited love of mine was destined to be one-sided. Trust me, I've tried to make you forego Arielle."

"I know," said Majid simply, interrupting her.

Assa's mouth quivered. Tears pooled in her large black eyes.

"Please forgive me, Majid. I didn't know what else to do. Going to my father for help was unforgivable. I wanted to save our marriage." Majid took her hands in his and his eyes beseeched her to continue. "And I know my father has used the information I gave him to bring you down."

"What's done is done," he replied philosophically.

"I don't think that's true. My mother will now go to my father and tell him what she has overheard and believe me, your performance was faultless." Assa managed a thin smile through her tears. "If I hadn't read those poems, I'd have fallen for it as well," she finished.

"Are you going to play along?' queried Majid dubiously, still unable to fathom the reasons for his wife's complete change in attitude.

"I don't ever want you to remember our marriage for my last deeds. What I've done is unforgivable. I did it out of desperation. I can only atone for it now."

"I don't blame you for what you've done. It shows how blessed I am as a man to be loved by two remarkable women. I'm not sure I deserve it. Part of me really wishes I wasn't forced to choose," he added truthfully. "So where do we go from here?"

"What do you need from me?"

"Time. I really need time. I need for your family to believe we're attempting to reconcile. You need to stop packing. We need to be seen together. Tonight, I've been invited to a Bulgari product launch. Please come with me. Being seen and photographed together will stop any rumours dead in their tracks."

"What should I wear?"

Majid hugged her tightly and wiped her tears from her cheeks in a very tender gesture.

"I'm sorry," he murmured in her hair. "And thank you. This is an amazing gift."

Assa removed herself from his embrace and looked up at him, her doe-shaped eyes, still shining with tears, meeting his.

"I wish it would have turned out differently for you and me, but I see little point in three people being miserable. I love you enough for wanting you to find true happiness at last."

Tears of gratitude silently rolled down Majid's cheeks.

When Assa's mother had heard Majid's car break to a stop, her heart had arrested. She did like her son-in-law, but right now she could not bear to face the man who had broken her daughter's heart. Helping her pack had made it even more poignant. As soon as she heard him come into the house requesting to speak with her, she had taken refuge in the adjoining kitchen, but had left the door ajar in case an argument followed which might have required her prompt intervention. However, what she'd overheard had confused her at first. Majid's voice had been tinged with an undercurrent of despair impossible to ignore. Slowly hope had shot through her. When a deep silence followed Majid's avowal, she'd peeked around the door to see what was happening and had witnessed the couple huddled together in a tight embrace. Without waiting another minute, she'd hurried out of the back door and into her car.

"Rashid!" she enthused, slightly out of breath as soon as she located her husband who was instructing their gardener. "You won't believe what's happened!"

"What?" replied Rashid somewhat gruffly. He hated being interrupted by any of his wives in front of staff, regardless of the motive. As far as he was concerned, they should request an audience to be heard. They owed it to his position.

"Majid has had a change of heart!" she trumpeted brightly. "He won't pronounce the last talaq. From what I observed they will reconcile. Your reputation will be safe," she added, knowing that it was all that mattered to him in the end. Rashid frowned suspiciously. The gardener, deferentially standing back, was all ears. As soon as Rashid realised he was still standing there, he motioned for his wife to follow him inside the house.

"What are you talking about?"

"I was at Assa's house helping her pack when Majid came home unexpectedly. I retreated to the kitchen but left the door ajar. During the discussion that followed Majid told her that, all things considered, he didn't believe he was making the right move. He was too old to start over again and he didn't believe the Australian woman would be happy away from home in the long run. He made it quite clear he had decided to stay!" She bubbled with excitement.

"That's wonderful news," said Rashid through clenched teeth. If he no longer had the excuse of his daughter's marriage annulment to bring Hamdam down, he would not be able to continue scheming.

"I will speak to him at the first opportunity to make sure there are no misunderstandings. Assa will be relieved, I'm sure, as I am," he added in a tone that belied his words. His wife shot him a quick look, not understanding his disappointment.

"Aren't you happy?" she pressed.

"Of course, but I'm running late. I have a meeting in 15 minutes. I'll see you later," he replied abruptly, heading down to the driveway where a fleet of cars was parked at the ready. Baysan shrugged. Sometimes her husband's moods were so volatile that trying to decipher them was akin to following a falcon's flight nigh in the sky. Regardless of his baffling lack of interest, she couldn't wait to share the exciting news with the rest of the family and she rushed to her phone.

In fact, Rashid was livid. Ever since his daughter had confided in him, he had dreamed of nothing else but stealing Hamdam's limelight. Since a man's word meant absolutely everything in his milieu, he had spent gratifying hours plotting the most effective ways of blotting Hamdam's reputation, albeit by proxy. He had to be careful about his methods since Hamdam had the Prince of Dubai's ear, not just due to his bloodline but also thanks to his role as advisor at large to the government. No matter how twisted his machinations, he had to be careful that nothing could ever be traced back to him, lest he signed his own death warrant. Since he could not attack Hamdam head on, he had formed the plan to propagate rumours about the horse's switch, planting the seeds which would undoubtedly blow up into a scandal of major proportions. He'd make sure no one missed the connection between Guillaume and Hamdam. However, with Majid's unforeseen change of heart, he'd no longer be able to hide behind a cloak of righteousness. He needed to change tack and revise his former plans, which consisted of dropping anonymous hints with major Australian newspapers, which he hoped would soon prompt an inquiry. Once doubt was seeded, he counted on human nature and its propensity for cutting down to size any successful man to do the rest. Even if nothing could ever be proven, Guillaume would come under close scrutiny for his past and present actions and the pressure was bound to affect him. Hamdam's reputation would be irrevocably tarnished by association. It would mark the beginning of his fall from grace, Rashid would make sure of it.

The businessman had tasted victory so many times in the last few days that he could no longer give up its allure. He wondered whether he would be lucky enough to locate someone in Australia capable of corroborating his daughter's earlier story. Surely, no one could commit fraud of such magnitude without accomplices or witnesses. Despairing to find a solution to his conundrum, he recalled the Joe Guarini link just in time. According to the newspapers he had read through on-line, the Corsican's body had been found on a stud farm neighbouring Guillaume's. Perhaps the owner would be interested in what he had to say.

Two hours later he retrieved Stefano's number. In his impatience, he had forgone due diligence. It would prove a costly mistake.

"Who's this?' asked Stefano after quickly snatching the phone from its cradle. Lately his patience was at an all-time low.

"Is this Mr Cavalieri's house? You don't know me but..."

Rashid did not finish his sentence. The line had gone dead. Puzzled, he redialled the number. The same gruff voice answered the call.

"I'm not interested," said Stefano. "I'm not interested in anything you have to sell," he repeated for emphasis. "Leave me alone and lose this number or I'll report you for harassment."

Dumbfounded, Rashid took a few seconds to find his words.

"Mr Cavalieri, I'm sorry to bother you. My name is Sheikh Rashid..."

Again he was interrupted in mid-sentence.

"Yes, I know who you are. You're the thief who sold me that dud stud. You've nerve calling me here! What the hell do you want? Ruining me wasn't enough? Called me to gloat?"

Rashid bristled at the aggressive tone. He had not expected the conversation to start on such hostile grounds. He cursed himself for realising too late that there could have been only one Cavalieri family and that the man he was talking to for the very first time was no other than the alleged anonymous buyer Trent had brokered for.

"Didn't the cryogenic sperm I shipped over work?" asked Rashi, confused, trying to regain the upper hand. "I thought Winnings told me it had worked a treat."

"Oh it worked! He involuntarily cheated the system thanks to you! Do you expect me to be thankful?" yelled Stefano. "What were you both thinking? If this gets out, I'm ruined, absolutely ruined! I repeat. What the hell do you want now?"

"I wasn't calling you in regards to Napoleon," replied Rashid, his tone subdued, trying to calm his interlocutor's anger. "I'm calling you regarding the Melbourne Cup."

"What about the Melbourne Cup?" asked Stefano tightly.

"It has come to my attention that perhaps there was something amiss with the winning horse..." began Rashid.

"You're speaking in riddles."

"I have it on good authority that the horses were switched," ventured Rashid. Stefano broke into raucous laughter.

"Old man, I don't know what's in the water over there, but you should stop drinking it! I can tell you what you're suggesting is impossible. Whoever your so-called impeccable source is, he or she is pulling your leg." Then suddenly remembering Trent's dying words he added in a more serious tone. "It can't be done, I assure you."

"I was hoping you might be able to use the information. If I understand it correctly you're not exactly best of friends with the horse's owner."

"Your sources are only partially correct," replied Stefano carefully, waiting to see where the strangely timed conversation was heading.

"The way I see it, it would be to your advantage to cast doubts on the horse," pursued Rashid doggedly.

"Why is that?"

"Well, if the horse was switched, then all bets are off, aren't they? Wasn't your horse next in the lead? He'd have to give the money back, wouldn't he? There'd be a good chance he'd be sent to jail, isn't that right?"

"What is it to you?" questioned Stefano, bemused.

"Let's say I'm a concerned citizen. Or perhaps I'm just a punter who shouldn't have lost. Or simply I'm a man who dislikes LaSalle. Take your pick."

"This smells like a trap," replied Stefano crossly. "I'm not sure what game you're playing at, but I'm not falling for it. You've no proof whatsoever or you wouldn't have come to me with your wild allegations. You'd have gone straight to the race stewards. You've made a fool of me twice already, Mr Rashid. There won't be a third time!" boomed Stefano, his temper quickly rising.

"Twice?" queried Rashid, uncomprehending.

"First time when you sold me a dud, and the second time when you conspired to give my studmaster frozen sperm so he could impregnate the mares and pull wool over my eyes! You're a despicable man. This conversation is over."

Without waiting for a reply and livid with rage, Stefano hung up the phone. Back in Dubai, Rashid stared at it, dumbfounded, his plan dead in its tracks.

However, at home, as far as Detective Zack Summers was concerned, the conversation was just beginning. Tapping Stefano's phone had finally paid off. He couldn't believe what he had heard.

When he accidentally ran into Guillaume minutes later at the downtown post office, Zack's face was set into an unreadable mask. Guillaume was quick to smell the whiff of hostility emanating from his entire persona.

"Good morning, Zack. You look preoccupied. Something on your mind?" he queried cheerfully, stepping out of the queue to salute him.

"It seems this town harbours way too many secrets for its size. It seems that when I try to decipher a murder for example, or let's even say two for good measure, crimes I didn't even suspect in the first place rise to the surface all on their own," he replied instead, his teeth clenched, his forehead frozen in an expression of pained concentration.

"Do you have time for a coffee?" suggested Guillaume who had no intention of making public whatever the detective had to say.

"Why not?'

The two men stepped out of the small post office building and onto the main street. Within minutes they reached a small coffee shop with a couple of tables placed outside along the retaining wall. Mid-morning the shop was deserted. They ordered their lattes and went to sit on the sidewalk. Steady traffic prevented them from being overheard.

"What's up?" queried Guillaume, looking at the detective's tension-filled face. "Something of importance must have happened. It concerns me because you look rather startled and peeved to have run into me unexpectedly," his tone and demeanour trying to make the other man at ease.

"I'm not sure what to do at this point," replied Zack truthfully. "Let me explain. I've tapped Stefano's phones. For two weeks nothing has happened and then suddenly last night, I learned a lot more than I ever intended doing." He sighed and looked straight at Guillaume. "I'm not sure I like it and the implications simply make my head spin."

"Perhaps I can be of help?"

"I should probably do this formally at the station," replied Zack pensively. "But let's pretend for a minute we're just mates shooting the breeze."

"Then I'm all ears," encouraged Guillaume, puzzled by the preamble.

"Last night Stefano received a call from a man who called himself Sheik Rashid. Does the name ring a bell?"

"It does."

"I was afraid it might. From what I gathered this Rashid person was the same man who sold Stefano the famous stud Napoleon a couple of years back or so. It seems that the horse never settled, which I gather means that he was no good at his job and the mares didn't fall pregnant. The now deceased Trent Winnings had subsequently contacted the original seller and convinced him to ship him frozen semen previously extracted from the same stud. I presume he inseminated the mares with that import the following season. Stefano didn't seem pleased with this at all. What am I missing?"

"Artificial insemination is forbidden by the Australian Jockey Club and the Victorian Racing Club. Regardless, so is the use of frozen sperm. Trent would have known that. I'm surprised to hear Trent impregnated the mares without his boss' knowledge but it's possible."

"What are the implications?"

"Through this method Napoleon has sired several champions. Stefano has kept one of the fillies and the other colts belong to various other owners. All the horses sired by Napoleon would have been denied registration had anyone known artificial insemination had been involved. Since no one knew about it, this would basically upset the result of many races over the past two years. It would be a scandal of unfathomable proportions," whistled Guillaume softly.

"I'm not finished," interrupted Zack. "This Rashid character also implied that horses were switched during the Melbourne Cup. You wouldn't know anything about that either, would you?"

Guillaume blanched but remained impassable, forcing himself to stay calm under Zack's unflinching stare. "I suppose that's where I come in?" queried Guillaume, his eyebrow arched questioningly.

"From what I gathered, the purpose of the call was to convince Stefano to out you. I gather this Rashid has it in for you. It would be easy to believe that this foreign sheikh was the one to hire Guarini in the first place. But I'm missing a few pieces of the puzzle."

Their coffee finally arrived, giving Guillaume pause.

"Look, Zack," replied Guillaume, slowly measuring each word. "Switching horses under the nose of the stewards would be virtually impossible. I don't know how it could be done unless the treachery was planned months ahead of time. It would also require many accomplices, not the least amongst race officials. From what you say, it is obvious Rashid is desperately trying to cast shadows on my character."

"Why would he want to do that?"

"Because my daughter is about to marry his soon-to-be ex-son-in- law," explained Guillaume. "He must believe that if he were successful in destroying my reputation along with Arielle's, his daughter's husband would back out of the divorce."

"That's insane," murmured Zack. "But why would he call on Stefano for help?"

"He probably assumed Stefano is cut of the same venal cloth as his studmaster. Trent's moral compass was obviously askew. He panicked when Napoleon's first season turned out to be a scratch. Talk to Stefano but you'll probably discover that Trent was highly instrumental in selecting the horse and in brokering the purchase. With a horse that didn't perform his reputation would have been on the line and in all likelihood, so would have his job. He tried to repair the breach the only way he knew how. Rashid helped him because it would have been seriously detrimental to his reputation if it became known that he sold a deadbeat horse for stud."

Zack polished his eye glasses for a full minute, lost in thought. When he perched them back on his nose, he looked up squarely at Guillaume.

"Do you want to know what I think?"

"By all means," replied Guillaume, smiling thinly.

"At some point in the last month, Trent must have divulged his treachery to Stefano. I'm not sure what prompted it, but it doesn't sound as if he had done so since the very beginning. Stefano rightly panicked because he assumed you'd know for sure. He believed that his secret would never come to the fore if you were to disappear. By chance, but undoubtedly through concerted efforts, he came across Joe Guarini. He realised he could use the man's all-consuming hate for you without implicating himself. But Joe Guarini got lost and came upon Pandora Estates by mistake. Somehow he surprised Pat and Trent together when Pat had fled Chantilly Farms after the rape. Gunfire followed and both Guarini and Pat met their maker. Again Stefano must have realised his plan had backfired when Guarini was identified as one of the victims. He is now cornered. He backs out of the negotiations for Apple Legends so you'd keep your mouth shut. However, if he were in possession of a secret as explosive as your alleged switching of the horses to win the race, why wouldn't he use it against you? Why wouldn't he approach you for a truce, trading one secret for another? Especially after Rashid tried to nudge him in that direction?"

"I can't answer that," replied Guillaume sincerely. "But he'd need proof and there is no proof."

"Oh, that's right, isn't it? The thoroughbred in question is dead, isn't he?" His eyes bore into Guillaume's.

"The post-partum paperwork was sent to the Stud book registry. If you care to check it out, you'll see there was no anomaly. There were plenty of photos taken of Obsidian during all the races that qualified him beforehand, as well as during and after the Flemington course race. Compare them to your heart's content. The idea of switching such a distinctive horse is preposterous."

"Why would Rashid suggest it?"

"I'm afraid you'd have to ask him. I've no idea. What bothers me is that obviously Sheikh Rashid won't stop at anything to force my daughter to back out of her betrothal. Moreover, Stefano still believes I'd use the artificial insemination scandal against him at the very first opportunity. So, in the cold light of day, it appears that two men want me dead or at the very least, out of the way. Being Guillaume de la Selle nowadays is far from an enviable position." Guillaume tried to joke but the reality of his situation sent a shiver down his spine regardless. Zack agreed.

"I'll keep an eye on Stefano. Meanwhile, watch your back," he advised, "and let me know if this Rashid tries to intimidate you in the first instance. There are laws against it, even though trying to enforce them with someone residing on another continent is basically a waste of time. Guillaume? One more thing?"

"Yes?" replied Guillaume who had already stood up.

"Nathan would have known the horses had been artificially inseminated, wouldn't he?"

"Not necessarily. It's not uncommon for a stallion's performance to decrease or stop all together in any given season. When the mares were with foals a season later, Nathan would have assumed like everyone else that he had reverted back to his old self. Nathan's presence isn't required as a witness to each live covering. If Trent had artificially inseminated the mares at night for example, no one would have seen him. If you wanted to cheat the system, that'd be the way to do it."

"I see," retorted Zack, still deep in thought.

"Why do you ask?"

"Nathan is the only common denominator between the two farms who is still alive."

"I'm not following you."

"The forensic ballistics don't quite work, unless there was a third man there at Pandora Estates that night."

"Trent Winnings was there."

"I know but I still can't reconstruct the scene. Unless someone else was there who fled the scene."

"But Nathan was home with us," rectified Guillaume.

"I know. It still bothers me though. There is nothing simple and clear cut with this case. Well, I'll be on my way. Good day."

Zack touched the rim of his cap and walked off to find his car. Guillaume watched him go, wondering whether the detective had withheld any further information and was stringing him along.

After replaying the conversation in his mind, he concluded that Zack was guileless; he had shared exactly what had been on his mind, without afterthought. He also seemed to have accepted at face value the unfeasibility of switching a thoroughbred at the last minute, especially in the context of such a high profile race. At least for the time being, Guillaume was off the hook.

The fax from Total Genetics, the London-based laboratory whose services had been contracted a week earlier, was over four pages long. It first explained that if Nathan had provided them with a sperm sample, no matter how small, the presence of non-permeable sugars would have been easily detected. Indeed monosaccharides and trisacharrides were commonly used as semen extenders to aid in the partial dehydration of the sperm prior to freezing. Undoubtedly, Glycerol, as the primary cryoprotectant, would have also been present. Unfortunately, none of these would be detectable once the foal was born. Thus, without a cryogenic vial sample of the sperm, the only way to prove that the horses born out of artificial insemination differed from those born out of live coverings was to patiently and systematically deconstruct the DNA sequencing. Indeed, in appearance, behaviour and metabolism of the sequencing remained otherwise unchanged on the surface. The geneticist explained how they had used RFLP analysis by collecting DNA from blood cells and cutting them into small pieces using a restriction enzyme. According to him, this method helped generate thousands of DNA fragments of different sizes as a consequence of variations between DNA sequences of different individuals. The fragments were then separated on the basis of size using gel electrophoresis. They were then transferred to a nylon filter in a procedure called the Southern Blot. Thanks to this meticulous process, the minuscule pieces became permanently fixed to the filter and the DNA strands were thereby denatured. Various radio-labelled molecules were then added. Their purpose was to hybridise the DNA fragments now containing repeat sequences. Excess probe molecules were then washed away. The blot was subsequently exposed to an X-ray film. The results were clear. Blood samples extracted from animals resulting from live covering and those suspected as the result of artificial insemination using frozen sperm produced dark bands on the film of varying consistency and darkness. There was no mistake. Science had vindicated Nathan's suspicions. A crime had been committed and the English laboratory would stand behind its discovery. Actually it couldn't wait to go to press.

Meanwhile, Detective Zack Summers sat in his car, pondering his earlier conversation with Guillaume. As he shifted in his seat, his jacket slid over the front seat. As he righted it, his fingers came across an envelope crunched underneath the seat, an old bill he had thought misplaced. In retrieving it, he had flashbacks to Trent Winnings' property when he had searched for clues of the crimes at Pandora Estates. He had looked everywhere but inside the old Toyota Corolla parked under the shed since the studmaster had driven the hatchback truck to the property that day. Instinctively he decided to return to the small worker's cottage located at the southern end of Pandora's Estates.

He was quickly rewarded when in the small trunk under heavy tarpaulin he located a semi-crushed insulated shipping box with the address label half-peeled off. On what remained a return address to a company in the UAE was still clearly legible. There was now irrefutable evidence that Trent Winnings had conspired to defraud the Australian Stud Book. Zack had no doubt that an analysis of the box would reveal it was exactly the type of container one would use to ship frozen material to ensure its even temperature during transportation. However, the date, almost two years prior, confirmed that Stefano was unlikely to have known or he would have reacted very differently. Threatened by what he thought was Guillaume's knowledge of his treachery, he would have brought Guarini or someone just like him well beforehand. Stefano was in the clear. Trent had acted alone. Thus it made

Stefano's actions all the more puzzling. Zack slammed his palm against his forehead, and started laughing. He had finally figured it out. Stefano had been found that night still cradling his studmaster's head when the police had arrived at the property. Stefano had been in shock: his entire demeanour that evening had proved it. Yet for a man of his antecedents, the profound shock registered on his face couldn't have come from watching a man die, something he would have often witnessed, or from seeing his barns burn, an often sad reality on very hot summers. His obvious distress would have come on the back of a dying man's confession: Trent had spilled his secret, refusing to take it to the grave. That is why Stefano backed out of the negotiations two days later when it came to the purchase of Apple Legend. So why had he called upon Guarini to kill Guillaume? When he had initially contacted the illustrious Mafioso's son he'd known nothing of Trent's treachery. In his experience professional rivalries could often turn level-headed men into cold-blooded killers out for revenge. Was it simply a question of losing to Guillaume one too many times on the track? He wondered if Maria, Stefano's wife, might bring him the answers he sought. He knew she played bridge in Maitland every Wednesday. It was time to brush up on his card skills.

CHAPTER XVII

The first in-depth article landed in Racing Ahead, Equus and Equestrian Life in the same week, covering each continent at once. Confronted with the explosive revelations, the popular monthly magazines had been happy to set aside their already planned articles to accommodate the London lab's findings. Hamdam's offer to take out a half-dozen full-page colour ads in the same issue had been the only added incentive any of them had required. The scientific articles explained how Total Genetics' lab had just discovered that it was possible to distinguish between animals born from artificial insemination and those born from live mare covering, even when sired by the same stud. Indeed the resultant DNA sequence turned out to be unexpectedly different.

While many countries allowed the practice of artificial insemination since it facilitated reproduction ease by eliminating transport logistics of live stock, some sports, especially in the racing of thoroughbreds, banned it specifically. The scientific breakthrough was exposed likewise on business channels, sending the stocks of Total Genetics through the roof.

Three days later, it had run through international racing circles like wildfire. Interviewed experts claimed that the discovery closed yet another loophole. As a result, it would take artificial insemination practices completely off the agenda, keeping current modus operandi and thereby saving once and for all the livelihood of a great many people. The next step in the research was obvious, but would still take years to prove: were thoroughbreds born of live covering better or worse than their frozen counterparts? Was there indeed a systemic advantage to one method over the other? The answer would prove key to racing for decades ahead.

At first neither Rashid nor Stefano had paid attention to the headlines. However, by the end of the week, the news had been impossible to ignore. In the UAE, Hamdam had furthered his assault by commissioning news which elaborated on breeding standards at home and abroad, comparing practices endemic to the Arab world and elsewhere, weighing the scientific and ethical pros and cons. Some of the articles shamed those breeders who, having sold stallions for stud for large sums of money, had nonetheless withheld some of the animal's sperm, selling it at a later date. Thus, unbeknown to the new registered stud owner, new generations of colts and fillies had seen the light. It was made abundantly clear that this process in fact substantially decreased the perceived value of those born elsewhere through live covering.

Little by little, Rashid grew increasingly uncomfortable with the avalanche of articles on the subject that were filling the newsstands day after day. In his view, the media furore around Total Genetics' discovery was unwarranted. The ethical debate it appeared to have sparked couldn't have come at a worst time. He blamed the situation largely on a lack of luck, never imagining that he had been specifically targeted. Pacing in the office near his tack room, he wondered for the umpteenth time in the past week alone whether it was just a matter of time before breeders like him were investigated and publicly denounced. The timing irritated him: how could a disgraced man turn the tables on Hamdam by exposing his friend Guillaume as a cheat if he was himself under investigation for knowingly defrauding the system? His dream of exposing Guillaume, ruining his reputation and that of Hamdam by association, seemed to run through his fingers, the chance more remote with each passing day, especially without any tangible proof. He had hoped that Stefano could have shed some light on the rumour of a substitution or at the very least be willing to cast doubts on the race outcome. However he had struck out. He was still pacing when he was suddenly interrupted by his stable manager.

"Good morning, Farouk. What is it you want?" he barked in his usual gruff manner.

"I'm sorry to bother you but I have it on good authority that the Prince is sending investigators to all breeding farms to make sure that no one in his country can be accused of duplicity when it comes to trading studs."

"What are you saying?" demanded Rashid, ashen.

"Apparently your name has come up. They should be here any minute. They have the right to requisition everything in the stables pertaining to our breeding practices."

Rashid had turned a deeper shade of grey.

"What does that mean?" he asked through clenched teeth, sweat pearling on his knotted brows.

Without looking at his employer, Farouk answered quickly. "In other facilities, the police have gone straight to the cool room safe. Every cryogenic vial found was destroyed on the spot, no questions asked. Every shipping invoice for the last three years was confiscated. Every record book with foaling dates has been photocopied. Since dawn, over nine compounds have already been searched and hefty fines issued. It's my understanding that our Prince wants to be able to hold his head high in international racing circles and proclaim that UAE-owned horses would never participate in defrauding breeding laws in place in any other country."

Frozen to the spot by the Prince's unexpectedly swift actions, Sheikh Rashid took precious minutes to react. By the time he decided to quickly delete possible evidence left on his premises, the police were at his door.

★ ★

Hamdam had thoroughly enjoyed watching Rashid squirm. One of his nephews, a police deputy commander, had been part of the raid effected on Rashid's farm that morning. He had called him immediately thereafter. In Rashid's safe room, more than 200 vials of frozen sperm had been found each clearly labelled with the individual stallion's name. They were worth millions. According to the recovered letters of shipping, frozen sperm had been sent for years to the four corners of the globe, often destined to losing bidders when they had missed out on a notorious stallion just sold for stud. Rashid had never bothered to cover his tracks. All previous auctions for studs and private parties' treaties had all been duly recorded as well as the names of all principal contenders. It had been easy to follow the trail. Within days of any worthy auction, Rashid had personally contacted the unsuccessful bidders and proposed the frozen sperm from the very same stallion, at a discounted price. Turning over his money twice, once when he sold a promising horse for stud and the second time when he sold that horse's sperm to other parties and most often to direct competitors was simply good business sense. The police chief handed him an on-the-spot fine for over 1,000,000 dirhams. Rashid was given 24 hours to pay it, lest he faced jail time. Meanwhile, his operations would be suspended under further notice.

Rashid had exploded in a wrath so violent, even threatening the police, that he'd had to be restrained. Within hours, the whole of Dubai had heard the story; very few people had felt sorry for him. As a favour to Hamdam, the Prince had turned Rashid into his poster boy, making an example of him. The latter had not been prepared for the public humiliation and social disgrace, nor for the ensuing scandal. When his confidential sources confirmed his nemesis had played a large part in bringing him down, his rage knew no boundaries, his hate reaching a new pinnacle. With his honour in tatters, his need for revenge overwhelmed him.

On the very same Friday, when the day went by without the dreaded overseas call, Guillaume wondered what had happened. Like everyone else in the business, he had attentively read the articles disseminated by Total Genetics' PR machine. He had hoped that Rashid had felt the pressure, but was not sure whether men of his calibre actually ever took responsibility for their own actions. By 10 o'clock that night, he called Hamdam. His friend answered on the first ring. His tone was jovial.

"I bet you haven't heard from our friend today, have you?" he asked playfully.

"As a matter of fact, that's why I'm calling you. I didn't think a handful of articles would lead him to back down from his threat of blackmail. I didn't even think he'd consider they were aimed at him."

Hamdam laughed heartily until a coughing fit stopped him abruptly.

"Are you all right, old man? That didn't sound too healthy," he observed, immediately worried.

"Who are you calling an old man? No, I'm fine," replied Hamdam, catching his breath. The pain these days came in waves and more often than it used to. "A few articles didn't seem to panic him," he agreed. "However, a police raid certainly did!" he added, his voice filled with merriment.

"A police raid?" repeated Guillaume, uncomprehending.

"When the first articles were published in Racing Ahead, since apparently he has been a subscriber for years, my uncle called me to ask whether I knew anything about the ethical dilemma raised by this latest scientific discovery. It was my pleasure to tell him the entire saga minus a few prejudicial details as far as you're concerned. Together, we made sure that ensuing articles received plenty of attention. Owning prestigious stables, many prominent sheikhs quickly requested audiences and promised to eradicate such practices from their operations. They were spared further scrutiny. Others, believing they would never be caught, ignored the warning signs. This morning the police descended on several properties with search warrants. Frozen sperm was confiscated. Heavy fines were handed out. I'm certain it was purely coincidental that Rashid's breeding farm was included in that first raid." Hamdam's laugh boomed down the line. This time he kept any coughing at bay. In his office, mutely lit thanks to a single desk lamp, Guillaume smiled.

"I guess after that he didn't find the time to exercise his threat."

"Be still on your guard, my friend. Across the desert, a man's honour is all he has. Rashid will not take kindly to have been publicly denounced. He will seek revenge. One of us will be in the firing line for sure. By now he must have guessed I was instrumental in his disgrace. Harming me might prove difficult. Harming those I love might be less so. I'll warn Majid to be on his guard."

"Don't worry about me. I can take care of myself. Do you think he might be vindictive enough to spread nefarious rumours regardless, without informing me first?"

"It's my understanding that both Majid and his wife have manipulated him into thinking the divorce will no longer go ahead. Without the fear of further social alienation due to his daughter's divorce, he has no reason to come back and hunt you. All he wanted was for Majid to renounce his plans. He believes he has succeeded. Moreover, who would ever take him seriously now? He has been shown to wilfully defraud buyers and to have done so for decades. His word is no more than a mirage. No one will ever believe him."

"Thank you," said Guillaume humbly. "Once again I owe you."

"Nonsense!" replied Hamdam forcefully. "Why would you owe me? And why again?" he added, his curiosity getting the better of him.

"I know you bought my horses, once upon a time, back when tragedy forced my hand, all those years ago. As your house guest, you gave Arielle a chance to become who she was meant to be. And last but certainly not least, you've let me unburden myself with a secret that would have otherwise eaten at my heart," explained Guillaume without guile.

"In that case, my friend, trust me, we are even. Those horses I bought were winners and brought me luck. They were by far the best horses in my stables and I owe my first successes on the track to them. Without Arielle, my name wouldn't have become a household name in racing circles. Thanks to the publicity boost her presence gave the city in that particular year, my uncle offered me a chair in his government. Without you, I'd have no one except for my doctors to lean on in regards to my deteriorating health. Moreover, your daughter has brought Majid into my life. From where I sit, I owe you a great deal more than I could ever do for you."

Guillaume's eyes misted as he listened to him. Humility was a trait in Hamdam he most admired. The man had a remarkable knack for making those around him always feel whole and above all always morally debt-free.

"Hamdam," said Guillaume after a second pause, "Sarah and I thought we might come and visit some time soon. Winter has definitely set in and there is little to do at this time of year. The desert heat is most appealing right now. Would that be all right with you or were you planning to be out of town in the near future?"

"It'd be my pleasure. And please don't insult me by booking a hotel anywhere. It will be excruciatingly hot in a month's time but my house remains most pleasant."

"I'll call you with the final details. Hamdam, thanks again for everything."

Hanging up, Hamdam hoped it wouldn't be too late. Pain surged through his entire body and he tensed accordingly. Quickly he reached for his liquid morphine before the stabbing pangs prevented him from moving once again. He would love to have his friend by his side once more. He prayed Allah would grant him the favour.

Nadhir, aged 29, sported the physique of a boxer, with the nimble grace of a ballet dancer. Rashid's youngest son, light on his feet and quick with his fists, but with the mind of a child, had early on opted out of university which had proved well beyond his capabilities. Once tested, his business acumen had likewise proved disastrous. With more brawn than brain, leaning on his strengths, he'd decided for a career in private security. He soon spent most of his time at his father's side, acting as his bodyguard. Not only did

Rashid believe his status as a prominent businessman demanded it, but his often shady dealings had turned it into a necessity, regardless.

Pleasing his mercurial father was Nadhir's whole world. He regarded himself as his father's favourite, albeit by default, since he was glued to his side most days. So when his father had placed the blame of his dishonour squarely on a foreigner by the name of Guillaume de La Selle, explaining that the man had wished to destroy him out of simple spite, it had not taken long for Nadhir to come to the rescue. He proposed to deal with the situation personally. He knew his fists to be enough to incapacitate most men. In the past, the use of a weapon had often proven superfluous, his stealthy skills enough to control most situations. Travelling all the way to Australia though had necessitated slightly more convincing. In the end, with the promise of two new servant girls to add to his household, he had relented. He favoured Malaysian girls over other ethnicities and his father promised he would hire a new pair of cooks who'd wait for him upon his return. The deal had thus been sealed.

They started planning Nadhir's trip carefully. To avoid attracting unwarranted attention they agreed first of all that he would travel in westernised clothing. Nadhir would go to Chantilly Farms under the guise of checking out the boarding facilities for his alleged client's horses. His client would be introduced as a prominent businessman with an instantly recognisable face who wished to remain anonymous at the start, with all transactions remaining as discreet as possible. His father would forge the letter of introduction. They agreed Nadhir would be booked on an Etihad flight departing from Abu Dhabi the very next day. Whilst it would have been more practical to leave from Dubai on an Emirates flight, they would have run the risk of running into acquaintances. Undoubtedly, the latter would feel duty bound to ask dozens of inopportune questions. It never crossed Rashid's mind that on his way out of town his son would come to share his plans with anyone. However, it was Nadhir's very first overseas trip. He knew full well that Assa alone would sufficiently understand and would allay his fear of flying and calm his nerves at leaving home for the first time.

Stefano felt like a man who had not slept in weeks. In fact, sound sleep had eluded him ever since Melbourne Cup day, when he had wagered his future on a positive outcome. Unlike Guillaume, he had not bet on his own horse. Not that he was averse to some betting here and there, but he preferred roulette to the races. In racing, he knew only too well how quickly the best-laid plans could be derailed for unfathomable reasons. At least in a casino he could blame his losses on Lady Luck: it suited his temperament a lot better. On the track, it was much harder. Winning the race that particular year had meant everything to him: he desperately needed the money to increase his land holdings. Pandora Estates had badly needed larger pastures and the addition of more buildings to board and train more horses lest it risked bankruptcy. The purchase of Napoleon had proved a risky move initially designed to lift the farm's profile by injecting new blood into his broodmares' lines. When the horse had failed to settle, the brothers had walked a tightrope. Whilst they had recovered some of the outlay during the second season, not nearly enough mares had been covered to rationalise the initial purchase. When a month later the stud had to be put down, Stefano believed he had been cursed. Losing the Apple Legends property days later had been the nail in his coffin. Watching his barns burn to the ground and finding three corpses on his property had been too much to bear.

For days he had been mulling over the repeated insinuations that something had not been quite right with the Melbourne Cup upset win. Where he came from there was rarely smoke without fire, even if you had to first dig deep to locate the ambers. Instinctively, he knew something had happened on the day, but he had not seen anything amiss. On the other hand, Guillaume's win had been too fortuitous, too unexpected and, in the end, too spectacular not to hide deeper secrets. Trent's dying words pointed him in the direction of Will's champion. Rashid's call had confirmed everything was not what it seemed with Obsidian. However, he also knew that Guillaume would have covered his tracks and that no one was likely to find any proof at all, no matter how hard they tried. When men like Guillaume walked on the wrong side of ethics, they usually did so in such a way as to not leave any footprints at all. However, lest he went mad by churning over the problem, for his own peace of mind and to finally be able to sleep, it became vital to understand how Guillaume had engineered it all – the incredible win, the lifesaving purchase and the well-timed fire. They were all connected: he was sure of it. Lately he had been on a losing streak: it was time it stopped. However without knowing which strings to pull, recovery would be slow and time wasn't on his side. Confronting Guillaume was the only way.

Resolved to obtain the answers he sought, Stefano drove to Chantilly Farms later that afternoon. Since one of his fillies was due back to its owner, he had not needed an excuse other than wanting to organise the transfer. As expected, Guillaume was already at the stables, supervising the horse's transport. Likewise, he had yet to find a studmaster. Meanwhile, he covered all bases.

"Hello, Stefano," he said cautiously to his neighbour, surprised to see him. "I didn't expect you to come. All's fine so far. Paperwork's all in order."

"I'm sure it is. I thought it might be an opportunity for us to talk," replied Stefano uncharacteristically.

"Something specific on your mind?" queried Guillaume, unsure as to whether he wanted to have an open chat with Stefano after the latter had threateningly walked out of the meeting with Apple Legends.

"I see you haven't found a studmaster," said Stefano, looking around to check whether any staff members were susceptible to witness their exchange. With the lorry now loaded, Guillaume signalled the driver to take off.

"I heard you've been likewise unlucky," he retorted, turning back around to face his interlocutor, wondering what Stefano was up to.

For a few minutes the two men exchanged their views on how difficult it was to find trained and reliable staff, each astonished at finding so much in common with the other in regards to their instinctive reactions to the job market and their specific conundrum born from a recently shared violent past.

"Well," said Guillaume finally, "I'm sure you haven't come here to discuss our respective woes when it comes to employees. What's on your mind? Your horse is now gone."

For a minute, Stefano hesitated. It would be easy enough for him to back out of a confrontation now. All he had to do was simply state he had just wanted to be present when the filly was loaded onto the lorry. However, when he looked up, Guillaume was standing there, proud and erect, with an air of defiance and his usual steely quietness, which Stefano immediately interpreted as arrogance, pure and simple. He stared at the man facing him. Nothing ever seemed to ruffle him. Moreover, he had to admit that Guillaume looked much younger than his 60 years of age, whereas he felt in his bones every single one of them. Envy and resentment built over decades suddenly erupted.

"You know Trent accused you of cheating at Melbourne Cup," he spat venomously. "I believe him. Obsidian wasn't meant to win that day! You hadn't raised a winner! I know it and you know it!"

Taken aback by the unexpected attack, Guillaume looked at him.

"How the hell would he know?"

"Pat told him!" bluffed Stefano, since it was the only logical explanation as to how his manager could have come into any reliable information.

Guillaume clenched his teeth.

"And when would that have been?" he seethed. "Before or after he raped my daughter? Before or after he artificially inseminated your mares?"

The unadulterated violence in Guillaume's tone slapped Stefano hard.

"What are you talking about? What rape?" queried Stefano, completely taken aback. In his old-fashioned way, he considered that, regardless of circumstances, no man should ever raise a hand against a woman. In his mind, rape was the ultimate act of cowardice and it repulsed him.

"Pat sexually assaulted my daughter," explained Guillaume, livid. "Then he ran to your farm. I presume it was to share the details of his disgusting deed with his friend, Trent. Coincidentally, it happened on the very same night someone set fire to your barns and three men were later found dead. A lot happened that night, wouldn't you agree? Would you be trying to say it was in the middle of this chaos that Trent, out of the blue, accused me of cheating? Is that right?"

Trying to absorb the sequence of events as described by Guillaume, Stefano remained silent.

"I'm sorry, Will. What Pat did is inexcusable. I had no idea. How awful!" he finally managed to say.

"It's unconscionable!" agreed Guillaume, trying to control his anger. "As it is for you to accuse me without any tangible proof!"

"I swear it on Maria's head, those were his dying words. Why would he say something like that just as he took his last breath?"

"I agree, it makes no sense at all. In his shoes, I would have begged for forgiveness instead!" stormed the Frenchman.

"Forgiveness?" repeated Stefano, uncomprehending.

"It's true I'm still giving you the benefit of the doubt!" Guillaume exclaimed. "You probably knew Napoleon was a dud and you probably agreed to have the mares artificially inseminated! I should have known better. You'll stop at nothing! How could I ever think that a man like you was above this type of treachery?" continued Guillaume.

"I knew nothing about it!" screamed Stefano, furious. "I knew nothing of it until that night!" he repeated for emphasis.

"That's your claim, really? How gullible do you think I am? And if you did not know until then, why would you have contacted

Guarini? He was already here when you allegedly heard the rumours for the first time!"

As the two men continued to sling heated accusations at one another, night had quietly fallen around them. A nebulous moon had slowly risen above the tree line, its faint light bouncing off the corrugated roofs of the stables. Their voices boomed eerily across the deepening silence. Inexplicably a shiver ran down Guillaume's spine and a sense of déjà vu stopped him short in his rant. Likewise, Stefano caught the same low bristle in the leaves and heard the threatening crackle of brittle branches. Confused, both men held their breath, their anger momentarily put on hold. Together they peered into the darkness, which now hung ominously. The tension was palpable.

Unsettled by the deep, constant roar of the engines, Nadhir had slept little during the 13-hour flight, his heart dipping with every air pocket. For the first time in his life he had been tempted to resort to alcohol to calm his jagged nerves. Instead, he had prayed and ceaselessly cycled through the 33 amber beads of his Misbaha. By the time the Etihad jet had landed in Sydney, he had been haggard with fatigue and jet lag. Immigration proceedings seemed interminable, but he had been well coached. When questioned as to the exact nature of his visit since it showed less than a week's stay on his entry documents, he had presented himself as an emissary. He claimed to have travelled Down Under for the specific purpose of finding suitable boarding facilities for his father's thoroughbreds ahead of the racing season. One of the agents, who regularly bet more than he could afford at the local TAB, accepted the explanation at face value. He welcomed him to Australia with open arms and a friendly wink. It took Nadhir another hour to collect his luggage. A taxi brought him to the Intercontinental Hotel near Circular Quay, selected by his father as a convenient neutral base of operations, a place to which his son could return inconspicuously once the deed was done, right before his flight home.

As the first order of business, Nadhir booked a private guide, allegedly to tour the wineries around the Hunter Valley. Once in the Valley though he would decline to be bussed around and indicate a preference for renting a bike to cycle around at his leisure, offering the driver to meet him for a late tea. It was his plan, however, to call him instead by five o'clock to let him know that he had over-indulged and would rather sleep it off by remaining at one of the local hotels. He'd return to town only the following morning. Naturally, the guide would be handsomely compensated for this unorthodox turn of events. Nadhir had hoped the stratagem would not only give him plenty of time to locate Chantilly Farms and get rid of its owner once and for all, but also provide him with a solid alibi if required. He had passed the time on the flight over-memorising his victim's face. Rashid had provided him with the front-page photograph following the Melbourne Cup win when Guillaume was captured brandishing his trophy. The man's face was distinctive. There would be no case of mistaken identity. After all their preparations, father and son firmly believed they had left little to chance.

Minutes after arrival at his downtown hotel, Nadhir contacted the concierge, explaining what he wanted to do. The latter was quick to propose a cousin of his, who could certainly accommodate his request and at a fraction of the cost compared to an official tour. The only stipulation for such an arrangement was that the transaction be done in cash and not billed to the room. Nadhir didn't hesitate. They quickly agreed that the cousin in question would drop his client off at the Grapemobile Bicycle Hire shed. Nadhir would give him a call later that day to let him know exactly where he wished to be picked up to drive back to town. Due to his buffed physique, no one questioned the young man's desire for physical activity.

It was close to one o'clock when the driver dropped him off at the bike-hire shed, after a long drive during which there had been little communication between the two men, thanks to the Arabic man's limited English. Nadhir traced his route on his iPhone's Google map. From his bike-hire spot, it was a mere 24 kilometres to Chantilly Farms. He calculated it would take him less than a couple of hours, leaving plenty of time for an imponderable, such as a flat tire. He planned on getting to the property before nightfall, leaving enough time to understand the lay of the land. He would wait for dusk before striking. He always preferred the time when shadows lengthened on the ground and the waning light changed the contour of buildings and blurred the edges of landmarks, the lack of definition somehow adding another dimension to his sinister aims.

Right away he requested the feasibility of keeping the bike for a couple of days, explaining to the teenager behind the counter that he didn't wish to feel compelled to come back to base before closing if he was enjoying himself somewhere on the other side of the valley. He was in Australia just for a few days and wanted to get better acquainted with the Hunter Valley by taking in the scenery at a leisurely pace. Once again his luck held and his motives weren't questioned. After agreeing on an exorbitant two-day rental fee, and a substantial security deposit besides, the owner relented.

Once in town, Nadhir purchased at the only visible hardware store a backpack, a short length of steel wire, a pair of pliers, a pair of leather gloves and a powerful flashlight. Securing a bottle of water to the bike, he then started off. It was already well after two which, in his mind, still left him plenty of time to reach the property. However, he had not expected the challenge of the undulating landscape that stretched before him. Overwhelmed by jet lag, the steep hills soon slowed him down to a crawl. A nebulous moon was already appearing above the paddocks by the time he pedalled his way to Chantilly Farms. The gates were wide open.

After leaning his bike against the enormous trunk of a tree, he stealthily approached on foot alongside the drive framed by chestnut and maples. Overhearing a loud argument as he

303

approached the first set of buildings, he crouched in the low-lying bushes growing at the fork between three large eucalypts whose immense canopy shaded the yard. He checked out the dispute. Instantly he recognised one of the men standing a few feet away from him as his prey. However, he could not understand a word of the heated argument. He decided to wait for the opportunity to strike. With his victim identified, he was no longer in a hurry. He had no need for any potential witnesses either: with a bit of luck, the other man would soon leave the scene, leaving him alone with Guillaume. Without taking his eyes off the two men, he silently reached behind him to grab his backpack and remove the steel coil he had purchased earlier. At its extremities he had already twisted the steel with the pliers until it formed a loop at both ends. The makeshift handles would allow him to hold the razor sharp coil steady when strangulating his quarry. However, touching a warm and hard muzzle where his pack had laid a minute before made him jump involuntarily. The guttural grunt and the headbutt push that followed startled him so as to make him step back out of the way onto a stack of dry wood that creaked under his weight, breaking the silence. He froze on the spot, waiting.

"Who's there?" yelled Guillaume in Nadhir's direction, all his senses on full alert.

"I heard it too," concurred Stefano. "Those branches cracked under some heavy weight," he added under his breath.

Both men peered into the darkness, incapable of distinguishing anything in the shadowy masses of low-lying bushes surrounding the bank of stables in front of which they had been arguing. Suddenly a dark, compact mass pushed forward, sprinting straight ahead, heading for them, making them both leap sideways to avoid a head-on collision.

"God, darn wombat!" exclaimed Guillaume, instantly recognising the compact animal that ran past them. "Gosh, it really scared me! I'm a bit paranoid lately," he admitted, laughing nervously, watching Stefano who was likewise catching his breath. "Let me get my rifle though. Don't want the beast to start digging holes all over the place! What a nuisance. I was sure I had gotten rid of all the local residents some time last year."

Stefano exhaled slowly. Even after all these years, some of the local fauna still took him by surprise and made him most uneasy. For the most part, wombats came out foraging at night. The holes they dug always signified danger for the horses in their care as the animals often trapped their hoofs in their burrows, accidentally breaking their legs. Nadhir, instinctively rolling on his side in the dark to avoid being trampled by the unknown animal, was also trying to slow down his heart rate.

"Our discussion isn't over yet," insisted Stefano after recovering from his fright.

"That's right!" agreed Guillaume but with much less venom in his tone. "So answer me, why did you contact Guarini? How did you know he'd come after me?" he added, raising his voice once again, unable to walk away from the question that haunted him.

"I have always known you weren't who you said you were! Where I come from men who hide their past either have terrible deeds to their names or try to escape persecution. I didn't know which. To cut a long story short, and through a series of fortuitous leads, I ended up giving him the information necessary to track you down."

"And kill me? Why?"

Stefano shrugged.

"I didn't think he'd risk killing you. I thought he'd just teach you a lesson."

"I repeat, why? Why go to all the trouble? What have I ever done to you?"

This time Stefano's temper boiled over and the pent-up jealousy he had suppressed for nearly three decades just exploded.

"You're always the best at everything! You're an immigrant just like me, but no one calls you a wog behind your back! Your wife is on everyone's social list and on the board of every high-profile charitable committee from here to the Queensland border. Despite her donations, both in kind and in money, my wife is never invited to put down her candidacy anywhere. I see how people look at her as if she were some illiterate peasant. We weren't even blessed with children! But of course, yours is not just beautiful but talented and smart. Even when my horses win races, it's you who steals the limelight, and you who ends up being quoted for memorable quips. Everyone calls upon your expertise and experience and whilst mine is equivalent to yours, no one ever cares about what I have to say. Pandora Estates is always compared to Chantilly Farms. Most times I come up second best. To add insult to injury, you've just won the Melbourne Cup. I've had it up to here with you and your business! I'd had enough of your smugness and success!" shot out Stefano angrily, wildly gesticulating with his hands, his face turning red, spitting his words in short angry bursts.

Wide-eyed, Guillaume stared at him, dumfounded and shaken to the core by the violent outburst. Plain old-fashioned jealousy? Really? His whole world had been tipped over due to simple envy? However, he could hardly empathise as it was an emotion he had never experienced. He certainly had never imagined that his neighbour – a very successful entrepreneur by any yardstick – would ever have held so much personal resentment towards him and his family. He was not quite sure how to react to the unexpected admission, although it had finally clarified many of the events of the last few weeks.

"I'm at a loss for words," said Guillaume, quietly looking at Stefano squarely. "I had no idea. All this time I thought it was all fair dinkum rivalry between you and me and nothing more."

"Here you go again!" shouted Stefano. "You've no idea because you live in a glass bubble, perched high in the same ivory tower as those of your kind. It is true my family were peasants and yours nobility. We both fled our past and ended up here. Australia should have been a great social equaliser but somehow you were already ahead, even before landing here. It's just not fair! That's what has been eating at me all these years – the bloody injustice of it all! And now you've not only produced a champion and a star jockey, but you've almost doubled your land holdings. No doubt, you've got plenty of money in the bank to boot. I should have killed you myself!" added Stefano in one last spurt, but the fight had already gone out of him and his shoulders slumped in resignation.

Guillaume stared at him. Now was his chance to understand the root of the problem: he did not think he would be afforded another opportunity such as this one.

"But didn't you start this whole conversation by pointing the finger at me on cheating charges?"

"And wasn't your reply to that allegation the not-so-subtle accusation that my horse running in the same race, including a number of others also foaled the same year, were all the result of artificial insemination? Did I misunderstand the implication that one illegal activity perhaps washes the hand of the other? Aren't we even?"

Guillaume smiled slowly. Stefano's brows were still as knotted as his stomach, but his head and his heart were telling him it was finally over: it was time to let bygones be bygones. They stood still opposite one another, unsure what to do next, when suddenly Guillaume jerked backwards, losing his footing. All Stefano saw was a flash of light dancing on the top of a wire and the dark hulk of a large man looming over Guillaume.

Lifted off his feet, his hands desperately trying to pull against the lethal bite of the steel cord against his throat, Guillaume emitted low gurgling sounds. Without hesitation, quickly appraising the situation, Stefano rammed the bulk of his entire body against that of the stranger in an attempt to unsteady him. Momentarily swayed, Nadhir released his chokehold for just a few seconds, leaving Guillaume time to catch his breath and reflexively defend himself by kicking his assailant hard. However, Nadhir had already punched Stefano out, leaving the Italian on his knees, coughing up blood in the dirt. Guillaume was no match for a man half his age and Nadhir soon had the wire slicing through his throat once again, Guillaume losing both blood and strength rapidly. Stefano had yet to find his feet, struggling to stand up.

"Papa, Papa? Where are you? What's going on? Why aren't you back home for dinner?" shouted Arielle, her voice coming from just a few feet away. Summoning all of his strength, Stefano yelled back, "Arielle, grab a gun! We're in trouble here! Call the police! Do something! Hurry!"

'Stefano's voice?' thought Arielle. 'What in hell is he still doing here?'

She had seen his truck earlier that afternoon but had assumed he had followed the transfer lorry out. She had come looking for her father when the latter had not returned home after bunkering their horses down for the night. She hadn't expected to hear from Stefano, but the anguish in his voice was unmistakable. Her father's shotgun was in the tack room, a few metres away from her, just to her right. As she ran to retrieve it, she dialled Detective Summers' number. He answered immediately. With a halting voice she explained what she had just heard. He requested she leave the phone on and hurry back to lend assistance. He'd be there as soon as possible. Ambulances would tag along.

When Arielle returned to the scene, the shotgun drawn and levelled at the intruder, Stefano was engaged in a tackle with a stocky man whilst her inert father was slumped on the ground nearby. She fired the first warning shot above their heads. The assailant instantly turned towards her to assess the oncoming danger. Her wispy frame was caught in the moonlight and he groaned inwardly at the badly timed interruption, dismissing Arielle as an unworthy enemy and resuming his punch-up immediately. The second time around though, there was no warning and the shot went straight through his shoulder. He roared in surprise and in pain, abandoning Stefano and surging towards Arielle, who had just reloaded. The third shot went through his stomach at very close range. Stefano, right behind him, having wrapped his arms around his legs so he couldn't lunge at Arielle, also gasped in pain, blood soon spreading below his collarbone. It had gone through his upper chest. Nadhir slumped backwards, falling on his rear, both hands now applying pressure to the gaping wound. In the far distance, piercing the night, sirens blared. Arielle ran to her father. He had not yet moved. His pulse was weak. His arteries pulsed at his throat, spurting bright red blood everywhere, soaking the dirt beneath him. Arielle didn't dare move him. She unbuttoned her shirt, bunched it into a ball and pressed it firmly against his throat. She did not dare move. Helplessly watching her father's life drain away, she began to pray.

THREE MONTHS LATER

Her eyes, light sparkles against the pale emerald-green hijab which delicately surrounded her face, focused solely on Majid's own. Clearly moved, Arielle nonetheless enunciated clearly, "An Kah'tu nafsaka a'lal mah'ril ma'loom." Her cheeks flushed slightly as she pronounced the traditional phrase, the long-sleeved, bateau-cut lace wedding gown matching exquisitely the headdress of the same translucent hue. Dressed immaculately in a snow white kandura, his eyes likewise brimming with emotion, Majid replied immediately, "Qabiltum Nikaha." The Imam looked from the groom to the bride and smiled benevolently.

"You're now wed. May Allah in His infinite Wisdom bless your union."

In the small unadorned room of the marriage section of the Islamic Courts, only a handful attended the private Nikaah ceremony. Besides the Imam, there were the newlyweds, Hamdam, Tiraq – Majid's best friend, whom he'd known since he was a boy – and Guillaume in his wheelchair with Sarah right behind him. No one else was present.

After the traumatic events at Chantilly Farms three months prior and after lengthy discussions with family and religious leaders, Majid, in the end, had not requested Arielle convert to Islam. According to the law, as long as the groom was of Muslim faith and background and an Emirati to boot, he could marry whomever he pleased, regardless of religious affiliations. Grateful to avoid starting her married life with compromises, Arielle had nonetheless been keen to respect her future husband's laws and customs. In the end, they had agreed upon an interfaith wedding, with the western-style wedding following the simple Islamic ceremony. Both had been scheduled for a Thursday evening, with the whole weekend ahead of them. Despite Majid's social and political clout, it had not been easy to set up. Indeed, Arielle, who was only carrying a simple visitor's visa, had first been subjected to invasive medical examinations. All paperwork, including her birth certificate, had undergone a painfully slow translation by a court-appointed translator. Moreover, she had to wait to be cleared by the Police Directorate which thoroughly checked she did not have a criminal record anywhere in the world. The authenticity of her identity by the Ministry of Foreign Affairs through the Australian Consulate had also taken some time. For the first time in his life, Majid tasted the difficulty met by expatriates when trying to make sense of Sharia Law. The number of hoops through which Arielle had been forced to jump had infuriated him.

When Arabian Nights covered the subject a couple of weeks later, the magazine broke all sales records, demonstrating how much this particular topic resonated with UAE residents. As soon as the Nikaah was over, the particularly challenging administrative nightmare finally behind them, the couple exited the courthouse, followed by their witnesses. Parked right up front, two limousines stood at the ready to drive them to Hamdam's palace where over 300 guests awaited them.

Three months earlier, when Detective Zack Summers had arrived at Chantilly Farms, with an ambulance and a fire truck in his tracks, it had taken him a few seconds to make sense of the scene that had confronted him. Eyes closed, rocking back and forth on her heels, Arielle had gently held Guillaume's hand, her lips moving in a silent litany. A shotgun had rested against her thigh. The front of Guillaume's sweater had been soaked with blood and he'd appeared unconscious. A couple of metres away from the duo, Stefano had sat against a post, his breathing laboured, shoulders hunched over, hands clasped against his breast, blood oozing through his fingers. At his feet, a man in his thirties, of dark complexion, dressed in black from head to toe, had laid in the dirt, his mouth agape, empty eyes staring at the moonless night. Gently, Zack had touched Arielle's shoulder and she had opened her eyes. The light had gone out of them. She had stared dully at the detective, visibly in shock.

"It's all right, Arielle. The ambulance is here. Your dad will make it, I promise. Can you stand?"

Arielle had nodded despondently and as soon as she had let go of her father, the two paramedics, having slid a stretcher under Guillaume's body, had lifted him out. Within minutes, the ambulance had roared down the hill towards the hospital.

"Stefano," Arielle had murmured, turning to where the man awkwardly sat.

"Don't worry. He's being taken care of," he had assured her, after seeing the firemen giving the man necessary first aid. With a quick gesture across his throat, a colleague had already motioned to him that the third man on the scene no longer required medical attention.

"What happened here?" the detective had queried, concentrating on his witness.

"Dad was late coming up for dinner. I came looking for him. I knew he'd be somewhere near the stables. As I approached, I heard Stefano's voice. He told me they were in trouble. He yelled for me to get the gun Papa always kept in the tack room and call the police. I ran to the tack room and grabbed the gun. I called you at the same time. When I got here, I saw Papa was already down and Stefano engaged in an all-out brawl with a stranger," she had recited without pathos, the sequence of events clear in her mind.

"And then?" Zack had prompted.

"I first fired a warning shot above their heads but somehow it didn't seem to detract the other guy. So I fired a second time and I hit him. He lunged at me and I fired a third time. Then everything went silent. I think I may have shot Stefano by mistake? Did I?"

"It's all right, Arielle. You did what you had to do. Let me speak with Stefano." He had whistled and one of his deputies had rushed over. He had requested a blanket be put around Arielle's shoulders. The deputy had remained at her side and had offered her a cigarette on which she had dragged gratefully.

"Stefano? How are you feeling?" Zack had asked him. The old man's breath had come in short staccato.

"I've been better," he had replied with effort, his whole face contorted in pain.

"What happened?"

"Came here to speak to Will and clear the air," Stefano had explained haltingly. "Then all of a sudden, this guy jumped out behind Will and held him in a chokehold. I tried to rush him but he held on tight, and I saw Will was losing lots of blood. He must have used a knife or a wire or something. I fought him but he's a bloody strong fellow, I tell you! Finally he let go of Will to defend himself and just at that moment I heard Arielle's calling out. I told her to get the gun. I heard three shots. One must have grazed me," he had added, coughing blood into the dirt, his eyes rolling back in his head.

"I need help here," Zack had yelled, aware that Stefano was losing consciousness. Minutes later, Stefano had been rushed to hospital. He had been pronounced dead on arrival, the bullet having lodged in his left ventricle. Zack had shaken his head in complete disbelief: five deaths under his watch in less than five weeks, four more than in the rest of his 27-year career! He certainly hoped the bloodshed was over. Once again its causes rested with the stranger in the midst.

Zack had not expected to find any identification on the body. What he'd found, however, had been a string of amber beads in the back pocket. He had been puzzled. Arielle had rescued him.

"It's a Misbaha," she'd clarified. "These are Muslim prayer beads. I've seen many such beads during my stay in Dubai 10

314

years ago. It indicates beyond a doubt that this man is a devout Muslim."

"Another Arabic friend?" Zack had asked, incredulous.

Admitting it had been an unlikely coincidence, Arielle had then suggested the police check all recent arrivals into the country by sending the man's photo to Immigration. It hadn't taken long to match the man with the Australian Customs' records. Finding out he'd not bothered to check into the Intercontinental Hotel under a false identity had amused the detective. Figuring out the stratagem employed to gain access to Chantilly Farms had been relatively simple police work: the bike leaning against a nearby tree bore the rental's property name all over the chassis. However, confirmation that the young man was no other than Rashid's youngest son had left everyone reeling. The Emirati had gone too far.

It had taken another week for the police to arrest Rashid at his compound in front of family and assembled staff. The charges of conspiring to commit murder, murder for hire, attempted murder and manslaughter by proxy had all been neatly laid out. Rashid had indeed been found to have engineered the conditions by which Stefano had lost his life. By sending his son overseas, he had sent him to his death. Assa had confirmed that, on his way to the airport, her brother Nadhir had confided that their father was sending him overseas on a secret mission. He had been scared of flying and she had done her best to appease him with a gift of the distinctive Misbaha.

Justice had been served, with the unforgiving Sharia court executing a swift judgement. With Rashid in jail, stripped of all power, there had been no more impediments to Majid's future. Immediately after the trial, Assa had returned to live with her mother, likewise free from her controlling husband. The latter had welcomed her with open arms. After overseeing her move, Majid

315

had flown to Australia. To a recovering Guillaume, he had requested Arielle's hand in marriage.

During the reception that followed the elegant Anglican ceremony, when the two lovers had exchanged their vows under a canopy of white flowers erected in the middle of Hamdam's gardens, Hamdam solicitously pushed Guillaume's chair near the water's edge. Guillaume looked up at his oldest friend, noticing his cheeks had acquired a slightly yellowish tint.

"How much longer do you have?"

"A couple of weeks at best."

"Why did you refuse further treatment?"

"The side-effects didn't seem worth it. I'd have to go and spend the rest of my days in London in a specialised facility, away from everything I hold dear. Moreover, I didn't like the odds. And to top it all, I'd have missed your daughter's wedding."

"Oh, come on!" replied Guillaume, exasperated. "Arielle would have understood! Not only did you propose to host her nuptials but you also gifted her a yacht so large that she could live on it for the rest of her life! I really don't believe she could ever be cross with you for anything."

"All right then. Let's just say there was really no point. I chose a shorter life, with the possibility of a few good days over a slow, agonising death filled with doctors, nurses and invasive tubes. I've no regrets," said Hamdam firmly.

"I wish I could say the same," replied Guillaume wistfully.

"The main thing is not to add to existing ones," said Hamdam with a smile, He squatted to be at eye level with Guillaume, who looked back at him without wavering.

"When I felt that wire cutting through my throat, just before I blacked out, I saw my life floating in front of my eyes. It's true what they say. The best and the worst in your life drifts past you, like amorphous dreams of exceptional vividness. And you know what, interestingly enough, Obsession wasn't one of them!"

"I'm not surprised," interrupted Hamdam.

"Really?" Guillaume questioned, curious. "I did cheat. It was the first and last time but it was monumental. In a perverted manner, it brought on Stefano's and Nadhir's death. I should feel guilty. It should lie as a blot on my conscience."

"By society's standards, you certainly did cheat. Legally, without a doubt, but you did so according to your own sense of right and wrong. Your actions were dictated by your heart. I'm pretty sure you would do it again, given the same circumstances. At the end of the day, you saved your family from ruin and dishonour."

"I don't follow your reasoning. Somehow that exonerates me?" queried Guillaume, clearly intrigued.

"No, it doesn't, but in my book, and the writings of Allah, family is sacred. It's your duty before all else to keep it together and look after them. An honourable man lives for his family. I'd have done the same."

"I don't believe you, but thank you for saying it. Thank you once again for your generosity of heart and spirit. You're a true friend."

"I know you'll keep your promise," replied Hamdam. "We'll both go to our grave with our secrets. We've reached a truce, however tainted."

"What else could we have done?" asked Guillaume. "Expose Trent's treachery and ruin the lives of many innocent bystanders? Confess to substitution during the most spectacular race in the world and create such a scandal that it would ruin the Sports of Kings forever? We both know that once we'd opened Pandora's box, we wouldn't have been able to put the lid back on."

"Literally."

The two old men chuckled softly. Still recovering from reconstructive surgery after his ordeal when his neck had almost been severed from his spinal cord, Guillaume leaned back in his wheelchair. On the honeyed sand, still warm from the day's heat,

Hamdam sat peacefully cross-legged at his side. Water lapped languidly at their feet. Behind them they could hear music and laughter wafting in and out with the desert breeze. Lost in thought, the two friends watched the immaculate blue sky where clouds leaped over each other, in a race towards infinity. Both were finally at peace.

THE END

Printed in Australia
AUOC02n1320121017
290425AU00002B/2/P